little black dress
· IT'S A GIRL THING ·

Dear Little Black Dress Reader,

Thanks for picking up this Little Black Dress book, one of the great new titles from our series of fun, page-turning romance novels. Lucky you – you're about to have a fantastic romantic read that we know you won't be able to put down!

Why don't you make your Little Black Dress experience even better by logging on to

www.littleblackdressbooks.com

where you can:

- ▾ Enter our **monthly competitions** to win **gorgeous** prizes
- ▾ Get **hot-off-the-press** news about our latest titles
- ▾ Read **exclusive** preview chapters both from your **favourite** authors and from brilliant new writing talent
- ▾ Buy **up-and-coming** books online
- ▾ Sign up for an essential slice of romance via our **fortnightly email** newsletter

We love nothing more than to curl up and indulge in an addictive romance, and so we're delighted to welcome you into the Little Black Dress club!

With love from,

The **little black dress** team

Five interesting things about Rachel Gibson:

1. Growing up, I didn't like to read. I liked to play tetherball and wanted to be a tetherball champion.

2. I have a deadly fear of grasshoppers.

3. I am a shoe-aholic. I think ugly shoes are an abomination of biblical proportion.

4. I love to read the tabloids. Especially the ones featuring stories such as Bat Boy and women having Big Foot's baby.

5. I write romance novels, but I hate overly sentimental movies and sappy love songs.

By Rachel Gibson

Daisy's Back in Town
Sex, Lies and Online Dating
I'm in No Mood for Love
The Trouble with Valentine's Day
Simply Irresistible
Tangled Up in You
It Must Be Love
True Confessions
Lola Carlyle Reveals All
Not Another Bad Date
Truly Madly Yours
See Jane Score

Truly Madly Yours

Rachel Gibson

little
black
dress

Published by arrangement with AVON
An imprint of HARPERCOLLINS PUBLISHERS, USA

The right of Rachel Gibson to be identified as the Author of
the Work has been asserted by her in accordance with the
Copyright, Designs and Patents Act 1988.

First published in 1999
by AVON BOOKS
An imprint of HARPERCOLLINS PUBLISHERS, USA

First published in Great Britain in 2008
by LITTLE BLACK DRESS
An imprint of HEADLINE PUBLISHING GROUP

A LITTLE BLACK DRESS paperback

1

978 0 7553 3744 6

Typeset in Transit511BT by Avon DataSet Ltd,
Bidford-on-Avon, Warwickshire

Printed and bound in Great Britain by Clays Ltd, St Ives plc

HEADLINE PUBLISHING GROUP
An Hachette Livre UK Company
338 Euston Road
London NW1 3BH

www.littleblackdressbooks.com
www.headline.co.uk
www.hachettelivre.co.uk

With love to my mother and father, Al and Mary Reed. Late at night when my mind is quiet, I can still remember the scent of my mother's skin and the texture of my father's spiky crewcut, and I know that I have been blessed.

Prologue

The red glow from a space heater touched the creases and folds of Henry Shaw's face, while the nicker of his beloved Appaloosas called to him on the warm spring breeze. He plugged an old eight-track cassette into its player, and the deep, whiskey-rough voice of Johnny Cash filled the small tack shed. Before Johnny had found religion, he'd been one kick-ass carouser. A man's man, and Henry liked that. Then Johnny had found Jesus and June and his career had gone to hell in a hand basket. Life didn't always go according to plan. God and women and disease had a way of interfering. Henry hated anything that interfered with his plans.

He hated not being in control.

He poured himself a bourbon and looked out the small window above his work bench. The setting sun hung just above Shaw Mountain, named after Henry's ancestors who'd settled the rich valley below. Sharp gray shadows sliced across the valley toward Lake Mary, named for Henry's great-great-grandmother, Mary Shaw.

More than Henry hated God and disease and not being in control, he hated friggin' doctors. They poked and prodded until they found something wrong, and none of them had ever said a damn thing he'd wanted to hear. Each time he'd tried to prove them wrong, but in the end he never had.

Henry splashed linseed oil on some old cotton rags and set them in a cardboard box. He'd always planned to have a passel of grandchildren by now, but he didn't have a single one. He was the last Shaw. The last in a long line of an old and respected family. The Shaws were nearly extinct, and it ate a hole in his gut. There was no one to carry his blood after he was gone . . . no one except Nick.

He sat down in an old office chair and raised the bourbon to his lips. He would be the first to admit he'd wronged that boy. For several years now, he'd tried to make it up to his son. But Nick was a stubborn, unforgiving man. Just as he'd been a defiant unlovable boy.

If Henry had more time, he was sure he and his son could have come to some sort of understanding. But he didn't have time, and Nick didn't make it easy. In fact, Nick made it damn hard to even like him.

He remembered the day Nick's mother, Benita Allegrezza, had pounded on his front door, claiming Henry had fathered the black-haired baby in her arms. Henry had turned his attention from Benita's dark gaze to the big blue eyes of his wife, Ruth, who had stood beside him.

He'd denied it like hell. Of course, there had been a real good chance that what Benita claimed was true, but he'd denied even the possibility. Even if Henry hadn't been married, he never would have chosen to have a child with a Basque woman. Those people were too dark, too volatile, and too religious for his taste. He'd wanted white, blond-haired babies. He didn't want his kids confused for wet-backs. Oh, he knew Basques weren't Mexicans, but they all looked alike to him.

If it hadn't been for Benita's brother, Josu, no one would have known about his affair with the young widow. But that sheep-loving bastard had tried to blackmail him into recognizing Nick as his son. He'd thought Josu had been bluffing when the man had come to him and threatened to tell everyone in town that Henry had taken advantage of his grieving sister and had knocked her up. He'd ignored the threat, but Josu hadn't been bluffing. Again Henry had denied paternity.

But by the time Nick was five, he looked enough like a Shaw that no one believed Henry anymore. Not even Ruth. She'd divorced him and taken half his money.

But back then, he'd still had time. He'd been in his late thirties. Still a young man.

Henry picked up a .357 and slipped six bullets into the cylinder. After Ruth, he'd found his second wife, Gwen. Even though Gwen had been a poor unwed mother of questionable parentage, he'd married her for several reasons. She obviously wasn't barren, as he'd suspected of Ruth, and she was so beautiful she made him ache. She and her daughter had been so grateful to him, and so easy to mold into what he wanted. But in the end, his stepdaughter had disappointed him bitterly, and the one thing he wanted most from Gwen, she had failed to give him. After years of marriage, she hadn't given him a legitimate heir.

Henry spun the cylinder then looked down at the revolver in his hand. With the barrel of the pistol, he pushed the box of linseed rags closer to the space heater. He didn't want anyone to clean up the mess after he was gone. The song he'd been waiting to hear crackled through the speakers, and he cranked up the eight-track player as Johnny sang about falling into a burning ring of fire.

His eyes got a little misty when he thought of his life and the people he would leave behind. It was a damn shame he wouldn't be around to see the looks on their faces when they discovered what he'd done.

'Death comes, as it must, to all men, and with it the inevitable separation from loved ones,' Reverend Tippet droned in his flat solemn tone. 'We will miss Henry Shaw, beloved husband, father, and prominent member of our community.' The reverend paused and glanced about the large group gathered to bid their final farewell. 'Henry would be pleased to see so many friends here today.'

Henry Shaw would have taken one look at the line of cars backed up to the gated entrance of Salvation Cemetery, and he would have regarded the respectable turnout as somewhat less than his due. Until he'd been voted out of office last year in favor of that yellow-dog Democrat George Tanasee, he'd been mayor of Truly, Idaho for over twenty-four years.

Henry had been a big man in the small community. He'd owned half the businesses and had more money then the whole town combined. Shortly after his first wife had divorced him twenty-six years ago, he'd gone out and replaced her with the prettiest woman he could find. He'd owned the finest pair of Weimaraners in the state, Duke and Dolores, and until recently, he'd lived in the biggest house in town. But that had been before those Allegrezza boys had started building all over the damn place. He'd had a stepdaughter too, but he hadn't talked about her in years.

Henry had loved his position in the community. He'd been warm and generous to the people who'd agreed with his opinions, but if you weren't Henry's friend, you were his enemy. Those who'd dared to challenge him usually regretted it. He'd been a pompous, redneck son of a bitch, and when they'd pulled his charred remains from the inferno which had claimed his life, there were some members of the community who felt that Henry Shaw got exactly what he deserved.

'To the earth we give the body of our loved one. Henry's life . . .'

Delaney Shaw, Henry's stepdaughter, listened to the bland Muzak quality in Reverend Tippet's voice and cast a sideways glance at her mother. The soft shadows of bereavement looked good on Gwen Shaw, but Delaney wasn't surprised. Her mother looked good in everything. She always had. Delaney returned her gaze to the spray of yellow roses on Henry's casket. The bright June sun shot sparks off the polished mahogany and shiny brass hardware. She reached inside the pocket of the mint-green suit she'd borrowed from her mother and found her sunglasses. Sliding the tortoiseshell frame onto her face, she hid from the sun's stabbing rays and the curious glances of the people around her. She straightened her shoulders and took several long deep breaths. She hadn't been home for ten years. She'd always meant to come back and make her peace with Henry. Now it was too late.

A light breeze tossed red and gold streaked curls about her face, and she pushed her chin-length hair behind her ears. She should have tried. She shouldn't have stayed away for so long. She shouldn't have allowed so many years to pass, but she'd never thought he'd die. Not Henry. The last time she'd seen him, they'd said some horrible things to each other. His anger had been so fierce, she could still remember it clearly.

A sound like the wrath of God rolled in the distance, and Delaney raised her gaze to the heavens, half expecting to see thunder and lightning bolts, certain the arrival of a man like Henry had created turbulence in paradise. The sky remained a clear blue, but the rumbling continued, drawing her attention to the iron gates of the cemetery.

Straddling gleaming black lacquer and shimmering chrome, windblown hair tousled about broad shoulders, a lone biker bore down on the crowd gathered to bid their farewells. The monster engine vibrated the ground and shook the air, the act of committal suffocated by a set of bad-dog pipes. Dressed in faded jeans and a soft white T-shirt, the biker slowed and brought the Harley to a rumbling stop in front of the gray hearse. The engine died, and his boot heel scraped the asphalt as he laid the bike on its kickstand. Then in one smooth motion, he rose. Several days' growth of beard darkened a strong jaw and cheeks, drawing attention to a firm mouth. A small gold hoop pierced his earlobe while a pair of platinum Oakley's concealed his eyes.

There was something vaguely familiar about the bad-ass biker. Something about his smooth olive skin and black hair, but Delaney couldn't place him.

'Oh, my God,' her mother gasped beside her. 'I can't believe he dared to show up dressed like that.'

Her incredulity was shared by other mourners who had the bad manners to break into loud whispers.

'He's trouble.'

'Always has been bad to the bone.'

Levi's caressed his firm thighs, cupped his crotch, and covered his long legs in soft denim. The warm breeze flattened his shirt against his broad muscular chest. Delaney lifted her gaze to his face again. Slowly he removed the sunglasses from the bridge of his straight nose and shoved them into the front pocket of his T-shirt. His light gray eyes stared directly back at her.

Delaney's heart stopped and her bones fused. She

recognized those eyes burning a hole in her. They were the exact copy of his Irish father's but much more startling because they were set in a face typical of his Basque heritage.

Nick Allegrezza, the source of her girlhood fascinations and the origin of her disillusions. Nick, the slick-talking, smooth-tongued snake. He stood with his weight on one foot as if he didn't notice the stir he'd caused. More than likely he *did* notice and simply didn't care. Delaney had been gone ten years, but some things obviously hadn't changed. Nick had filled out and his features had matured, but his presence still attracted attention.

Reverend Tippet bowed his head. 'Let us pray for Henry Shaw,' he began. Delaney tucked her chin and closed her eyes. Even as a child, Nick had attracted more than his share of attention. His older brother Louie had been wild too, but Louie had never been as wild as Nick. Everyone knew the Allegrezza brothers were crazy, impulsive Bascos, quick-fingered and as horny as parolees.

Every girl in town had been warned to stay far away from the brothers, but like lemmings to the sea, many had succumbed to the call of the wild and thrown themselves at 'those Basque boys.' Nick had earned the added reputation for charming virgins out of their undies. But he hadn't charmed Delaney. Contrary to popular belief, she hadn't knocked boots with Nick Allegrezza. He hadn't taken *her* virginity.

Not technically anyway.

'Amen,' the mourners recited as one.

'Yeah. Amen,' Delaney uttered, feeling a bit guilty for her irreverent thoughts during a prayer to God. She glanced over the top of her sunglasses, and her eyes narrowed. She watched Nick's lips move as he made a quick sign of the cross. He was Catholic of course, like the other Basque families in the area. Still, it seemed sacrilegious to see such an overtly sexual, long-haired, earring-wearing *biker* cross himself as if he were a priest. Then as if he had all day, he lifted his gaze up the front of Delaney's suit to her face. For an instant, something flickered in his eyes, but just as quickly it was gone, and his attention was drawn to a blond woman in a pink slip dress by his side. She raised on her toes and whispered something into his ear.

Mourners crowded around Delaney and her mother, stopping to give their condolences before moving toward their cars. She lost sight of Nick and turned to people passing in front of her. She recognized most of Henry's friends, who paused to speak to her, but saw very few faces under the age of fifty. She smiled and nodded and shook hands, hating every minute of their close scrutiny. She wanted to be alone. She wanted to be by herself so she could think about Henry and the good times. She wanted to remember Henry before they'd disappointed each other so terribly. But she knew she wouldn't get the opportunity until much later. She was emotionally exhausted, and by the time she and her mother made their way to the limousine that would take them back home, she wanted nothing more than to hibernate.

The rumble of Nick's Harley drew her attention and she glanced over her shoulder at him. He revved the engine twice then flipped a U and gunned the big bike. Delaney's brows lowered as she watched him shoot past, her eyes focused on the blond pressed against his back like a human suction cup. He'd picked up a woman at Henry's funeral, picked her up as if he were out trolling bars. Delaney didn't recognize her, but she wasn't really surprised to see a woman leaving the funeral with Nick. Nothing was sacred to him. Nothing off limits.

She climbed into the limousine and sank into plush velvet seats. Henry was dead, but nothing had changed.

'That was a real nice service, don't you think?' Gwen asked, interrupting Delaney's thoughts as the car pulled away from the gravesite and headed toward Highway 55.

Delaney kept her gaze on the blue flashes of Lake Mary barely visible through dense pine forest. 'Yes,' she answered, then turned her attention to her mother. 'It was real nice.'

'Henry loved you. He just didn't know how to compromise.'

They'd had this same discussion many times, and Delaney didn't feel like talking about it. The conversation always began and ended the same, yet nothing ever got resolved. 'How many people do you think will show up?' she asked, referring to the after-funeral buffet.

'Most everyone, I imagine.' Gwen reached across the distance that separated them and pushed the sides of Delaney's hair behind her ears.

Delaney half expected her mother to wet her fingers and make spit curls on her forehead as she'd done when Delaney had been a child. She'd hated it then, and she hated it now. The constant fixing, as if she wasn't good enough the way she was. The constant fussing, as if she could be made into something she wasn't.

No. Nothing had changed.

'I'm so glad you're home, Laney.'

Delaney felt suffocated and pressed the electric window switch. She breathed in the fresh mountain air and let it out slowly. Two days, she told herself. She could go home in two days.

Last week, she'd received notification that she was named in Henry's will. After the way they'd parted, she couldn't imagine why he'd included her. She wondered if he'd included Nick, too, or if he would ignore his son, even after his death.

Briefly she wondered if Henry had left her money or property. More than likely it was some kind of a gag gift, like an old rusted fishing boat or a stuffed mackinaw. Whatever it was didn't matter, she was leaving directly after the will was read. Now all she had to do was gather the courage to tell her mother. Maybe she'd call her from a pay phone somewhere around Salt Lake City. Until then, she planned to look up some of her old girlfriends, hit a few local bars, and wait it out until she could head home to the big city where she could breathe. She knew if she stayed more than a few days, she'd lose her mind – or worse, herself.

'Well, look who's back.'

Delaney set a plate of stuffed mushrooms on the buffet table then looked into the eyes of her childhood adversary, Helen Schnupp. Growing up, Helen had been a thorn in Delaney's side, a rock in her shoe, and a colossal pain in the ass. Every time Delaney had turned around, Helen had been there, usually one step ahead. Helen had been prettier, faster in track, and better in basketball. In the second grade Helen had unseated her for first place in the county spelling bee. In the eighth grade Helen had beaten her out for head cheerleader, and in the eleventh she'd been caught at the drive-in with Delaney's boyfriend, Tommy Markham, riding the bologna pony in the back of the Markham family station wagon. A girl didn't forget a thing like that, and Delaney took silent pleasure in Helen's split ends and overprocessed highlights.

'Helen Schnupp,' she said, hating to admit to herself that except for the hair, her old nemesis was still pretty.

'It's Markham now.' Helen grabbed a croissant and stuffed it with sliced ham. 'Tommy and I have been happily married for seven years.'

Delaney forced a smile. 'Isn't that just great?' She told herself she didn't give a damn about either one of them, but she'd always entertained the fantasy of a Bonnie and Clyde style ending for Helen and Tommy. The fact that she still harbored such animosity didn't bother her as much as she thought it probably should. Maybe it was time for that psychotherapy she'd been putting off.

'Are you married?'

'No.'

Helen gave her a look filled with pity. 'Your mother tells me you live in Scottsdale.'

Delaney fought an urge to shove Helen's croissant up her nose. 'I live in Phoenix.'

'Oh?' Helen reached for a mushroom and scooted down the line. 'I must not have heard her right.'

Delaney doubted there was anything wrong with Helen's hearing. Her hair was another matter, however, and if Delaney hadn't already planned to leave in a few days, and if she were a nicer person, she might have offered to snip some of the damage. She might have even slapped a protein pack on Helen's frizzy hair and wrapped her whole head in cellophane. But she wasn't that nice.

Her gaze scanned the dining room filled with people until she located her mother. Surrounded by friends, every blond hair in perfect order, her makeup flawless, Gwen Shaw looked like a queen holding court. Gwen had always been the Grace Kelly of Truly, Idaho. She even resembled her somewhat. At forty-four, she could pass for thirty-nine and, as she was fond of saying, looked much too young to have a daughter who was twenty-nine.

Anywhere else, a fifteen-year age difference between mother and daughter might have raised more than a few brows, but in small-town Idaho, it wasn't uncommon for high school sweethearts to marry the day after graduation, sometimes because the bride was about to go into labor. No one thought anything of teenage pregnancy, unless of course the teen wasn't married. *That* sort of scandal fueled the gossip fires for years.

Everyone in Truly believed the mayor's young wife had been widowed shortly after she'd married Delaney's biological father, but it was all a lie. At fifteen, Gwen had been involved with a married man, and when he'd found out she was pregnant, he dumped her and she left town.

'I see you came back. I thought you might be dead.'

Delaney's attention was drawn to Old Mrs Van Damme hunched over an aluminum walker and teetering toward a deviled egg, her white hair plastered with finger waves just as Delaney remembered. She couldn't recall the woman's first name. She didn't know if she'd ever heard it used. Everyone had always referred to her as Old Mrs Van Damme. The woman was so ancient now, her back bowed with age and osteoporosis, she was turning into a human fossil.

'Can I help you get something to eat?' Delaney offered, standing a little straighter while counting back to the last time she'd had a glass of milk, or at the very least a calcium-enriched Tums.

Mrs Van Damme snagged an egg, then handed Delaney her plate. 'Some of that and that,' she directed, pointing to several different dishes.

'Would you like salad?'

'Makes me gassy,' Mrs Van Damme whispered, then pointed at a bowl of ambrosia. 'That looks good, and some of those chicken wings, too. They're hot, but I brought my Pepto.'

For such a frail little thing, Old Mrs Van Damme ate like a lumberjack. 'Are you related to Jean-Claude?' Delaney joked, attempting to interject a little levity in the otherwise somber occasion.

'Who?'

'Jean-Claude Van Damme, the kickboxer.'

'No, I don't know any Jean-Claude, but maybe they got one living in Emmett. Those Emmett Van Dammes are always in trouble, always kicking up about something or another. Last year Teddy – my late brother's middle grandchild – got arrested for stealing that big Smokey the Bear they had standing in front of the forest service building. Why'd he want something like that, anyway?'

'Maybe because his name is Teddy.'

'Huh?'

Delaney frowned. 'Never mind.' She shouldn't have tried. She'd forgotten that her sense of humor wasn't appreciated in redneck towns where men tended to use their shirt pockets for ashtrays. She sat Mrs Van Damme at a table near the buffet, then she headed for the bar.

She'd often thought the whole after-the-funeral ritual of gathering to eat like hogs and get drunk was a bit odd, but she supposed it existed to give the family comfort. Delaney didn't feel comforted in the least. She felt on display, but she'd always felt that way living in Truly. She'd grown up as the daughter of the mayor and his very beautiful wife. Delaney had always fallen a little short somehow. She'd never been outgoing or boisterous like Henry, and she'd never been beautiful like Gwen.

She walked into the parlor where Henry's cronies from the Moose Lodge were holding down the bar and reeking of Johnnie Walker. They paid her little attention as she poured herself a glass of wine and stepped out of the low heels her mother had insisted she borrow.

Even though Delaney knew that she was sometimes compulsive, she really had only one addiction. She was a shoe-aholic. She thought Imelda Marcos got a bad rap. Delaney loved shoes. All shoes. Except little pumps with stubby heels. Too boring. Her tastes leaned toward stilettoes, funky boots, or Hercules sandals. Her clothes weren't exactly conventional, either. For the last few years she'd worked at Valentina, an upscale salon where customers paid a hundred dollars to get their hair cut and expected to see their stylist in trendsetting clothes. For their money, Delaney's customers wanted to see short vinyl skirts, leather pants, or sheer blouses with black bras. Not exactly proper funeral attire for the stepdaughter of a man who'd ruled the small town for many years.

Delaney was just about to exit the room when the conversation stopped her.

'Don says he looked like a charcoal briquette by the time they got him out.'

'Hellva way to die.'

The men shook their collective heads and drank their Scotch. Delaney knew the fire had occurred in a shed Henry had built across town. According to Gwen, he'd taken a recent interest in breeding Appaloosas, but he hadn't cared for the smell of manure near his house.

'Henry loved those horses,' said a Moose in a cowboy-cut leisure suit. 'I heard tell a spark caught the barn on fire, too. There wasn't much left of those Appaloosas, just some femur bones and a hoof or two.'

'Do you think it was arson?'

Delaney rolled her eyes. *Arson.* In a town that had yet to plug into cable television, Truly loved nothing more than listening to gossip and spreading intrigue. They lived for it. Ate it up like a fifth food group.

'The investigators from Boise don't really think so, but it hasn't been ruled out.'

There was a pause in the conversation before someone said, 'I doubt the fire was intentional. Who would do that to Henry?'

'Maybe Allegrezza.'

'Nick?'

'He hated Henry.'

'So did a lotta people, if the truth be told. Burning a man and his horses is a helluva lotta hate. I don't know if Allegrezza hated Henry that much.'

'Henry was plenty ticked about those condos Nick is buildin' out on Crescent Bay, and the two of them almost got into a fistfight about it down at the Chevron a month or two ago. I don't know how he got that piece of property from Henry, but he sure as hell did. Then he went and built condos all over the damn place.'

Again they shook their heads and tipped their glasses. Delaney had spent a lot of hours lying on the white sands and swimming in the clear blue water of Crescent Bay. Coveted by most everyone in town, the Bay was a prime piece of real estate located on a large expanse of undeveloped beach. The property had been in Henry's family for generations, and Delaney wondered how Nick had gotten his hands on it.

'Last I heard, those condos are making Allegrezza a fortune.'

'Yep. They're being snapped up by Californians. Next thing you know, we'll be overrun by latte-sippin,' dope-smokin' pantywaists.'

'Or worse – actors.'

'Nothin' worse then a do-gooder like Bruce Willis moving in and trying to change everything. He's the worse thing that ever happened to Hailey. Hell, he moves up there, renovates a few buildings, then thinks he can tell everyone in the whole damn state how to vote.'

The men concurred with a mutual nod and disgruntled scoff. When the conversation turned to movie stars and action films, Delaney walked unnoticed from the room. She moved down the hall to Henry's study and closed the pocket doors behind her. On the wall behind his massive mahogany desk, Henry's face stared down at her. Delaney remembered when he'd had the portrait painted. She'd been thirteen, about the time she'd first attempted to exert a little independence. She'd wanted to pierce her ears. Henry had said no. It was neither the first nor certainly the last time he'd exercised his control over her. Henry had always had to have control.

Delaney sat in the huge leather chair and was surprised to

see a picture of herself sitting on the desk. She recalled the day Henry had taken the photograph. It was the day her whole life had changed. She'd been seven and her mother had just married Henry. It was the day she'd walked out of a single wide on the outskirts of Las Vegas and, after a short flight, into a three-story Victorian in Truly.

The first time she'd seen the house, with its twin turrets and gabled roof, she'd thought she was moving into a palace, which meant Henry was obviously a king. The mansion was surrounded by forest on three sides, cut back to allow beautifully landscaped lawn while the backyard gently sloped toward the cool waters of Lake Mary.

Within hours, Delaney had departed poverty and landed in a storybook. Her mother was happy and Delaney felt like a princess. And on that day, sitting on the steps in a frilly white dress her mother had forced her to wear, she'd fallen in love with Henry Shaw. He was older than the other men in her mother's life had been – nicer, too. He didn't yell at Delaney, and he didn't make her mother cry. He made her feel safe and secure, something she'd felt all too infrequently in her young life. He'd adopted her and he was the only father she'd ever known. For those reasons, she loved Henry and she always would.

It was also the first time she'd laid eyes on Nick Allegrezza. He'd popped out of the bushes in Henry's yard, his gray eyes blazing hatred, his cheeks mottled with anger. He'd scared her, yet she'd been fascinated by him at the same time. Nick had been a beautiful boy, black hair, smooth tan skin, and eyes like smoke.

He'd stood in the buckbrush, his arms at his sides, stiff with rage and defiance. All that rebellious Basque and Irish blood raging within his veins. He'd looked at the two of them, then he'd spoken to Henry. Years later Delaney couldn't remember the exact words, but she would never forget the angry sentiment.

'You make sure you steer clear of him,' Henry had said as they'd watched him turn and leave, his chin up, back straight.

It wouldn't be the last time he would warn her to stay away from Nick, but years later, it was one warning she wished she'd listened to.

Nick shoved his legs into his Levi's, then stood to button the fly. He glanced over his shoulder at the woman tangled in motel sheets. Her blond hair fanned about her head. Her eyes were closed, her breathing slow and easy. Gail Oliver was the daughter of a judge and the recently divorced mother of a young son. To celebrate the end of her marriage, she'd had her tummy tucked and her breasts implanted with saline. At Henry's funeral she'd walked up to him as bold as brass and announced she wanted him to be the first to see her new body. He could tell by the look in her eyes that she'd thought he should feel flattered. He wasn't. He'd wanted a distraction, and she'd offered it. She'd acted offended when he'd pulled the Harley to a stop in front of the Starlight Motel, but she hadn't asked him to take her back home.

Nick turned from the woman in bed and moved across the green carpet to a sliding glass door that led onto a small deck overlooking Highway 55. He hadn't planned on attending the old man's funeral. He still didn't know exactly how it had happened. One minute he'd been standing on Crescent Beach going over some specs with a subcontractor, then the next thing he knew, he was on his Harley heading for the cemetery. He hadn't meant to go. He'd known he was *persona non grata*, but he'd gone anyway. For some reason he didn't want to examine too closely, he'd had to say good-bye.

He moved to a corner of the deck, away from the light spilling onto the wooden planks, and was quickly enveloped in darkness. Reverend Tippet had hardly uttered the word 'amen' before Gail, wearing that filmy little dress with the tiny straps, had propositioned Nick.

'My body is better at thirty-three than it was at sixteen,' she'd whispered in his ear. Nick couldn't remember clearly what she'd looked like at sixteen, but he did remember she'd liked sex. She'd been one of those girls who loved to get laid but wanted to act like a virgin afterward. She used to sneak out of her house and scratch on the back door of the Lomax Grocery where he'd worked after hours sweeping the floor. If he'd been in the mood, he'd let her in and bang her on a box of freight or on the checkout counter. Afterward she'd behave as if she were doing him a favor. They'd both known different.

The cool night air tossed his hair about his shoulders and brushed across his bare skin. He hardly noticed the chill. Delaney was back. When he'd heard about Henry, he'd figured she'd come home for his funeral. Still, seeing her on the other side of the old man's casket, with her hair dyed about five shades of red, had been a shock. After ten years she still reminded him of a porcelain doll, smooth as silk and delicate. Seeing her brought it all back, and he remembered the first time he'd laid eyes on her. Her hair had been blond then, and she'd been seven years old.

On that day over two decades ago, he'd been standing in line at the Tasty Freeze when he'd first heard about Henry Shaw's new wife. He couldn't believe the news. Henry had married again, and since everything Henry did interested Nick, he and his older brother Louie had hopped on their old stingrays and peddled around the lake to Henry's huge Victorian house. With the spinning of his bicycle tires, Nick's head spun, too. He knew Henry would never marry his mother. They'd hated each other for as long as Nick could remember. They didn't even speak. Mostly Henry just ignored Nick, but maybe that would change now. Maybe Henry's new wife would like kids. Maybe she'd like him.

Nick and Louie hid their bikes behind pine trees and crawled on their bellies beneath the thick buckbrush edging the terraced lawn. It was a spot they knew well. Louie was twelve, older than Nick by two years, but Nick was better at waiting than his brother. Maybe it was because he was used to waiting, or because his interest in Henry Shaw was more personal than his brother's. The two boys made themselves comfortable and prepared to wait.

'He ain't comin' out,' Louie complained after an hour of surveillance. 'We've been here for a long time, and he ain't comin' out.'

'He will sooner or later.' Nick looked at his brother, then returned his attention to the front of the big gray house. 'Has to.'

'Let's go catch some fish in Mr Bender's pond.'

Every summer Clark Bender stocked the pond in his backyard with brown trout. And every summer the Allegrezza boys relieved him of several twelve-inch beauties. 'Mom will get mad,' Nick reminded his brother, last week's experience with the wooden spoon across his palms still fresh in his mind. Usually Benita Allegrezza defended her boys with blind ferocity. But even she couldn't deny Mr Bender's accusation when the two had been escorted home stinking of fish guts, several choice trout dangling from their stringer.

'She won't find out 'cause Bender's out of town.'

Nick looked at Louie again, and thinking of all those hungry trout made his hands itch for his fishing rod. 'You sure?'

'Yep.'

He thought of the pond and all those fish just waiting for a Pautzke's and a sharp hook. Then he whipped his head back and forth and clenched his jaws. If Henry got married again, then Nick was going to stick around to see his wife.

'You're crazy,' Louie said with disgust and scooted backward, out of the buckbrush.

'Are you goin' fishing?'

'No, I'm goin' home, but first I gotta drain the lizard.'

Nick smiled. He liked it when his older brother said cool stuff like that. 'Don't tell Mom where I am.'

Louie unzipped his pants and sighed as he relieved himself on a Ponderosa. 'Just don't be gone so long she figures it out.'

'I won't.' When Louie jumped on his bike and peddled away, Nick returned his gaze to the front of the house. He propped his chin in his hand and watched the front door. While he waited, he thought about Louie and about how lucky he was to have a brother who was going into the seventh grade. He could talk to him about anything and Louie never laughed. Louie had already seen the puberty film in school, and so Nick could ask him important questions, like when he was likely to get hair on his balls, stuff a guy just couldn't come right out and ask his Catholic mother.

A wood ant crawled up Nick's arm, and he was just about to smash it between his fingers when the front door opened and he froze. Henry walked out of the house and paused on the veranda to look over his shoulder. He motioned with his hand, and a little girl stepped through the doorway. A mass of blond curls framed her face and cascaded down her back. She placed her hand in Henry's and the two of them walked across the porch and down the front steps. She wore a frilly white dress with lacy socks like girls wore to their First Communion, but it wasn't even Sunday. Henry pointed in Nick's general direction, and Nick held his breath, fearing he'd been detected.

'Right back there,' Henry said to the little girl as they moved across the lawn toward Nick's hiding place. 'There's a great big tree that I've thought could use a treehouse in it.'

The little girl looked up at the towering man by her side

and nodded. Her golden curls bounced like springs. The girl's skin was a lot paler than Nick's, and her big eyes were brown. Nick thought she looked like those little dolls his Tia Narcisa kept locked in a glass cabinet, away from clumsy boys with dirty hands. Nick had never been allowed to touch the pretty little dolls, but he'd never really wanted to anyway.

'Like Winnie the Pooh?' she asked.

'Would you like that?'

'Yes, Henry.'

Henry lowered to one knee and looked into the girl's eyes. 'I'm your father now. You can call me Daddy.'

Nick's chest caved in and his heart pounded so hard he couldn't breathe. He'd waited his whole life to hear those words, but Henry had said them to a pale-faced stupid girl who liked Winnie the Pooh. He must have made a sound because Henry and the girl looked right at his hiding spot.

'Who's in there?' Henry demanded as he stood.

Slowly, with fear gripping his stomach, Nick rose to his feet and faced the man his mother had always said was his father. He stood straight with his shoulders back and stared into Henry's light gray eyes. He wanted to run, but he didn't move.

'What are you doing in there?' Henry demanded again.

Nick shoved his chin in the air but he didn't answer.

'Who is he, Henry?' the girl asked.

'Nobody,' he answered and turned to Nick. 'You go on home. Now get, and don't come around here anymore.'

Standing in buckbrush up to his chest, with his knees shaking and his stomach hurting, Nick Allegrezza felt his hopes die. He hated Henry Shaw. 'You're a lizard-sucking son of a bitch,' he said, then lowered his gaze to the golden-haired girl. He hated her, too. With his eyes burning hatred and stinging with anger, he turned and walked from his hiding place. He never returned. He was finished waiting in the shadows. Waiting for things he would never have.

*

Footsteps pulled Nick from thoughts of his past, but he didn't turn around.

'What do you think?' Gail moved behind him and wrapped her arms around his waist. The thin material of her dress was the only thing separating her bare breasts from his back.

'About what?'

'About the new and improved me.'

He turned then and looked at her. She was bathed in darkness and he couldn't see her very well. 'You look fine,' he answered.

'Fine? I spent thousands on a boob job, and that's the best you can do? "You look fine"?'

'What do you want me to say, that you would have been smarter to invest your money in real estate rather than saltwater?'

'I thought men liked big breasts,' she said with a pout in her voice.

Big or small didn't matter as much as what a woman did with her body. He liked a woman who knew how to use what she had, who lost control in bed. A woman who could let go and get down and dirty with him. Gail was too worried about how she looked.

'I thought all men fantasize about big breasts,' she continued.

'Not all men.' Nick hadn't fantasized about a woman in a very long time. In fact, he hadn't fantasized since he'd been a kid, and all those fantasies had been the same.

Gail wrapped her arms around his neck and rose onto the balls of her feet. 'You didn't seem to mind a while ago.'

'I didn't say I minded.'

She slid her hand down his chest to his stomach. 'Then make love to me again.'

He wrapped his fingers around her wrist. 'I don't make love.'

'Then what did we just do half an hour ago?'

He thought about giving her a one-word answer, but he knew she wouldn't appreciate his candor. He thought about taking her home, but she slid her hand to the front of his jeans, and he thought maybe he'd wait a while to see what she had on her mind. 'That was sex,' he said. 'One has nothing to do with the other.'

'You sound bitter.'

'Why, because I don't confuse sex and love?' Nick didn't consider himself bitter, just uninterested. As far as he was concerned, there was no payoff in love. Just a lot of wasted time and emotion.

'Maybe you've never been in love.' She pressed her hand into his fly. 'Maybe you'll fall in love with me.'

Nick chuckled deep within his chest. 'Don't count on it.'

The morning after the funeral, Delaney slept late and narrowly escaped a meeting of the Charitable Society of Truly, the small town's equivalent of the Junior League. She'd hoped to lie around the house all afternoon and spend some time with her mother before leaving that evening to meet her best friend from high school, Lisa Collins. The two had plans to meet at Mort's Bar for a night of margaritas and gossip.

But Gwen had different plans for Delaney. 'I'd like you to stay for the meeting,' Gwen said as soon as she walked into the kitchen, looking like a catalog model dressed in powder-blue silk. A slight wrinkle furrowed her brow as she glanced at Delaney's shoes. 'We're hoping to buy new playground equipment for Larkspur Park, and I think you could help us come up with creative ways to raise money.'

Delaney would rather chew on tinfoil than get sucked into attending one of her mother's boring meetings. 'I have plans,' she lied, and spread strawberry preserves onto a toasted bagel. She was twenty-nine but still couldn't bring herself to purposely disappoint her mother.

'What plans?'

'I'm meeting a friend for lunch.' She leaned her behind against the cherrywood island and bit into her bagel.

Tiny creases settled in the corners of Gwen's blue eyes. 'You're going into town looking like that?'

Delaney glanced down at her white sleeveless sweater, her black jean shorts, and the thin patent leather straps of her Hercules sandals with the rubber wedgie soles. She'd dressed conservatively, but maybe her shoes were slightly different by small-town standards. She didn't care; she loved them. 'I like what I'm wearing,' she said, feeling like a nine-year-old again. She didn't like the feeling, but it reminded her of the biggest reason why she planned to leave Truly quickly the following afternoon after Henry's will was read.

'I'll take you shopping next week. We'll drive down to Boise and spend the day at the mall.' Gwen smiled with genuine pleasure. 'Now that you're home again, we can go at least once a month.'

There it was. Gwen's assumption that Delaney would be moving back to Truly now that Henry was dead. But Henry Shaw hadn't been the only reason Delaney kept at least an entire state between herself and Idaho.

'I don't need anything, Mother,' she said and polished off her breakfast. If she stayed more than a few days, there wasn't a doubt in her mind that Gwen would have her in Liz Claiborne and turn her into a respectable member of the Charitable Society. She'd grown up wearing clothes she didn't like and pretending to be someone she wasn't just to please her parents. She'd killed herself to make honor roll in school, and she'd never so much as received a fine on a library book. She'd grown up the mayor's daughter. That meant she'd had to be perfect.

'Aren't those shoes uncomfortable?'

Delaney shook her head. 'Tell me about the fire,' she said, purposely changing the subject. Since she'd arrived in Truly, she'd learned very little of what had actually happened the night of Henry's death. Her mother was reluctant to talk about it, but now that the funeral was over, Delaney pressed for information.

Gwen sighed and reached for the butter knife Delaney had used to spread preserves. The heels of her blue pumps clicked on the red brick tiles as she moved toward the kitchen sink. 'I don't know anything more now than I did when I called you last Monday.' She set down the knife then gazed out the big window above the sink. 'Henry was in his tack shed and it caught on fire. Sheriff Crow told me they think it started in a pile of linseed rags he'd left by an old space heater.' Gwen's voice wavered as she spoke.

Delaney moved toward her mother and put her arm around Gwen's shoulders. She looked out at the backyard, at the boat dock swaying on gentle waves, and asked the question she'd been afraid to voice, 'Do you know if he suffered very much?'

'I don't think so, but I don't want to know if he did. I don't know how long he lived or if God was merciful and he died before the flames got to him. I didn't ask. Everything that has happened this past week has been hard enough.' She paused to clear her throat. 'I've had so much to do, and I don't like to think about it.'

Delaney turned her gaze to her mother, and for the first time in a very long time, she felt a connection with the woman who'd given her life. They were so different, but in this, they were the same. Despite his faults, they had both loved Henry Shaw.

'I'm sure your friends would understand if you canceled your meeting today. If you'd like, I'll call them for you.'

Gwen turned her attention to Delaney and shook her head. 'I have responsibilities, Laney. I can't put my life on hold forever.'

Forever? Henry had been dead less than a week, buried less than twenty-four hours. She dropped her hand from her mother's shoulders, feeling the connection snap. 'I'm going outside for a bit,' she said, and walked out the back door before she could give in to the disappointment. A late morning breeze rustled the quaking aspen, filling the pine-scented air with the whisper of leaves. She took a deep breath and moved across the back patio.

Disappointment seemed the best word to describe her family. They'd lived a facade, and as a result, they'd been doomed to disappoint one another. A long time ago she'd come to terms with the fact that her mother was superficial, far more concerned with appearance than substance. And Delaney had accepted that Henry was an over-the-top control freak. When she'd behaved as Henry expected, he'd been a wonderful father. He'd given her his time and attention, taken her and her friends boating or camping in the Sawtooths, but the Shaws had lived a life of reprimand and reward, and she'd always felt disappointed that everything, even love, had been conditional.

Delaney walked past a towering Ponderosa to the large dog run on the edge of the back lawn. Two brass name plates tacked above the door of the kennel declared the Weimaraners inside were Duke and Dolores.

'Aren't you pretty babies?' she cooed, touching their smooth noses through the chain link and talking to them as if they were lap dogs. Delaney loved dogs, having been raised with Dolores and Duke's predecessors, Clark and Clara. But these days, she moved too often to have a goldfish, let alone a real pet. 'Poor pretty babies all penned up.' The Weimaraners licked her fingers, and she lowered to one knee. The dogs were well-groomed, and since they'd belonged to Henry, no doubt well-trained. Their long brown faces and sad blue eyes silently begged her to set them free. 'I know how you feel,' she said. 'I used to be trapped here, too.' Duke let loose with a pitiful whine that tugged at Delaney's sympathetic heart. 'Okay, but don't go out of the yard,' she said as she stood.

The kennel door swung open and Duke and Dolores threw themselves forward, shooting past Delaney like two streaks of lightening. 'Damn it, get back here!' she yelled, turning just in time to see their stubby tails disappear into the forest. She thought about letting them go with the hope they'd return on their own. Then she thought of the highway less than a mile from the house.

She grabbed two leather leashes from inside the kennel and took off after them. She didn't feel any attachment toward the dogs, but she didn't want them to end up as roadkill either. 'Duke! Dolores!' she called, running as fast as she could, carefully balancing her weight over a pair of wedgie sandals. 'Dinnertime. Steak. Kibbles and Bits.' She chased them into the forest and on old trails she'd roamed as a child. Towering pines enclosed her in shadows and shrubbery slapped at her shins and ankles. She caught up with the dogs at the old treehouse Henry had built for her as a child, but they took off just as she made a grab for their collars. 'Milk-Bones,' she called out as she pursued them past Elephant Rock and through Huckleberry Creek. She might have given up if the two animals hadn't stayed within spitting distance, teasing her, taunting her with their closeness. She chased them under low-hanging aspen branches and scraped her hand as she hoisted herself over a fallen pine.

'Damn it!' she cursed as she inspected her scratches. Duke and Dolores sat on their haunches, wagging their stubby tails and waiting for her to finish. 'Come!' she commanded. They lowered their heads in submission, but as soon as she took a step, they jumped up and took off. 'Get back here!' She considered letting them go, but then she remembered the Truly Charitable Society meeting at her mother's house. Chasing stupid dogs through the forest suddenly sounded like a good time.

She followed them up a small hill and paused beneath a

pine tree to catch her breath. Her brows lowered as she gazed at the meadow in front of her, subdivided and cleared of trees. A bulldozer and a front-end loader sat idle next to a huge dump truck. Neon orange paint marked the ground in several spots beside big sewer trenches, and Nick Allegrezza stood in the midst of the chaos next to a black Jeep Wrangler, Duke and Dolores at his feet.

Delaney's heart jumped to her throat. Nick was the one person she'd hoped to avoid during her short visit. He was the source of the single most humiliating experience of her life. She fought to suppress the urge to turn and go back the way she'd come. Nick had seen her and there was no way she was going to run. She had to force herself to walk calmly down the incline toward him.

He was dressed the same as he had been yesterday at Henry's funeral. White T-shirt, worn Levi's, gold earring, but he'd shaved today and his hair was pulled back in a ponytail. He looked like he belonged on a billboard wearing nothing but his Calvin's.

'Hello,' she called out. He didn't say anything, just stood there, one of his big hands leisurely scratching the top of Duke's head as his gray eyes watched her. She fought the apprehension weighing the pit of her stomach as she came to stand several feet before him. 'I'm walking Henry's dogs,' she said, and was again treated with silence and his steady, unfathomable gaze. He was taller than she remembered. The top of her head barely reached his shoulder. His chest was broader. His muscles bigger. The last time she'd stood this close, he'd turned her life inside out and changed it forever. She'd thought he was a knight in shining armor, driving a slightly battered Mustang. But she'd been wrong.

He'd been forbidden to her all her life, and she'd been drawn to him like an insect to a bug light. She'd been a good girl longing to be set free, and all he'd had to do was crook his finger at her and utter four words. Four provocative words from his bad-boy lips. 'Come here, wild thing,' he'd said, and her soul had responded with a resounding *yes*. It had been as if he'd looked deep inside her, past the facade, to the real Delaney. She'd been eighteen and horribly naive. She'd never been allowed to spread her wings, to breathe on her own, and Nick had been like pure oxygen that went straight to her head. But she'd paid for it.

'They're not as well-behaved as Clark and Clara were,' she continued, refusing to feel intimidated by his silence.

When he finally did speak, it wasn't what she expected. 'What did you do to your hair?' he asked.

She touched her fingers to the soft red curls. 'I like it.'

'You look better as a blond.'

Delaney's hand fell to her side, and she lowered her gaze to the dogs at Nick's feet. 'I didn't ask for your opinion.'

'You should sue.'

She really did like her hair, but even if she didn't, she couldn't very well sue herself. 'What are you doing up here?' she asked as she leaned forward and snapped the leash on Duke's collar. 'Looting?'

'No.' He rocked back on his heels. 'I never plunder on the Lord's day. You're safe.'

She looked into his dark face. 'But funerals are fair game, right?'

A frown creased his forehead. 'What are you talking about?'

'That blond yesterday. You treated Henry's funeral like a pick-up bar. That was disrespectful and gauche, Nick. Even for you.'

The frown disappeared, chased away by a licentious smile. 'Jealous?'

'Don't flatter yourself.'

'Want the details?'

She rolled her eyes. 'Spare me.'

'You sure? It's pretty juicy stuff.'

'I think I'll live.' She pushed one side of her hair behind her ear, then reached for Dolores.

Before she touched the dog, Nick reached out and grabbed her wrist. 'What happened here?' he asked and cupped the back of her hand. His palm was big and warm and callused, and he lightly brushed his thumb across the scratch on her own palm. A surprising little tingle tickled her fingertips, then swept up her arm.

'It's nothing.' She pulled away. 'I scraped it climbing over a blowdown.'

He looked into her face. 'You climbed over a blowdown in those shoes?'

For the second time in less than an hour, her favorite shoes were being maligned. 'There's nothing wrong with them.'

'Not if you're a dominatrix.' His gaze slid down her body, then slowly climbed back up. 'Are you?'

'Dream on.' She reached for Dolores again, and this time successfully clipped the leash on the dog's collar. 'Whips and chains aren't my idea of a good time.'

'That's a shame.' He folded his arms across his chest and leaned his butt against the tire well of the Jeep. 'The closest thing Truly has to an experienced dominatrix is Wendy Weston, 1990 state champion calf roper and barrel racer.'

'Can you afford two women spanking your bum?'

'You could steal me away,' he said through a grin. 'You're better-looking than Wendy, and you have the right shoes.'

'Gee thanks. Too bad I'm leaving tomorrow afternoon.'

He looked a little surprised by her answer. 'Short trip.'

Delaney shrugged and pulled the dogs toward her. 'I never intended to stay long.' She would probably never see him again, and she let her gaze roam the sensual line of his dark face. He was too handsome for his own good, but maybe he wasn't as bad as she remembered. He would never pass for a *nice* guy, but at least he hadn't reminded her of the night she'd sat on the hood of his Mustang. It had been ten years; maybe he'd mellowed. 'Good-bye, Nick,' she said and took a step backward.

He touched two fingers to his brow in a mock salute, and she turned and headed back the way she'd come, dragging the dogs along with her.

At the top of the small hill, she glanced over her shoulder one last time. Nick stood just as she'd left him beside his Jeep, arms folded across his chest, watching her. As she stepped into the shifting forest shadows, she remembered the blond he'd picked up at Henry's funeral. Maybe he'd mellowed, but she'd bet pure testosterone, not blood, ran through his veins.

Duke and Dolores tugged at their leashes and Delaney tightened her grasp. She thought about Henry and about Nick and wondered once again if Henry had included his son in his will. She wondered if they'd ever tried to reconcile, and she wondered what Henry had bequeathed her. For a few brief moments, she let herself imagine a gift of money. She let herself imagine what she could do with a chunk of cash. First, she'd pay off her car, then she'd buy a pair of shoes from some place like Bergdorf Goodman. She'd never owned an eight-hundred-dollar pair of shoes, but she wanted to.

And if Henry had left her a *huge* chunk a cash?

She'd open her own salon. Without a doubt. A modern salon with lots of mirrors, and marble, and stainless steel. She'd dreamed of her own business for quite a while now, but two things stood in her way. One, she hadn't found a city where she wanted live for more than a couple of years. And two, she didn't have the capital or the collateral to get the capital.

Delaney stopped in front of the fallen tree she'd climbed over earlier. When Duke and Dolores began to crawl beneath, she pulled on their leashes and took the long way around. Her wedgies teetered on rocks, and her toes were covered with dirt. As she trudged through a crop of buckbrush, she thought of bug bites and blood-sucking ticks. A shiver ran up her spine, and she pushed aside the thought of contracting Rocky Mountain spotted fever and replaced it with designing the perfect upscale salon in her head. She'd start out with five chairs, and stylists would lease space from *her* for a change. Since she didn't like to give manicures and hated pedicures, she'd hire someone else to do it. She'd stick to what she loved: cutting hair, schmoozing, and serving her customers lattes. She'd start out charging her customers seventy-five dollars for a cut and blow-dry. A bargain for her services, and once she had a steady client base, she'd raise her prices on them gradually.

God bless America and a free market system where everyone had the right to charge whatever they wanted. That thought brought her full circle to Henry and his will. As much as she liked to dream about her own salon, she seriously doubted he'd left her money. Probably her gift was something he would know she didn't want.

As Delaney carefully picked her way across Huckleberry Creek, the two dogs jumped in and splashed her with icy water. Henry had probably left her a gag gift. Something to torture her for a long time. Something like two unruly Weimaraners.

Downtown Truly boasted two grocery stores, three restaurants, four bars, and one recently installed traffic light. The Valley View Drive-In had been closed for five years due to lack of business, and one of only two beauty salons, Gloria's: A Cut Above, had closed the month before due to Gloria's unexpected demise. The three-hundred-pound woman had suffered a massive heart attack while giving Mrs Hillard a shampoo and set. Poor Mrs Hillard still had nightmares.

The old courthouse was located next to the police station and forestry service building. Three churches competed for souls, Mormon, Catholic, and born-again Christian. The new hospital had been built next to the combination elementary and middle school, but the most celebrated establishment in town, Mort's Bar, was in the older section of Truly, on Main between Value Hardware and the Panda Restaurant.

Mort's was more than a place to get tanked. It was an institution, famous for its cold Coors and array of antlers. Deer, elk, antelope, and moose decorated the wall above the bar, their magnificent racks adorned with bright panties. Bikinis. Briefs. Thongs. All colors, all signed and dated by the donor drunk. A few years back, the owner had nailed a jack-o-lope head next to the moose, but no respectable woman, drunk or sober, wanted her panties hanging from something as goofy-looking as a jack-o-lope. The head had been quickly moved to the back room to hang above the pinball machine.

Delaney had never been in Mort's. She'd been too young ten years ago. Now as she sipped margaritas in a booth toward the back, she wondered at the attraction. Except for the wall above the bar, Mort's was like a hundred other bars in a hundred other small towns. The lights were dim, the juke-box was constant, and the smell of tobacco and beer permeated everything. The dress was casual, and Delaney felt perfectly at home in a pair of jeans and a Mossimo T-shirt.

'Did you ever donate your undies?' she asked Lisa, who sat across the blue vinyl booth. Within minutes of meeting her old friend, the two had fallen into easy conversation, as if they'd never been apart.

'Not that I recall,' she answered, her green eyes alight with humor. Lisa's easy smile and laughter had been what had drawn the two together in the fourth grade. Lisa had been carefree, her brunette hair always in a scraggly ponytail. Delaney had been uptight, her blond hair perfectly curled.

Lisa had been a free spirit. Delaney had been a spirit longing to be free. They'd loved the same music and movies, and they'd loved to argue like sisters for hours. The two had balanced each other out.

After Lisa had graduated from high school, she'd received her degree in interior design. She'd lived in Boise for eight years, employed at a design firm where she'd done all the work and received none of the credit. Two years ago she'd quit and moved back to Truly. Now, thanks to computers and modems, she operated a busy design business from her home.

Delaney's gaze took in her friend's pretty face and disheveled ponytail. Lisa was smart and attractive, but Delaney still had the better hair. If she were staying in town longer, she'd grab her friend and cut her hair to accent her eyes, then maybe brush a few light streaks around her face.

'Your mother tells me you're a makeup artist down in Scottsdale. She said you have celebrity clients.'

Delaney wasn't surprised by her mother's embellishment and took a sip of her margarita. Gwen hated Delaney's career, perhaps because it reminded her mother of their life before Henry – the life Delaney had never been allowed to talk about, when Gwen had styled hair for dancers on the Vegas strip. But Delaney was nothing like her mother. She loved working in a salon. It had taken years to finally discover her niche. She loved the tactile sensations, the smell of Paul Mitchell, and the gratification of a pleased client. And it didn't hurt that she was extremely good. 'I'm a hairstylist in a salon in Scottsdale, but I live in Phoenix,' she said and licked the salt from her top lip. 'I love it, but my mother is embarrassed by what I do for a living. You'd think I was a hooker or something.' She shrugged. 'I don't do makeup because of the hours, but I did trim Ed McMahon's hair once.'

'You're a beautician?' Lisa laughed. 'This is too good. Helen Markham has a salon over on Fire-weed Lane.'

'You're kidding? I saw Helen yesterday. Her hair looked like shit.'

'I didn't say she was any good at it.'

'Well, I am,' Delaney said, having found something at last that she was a lot better at than her old rival.

A waitress approached and set two more margaritas on the table. 'That gentleman over there,' the woman said, pointing toward the bar, 'bought you two another round.'

Delaney glanced at the man she recognized as one of Henry's friends. 'Tell him thank you,' she said and watched as the waitress left. She hadn't bought a drink since she'd stepped foot in Mort's. Men she vaguely remembered from her youth kept a steady supply of booze coming to her table. She was on her third, and if she weren't careful, she'd be drunk in no time.

'Remember when you caught Helen and Tommy doing it in the back of his mother's Vista Cruiser?' Lisa asked, beginning to look a little glassy-eyed.

'Of course I remember. He'd told me he was going to the drive-in with some friends.' She drained one glass and reached for the third. 'I decided to surprise him. And I did.'

Lisa laughed and downed her drink. 'That was so funny.'

Delaney's laughter joined her friend's. 'Not at the time though. Having Helen Schnupp, of all girls, steal my first boyfriend sucked.'

'Yeah, but she did you a favor. Tommy has turned into a real bum. He only works long enough to collect unemployment. He has two kids, and Helen supports them most of the time.'

'How does he look?' Delaney asked, cutting to the important stuff.

'Still good-lookin'.'

'Damn.' She'd hoped for a report of a receding hairline at the very least. 'Who was that friend of Tommy's? Do you remember? He always wore that John Deere baseball cap, and you had a mad crush on him.'

A frown appeared between Lisa's brows. 'Jim Bushyhead.'

Delaney snapped her fingers. 'That's right. You dated him for a while, but he dumped you for that girl with the mustache and big boobs.'

'Tina Uberanga. She was Basque *and* Italian . . . poor thing.'

'I remember you were madly in love with him for a long time after he dumped you.'

'No, I wasn't.'

'Yes, you were. We used to have to drive by his house at least five times a day.'

'No way.'

Two more drinks appeared, provided by another of Henry's associates. Delaney waved her thanks and turned back to her friend. They resumed their gossip over a steady stream of free margaritas. At nine-thirty Delaney glanced at her watch. She'd lost count of her drinks, and her cheeks were beginning to feel a little numb. 'I don't suppose Truly has a taxi service these days.' If she cut herself off now, she'd have over three hours to sober up before the bar closed and she had to drive home.

'Nope. We finally got a gas station with a minimart. But it closes at eleven.' She pointed a finger at Delaney and said, 'You don't know how lucky you are to live in a city with a Circle K. You can't just grab a box of Ding Dongs or a burrito at two in the morning around here.'

'Are you drunk?'

Lisa leaned forward and confessed, 'Yes, and guess what else? I'm getting married.'

'What?' Delaney sputtered. 'You're getting married and you waited all this time to tell me?'

'Well, we're not telling anyone for a while. He wants to talk to his daughter first, before it's common knowledge. But she's in Washington with her mother until next week.'

'Who? Who's the lucky guy?'

Lisa looked her straight in the eyes and said, 'Louie Allegrezza.'

Delaney blinked several times then burst into laughter. 'That's a good one.'

'I'm serious.'

'Crazy Louie.' She continued to laugh as she shook her head. 'You've got to be pulling my leg.'

'I'm not. We've been seeing each other for eight months. Last week he asked me to marry him, and of course I said yes. We're getting married November fifteenth.'

'Nick's brother?' Her laughter died. 'You're serious, aren't you?'

'Very, but we can't tell anyone until he talks to Sophie.'

'Sophie?'

'His daughter from his first wife. Sophie's thirteen and a real daddy's girl. He thinks if he tells her when she gets back, she'll have almost six months to get used to the idea.'

'Crazy Louie,' Delaney repeated, stunned. 'Isn't he doing time in prison?'

'No. He doesn't do crazy things anymore.' She paused and shook her head. 'Besides, he was never really *that* crazy.'

Delaney wondered if her friend had fallen on her head in the past ten years and suffered memory loss. 'Lisa, he stole a car in the fifth grade.'

'No. We were in the fifth grade. He was in the ninth, and in all fairness, he was on his way to take it back when he hopped the curb and got high-centered on that bench in front of Value Drug.' Lisa shrugged. 'He might not have even gotten caught if he hadn't swerved to miss the Olsens' dog, Buckey.'

Delaney blinked to clear her head. 'Are you blaming Buckey?'

'That dog always did run loose.'

All dogs ran loose in Truly. 'I can't believe you're blaming poor Buckey? You must be in love.'

Lisa smiled. 'I am. Haven't you ever felt so in love you wanted to crawl inside a man's skin and stay there?'

'A few times,' Delaney confessed, feeling a little envious of her friend. 'But I got over it after a while.'

'Too bad you live so far away, I'd ask you to be in my wedding. Remember how we were always going to be each other's maid of honor?'

'Yeah.' Delaney sighed. 'I was going to marry Jon Cryer and you were going to marry Andrew McCarthy.'

'*Pretty in Pink*.' Lisa sighed, too. 'That was a great movie. How many times do you think we sat there and cried when Andrew McCarthy dumped Molly Ringwald because she was from the wrong side of the tracks?'

'At least a hundred. Remember when—' she began but the bartender's voice interrupted her.

'Last call,' he bellowed.

Delaney checked her watch again. 'Last call? It's not even ten.'

'It's Sunday,' Lisa reminded her. 'Bars close at ten on Sunday.'

'We're both too drunk to drive.' Delaney panicked. 'How are we going to get home?'

'Louie's picking me up 'cause he knows I'm a cheap date and thinks he's going to get lucky. I'm sure he'll take you home, too.'

She pictured her mother's horrified face peering out the front window, crazy Louie Allegrezza careening up the driveway. Delaney smiled at the thought, and she knew she was a few margaritas past sobriety. 'If you don't think he'll mind.'

But it wasn't Louie who blew into the bar five minutes later like he owned the place. It was Nick. He'd slipped a plaid flannel shirt over his T-shirt. He'd left the shirt unbuttoned, and the ends hung open at his hips. Delaney sank down in her seat. Drunk or sober, she wasn't in the mood to face him. He hadn't mentioned their past when she'd seen him earlier that day, but she still didn't trust that he wouldn't.

'Nick!' Lisa waved as she called across the bar. 'Where's Louie?'

He looked toward the booth at Lisa, then his gaze locked on Delaney as he moved toward her. 'Sophie called upset about something,' he explained, coming to stand by the table. He paused, then switched his attention to his future sister-in-law. 'He asked me to come and get you.'

Lisa scooted across the booth seat and stood. 'Would you mind giving Delaney a ride home?'

'That's okay,' Delaney quickly assured them. She grabbed her crocheted purse and rose to her feet. 'I can find my own way.' The room tilted slightly, and she placed a hand on the wall beside her. 'I don't think I'm that drunk.'

The corners of Nick's mouth pulled into a frown. 'You're wasted.'

'I just stood up a little too fast,' she said and stuck her hand in her peach-colored bag, searching for a quarter. She'd have to call her mother. She really wasn't looking forward to it, but if she thought her mother would be horrified to see Louie, Nick would send her over the top.

'You can't drive,' Lisa insisted.

'I wasn't— heeey!' she called out to Nick's retreating back as she watched him head across the bar with her purse in his hand. Any other man might have been in danger of looking a little swishy clutching a woman's peach bag, but not Nick.

She and Lisa followed him out the door and into the black night. She hoped her mother was already in bed asleep. 'Damn it's cold,' she muttered, the mountain chill seeping into her pores. Crossing her arms over her breasts, she practically ran down the sidewalk to keep up with Nick's long strides. She wasn't used to summer nights in the mountains of Idaho anymore. In Phoenix temperatures dipped to ninety-four – not fifty-four – and she couldn't wait to get back.

'It's not that cold,' Lisa argued as they passed Delaney's yellow Miata parked by the curb. 'You've turned into a wimp.'

'You're a bigger wimp than I am. You always were. Remember when you fell off the monkey bars in sixth grade and cried for three hours?'

'I hurt my tailbone.'

They stopped by Nick's black Jeep. 'It didn't hurt that much,' she said. 'You were just a big wimp.'

'At least I didn't cry like a baby when I had to dissect a frog in high school.'

'I got frog guts in my hair,' Delaney defended. 'Anyone would cry if frog guts flew in their hair.'

'Jesus, Joseph, and Mary.' Nick sighed like a weary priest and opened the car passenger door. 'What did I do to deserve this?'

Lisa pushed the seat forward. 'Something sinful I'm sure,' she said and climbed into the back.

Nick laughed and flipped the backrest into place for Delaney. Like a perfect gentleman, he held the door for her. She knew she was drunk, her judgment impaired, but maybe he had changed. She looked at him cast in shadows, only the lower half of his face illuminated by a street lamp. She knew he could charm the pants off anyone when he wanted, and there had been a few times in her life when he'd been uncharacteristically nice to her. Like the time in fourth grade when she'd come out of the market with a plenty pack of Trident and discovered a flat tire on her bicycle. Nick had insisted on pushing it all the way home. He'd shared his candy with her, and she'd given him some of her gum. Maybe he'd actually changed and *turned* into a nice guy. 'Thank you for the ride home, Nick.' Or better yet, maybe he'd forgotten about the single worst night of her life. Maybe he'd forgotten that she'd thrown herself at him.

'Any time.' A smile curved his sensuous mouth and he handed the purse to her. 'Wild thing.'

Delaney zipped her suitcase and looked about her bedroom one last time. Nothing had changed since the day she'd walked out ten years ago. The rose wallpaper, the lace canopy, and her music collection were all just as she'd left them. Even the snapshots stuck to the vanity mirror were the same. Her things had been kept waiting for her, but instead of feeling comforting and welcoming, the room felt oppressive. The walls were closing in on her. She had to get out.

Now all she had to do was listen to the will and, of course, tell her mother she was leaving. Gwen would do her best to make Delaney feel guilty, and Delaney wasn't looking forward to the confrontation.

She left the room and headed downstairs to Henry's office to hear the reading of his will. She'd dressed for comfort in a sleeveless T-shirt dress made of soft blue cotton, and she'd shoved her feet into a pair of platform slides that she could kick off easily during the long drive ahead of her.

At the entrance to the office, a long-time friend of Henry's, Frank Stuart, greeted her as if he were a doorman at the Ritz-Carlton. 'Good morning, Miss Shaw,' he said as she walked into the room. Max Harrison, Henry's estate lawyer, sat behind the heavy desk and looked up as Delaney entered. She shook his hand and spoke to him briefly before taking a seat beside her mother in the front row.

'Who isn't here?' she asked, referring to the remaining empty chair next to hers.

'Nick.' Gwen sighed as she fingered the three strands of her pearl necklace. 'Although I can't imagine why Henry would provide for him in his will. He'd tried to reach out many times in the past few years, but Nick threw every attempt back in his father's face.'

So Henry had attempted a reconciliation. She wasn't really surprised. She'd always assumed since Henry had failed to produce a legitimate heir with Gwen, he'd eventually turn his attention to the son he'd always ignored.

Less than a minute later, Nick walked into the room, managing to look almost respectable in a pair of charcoal corduroys and a ribbed silk polo the same color as his eyes. Unlike the funeral, he'd dressed for the occasion. His hair was pulled back, and he'd left his earring at home. His gaze moved over the room, then he took the chair next to Delaney. She glanced up at him out of the corner of her eye, but he stared straight ahead, feet apart, his hands resting on his thighs. The clean scent of his aftershave teased her nose. She hadn't spoken to him since he'd called her 'wild thing' the night before. She'd ignored him all the way to her mother's house, feeling the same humiliation she thought she'd overcome years ago. She had no intention of speaking to the jerk now.

'Thank you all for coming,' Max greeted, drawing Delaney's attention. 'In order to save time, I would ask that you hold all questions until I am finished.' He cleared his throat, squared the documents in front of him, and began in his smooth lawyer's voice, ' "I, Henry Shaw, now of Truly, resident of Valley County, State of Idaho, do make and declare this to be my Last Will and Testament, hereby revoking all Wills and Codicils I have made before this.

' "Article I: I nominate and appoint my trusted friend Frank Stuart as Executor of this Will. I request that no Executor or successor in such capacity shall be required to furnish any sureties on his official bond . . ." '

Delaney looked at a point behind Max's head and listened with half an ear as he read the part of the will that outlined the duty of the executor. She didn't care about executor duties. Her mind was filled with more important concerns, like her mother seated on one side and Nick on the other. The two disliked each other intensely. They always had, and the tension that filled the room was almost tangible.

Nick's shoulder brushed Delaney's as he placed his elbows on the arms of his chair. His shirt grazed her bare skin, then was gone. Delaney forced herself to remain perfectly still, as if the touch hadn't happened, as if she hadn't felt the smooth texture of his sleeve on her skin.

Max proceeded to the section of the will that provided for Henry's long-time employees and his brothers at the Moose Lodge. Then he paused and Delaney returned her gaze to him. She watched him carefully set one page aside before he continued.

' "Article III: (A) I give and bequeath half of my tangible property and half of my estate not otherwise disposed of hereunder, together with any unexpired insurance policies thereon, to my wife, Gwen Shaw. Gwen was an excellent wife, and I loved her deeply.

' "(B) To my daughter, Delaney Shaw, I give and bequeath the remainder of my tangible property and the remainder of my estate not otherwise disposed of hereunder on the condition that she reside strictly within the city limits of Truly, Idaho, and may not leave, for a period of one year so that she may look after her mother. The subsequent year to begin upon notification of this Will. If Delaney refuses to comply with the terms of this Will, the property referred to in this

Article III (B) shall pass to my son, Nick Allegrezza." '

'What does all that mean?' Delaney interrupted. Her mother's sudden grasp on her arm was the only thing keeping her from jumping to her feet.

Max glanced at her, then returned his gaze to the document on the desk before him. ' "(C) I give to my son, Nick Allegrezza, the properties known as Angel Beach and Silver Creek, to do with as he wishes, provided that he refrain from entering into a sexual relationship with Delaney Shaw for one year. If Nick refuses, or goes against my wishes in regard to this stipulation, then the above property shall revert to Delaney Shaw." '

Delaney sat rigid in her chair, feeling as if she'd been zapped with a stun gun. Heat flushed her face and her heart felt like it had stopped. Max's voice continued for several more moments, but Delaney was too confused to listen. It was all too much to take in at one time, and she didn't really understand most of what had been read. Except the last part forbidding Nick to 'enter into a sexual relationship' with her. That part had been a slap directed at them both. A reminder of the past when Nick had used her to get back at Henry, and she'd begged him to do it. Even after his death, Henry wasn't finished punishing her. She was so mortified she wanted to die. She wondered what Nick thought, but she was too afraid to look at him.

The lawyer finished and glanced up from the will. Silence filled the office, and no one spoke for several long moments, until Gwen voiced the question on everyone's mind.

'Is that legal and binding?'

'Yes,' Max answered.

'So, I am to receive half of the estate free of conditions, yet in order for Delaney to inherit, she must stay in Truly for one year?'

'That's correct.'

'That's ridiculous,' Delaney scoffed, trying her best to forget about Nick and concentrate on her own bequest. 'This is the 1990s. Henry can't play God. This can't be legal.'

'I assure you it is. In order to inherit your share, you must agree to the conditions expressed in the will.'

'Forget it.' Delaney stood. Her bags were packed. She wasn't about to let Henry control her from the grave. 'I'll give my share to Mother.'

'You can't. The bequest was conditional. You will receive your share of the estate on the condition you reside in Truly for one year. The estate is held in trust until after the provisionary period. In short, you can't give your mother what you don't have. And if you decided to reject the terms of the will, your portion of the estate will revert to Nick, not Gwen.'

And if Delaney did that, her mother would kill her. But Delaney didn't care. She wasn't going to sell her soul to spare her mother. 'What if I contest the will?' she asked, becoming desperate.

'You can't contest the will simply because you don't like the provisions. You have to have grounds, such as lack of mental capacity or fraud.'

'Well, there you go.' Delaney lifted her hands, palms up. 'Henry was obviously out of his mind.'

'I'm afraid the court would hold a different view. The provision has to be proven illegal or against public policy, and it is neither. It may be considered capricious, but it meets the requirements of the law. The fact is, Delaney, your portion of the estate is estimated at just over three million dollars. Henry has made you a very wealthy young woman. All you have to do is live in Truly for one year, and no court is going to consider the condition impossible to perform. You can accept or refuse. It's that simple.'

Delaney sat back down, the breath knocked from her lungs.

Three million. She'd assumed they were talking about several *thousand.*

'If you agree to the terms,' Max continued, 'an adequate monthly allowance will be provided for your care and support.'

'When did Henry make this will?' Gwen wanted to know.

'Two months ago.'

Gwen nodded as if it all made perfect sense, but it didn't. Not to Delaney.

'Do you have any questions, Nick?' Max asked.

'Yeah. Does one fuck constitute a sexual relationship?'

'Oh, my God!' Gwen gasped.

Delaney clenched her hands into fists and turned her gaze to him. His gray eyes burned with fury, and anger thinned his lips. That was okay with Delaney; she was furious, too. They stared at each other, two combatants spoiling for a fight. 'You,' she said, lifting her chin and looking at him as if he were something she needed to scrape off her shoes, 'are evil.'

'And what about oral sex?' Nick asked, keeping his gaze locked on Delaney.

'Uh . . . Nick,' Max spoke into the tension. 'I don't think we—'

'I think we do,' Nick interrupted. 'Henry was obviously concerned about it. So concerned he included it in his will.' He turned his hard gaze to the lawyer. 'I think we need to know the rules right up front so there's no confusion.'

'*I'm* not confused,' Delaney told him.

'For instance,' Nick continued as if she hadn't spoken. 'I've never considered a one-night stand a relationship. Just two naked bodies rubbing up against each other, getting all sweaty, and having a good time. In the morning you wake up alone. No promises you never intend to keep. No commitment. No looking at each other over breakfast. Just sex.'

Max cleared his throat. 'I believe Henry's intent was no sexual contact at all.'

'How's anyone going to know?'

Delaney glared at him. 'Easy. I wouldn't have sex with you to save my life.'

He looked at her and lifted a skeptical brow.

'Well,' Max interjected, 'as executor, it is Frank Stuart's duty to see that the terms are enforced.'

Nick turned his attention to the executor, who stood at the back of the room. 'Are you going to spy on me, Frank? Peek in my windows?'

'No, Nick. I'll take your word that you'll agree to the conditions of the will.'

'I don't know, Frank,' he said and turned his gaze to Delaney once again. His eyes lingered on her mouth before sliding down her throat to her breast. 'She's pretty hot. What if I just can't control myself?'

'Stop it right now!' Gwen stood and pointed at Nick. 'If Henry were here, you wouldn't behave this way. If Henry were here, you'd have more respect.'

He looked at Gwen as he rose to his feet. 'If Henry were here, I'd kick his ass for him.'

'He was your father!'

'He was nothing more than a sperm donor,' he scoffed, then he moved to the door and delivered one last parting shot before he left. 'Too bad for all of us he was a one-shot wonder,' he said, leaving the room filled with stunned silence.

'Leave it to Nick to make everything unpleasant,' Gwen said after they heard the front door close. 'Henry tried to make amends, but Nick rejected him every time. I think it's because he's always been jealous of Delaney. His behaviour here today proves it, don't you think?'

Delaney's head began to pound. 'I don't know.' She raised her palms to the sides of her face. 'I've never known why Nick does the things he does.' Nick had always been a mystery to her, even when they were kids. He'd always been unpredictable, and she'd never pretended to understand why he behaved the way he did. One day he acted like he could hardly tolerate her presence in the same town, then the very next day he might say something nice to her, or make the boys at her school stop teasing her. And just when she would start to think he was nice, he'd blindside her, leaving her stunned and gasping. Like today, and like the time he'd hit her between the eyes with a snowball. She'd been in the third grade, standing in front of the school, waiting for her mother to pick her up. She remembered standing to one side, watching Nick and a group of his friends build a snow fort by the flagpole. She remembered how his thick black hair and olive skin had been such a sharp contrast against all that white. He'd worn a navy wool sweater with leather patches on the shoulders, and his cheeks had turned red from the cold. She'd smiled at him, and he'd thrown a snowball at her and practically knocked her unconscious. She'd had to go to school with two black eyes, which eventually turned green and yellow before fading completely.

'What now?' Gwen asked, pulling Delaney's attention from the past and Nick.

'If no one contests the will we can proceed fairly quick.' Max looked at Delaney. 'Do you plan to challenge the will?'

'What's the point? You made it clear that Henry's provision for me was a take it or leave it proposition.'

'That's correct.'

She should have known Henry would attach conditions to his will. She should have known he would try to make her take over his business, to control her and everyone else from the grave. Now all she had to do was choose. Money or her soul. Half an hour ago she would have said that her soul wasn't for sale, but that had been before she'd heard the asking price. Half an hour ago everything had been so clear. Now suddenly the lines were blurred, and she didn't know what to think anymore.

'Can I sell off Henry's assets?'

'As soon as they legally belong to you.'

Three million dollars in exchange for one year of her life. After that, she could go anywhere she liked. Since leaving Truly ten years ago, she'd never stayed in one place for more than a few years. She always became too restless and edgy to stay in one place for very long. When the urge to move called, she always answered on the first ring. With all that money, she could go anywhere she wanted. Do whatever she wanted, maybe find a place she'd want to call home.

The last thing in the world she wanted was to move back to Truly. Her mother would make her crazy. She'd be crazy to stay here and give up a year of her life.

She'd be crazy if she didn't.

The Jeep Wrangler slid to a stop a few feet from the burned remains of what had once been a large barn. The fire had burned so hot, the building had caved in on itself, leaving behind a pile of mostly unrecognizable debris. To the left, a blackened foundation, a heap of cinders, and shards of broken glass were all that was left of Henry's tack shed.

Nick popped the Jeep's clutch and killed the engine. He would have bet anything that the old man hadn't intended to torch his horses too. He'd been there the morning after the fire when the coroner pulled what had been left of Henry from the ashes. Nick hadn't expected to feel anything. He was surprised that he did.

Except for the five years Nick had lived and worked in Boise, he'd resided in the same small town as his father, both of them ignoring each other. It wasn't until he and Louie had moved their construction company to Truly that Henry decided he would finally acknowledge Nick. Gwen had just turned forty and Henry finally accepted the fact that he would never father children with her. Time had run out, and he turned his attention to his only son. By then, Nick was in his late twenties and had no interest in a reconciliation with the man who'd always refused to acknowledge him. As far as he was concerned, Henry's sudden interest was a case of too little too late.

But Henry was determined. He made Nick persistent offers of money or property. He offered him thousands of dollars to change his name to Shaw. When Nick refused, Henry doubled the offer. Nick promptly told him to shove it.

He offered Nick a share of his businesses if Nick would act like the son Henry wanted. 'Come over for dinner,' as if that would make up for a lifetime of indifference. Nick turned him down.

Eventually though, they did enter into a somewhat strained coexistence. Nick gave his father the courtesy of listening to his offers and enticements *before* he refused. Even now, Nick had to admit some of the offers had been pretty good, but he'd easily turned them down. Henry accused him of obstinacy, but it was more disinterest than anything else. Nick just didn't care anymore, but even if he'd been seriously tempted, everything had a price. Nothing was free. There was always a trade-off. Quid pro quo.

Until six months ago. In an effort to bridge the gap between them, Henry gave Nick a very generous gift, a peace offering with no strings attached. He outright deeded him Crescent Bay. 'So my grandchildren will always have the best beach in Truly,' he'd said.

Nick took the gift, and within a week, submitted plans to the city to develop condominiums on the five acres of beach-front property. The preliminary plat was approved remarkably fast, before Henry knew and could raise an objection. The fact that the old man didn't find out until after the fact was incredible luck.

Henry had been furious. But he got over it quickly because there was something Henry wanted more than anything else. He'd wanted the one thing that only Nick could give him. He'd wanted a grandchild. A direct blood descendant. Henry had money and property and prestige, but he hadn't had time. He'd been diagnosed with advanced prostate cancer. He'd known he was going to die.

'Just pick a woman,' Henry had ordered several months ago after barging into Nick's down-town offices. 'You should be able to get someone pregnant. God knows you've practiced enough to get it right.'

'I've told you, I've never met a woman I'd consider marrying.'

'You don't have to get married, for God's sake.'

Nick wasn't willing to produce a bastard for anyone, and he hated Henry for suggesting it to him, his bastard son, as if the consequences were unimportant.

'You're doing this to spite me. I'll leave you everything when I'm gone. Everything. I've talked to my attorney, and I'll have to leave Gwen a little something so she won't contest my will, but you'll get everything else. And all you have to do is get a woman pregnant before I die. If you can't choose someone, I'll pick the girl for you. Someone from a good family.'

Nick had shown him the door.

The cell phone chirped on the seat next to him, but he ignored it. He hadn't been all that surprised when he'd learned the cause of Henry's death had been a gunshot wound to the head and not the fire. He'd known Henry was getting worse, and Nick would have done the same thing.

Sheriff Crow had been the one to tell Nick that Henry had killed himself, but very few people knew the truth. Gwen wanted it that way. Henry had gone out on his own terms, but not before he'd created one hell of a will.

Nick had figured Henry would pull something in his will, but he'd never expected Henry to place the condition on what Nick did or didn't do with *Delaney*. Why her? A real bad feeling tweaked the base of his skull, and he feared he knew the answer. It sounded perverse, but he had a feeling Henry was trying to pick the mother of his grandchild.

For reasons he didn't want to examine too closely, Delaney had always spelled trouble for him. From the start. Like the time she'd been standing in front of the school bundled up in a fancy blue coat with a furry white collar, her blond hair a mass of shiny curls about her face. Her big brown eyes had looked into his, and a little smile had tilted her pink lips. His chest had grown tight and his throat closed. Then before he'd realized what he was doing, he'd picked up a snowball and nailed her in the forehead. He hadn't known why he'd done it, but it had been the one and only time his mother took a belt to his behind. Not so much because he'd hit Delaney, but because he'd hit a girl. The next time he'd seen her at school, she'd looked like Zorro, with twin black eyes. He'd stared at her, feeling sick to his stomach and wishing he could race home and hide. He'd tried to apologize, but she'd always run away when she'd seen him coming. He guessed he didn't blame her.

After all these years, she still had a way of getting to him. It was the way she looked at him sometimes. Like he was dirt, or worse, when she looked *through* him as if he didn't even exist. It made him want to reach out and pinch her, just to hear her say ouch.

Today he hadn't meant to hurt or provoke her. Well, not until she'd given him that 'you're scum' look. But listening to Henry's will had provoked *him*. Just thinking about it pissed him off all over again. He thought about Henry and Delaney, and that real bad feeling tweaked the back of his neck once more.

Nick reached for the ignition key and headed back toward town. He had a few questions, and Max Harrison was the only person who knew the answers.

'What can I do for you?' the lawyer asked as soon as Nick was shown into a spacious office near the front of the building.

Nick didn't waste time on idle conversation. 'Is Henry's will legal, and can I contest?'

'As I told you earlier when I read the will, it's legal. You can waste your money on a contest.' Max gave Nick a wary look before he added, 'But you won't win.'

'Why did he do it? I have my suspicions.'

Max looked at the younger man standing in his office. There was something unpredictable and intense lurking just beneath that cool exterior. Max didn't like Allegrezza. He didn't like the way he'd behaved earlier. He didn't like the disrespect he'd shown Gwen and Delaney – a man should never swear in the presence of ladies. But he'd liked Henry's will even less. He sat in a leather chair behind his desk, and Nick sat across from him. 'What are your suspicions?'

Nick leveled his wintry gaze on Max and said without reservation, 'Henry wants me to get Delaney pregnant.'

Max debated whether to tell Nick the truth. He felt no love or loyalty toward his former client. Henry had been a very difficult man and had ignored his professional advice repeatedly. He'd cautioned Henry about drafting such a capricious and potentially injurious will, but Henry Shaw always had to have things his own way, and the money had been too good for Max to let his client find another lawyer. 'I believe that was his intent, yes,' he answered truthfully, perhaps because he felt a little guilty for his part in it.

'Why didn't he just say so in the will?'

'Henry wanted his will drafted that way for two reasons.

First, he didn't think you'd concede to father a child for property or money. Second, I informed him that if you contested a condition stipulating you impregnate a woman, you might possibly win on the grounds of a conflict of morals. Henry didn't seem to think there was a judge around who would believe you have any morals when it comes to women, but contesting the will would defeat the purpose.' Max paused and watched Nick's jaws tighten. He was pleased to see a reaction, however slight. Maybe the man wasn't completely void of human emotion. 'There is always a chance you might get a judge who would declare the condition void.'

'Why Delaney? Why not another woman?'

'He was under the impression that you and Delaney had a clandestine past together,' Max said. 'And he thought if he forbade you to touch Delaney, you'd feel compelled to defy him, as I take it you have in the past.'

Anger tightened Nick's throat. There had been no clandestine past between himself and Delaney. 'Clandestine' made it sound like Romeo and freakin' Juliet. As far as the other, that whole forbidden theory, what Max said might have been true once, but Henry had overplayed his hand. Nick wasn't a kid anymore, drawn to the things he couldn't have. He didn't do things just to defy the old man, and he wasn't drawn to the porcelain doll who always got his hands slapped for him.

'Thank you,' he said as he stood. 'I know you didn't have to tell me anything.'

'You're right. I didn't.'

Nick shook Max's extended hand. He didn't think the lawyer liked him much, which was okay with Nick.

'I hope Henry went to all the trouble for nothing,' Max said. 'I hope, for Delaney's sake, he won't get what he wants.'

Nick didn't bother with a reply. Delaney's virtue was safe from him. He walked out the front door of the office and down the sidewalk toward his Jeep. He could hear his cell phone chirping even before he opened the door. It stopped only to start once again. He started the engine and reached for the small phone. It was his mother wanting information about the will and reminding him to come to her house for lunch. He didn't need reminding. He and Louie ate lunch at their mother's house several times a week. It calmed her worries about their eating habits and kept her from coming to their houses and rearranging the sock drawers.

But today he didn't particularly want to see his mother. He knew how she'd react to Henry's will and really didn't want to talk to her about it. She'd rant and rage and direct her angry diatribes at anyone with the last name Shaw. He supposed she had many legitimate reasons to hate Henry.

Her husband Louis had been killed driving one of Henry's logging trucks, leaving her with a small son, Louie, to raise by herself. A few weeks after Louis's funeral, Henry had gone to the house to offer his comfort and sympathy. When he'd left late that night, he'd left with the vulnerable young widow's signature on a document releasing him from further responsibility in Louis's death. He'd placed a check in her hand, and a son in her womb. After Nick had been born, Benita had confronted Henry, but he'd denied the baby could possibly be his. He'd kept denying it for most of Nick's life.

Even though Nick figured his mother had a right to her anger, when he arrived at her house, he was surprised at the vehemence of today's tirade. She cursed the will in three languages: Spanish, Basque, and English. Nick understood only part of what she said, but most of her outrage was directed toward Delaney. And he hadn't even told her about the absurd no-sex stipulation. He hoped he wouldn't have to.

'That girl!' she fumed, sawing her way through a loaf of bread. 'He always put that *neska izugarri* before his son. His own blood. She is nothing, nothing. Yet she gets everything.'

'She might leave town,' Nick reminded her. He didn't care

whether Delaney stayed or was already on her way back home. He didn't really want Henry's business or the money. Henry had already given him the only property he would have wanted.

'Ba! Why should she leave? Your uncle Josu will have something to say about this.'

Josu Olechea was his mother's only brother. He was a third-generation sheep rancher, and owned land near Marsing. Since Benita had no husband, she counted on Josu to be head of the family, no matter that her sons were grown.

'Don't bother him with this,' Nick said and leaned a shoulder against the refrigerator. As a boy, whenever he'd gotten in trouble or his mother figured he and Louie needed a positive male influence, she'd sent them to spend the summer with Josu and his sheepherders. Both of them had loved it until they'd discovered girls.

The back door opened and his brother stepped into the kitchen. Louie was shorter than Nick. Solid, with the black hair and eyes he'd inherited from both his mother and father. 'So,' Louie began, closing the screen door behind him. 'What did the old man leave you?'

Nick smiled and straightened. His brother would appreciate the inheritance. 'You're going to love it.'

'He got practically nothing,' his mother interjected, carrying a plate of sliced bread into the dining room.

'He left me his Angel Beach property and the land at Silver Creek.'

Louie's thick brows rose up his forehead and a glint sparkled in his dark eyes. 'Holy shit,' the thirty-four-year-old land developer whispered so his mother wouldn't hear him.

Nick laughed and the two of them followed Benita into the dining room, then sat at the polished oak table. They watched their mother neatly fold back the lace tablecloth, then leave to get their lunch.

'What are you going to put on the Angel Beach property?' Louie asked, assuming correctly that Nick would want the land developed. Benita might not realize the worth of Nick's inheritance, but his brother did.

'I don't know. I have a year to think about it.'

'A year?'

Benita set bowls of *guisado de vaca* in front her sons, then took her seat. It was hot outside, and Nick really didn't feel like stew. 'I get the property if I do something. Or *not* do something, actually.'

'Is he trying to get you to change your name again?'

Nick looked up from his bowl. His mother and brother stared back at him. There was no way around it. They were family, and they believed family had the God-given right to stick their noses in his business. He snagged a piece of bread and took a bite. 'There was a condition,' he began after he swallowed. 'I get the property in one year if I don't become involved with Delaney.'

Slowly Louie picked up his spoon. 'Involved? How?'

Nick cast a sideways glance at his mother, who was still staring at him. She'd never talked to either boy about sex. She'd never even so much as mentioned it. She'd left *the talk* up to Uncle Josu, but by that time, both Allegrezza boys had known most of it anyway. He returned his gaze to his brother and lifted one brow.

Louie took a bite of stew. 'What happens if you do?'

'What do you mean what happens?' Nick scowled at his brother as he reached for his spoon. Even if he were crazy enough to want Delaney, which he wasn't, she hated him. He'd seen it in her eyes today. 'You sound as if there's a possibility.'

Louie didn't say anything. He didn't have to. He knew Nick's history.

'What happens?' his mother asked, who didn't know anything but felt she had the right to know everything.

'Then Delaney inherits the property.'

'Of course. Isn't it enough that she got everything that is rightfully yours? Now she will be after you to get her hands on your property, Nick,' his mother predicted, generations of suspicious and secretive Basque blood running through her veins. Her dark eyes narrowed. 'You watch out for her. She's as greedy as her mother.'

Nick seriously doubted he would have to *watch out* for Delaney. Last night when he'd driven her to her mother's house, she'd sat in his Jeep doing a really good impersonation of a statue, the moonlight casting her profile in gray shadows and letting him know she was royally pissed off. And after today, he was pretty sure she'd avoid him like a leper.

'Promise me, Nick,' his mother continued. 'She always got you into trouble. You watch out.'

'I'll watch out.'

Louie grunted.

Nick frowned at his brother and purposely changed the subject. 'How's Sophie?'

'She's coming home tomorrow,' Louie answered.

'That's wonderful news.' Benita smiled and set a slice of bread next to her bowl.

'I'd hoped to have a little more time alone with Lisa before I tell Sophie about the wedding,' Louie said. 'I don't know how she'll take the news.'

'She'll adjust to her new stepmother eventually. Everything will turn out fine,' Benita predicted. She liked Lisa okay, but she wasn't Basque and she wasn't Catholic, which meant that Louie couldn't marry *in the church*. Never mind that Louie was divorced and couldn't marry *in the church* anyway. Benita wasn't worried about Louie. Louie would be okay. But Nick. She worried about Nick. She always had. And now *that girl* was back and she would worry even more.

Benita hated anyone with the last name Shaw. Mostly she

hated Henry for the way he'd treated her and the way he'd treated her son, but she hated that *girl* and her mother too. For years she'd watched Delaney parade around in fancy clothes while Benita had to patch Louie's hand-me-downs for Nick. Delaney got new bicycles and expensive toys while Nick went without or had to settle for secondhand. And while she'd watched Delaney get more than one little girl needed, she'd also watched her son, his proud shoulders straight, chin in the air. A stoic little man. And each time she watched him pretend it didn't matter, her heart broke a little more. Each time she watched him watch that girl, she grew a little more bitter.

Benita was proud of both her sons and she loved them equally. But Nick was different from Louie. Nick was so very sensitive.

She looked across the table at her younger son. Nick would always break her heart.

4

The plastic doggie scooper bags in the pocket of Delaney's shorts seemed like some pathetic metaphor of her life. Shit, that's what it was. Ever since she'd sold her soul for money, that's what her life had become, and she didn't see that it would get any better for another eleven months. Almost everything she owned resided in a storage shed on the outskirts of town, and her closest companions were the two Weimaraners walking beside her.

It had taken Delaney less than five hours to decide to accept the terms of Henry's will. An appallingly short amount of time, but she wanted the money. She'd been given a one-week reprieve to travel to Phoenix, quit her job, and close her apartment. Saying good-bye to her friends at Valentina had been hard. Saying good-bye to her freedom was even harder. It had been only a month, but it felt like she'd been a prisoner for a year.

She had no job and wore boring clothes she didn't particularly like because she lived with her mother.

The hot sun baked the top of her head as she made her way down Grey Squirrel Lane toward the center of town. When she'd lived in Truly ten years ago, most of the streets hadn't had names. There had been no need, but with the recent influx of summer residents, and the boom in real estate, the city council had knocked itself out to come up with really inventive street names like Gopher, Chipmunk, and Grey Squirrel. Delaney, it seemed, lived in the rodent section of town, while Lisa fared somewhat better over on Milkweed, which of course was next to Ragweed and Tumbleweed.

Since she'd been back, she'd noticed a lot of other changes, too. The business district had quadrupled, and the old part of town had been given a facelift. There were two public boat ramps to accommodate the heavy invasion of boats and Jet Skis, and the city had added three new parks. But beyond those changes, there were two other very visible and telling signs that the town had finally been pulled into the 1990s. First, there was the Mountain Java Espresso Shop located between Sterling Realty and the Grits and Grub Diner. And second, the old lumber mill had been converted into a microbrewery. When Delaney had lived in Truly before, the people drank Folgers and Coors. They would have declared a double-shot skinny latte 'sissy coffee' and would have beat the crap out of anyone who dared to utter the words 'raspberry beer.'

It was the Fourth of July and the town was smothered in patriotism. Red, white, and blue flags and ribbons decorated everything from the 'Welcome to Truly' banner to the wooden Indian standing outside Howdy's Trading Post. There would be a parade later, of course. In Truly, there were parades for just about every occasion. Maybe she'd stick around downtown and watch the parade. It wasn't like she had anything else to do.

At the corner of Beaver and Main, Delaney stopped and waited for an RV to lumber by. For walking so nicely beside her, she reached into her pocket and rewarded Duke and Dolores with Milk-Bones. It had taken several frustrating weeks to assert her role as the alpha dog and teach them who was boss. She'd had the time. For the past month she'd spent some of her time catching up with a few old school friends. But they were all married and had families and looked at her as if she were abnormal because she didn't.

She would have loved to spend more time with Lisa, but unlike Delaney, Lisa had a job and a fiancé. She would have loved to sit down with her old friend and talk about Henry's will and the real reason she was back in Truly. But she didn't dare. If its stipulation became public, Delaney's life would turn into a burning hell. She would become the subject of endless speculation and the topic of never-ending gossip. And if the part of the will concerning *Nick* was revealed, she'd probably have to kill herself.

As it was, she was just likely to die of boredom before it was all over. She spent her days watching talk shows, or she walked Duke and Dolores as a means to get out of the house and escape the life her mother had planned for her. Gwen had decided that since Delaney would be living in Truly for a year, they should be involved in the same projects, belong to the same social organizations, and attend the same civic meetings. She'd even gone so far as submitting Delaney's name to spearhead a committee concerned with the drug problem in Truly. Delaney had politely turned down the offer. First of all, Truly's drug problem was laughable. Second, Delaney would rather drink bong water than get involved in the community.

She and the dogs moved down Main, passing a deli and T-shirt shop. Both were recent additions to the downtown area, and judging by the foot traffic, seemed to do a fair amount of business. With the soles of her Lycra sling-backs slapping her bare heels, she walked past a tiny bookstore with a poster stuck on the door advertising an upcoming R&B festival. The poster surprised Delaney, and she wondered when the town had abandoned Conway Twitty for James Brown.

She stopped in front of a thin two-story building flanked on one side by an ice-cream shop and on the other by the offices of Allegrezza Construction. Painted across the big plate glass window were the words: 'Gloria's: A Cut Above. Any cut and style $10.' Delaney didn't think the sign spoke well for Gloria's abilities.

Duke and Dolores sat at her feet, and she scratched them between the ears. Leaning forward, she peered into the huge plate-glass window to see the red Naugahyde salon chairs. Each time she'd driven through town, she'd noticed the salon had been closed.

'Hey there, what's up?'

Delaney recognized Lisa's voice and turned to her friend. She wasn't surprised to see Louie standing by Lisa's side. His gaze was direct and a bit unnerving. Or maybe she found him unnerving because he was Nick's brother. 'I was just checking out this salon,' she answered.

'I gotta get going, *alu gozo*,' Louie said, then bent his head and kissed his fiancée. The kiss lingered and Delaney lowered her gaze to a point between Duke's ears. She hadn't had a boyfriend in over a year, and that relationship hadn't lasted more than four months. She couldn't remember the last time a man had kissed her like he meant to eat her up and didn't care who watched.

'See you around, Delaney.'

She glanced up. 'See ya, Louie.' She watched him walk into the building next to the salon. Maybe she found him unnerving because, like his brother, he was extremely masculine. Nick was taller, more sculpted, like a statue. Louie was built like a bull. You'd never see an Allegrezza in a Versace neck-cloth or a tiny Speedo. 'What does *alu gozo* mean?' she asked, having a little difficulty pronouncing the foreign words.

'It's an endearment, like sweetheart. Louie can be so romantic.'

Unexpected envy tugged at her. 'What are you up to?'

Lisa lowered to one knee and scratched Duke and Dolores

beneath the chin. 'I took Louie to lunch, and I was just dropping him back off.'

'Where'd you go?'

Lisa smiled as the dogs licked her hands. 'My house.'

Delaney felt a twinge of jealousy and realized she was lonelier than she'd thought. It was the Fourth of July and a Friday night. The weekend stretched before her – empty. She missed the friends she'd had in Phoenix. She missed her busy life.

'I'm glad I ran into you. What are you doing tonight?' Lisa asked.

Not a damn thing, she thought. 'I don't know yet.'

'Louie and I thought we'd have some friends over. I want you to come, too. His house is on Horseshoe Bay, not far from where they'll shoot the fireworks out over the lake. The show is pretty awesome from his beach.'

Delaney Shaw at Louie Allegrezza's? Nick's brother? Mrs Allegrezza's son? She'd seen Benita the other day at the grocery store, and everything she remembered about the woman was still true. No one showed such cold contempt as Benita Allegrezza. No one could convey both superiority and disdain in the same look of her dark eyes. 'Oh, I don't think so, but thanks.'

'Chicken.' Lisa stood and wiped her hands on her jeans.

'I'm not a chicken.' Delaney shifted her weight to one foot and tilted her head to the side. 'I just don't want to go someplace where I know I'm not welcome.'

'You're welcome. I talked to Louie, and he doesn't have a problem with you coming.' Lisa took a deep breath, then said, 'He said he likes you.'

Delaney laughed. 'Liar.'

'Okay, he said he didn't *know* you. But if he gets to know you, he'll like you.'

'Will Nick be there?' One of her main goals for surviving

the entire year was to avoid him as much as humanly possible. He was rude and crude and purposely reminded her of things best forgotten. She was stuck in the same city, but that didn't mean she had to socialize with him.

'Nick will be out on the lake with some of his friends, so he won't be there.'

'What about Mrs Allegrezza?'

Lisa looked at her as if she were an idiot. 'Of course not. Louie is going to invite some of the guys who work for him, and Sophie will be there with some of her friends. We're going to get together for hot dogs and burgers about six. You should come. What else are you going to do?'

'Well, I was going to watch the parade.'

'That's over by six, Delaney. You don't want to sit home alone do you?'

Her obvious lack of a life embarrassed Delaney, and she glanced across the street toward Sterling Realty. She thought of the night ahead of her. After *Wheel of Fortune*, what was there to do? 'Well, I guess I could drop by. If you're sure Louie won't mind my being there.'

Lisa waved aside Delaney's concern and took a few steps backward to leave. 'I told you, we talked it over, and he doesn't care. Once he gets to know you, he'll like you.'

Delaney watched her friend walk away. She wasn't as optimistic as Lisa. Louie was Nick's brother, and the tension and animosity between herself and Nick was a tangible thing. She hadn't spoken to Nick since the reading of Henry's will, but she'd seen him several times. She'd seen him bombing down Wagon Wheel Road on his Harley, then a few days later walking into Mort's with a redhead pressed up against his side. The last time she'd laid eyes on him was at the intersection of Main and First. She'd been stopped at the traffic light, and he'd crossed the street in front of her. *I don't know, Frank. She's pretty hot. What if I just can't control myself?*

Her grip had tightened on the steering wheel, and she'd felt her cheeks burn. His attention had been focused on the folder in his right hand, and she'd wondered what he would do if she *accidentally* bumped into him? If her foot accidentally slipped from the brake and hit the gas. If she accidentally mowed him down, then backed up just to make sure?

She'd revved the Miata's engine like she was Cha-Cha Muldowney waiting for the flag to drop, then she'd eased the clutch just enough so the car lunged into the crosswalk. Nick's head had jerked up, and he'd jumped out of the way. His brows lowered and his cool gray eyes bored into her. In another split second the bumper would have clipped his right leg.

She'd smiled at him. For that moment, life had been good.

Delaney vacillated for hours over whether she should show up at Lisa's party. She hadn't fully decided until she caught herself thinking about curling up with a stack of magazines and a box of wine. She was twenty-nine, and if she didn't do something quick, she was afraid she'd become one of those women who wore hats instead of brushing their hair and traded in their red platforms for Easy Spirit walking shoes. Before she could change her mind, she pulled on a black turtleneck and a quilted leather vest the color of limes. Her jeans were black also, but her ankle boots matched her vest. She scrunched mousse in her soft curls and hung little gold hoops in the four piercings she had in each ear.

By the time Delaney arrived at the party, it was a little after eight. Three giggling thirteen-year-old girls answered the door and led her toward the rear of a spacious home constructed of river rock and cedar.

'They're all back here,' one of the girls with dark eyes informed her. 'Do you wanna put your purse in my dad's room?'

She'd shoved her wallet and a tube of burgundy lipstick into a little patent leather bag that looked like a hatbox. The wallet she could live without, but she wouldn't be able to replace her Estee Lauder lipstick for a year. 'No thanks. Are you Sophie?'

The girl barely glanced over her shoulder at Delaney as they moved through the kitchen. 'Yep. Who are you?'

Sophie had braces and pimples and wonderfully thick hair with horrible dried and split ends. Split ends drove Delaney nuts. They were like a crooked picture that drove a person mad until it was straightened. 'I'm Lisa's friend, Delaney.'

Sophie's head whipped around and her eyes widened. 'Oh my gosh! I heard Grandma talk about you.'

By the look on Sophie's face, Benita hadn't been dispensing compliments. 'Great,' Delaney muttered as she stepped around the three girls. She walked through a set of double glass doors onto a deck. The white sandy beach below was shaded by two enormous Ponderosas, and several boats were tied to the dock riding the gentle waves of Lake Mary.

'Hey there,' Lisa greeted and excused herself from the semicircle of people around her. 'I was worried you wouldn't make it. Did you have to go to something fancy first?'

Delaney glanced down at her clothes, then lifted her gaze to the other guests who wore T-shirts and shorts. 'No. I still get cold,' she answered. 'Are you sure it's okay that I'm here?'

'Sure. How was the parade?'

'It was almost exactly the same as it was the last time I saw it, except the group of World War veterans has dwindled to two old guys in the back of a school bus.' She smiled, more relaxed than she'd been in over a month. 'And the biggest thrill is still the anticipation over which unsuspecting tuba player will step in the horse crap.'

'How was the junior high school band? Sophie told me they were pretty good this year.'

Delaney struggled for a compliment. 'Well, the uniforms are better than when we were in school.'

'That's what I thought.' Lisa laughed. 'Are you hungry?'

'I've eaten already.'

'Come on, and I'll introduce you around. There are some people here you might remember.'

Delaney followed Lisa to a knot of people gathered around two barbecues. The fifteen or so guests were a combination of friends Lisa and Louie had known most of their lives and people who worked for Allegrezza Construction.

Delaney chatted with Andrea Huff, the best baseball pitcher in elementary school. Andrea was married to John French, the boy who'd taken one of Andrea's knuckleballs in the stomach and had hurled macaroni and cheese on the playground. The two seemed happy together, and Delaney wondered if there was a connection.

'I have two sons.' She pointed to the beach below, then paused to lean over the rail and bellow at a cluster of children wading in the lake, 'Eric! Eric French, I told you not to get into that water so soon after you've eaten.'

A tow-headed boy turned and raised a hand to shade his eyes. 'I'm only up to my knees.'

'Fine, but if you drown don't come crying to me.' Andrea sighed as she straightened. 'Do you have children?'

'No. I've never been married.'

Andrea looked at her as if she were an alien, and in Truly, Delaney supposed a twenty-nine-year-old, never-been-married woman was an oddity.

'Now, tell me what you've been up to since high school.'

Delaney told her about the places she'd lived, and then the conversation turned to the memories each had of growing up in a small town at the same moment in time. They chatted about sledding at the base of Shaw Mountain, and laughed about the time Andrea had lost her bikini top waterskiing across the lake.

Something warm and unexpected settled near Delaney's

soul. Talking to Andrea felt like finding something she hadn't even known she'd missed, like old worn slippers long ago discarded for a newer flashier pair.

After Andrea, Lisa introduced Delaney to several single men who worked for Louie, and Delaney found herself on the receiving end of some very flattering male attention. Most of the single construction workers were younger than Delaney. Several were deeply tanned, had buns of steel, and looked like they'd jumped out of a Diet Coke commercial. Delaney was glad she hadn't settled for that box of Franzia. Especially when a backhoe operator named Steve handed her a bottle of Bud and looked at her through clear baby blues. His hair was like sun-bleached butterscotch, and there was a scruffiness about him Delaney might have found enormously appealing if it hadn't been so contrived. His hair was strategically tousled and too gelled to be natural. Steve knew he was gorgeous.

'I'm going to check on Louie.' Lisa grinned, then gave Delaney a cheesy thumbs-up sign behind Steve's back as if they were still back in high school and had to approve each other's dates.

'I've seen you around,' Steve said as soon as it was just the two of them.

'Really?' She raised the beer to her lips and took a drink. 'Where?'

'In your little yellow car.' His smile showed his very white, slightly crooked teeth. 'You're hard to miss.'

'I guess my car draws attention.'

'Not your car. You. You're hard to miss.'

She'd felt so invisible in the plain T-shirts and shorts she'd worn lately that she pointed to herself and asked, 'Me?'

'Don't tell me you're one of those girls who likes to pretend they don't know they're beautiful?'

Beautiful? No, Delaney knew she wasn't beautiful. She was attractive and could make herself look damn good when she tried. But if Steve wanted to tell her she was beautiful, she would let him. Because, contrived or not, he wasn't a dog – figuratively or literally. She spent so much time with Duke and Dolores that if she let herself, she could melt beneath such attention.

'How old are you?' she asked him.

'Twenty-two.'

Seven years. At twenty-two Delaney had been experimenting with life. She'd been like a convict on a prison break – a five-year prison break. Between the ages of nineteen and twenty-four, she'd lived a life of reckless abandon and absolute freedom. She'd had a great time, but was glad she was older and wiser.

She turned her gaze to the teenage girls on the beach below waving their arms and running to the edge of the water. She wasn't *that* much older than Steve, and it wasn't like she was looking for a commitment. Delaney raised the bottle to her lips again and took a drink. Maybe she could just use him for the summer. Use him, then dump him. Men had certainly used and dumped her. Why couldn't she treat men the same way men treated her? What was the difference?

'Uncle Nick's back,' Sophie called up to Louie, who stood in a knot of people.

Everything inside Delaney stilled. Her gaze flew to the boat slowly cruising toward the end of the dock, to the man standing behind the wheel of the Bayliner, his feet wide apart, his dark hair blowing about his shoulders. Shade from the towering pine fell across the surface of the water and bathed him and his three female passengers in shadows. Sophie shot down the dock with her friends trailing behind her, their excited chatter rising above the noise of the outboard engine. Nick's responding laughter reached Delaney on the breeze. She set her beer on the rail and turned to find Lisa several feet away, looking very guilty.

'Excuse me, Steve,' she said and moved to her friend.

'Don't kill me,' Lisa whispered.

'You should have told me.'

'Would you have come?'

'No.'

'Then I'm glad I lied.'

'Why, so I could get here then leave again?'

'Don't be such a wimp. You need to get past your hostile feelings for Nick.'

Delaney looked into her childhood friend's eyes and tried not to feel hurt by her remark. She reminded herself that Lisa didn't know about Henry's will or the night Nick had used her ten years ago. 'I know he's going to be your brother-in-law, but there are some very good reasons why I feel "hostile" toward him.'

'Louie told me.'

A myriad of horrible questions ran through Delaney's head. She wondered who knew what. What they knew, and who had said what to whom. 'What did he tell you?'

'He told me about the will.'

Delaney glanced over her shoulder at Louie, who was staring out at the lake. She would have preferred that no one know about the will, but it wasn't her biggest concern. Hopefully, her greatest fear was still buried in the past. 'How long have you known?'

'About a month, and I wish you would have told me. I wanted to ask you to be in my wedding, but I was waiting for you to tell me you were going to be here. Pretending I don't know has been really hard, but now I can ask you to be one of my bridesmaids. I wanted you to be my maid of honor, but I couldn't, so I had to ask my sister. But I—'

'Exactly what did Louie tell you?' Delaney interrupted as she reached for Lisa's arm and pulled her to a deserted part of the deck.

'That if you leave Truly, Nick inherits your share of Henry's estate, and if the two of you have sex, you inherit his.'

'Who else knows?'

'Benita, I think.'

Of course. 'And maybe Sophie. She said something about overhearing her grandmother.' Dread settled in the pit of her stomach, and she let go of Lisa's arm. 'This is so humiliating. Now everyone in town will know, and I won't be able to go anywhere without people watching me to make sure I don't leave town or have sex with Nick.' She felt her skull tighten at the very thought. 'As if that would ever happen anyway.'

'No one else will find out. If you're worried about Sophie, I'll talk to her.'

'And she'll listen to you?'

'If I tell her the gossip could hurt Nick, she'll listen. She worships him. In Sophie's eyes, Nick is a saint and can do no wrong.'

Delaney looked over her shoulder and watched Saint Nick with his harem of females make their way up the dock. He handed a large paper sack to Sophie, and she and her friends took off toward a picnic table on the beach. In his loose green tank top, battered Levi's with the large three-corner tear above the right knee, and rubber flip-flops, he looked like he'd just gotten out of bed. Delaney's gaze moved to the three women. Maybe he had.

'I wonder where he picked them up,' Lisa said, referring to the blond by his side and the two brunettes following close behind. 'He was just going to his house to get some fireworks for Sophie.'

'Apparently he picked up more than a few smoke bombs. Who are those women?'

'The blond is Gail something, I don't know her married name, but her dad was Judge Tanner. The two behind him look like the Howell twins, Lonna and Lanna.'

Delaney remembered Gail Tanner. She'd been several years older than Delaney, and their families had occasionally socialized. She also recognized her as the woman Nick had pick up at Henry's funeral. The Howell twins she didn't know. 'Gail's married?'

'Divorced.'

Delaney turned around for a better look. The women wore tight tank tops tucked into jeans. Delaney would have loved to dismiss them as tramps, but she couldn't. They looked more like centerfolds than hookers. 'Did Gail get a boob job? I don't remember her being that big.'

'A boob job and a little fat sucked out of her butt, too.'

'Hmm.' Delaney's gaze returned to Nick and the triangle of thigh visible through the tear in his jeans. 'Have you seen them do liposuction on TV? Damn, it hurt my buns just thinking about it.'

'It's disgusting. Looks just like chicken fat.'

'Would you ever have it done?'

'In a second. Would you?'

Delaney looked at her friend as she thought about it. 'I don't think so, but I'll probably have my breasts lifted when they start to sag past my belly button. Hopefully, that won't be for twenty more years.' Delaney's statement drew Lisa's attention to her chest.

'You always did have pretty good boobs. I never had great boobs, but I have a really nice butt.'

The two women switched their attention to Lisa's behind.

'Better than mine,' Delaney admitted, then returned her gaze to Nick and the three women making their way across the beach toward the bottom of the stairs leading to the deck. 'So, which one is his girlfriend?'

'I don't know.'

'Probably all three.'

'Probably,' Lisa agreed.

'None of them,' spoke Louie from behind.

Delaney did a mental groan and closed her eyes. She'd been caught gossiping about Nick. Worse, she'd been caught by Louie. She wondered how long he'd been standing there. She wondered if he'd heard her talking about getting her breasts lifted, but she didn't dare ask. Slowly she turned to face him, racking her brain for something to say.

Thankfully, Lisa didn't have the same problem. 'Are you sure he isn't dating the twins?'

'No,' he answered, then announced with a completely serious look on his face, 'Nick is a one-woman man.'

Delaney glanced at Lisa and the two of them burst into laughter.

'What's so funny?' Louie wanted to know. He crossed his arms over his chest, and his dark brows formed one prominent line across his forehead.

'You,' Lisa answered and kissed his firm mouth. 'You're crazy, but that's what I love about you.'

Louie put an arm around Lisa's waist and pulled her tight. 'I love you, too, *alu gozo*.'

No one had ever whispered exotic endearments to Delaney – unless she counted 'Do me, baby.' No man had ever loved her the way Louie obviously loved Lisa. And no man was likely to, either, as long as she was stuck in Truly with nothing to do but walk dogs. There had to be something better than picking up dog poop. 'Do you know who owns the building next to you?'

'You do now.' Louie shrugged. 'Maybe your mother. I guess it depends on how everything shakes out in your father's will.'

'I do?' As she absorbed the news a big smile parted her lips.

'Yep. Henry owned that whole block.'

'Your offices, too?'

'Yep.'

She had a lot to think about and took a step backward.

'Well, thanks for having me,' she said, fully intending to beat a retreat before she got within spitting distance of Nick.

'You just got here,' Lisa pointed out. 'Stay until after the fireworks. Louie, tell her we want her to stay.'

'Why don't you stay?' Louie said and took the bota he had hanging from his shoulder and held it toward her.

Great, now she'd look like a baby if she left. She took the pigskin bag from him and asked, 'What's in this?'

'*Txakoli.*' When she didn't drink, he added, 'Red wine. It's for special occasions and holidays.'

Delaney lifted the bag and hit her chin with a thin stream of wine before raising it to her mouth. The wine was sweet and very potent, and when she lowered it again, she got wine on her throat. 'I guess I should stick to a glass,' she joked and wiped her chin and neck.

From behind, the bota was plucked from her hand. She turned and stared at a wide chest and faded green cotton. Her stomach twisted like a pretzel as she slowly raised her gaze past Nick's lips to his gray eyes. The Allegrezza boys had a habit of sneaking up on her from behind.

'Open up,' he said.

She tilted her head to one side and stared at him.

'Open up,' he repeated and raised the bota to within several inches of her face.

'What are you going to do if I don't? Squirt wine all over me?'

He smiled, slow and sensual. 'Yes.'

She didn't doubt him for a moment. The second her mouth opened, wine shot between her parted lips. She watched helpless as Lisa and Louie walked away. She would have followed if she hadn't been forced to stand very still. Then the stream of wine was gone without leaving so much as a drop anywhere. She swallowed and licked the corner of her mouth. She didn't say a word.

'You're welcome.'

The breeze carried the scent of his skin and tossed strands of his thick dark hair about his bare shoulders. He smelled like clean mountain air and dark sensual man. 'I didn't ask for your help.'

'No, but you need a lot of *txakoli* to kill that bug up your butt.' He leaned back slightly and raised the bota. A red arc filled his mouth, and his throat worked as he swallowed. Fine black hair shadowed his armpit, and for the first time, Delaney noticed the tattoo circling his right biceps. It was a thin wreath of thorns, and the twists and barbs of black ink looked remarkably real against his smooth tan skin. He lowered the bag and sucked a bead of wine from his lower lip. 'Were you going to run me over the other day, wild thing?'

She tried not to react. 'Don't call me that, please.'

'What? Wild thing?'

'Yes.'

'Why not?'

'Because I don't like it.'

Nick didn't give a damn what she liked. She'd tried to run him over, no doubt about it. He slid his gaze down the curves of her body as he screwed the cap onto the spout of the bota. 'I guess that's too bad.' The second he'd stepped foot on the deck, he'd noticed her, and not just because she wore a turtleneck and green leather vest when everyone else had dressed for summer. It was her hair. The setting sun caught all those different shades of red and set them ablaze.

'Then I guess the next time I see you in a crosswalk, I won't put on the brake.'

Nick stepped forward until she had to tilt her head back to look up at him. His gaze moved over her flawless porcelain cheeks to her pink lips. The last time he'd been this close to her, she'd been naked. 'Give it your best shot.' White and pink. That's what he remembered about her most. Soft pink mouth and tongue. Firm white breasts and tight pink nipples. Silky white thighs.

She opened her mouth to say something, but whatever she meant to say was silenced by Gail's approach.

'There you are,' Gail said as she wove her arm through Nick's. 'Let's hurry and get a place on the beach before the show starts.'

Nick stared into Delaney's big brown eyes and felt a tightening in his groin that had nothing to do with the willing woman by his side. He stepped back and turned his attention to Gail. 'If you're in a hurry, go ahead without me.'

'No, I'll wait.' Gail turned her gaze from Nick to Delaney. Her grip on his arm tightened. 'Hello, Delaney. I hear you've moved back.'

'For a while.'

'The last time I talked to your mother, she told me you were a flight attendant with United.'

A slight frown wrinkled Delaney's brow and she glanced around as if she were desperately looking for a reason to escape. 'That was five years ago, and I was a baggage handler, not a flight attendant,' she said and took a step backward. 'Well, it was nice to see you again, Gail. I've got to go. I told Lisa I'd help her . . . ah . . . do something.' Without a glance in Nick's direction, she turned and walked away.

'What's going on between the two of you?' Gail asked.

'Nothing.' He didn't want to talk about Delaney, especially not with Gail. He didn't even want to think about her. She was trouble for him. She always had been. Since the first time he'd looked into her big brown eyes.

'When I walked up it certainly looked like something.'

'Drop it.' He shook free of Gail's grasp and moved into the house. Earlier, when he'd gone to his own house to get the fireworks he'd promised Sophie, Gail and the twins had been knocking on his front door. He didn't like women dropping by his house. It gave them unrealistic ideas of his involvement with them. But it was a holiday, and he'd decided to overlook the intrusion this one time and had invited them to Louie's. Now he wished he hadn't. He recognized that determined look in Gail's eyes. She wasn't about to drop anything.

Gail followed close behind Nick, but waited until they were in the deserted kitchen before she continued, 'Do you remember when Delaney left ten years ago? A lot of people said she was pregnant. A lot of people said you were the father.'

Nick tossed Louie's bota on the counter, then reached into a cooler. He grabbed two Miller's and twisted the caps off each. He remembered the rumors. Depending on who you listened to at the time, gossip had him and Delaney getting it on in a hundred different places and in very imaginative ways. But whichever version you heard, the ending was always the same. Nick Allegrezza had put his dirty hands on Delaney Shaw. He'd impregnated the princess.

Henry hadn't known what to believe. He'd been enraged at the very *possibility* that the rumor could be true. He'd demanded Nick deny it. Of course, Nick hadn't.

'Were you?'

Now it was ironic as hell. Ten years later, Henry wanted him to knock up Delaney. Nick handed Gail one of the cold beers. 'I told you to drop it.'

'I think I have a right to know, Nick.'

He looked into her blue eyes and laughed without humor. 'You don't have a right to know squat.'

'I have a right to know if you see other women.'

'You know I do.'

'What if I asked you to stop?'

'Don't,' he warned.

'Why not? We've gotten close since we've become lovers. We could have a wonderful life together if you'd let it happen.'

He knew for a fact he wasn't the only man on Gail's list of potential husbands. He just happened to be at the top. For a while, being number one on Gail's sexual hit parade had been amusing. But lately she'd begun to get possessive and that irritated him. 'I told you from the start not to expect anything from me. I never confuse sex and love. One has nothing to do with the other.' Nick raised the beer to his lips and said, 'I don't love you, but try not to take it personal.'

She crossed her arms beneath her breasts and leaned her behind against the edge of the counter. 'You're such a shit. I don't know why I put up with you.'

Nick took a long drink. They both knew why she put up with him.

Delaney felt Steve's strong masculine arm encircle her waist and pull her against his side. Red, white, and blue exploded in the black night, showering the lake with fiery sparks as Delaney tested the feeling of Steve's embrace. She decided she liked it. She liked the contact and the warmth. She felt alive again.

She glanced to the left and watched Nick bury the bottom half of a pipe in the sand. A few minutes earlier, she'd gotten a real good look at the fireworks 'Uncle Nick' had brought his niece. There wasn't so much as one legal sparkler in the sack.

A cascade of gold illuminated his profile for a few brief seconds, and she looked away. She wasn't going to avoid him anymore. She wasn't going to limit where she went because she didn't want to run into him. And she wasn't going to spend the rest of her time in Truly like she had the past month. She had a plan. Her mother wasn't going to like it, but Delaney didn't care.

And she had a wedding to look forward to in November, too. Lisa had approached her again about being in her wedding and Delaney had gladly said yes. She remembered the many times she and Lisa had pinned dishtowels in their hair and pretended to walk down the aisle. They'd speculated over who would marry first. They'd hoped for a big double wedding. Neither of them would have believed they would remain single until the ripe old age of twenty-nine.

Twenty-nine. As far as she could tell, she was the only one of her school friends who wasn't at least engaged. In February she would turn thirty. A thirty-year-old woman with no home of her own and no man in her life. The home she wasn't worried about. With three million she could buy a home. But the man. It wasn't that she *needed* a man in her life. She didn't, but it would have been nice to have one around sometimes. She hadn't had a boyfriend for a while and she missed the intimacy.

Her gaze was drawn again to the dark silhouette of the man lighting rockets from a pipe near the water's edge. He turned at the waist and looked over his shoulder in her direction. A funny little tickle settled in the pit of her stomach, and she quickly glanced up into the night sky.

The town sent up a finale so spectacular it lit the lake like dawn and caught the canopy of Colonel Mansfield's pontoon boat on fire. The people loved it and showed their appreciation by setting off their own bombs from beaches and balconies. Happy Dragons, Cobras, and Mighty Rebels burst in fiery showers of sparks. Legal fireworks like Whistling Pete's, modified to screech and take flight, buzzed the night sky.

Delaney had forgotten what pyromaniacs the people of Truly were. A shrieking missile whizzed past her head and exploded in a red shower on Louie's deck.

Welcome to Idaho. Land of potatoes and pyros.

5

The Miata's door handle dug into Delaney's behind as Steve pressed into her front. She placed her hands on his chest and ended the kiss.

'Come home with me,' he whispered above her ear.

Delaney pulled back just far enough to look into the dark shadows of his face. She wished she could use him. She wished she was tempted. She wished he wasn't so young and that his age didn't matter, but it did. 'I can't.' He was handsome, had pecs of steel, and seemed genuinely nice. She felt like a cradle robber.

'My roommate is out of town.'

A *roommate*. Of course he had a roommate. He was twenty-two. He probably lived on canned chili and Budweiser. When she'd been twenty-two, a well-rounded meal consisted mostly of corn chips, salsa, and sangria. She'd been living in Vegas, working at Circus Circus, not even concerned with the rest of her life. 'I never go home with men I've just met,' she told him and pushed until he took a step backward.

'What are you doing tomorrow night?' he asked.

Delaney shook her head and opened her car's door. 'You're a nice guy, but I'm not interested in seeing anyone right now.'

As she drove away, she looked into her rearview mirror at Steve's retreating back. At first she'd been flattered by the attention he'd paid her, but as the night had progressed, she'd become more uneasy. A lot of maturing happened in seven years. Matching furniture became as important as a killer stereo, and somewhere along the way, the phrase 'party till you puke' lost its appeal. But even if she'd been seriously tempted to use Steve's body for her own pleasure, Nick had ruined it for her. He ruined it by just being at the party. She was much too aware of him, and there was just too much history between them for her to ignore him completely. Even when she did manage to forget him for a few moments, she'd suddenly feel his gaze, like hot irresistible tractor beams pulling at her. But when she'd looked at him, he was never looking back.

Delaney turned up the long driveway and pressed the garage door opener on the dash. And even if Nick hadn't been there, and Steve hadn't been young, she doubted she would have gone home with him. She was twenty-nine, lived with her mother, and was too paranoid to enjoy a one-nighter.

After she parked next to Henry and Gwen's matching Cadillacs, she headed into the house through the door off the kitchen. A bug light and several citronella candles cast a dim glow on the porch out back, illuminating Gwen and the back of a man's head. It wasn't until Delaney walked outside that she recognized Henry's lawyer, Max Harrison. She hadn't seen Max since the day he'd read Henry's will. She was surprised to see him now.

'It's good to see you,' he said, standing as she approached. 'How do you like living in Truly again?'

It sucks, she thought as she sat in a wrought-iron chair across the matching table from her mother. 'It takes some getting used to.'

'Did you enjoy your party?' Gwen asked.

'Yes,' she answered truthfully. She'd met some nice people, and despite Nick Allegrezza, she'd enjoyed herself.

'Your mother was just telling me you've been busy training Henry's dogs.' Max took his seat once again, and his smile seemed genuine. 'Maybe you've found a new career.'

'Actually, I like my old career,' she said. Ever since her conversation with Louie, she'd been thinking about the vacant building downtown. She hadn't wanted to discuss her ideas with her mother until she was sure she could pull it off, but the person she needed to talk to most just happened to be sitting across the table, and her mother would find out sooner or later anyway. 'Who owns the building next to Allegrezza Construction?' she asked Max. 'It's a thin two-story with a hair salon on the bottom floor.'

'I believe Henry left that block of property at First and Main to you. Why?'

'I want to reopen the salon.'

'I don't think that's a good idea,' her mother said. 'There are a lot of other things you can do.'

Delaney ignored her. 'How do I go about doing it?'

'To get started, you'll need a small business loan. The previous owner is dead, so you'll need to contact the attorney representing her heirs to determine the value of the salon,' he began. When he was finished half an hour later, Delaney knew exactly what she had to do. First thing Monday, she'd pay a visit to the bank holding her money in trust and apply for a loan. As far as she could see, there was only one drawback to her plan. The salon was located next to Nick's construction company. 'Can I raise the rent on the building next door?' Maybe she could force him out.

'Not until the current lease expires.'

'When is that?'

'Another year I believe.'

'Damn.'

'Please don't swear,' her mother admonished while she reached across the table and placed her hand on top of

Delaney's. 'If you want to open a little business, why don't you think about a gift shop?'

'I don't want to open a gift shop.'

'You could open up in time to sell Christmas Spode.'

'I don't want to sell Spode.'

'I think it's a wonderful idea.'

'Then you do it. I'm a hairstylist, and I want to reopen the salon downtown.'

Gwen sat back in her chair. 'You're just doing this to spite me.'

She wasn't, but she'd lived with her mother long enough to know that if she argued, she'd end up looking childish. Sometimes talking to Gwen was like wrestling with flypaper. The more you fought to get free, the more you got stuck.

It took Delaney a little over three months to secure her loan and get the salon ready to open for business. While she waited, she did an unscientific study of the downtown business district, with emphasis on the number of customers who walked into Helen's Hair Hut. With legal pad and pen in hand, she parked in alleys and spied on her childhood nemesis, Helen Markham. When Lisa wasn't working or busy with wedding plans, Delaney had her report any activity she might notice as well. Delaney charted demographic statistics and visually gathered bad perm versus good perm data. She even went so far as concocting a phony English accent in case Helen recognized her when she called to ask what her competition charged for a color retouch. But it wasn't until she found herself digging through Helen's Dumpster one night to check out what kinds of cheap products Helen used that several thoughts struck her at the same time. As she'd stood there, up to her thighs in garbage, her foot sinking into a container of spoiled cottage cheese, she realized she'd gone a little overboard with her investigation. She also realized that the success of the salon had as much to do with fulfilling a dream as it did with kicking Helen to the curb. She'd been away for ten years, only to come back and fall into the same patterns. However, this time she wasn't going to lose anything to Helen.

By the end of the unscientific study, she could see that Helen did a thriving business, but Delaney wasn't worried. She'd seen Helen's hair. She could steal her old rival's clients – no problem.

Once the loan went through, Delaney put away her legal pad and got busy on the shop itself. A grimy layer of dust covered everything, from the cash register to the perming rods. Everything had to be scrubbed down and sterilized. She pored over the previous owner's books, but the numbers didn't match the inventory. Either Gloria had been completely inept, or someone had come in after her death and stolen cases of hair products. Not that Delaney minded the theft all that much since she didn't have to pay Gloria's heirs for the missing supplies, and everything in the shop was at least three years behind the current trends anyway. Still, it left her a little uneasy to think that someone might have access to the salon. In her mind, the prime suspect was of course Helen. Helen was a thief from way back, and who else would have use for things like cotton strips, shampoo towels, and wig pins?

Delaney had been assured that she had the only key to the front and rear entrances, as well as the only key to the apartment above. She wasn't convinced and called the sole locksmith in town, who promised he'd be out in a week. But she was living in Truly, where a week could sometimes mean a month depending on hunting season.

Nine days before she opened for business, she had the old name scraped from the front window, and the words THE CUTTING EDGE applied in gold. She had new products sitting in the storage room and new black lacquer chairs in the reception area. The hardwood floors were refinished and the walls painted a bright white. She hung up trade show posters and had the old mirrors replaced with bigger ones. When she was finished she was very pleased and very proud. It wasn't her dream salon. It wasn't chrome and marble and filled with the best stylists, but she'd accomplished a lot in a short amount of time.

She introduced herself to the owner of Bernard's Deli on the corner and the T-shirt shop next door. And on a day when she didn't see Nick's Jeep parked in the lot out back, she marched into Allegrezza construction and introduced herself to his secretary, Hilda, and office manager, Ann Marie.

Two nights before she opened, she gave a small party at the salon. She invited Lisa and Gwen and all of her mother's friends. She sent invitations to business owners in the area. She excluded Allegrezza Construction but had an invitation hand delivered to Helen's Hair Hut. For two hours her salon was packed with people eating her strawberries and drinking her champagne, but Helen didn't show.

Gwen did, but after half an hour she'd made up a dumb excuse about having a cold and left. It was just one more expression of her mother's disapproval. But Delaney had stopped living for her mother's approval a long time ago. She knew she would never get it anyway.

That next day, Delaney moved into the apartment above the salon. She hired a few men with trucks to haul her furniture from the storage unit to the small one-bedroom. Gwen predicted Delaney would be back in no time, but Delaney knew she wouldn't.

From a small common parking lot behind the salon, a set of old wooden stairs climbed the back of the building to the emerald green door of her new home. The apartment was run-down and needed linoleum, new curtains, and a decent stove post – *Brady Bunch* era. Delaney loved it. She loved the window seats in the small living room and bedroom. She loved the old clawfoot bathtub, and the huge arching window that looked down on Main. She'd certainly lived in nicer apartments, and the shabby little place couldn't begin to compete with the luxuries of her mother's house. But maybe that's why she loved it most of all. The things in it belonged to her. She hadn't even realized how much she missed having her stuff around until her own dishes filled the cupboards. She slept in her own wrought-iron bed and sat on her own cream linen sofa, with the zebra print pillows, to watch her own television. The black coffee and end tables belonged to her, as well as the pedestal table in the small dining area at the far left of the living room. The dining room and kitchen were separated by a half-wall, and a person could see most of the apartment all at once. Not that there was a lot to see.

Delaney unpacked what she considered her business clothes and hung them in her closet. She bought a few groceries, a clear plastic shower curtain with big red hearts on it, and two braided rugs for the worn patches on the kitchen floor.

Now all she needed was a phone and a few new locks.

Three days after she opened for business, she had her phone, but she was still waiting for those locks. She was waiting for the stampede of customers, too.

Delaney sat her first customer in the salon chair and took the towel from her head. 'Are you sure you want finger waves, Mrs Van Damme?' She hadn't done finger waves since beauty school. Not only had it been four years, but a whole head of finger waves was a pain in the backside.

'Yep. Just like I always get 'em. Last time I went to that shop around the corner,' she said, referring to Helen's Hair Hut. 'But she didn't do a very good job. She made it look like I had worms laying on my head. I haven't had a decent hairdo since Gloria passed on.'

Delaney shrugged out of her short vinyl jacket, then shoved her arms through a green smock. The smock covered her raspberry Lycra shirt and vinyl skirt, leaving her knees and shiny black boots exposed. She thought of her old job at Valentina in Scottsdale and of her clients who knew a little something about fashion and trends. She reached for her shaping comb and began to remove the tangles from the old woman's nape. She'd found some waving lotion in the storage room, left there by the former owner. Normally, she wouldn't have agreed to style Mrs Van Damme's hair, especially after the woman had bartered the price down to ten dollars. Delaney's intuitive talent lay in her ability to see nature's flaws and fix them with cut and color. The right cut could make noses look smaller, eyes bigger, and chins stronger.

But she was desperate. No one wanted to pay more than ten dollars for anything. In the three days she'd been open, Mrs Van Damme was the only person who hadn't taken one look at her prices and turned and run out. Of course, the woman could barely walk.

'If you do a good wave, I'll recommend you to my friends, but they won't pay more than I do.'

Oh goody, she thought, a whole year of frugal old ladies. A whole year of tight roller curls and back combing. 'Do you part your hair on the right, Mrs Van Damme?'

'On the left. And since you have your fingers in my hair, you can call me Wannetta.'

'How long have you worn your hair this way, Wannetta?'

'Oh, for about forty years. Ever since my late husband told me I looked like Mae West.'

Delaney seriously doubted Wannetta had ever looked anything like Mae West. 'Maybe it's time for a change,' she suggested and snapped on a pair of rubber gloves like a surgeon.

'Nope. I like to stick with what works.'

Delaney snipped off the tip of the bottle, then applied the lotion to the right side of the woman's head and began to shape the waves with her fingers and comb. It took her several tries to get the first ridge perfect so that she could move on to the second and third. While she worked, Wannetta chatted nonstop.

'My good friend Dortha Miles lives in one of those retirement villages in Boise. She really likes it. Food's good, she says. I've thought about moving to one of those villages myself. Ever since my husband, Leroy, passed on last year.' She paused to slip her bony hand from beneath the cape and scratch her nose.

'How'd your husband die?' Delaney asked as she formed a ridge with her comb.

'Fell off the roof and landed on his head. I don't know how many times I told that old fool not to climb up there. But he never listened to me, and look where he is now. He just had to get up there and fiddle with that TV antenna, so certain he could get channel two. Now I'm alone, and if it weren't for my worthless grandson, Ronnie, who can't keep a job and is always borrowing money, maybe I could afford to move into one of those retirement villages with Dortha. Only I'm not certain I would anyway being that her daughter is a' – she paused and lowered her voice – 'lesbian. I tend to think that sort of thing is genetic. Now, I'm not saying Dortha is a' – again she paused and whispered the next word – 'lesbian, but she always did have a tendency toward very short hair, and she wore comfortable shoes even before her arches fell. And I'd hate to live with someone and discover something like that. I'd be afraid to take a shower, and I'd be afraid she'd run around the apartment naked. Or maybe she'd try to get a peek at me when I'm naked.'

The mental picture that flashed through Delaney's head was frightening, and she had to bite her cheek to keep from laughing. The conversation moved from Wannetta's fear of naked lesbians to the other disturbing worries in her life. 'After that house out near Cow Creek was robbed last year,' she said, 'I had to start locking my doors. Never had to do that before. But I live alone now, and I can't be too careful I guess. Are you married?' she asked, peering at Delaney through the wall of mirrors in front of her.

Delaney was getting sick of that question. 'I haven't found the right man yet.'

'I have a grandson, Ronnie.'

'No, thanks.'

'Hmm. Do you live alone?'

'Yes, I do,' Delaney answered as she finished the last ridge. 'I live right upstairs.'

'Up there?' Wannetta pointed toward the ceiling.

'Yep.'

'How come, when your mamma has such a nice place?'

There were a million reasons. She'd hardly spoken to her mother since she'd moved out, and she couldn't say she was all that upset about it. 'I like living alone,' she answered and formed a row of tiny curls across the woman's forehead.

'Well, you just watch out for those crazy Basque Allegrezza boys next door. I dated a sheepherder once. They have mighty funny ways.'

Delaney bit her cheek again. Before she'd opened the shop, running into Nick had been a concern of hers, but although she'd seen his Jeep in the common lot behind the two buildings, and their back doors were only a few feet apart, she hadn't actually seen him. According to Lisa, she hadn't seen much of Louie lately, either. Allegrezza Construction was working overtime to complete several big jobs before the first snow, which could come as early as the beginning of November.

When Delaney was finished, Mrs Van Damme was still old

and wrinkled and looked nothing like Mae West. 'What do you think?' she asked and handed the woman an oval mirror.

'Hmm. Turn me.'

Delaney turned the chair so Wannetta could see the back of her head.

'Looks good, but I'm going to take off fifty cents for those little curls in the front. I never said I'd pay for extra curls.'

Delaney frowned and removed the neck strip and silver plastic cape.

'You give a senior citizen discount, don't you? Helen isn't as good as you, but she gives a discount to seniors.'

At this rate, she was going to be out of business in no time. As soon as Mrs Van Damme left, Delaney locked up and put away her green smock. She reached for her vinyl jacket and headed out the back. Just as she stepped outside and turned to shut the door behind her, a dusty black Jeep rolled to a stop in the slot reserved for Allegrezza Construction. She looked over her shoulder and almost dropped her keys.

Nick cut the Jeep's engine and stuck his head out the window. 'Hey, wild thing, where you headed dressed like a hooker?'

Slowly she turned and shoved her arms into her jacket. 'I am not dressed like a hooker.'

As he got out of the four-wheel drive, he looked her over. His gaze started at her boots and worked upward. A lazy smile curved his lips. 'Looks like somebody had a real good time wrapping you up in electrical tape.'

She pulled her hair from the back of her collar and subjected him to the same scrutiny he'd just given her. His hair was slicked back in a ponytail, and the arms had been hacked out of his blue work shirt. His jeans were worn almost white in places and his boots were dusty. 'Did you get that tattoo in prison?' she asked, pointing to the wreath of thorns circling his bare biceps.

His smile flatlined and he didn't answer.

Delaney couldn't remember a time when she'd gotten the best of Nick. He'd always been quicker and meaner. But that had been in the past with the old Delaney. The new Delaney stuck her nose in the air and pressed her luck. 'What were you in the slammer for, exposing yourself in public?'

'Strangling a smart-ass redhead who used to be blond.' He took several steps toward her and stopped close enough to touch. 'It was worth it.'

Delaney looked up at him and smiled. 'Did you bend over and pick up the soap?' She expected his anger. She expected him to say something cruel. Something to make her wish she'd run the second she'd seen his Jeep, but he didn't.

He rocked back on his heels and grinned. 'That was a good one,' he said, then he laughed, and it was the deep confident laughter of a man who knew with certainty that no one would think to question his sexual preference.

She couldn't remember a time when she'd ever heard his laughter that it hadn't been directed *at her*. Like the time her mother had made her dress up like a Smurf for the Halloween parade, and Nick and his hoodlum buddies had howled with laughter.

This Nick was disarming. 'Sounds like we're both going to be in Louie's wedding.'

'Yeah, who would have thought my best friend would end up with crazy Louie Allegrezza.'

His chuckle was deep and genuine. 'How's business?' he asked and really threw her off balance.

'Okay,' she answered. The last time he'd been pleasant to her, she'd let him strip her naked while he'd remained fully clothed. 'All I need is a few new locks and some deadbolts.'

'Why? Did someone try to break in?'

'I'm not sure.' She lowered her gaze to the folded papers

sticking out of his breast pocket, anywhere but his tractor-beam eyes. 'I was given only one key to the business and there have to be more somewhere. I called the locksmith, but he hasn't made it over yet.'

Nick reached for the door handle by Delaney's waist and jiggled it. His wrist brushed her hip. 'He probably won't. Jerry is a damn good locksmith when he works, but he works *just* enough to pay his rent and buy booze. You won't see him until he runs out of Black Velvet.'

'That's just great.' She looked down at the toes of her shiny boots. 'Has your business ever been broken into?'

'Nope, but I have steel doors and deadbolts.'

'Maybe I'll just do it myself,' she said, thinking out loud. How hard could it be? All she needed was a screwdriver and maybe a drill.

This time when he laughed, it was definitely *at* her. 'I'll send over a subcontractor in the next few days.'

Delaney looked up at him then. Up past his chin, his full sensuous mouth, and cool gaze. She didn't trust him. His offer was too nice. 'Why would you do that for me?'

'Suspicious?'

'Very.'

He shrugged. 'A person could easily crawl through the vents from one building to the other.'

'I knew your offer wasn't made out of the kindness of your heart.'

He leaned forward and planted his hands on the wall beside her head. 'You know me so well.'

His big body blocked the sunlight, but she refused to feel intimidated. 'What's it going to cost me?'

A wicked smile lit his eyes. 'Whatcha got?'

Okay, she refused to *show* him that he intimidated her. She lifted her chin a little. 'Twenty bucks?'

'Not enough.'

Trapped within his arms, she could hardly breathe. A thin slice of air separated her mouth from his. He was so close she could smell the scent of shaving cream still clinging to his skin. She had to turn her face away. 'Forty?' she asked, her voice all squeaky and breathless.

'Uh-uh.' He touched his index finger to her cheek and brought her gaze back to his. 'I don't want your money.'

'What do you want?'

His eyes moved to her mouth and she thought he would kiss her. 'I'll think of something,' he said and pushed away from the wall.

Delaney took a deep breath and watched him disappear into the building next door. She was afraid to think of what that something might be.

The next day at work, she made a sign offering free nail polish with a weave or color. No takers, but she did spray Mrs Vaughn's gray hair into the shape of a helmet. Laverne Vaughn had taught grade school in Truly until she'd been forced to retire in the late seventies.

Evidently, Wannetta had been true to her word. She told her friends about Delaney. Mrs Vaughn paid ten dollars, wanted her senior citizen discount, and demanded a free bottle of polish. Delaney took the sign down.

Friday she shampooed and styled another of Wannetta's friends, and Saturday, Mrs Stokesberry dropped off two wigs to be cleaned. One white for everyday wear, the other black for special occasions. She picked them up three hours later, and insisted on placing the white wig on her own head.

'You give a senior citizen discount, right?' she asked as she pulled at the hair about her ears.

'Yes.' Delaney sighed, wondering why she was putting up with so much crap from so many people. Her mother, the gray-haired ladies, and Nick. Especially Nick. The answer came to her like the ringing of her cash register. Three million dollars. She could put up with a lot for three million big ones.

As soon as the woman left, Delaney closed the salon early and went to visit her friends Duke and Dolores. The dogs trembled with excitement as they licked her cheeks. At last, friendly faces. She rested her forehead on Duke's neck and tried not to cry. She failed, just as she was failing with the salon. She hated finger waves and spraying hair into domes. She really hated washing and styling wigs. Most of all, she hated not doing what she loved. And what Delaney loved was making ordinary women look extraordinary. She loved the sound of blow-dryers, the tempo of rapid snipping, and the smell of dyes and perming solutions. She'd loved her life before she'd come back to Truly for Henry's funeral. She'd had friends and a job she loved.

Seven months and fifteen days, she told herself. Seven months and then she could move anywhere she wanted. She rose to her feet and reached for the dogs' leashes.

Half an hour later, she returned from walking the dogs and put them back in their pen. She was just about to open her car door when Gwen stepped outside.

'Can you stay for dinner?' her mother asked, wrapping a beige angora sweater around her shoulders.

'No.'

'I'm sorry I had to leave your party early.'

Delaney fished her keys from her pocket. Usually she bit her tongue and held it all inside, but she wasn't in the mood. 'No, I don't think you are.'

'Of course I am. Why would you say such a thing to me?'

She looked at her mother, at her blue eyes and blond hair cut in a classic bob. 'I don't know,' she answered, deciding to back down from an argument she would lose anyway. 'I've had a crappy day. I'll come to dinner tomorrow night if you want.'

'I have plans for tomorrow night.'

'Monday then,' Delaney said as she slid into her car. She waved good-bye, and as soon as she'd returned to her apartment, she called Lisa. 'Are you free tonight?' she asked when her friend picked up. 'I need a drink, maybe two.'

'Louie's working late, so I can meet you for a while.'

'Why don't we meet at Hennesey's? A blues band is playing there later tonight.'

'Okay, but I'll probably leave before they start.'

Delaney was a little disappointed, but she was used to being alone. After she hung up the telephone, she took a shower then dressed in a green belly sweater and a pair of jeans. She fluffed her hair, applied her makeup, and put on her Doc Marten's and leather jacket to walk the three blocks to Hennesey's. By the time she arrived, it was six-thirty and the bar was filled with the after-work crowd.

Hennesey's was a fair-sized bar, with the top level looking down on the lower. The tables on both levels were crowded together, and a portable stage had been set up on the large dance floor. For now, the lights inside the bar blazed and the dance floor was empty. Later, that would all change.

Delaney took a table near the end of the bar and was on her first beer when Lisa arrived. She took one look at her friend and raised a finger from her glass and pointed at Lisa's ponytail. 'You should let me cut your hair.'

'No way.' Lisa ordered a Miller Lite, then turned her attention back to Delaney. 'Remember what you did to Brigit?'

'Brigit who?'

'The doll my Great-grandmother Stolfus gave me. You cut off her long gold ringlets and made her look like Cyndi Lauper. I've been traumatized ever since.'

'I promise you won't look like Cyndi Lauper. I'll even do it for free.'

'I'll think about it.' Lisa's beer arrived and she paid the waitress. 'I ordered the bridesmaid dresses today. When they get here you'll have to come to my house for a final fitting.'

'Am I going to look like a tour guide on a Southern plantation?'

'No. The dresses are a wine-colored stretch velvet. Just a real simple A line so you don't draw attention away from the bride.'

Delaney took a sip of beer and smiled. 'I couldn't do that anyway, but you really should think about letting me do your hair for the big day. It'll be fun.'

'Maybe I'll let you do a braid or something.' Lisa took a drink. 'I booked the caterer for the wedding dinner.'

When the subject of Lisa's wedding was exhausted, conversation turned to Delaney's business.

'How is your salon doing these days?'

'Crappy. I had one customer, Mrs Stokesberry. She dropped off her wig, and I shampooed it like it was a roadkill poodle.'

'Cool job.'

'Tell me about it.'

Lisa took a drink then said, 'I don't want to make you feel worse, but I drove by Helen's Hair Hut today. She looked fairly busy.'

Delaney frowned into her beer. 'I've got to do something to steal her business.'

'Do a giveaway. People love to get something for nothing.'

She'd tried that already with the fingernail polish. 'I need to advertise,' she said, silently contemplating her options.

'Maybe you should do a little show or something at Sophie's school. Cut some hair, get some of those girls looking good. Then all the other girls will want you to cut their hair, too.'

'And their mothers will have to keep bringing them back.' Delaney sipped her beer, and thought about the possibilities.

'Don't look now, but Wes and Scooter Finley just walked

in.' Lisa raised her hand to the side of her face as a shield. 'Don't make eye contact or they'll come over.'

Delaney shielded her face also, but looked through her fingers. 'They're just as ugly as I remember.'

'Just as stupid, too.'

Delaney had graduated with the Finley brothers. They weren't twins, just repeat offenders. Wes and Scooter were two shades darker than albino with spooky pale eyes. 'Do they still think they're chick magnets?'

Lisa nodded. 'Go figure.' When the Finley threat had passed, Lisa lowered her hand and pointed toward two men standing at the bar. 'What do you think, boxers or briefs?'

Delaney took one look at their shirts with the big red Chevron logo, their Achy Breaky hair, and said, 'Briefs. White. Fruit of the Loom.'

'What about the guy third from the end?'

The man was tall, rail thin, with perfectly layered hair. The yellow sweater tied around his neck told Delaney he was either new in town or a man of great courage. Only a very brave man would walk the streets of Truly with a sweater of any color, let alone yellow, tied around his neck. 'Thong, I think. He's very daring.' Delaney took a drink of her beer and turned her attention to the door.

'Cotton or silk?'

'Silk. Now it's your turn.'

The two women turned and stared at the door, waiting for their next victim to walk through. He entered less than a minute later, looking as good as Delaney remembered. Tommy Markham's brown hair still curled about his ears and neck. He was still lean rather than beefy, and when his gaze landed on Delaney, his smile was still as charming as a wayward boy's. The kind of smile that could make a woman forgive him almost anything.

'You're driving my wife crazy. You know that, don't you?' he said as he approached their table.

Delaney looked up into Tommy's blue eyes and placed an innocent hand on her chest. 'Me?' There had been a time when the sight of his long lashes had made her heart flutter. She couldn't help the smile curving her mouth, but her heart was just fine. 'What have I done?'

'You moved back.'

Good, she thought. Helen had spent their whole childhood needling Delaney, driving *her* crazy. Turnabout was certainly fair play. 'So, where is the old ball and chain anyway?'

He laughed and sat in the chair next to her. 'She and the kids went to a wedding in Challis. They'll be back tomorrow sometime.'

'Why didn't you go?' Lisa asked him.

'I have to work in the morning.'

Delaney looked across the table at her friend, who was doing the 'he's married' signal with her eyes. Delaney grinned. Lisa had nothing to worry about. She didn't sleep with married men – ever. But Helen wouldn't know that. Let her worry.

Nick hung up the telephone and rolled his chair backward. The fluorescent lighting hummed overhead, and a smile played across his lips as he looked out the plate-glass window. The sun had set and his own reflection stared back at him. Everything was coming together. He had three contractors jumping to invest venture capital with him, and he was in the process of talking to several lenders.

He tossed his pencil onto the desk in front of him, then ran his fingers through the side of his hair. Half the town of Truly was going to shit bricks when they learned of his plans for Silver Creek. The other half was going to love it.

When he and Louie had decided to move the company to Truly, they'd known the older residents of the town would resist development and growth of any kind. But like Henry, those people were dying off and being replaced by a whole influx of yuppies. Depending on whom you listened to, the Allegrezza boys were either businessmen or land rapers. They were loved or hated. But then, they always had been.

He stood and stretched his arms over his head. The specifications for a nine-hole golf course and the blueprints for fifty-four two-thousand-square-foot condominiums lay before him. Even with a conservative projected budget, Allegrezza Construction stood to make a fortune. And that was just the first stage of development. The second stage was bound to make even more money, with million-dollar houses built within spitting distance of the green. Now all Nick needed was clear deed to the forty acres Henry had bequeathed him. In June he'd have it.

Nick smiled into the empty office. He'd made his first million building everything from starter houses to lavish homes in Boise, but a guy could always use spare cash.

He grabbed his bomber's jacket off the coat tree and headed out the back. After he finished with his plans for Silver Creek, he would think about what he wanted to build at Angel Beach. Or maybe he wouldn't build on it at all. He paused long enough to switch off the lights before locking the door behind him. His Harley Fat Boy sat in the space next to Delaney's Miata. He glanced up at her apartment, and the green door illuminated by a weak light. What a hole.

He could understand why she'd want to move from her mother's house. He couldn't be around Gwen for three seconds without wanting to choke her. But what he didn't understand was why Delaney had chosen to move into such a dump. He knew Henry's will provided her with a monthly income, and he knew she could afford a better place. It wouldn't take much for a man to kick the damn door off the hinges.

When he got the time, he still planned to replace the locks

on her shop. But Delaney herself wasn't his problem. Where she lived or what she chose to wear didn't concern him. If she wanted to live in a little hole and wear a strip of vinyl that barely covered her ass, that was her problem. He didn't give a damn. He was sure he wouldn't give her more than a passing thought if she weren't living practically on top of him.

Swinging one leg over the Harley, he righted the bike. If he'd seen any other woman in that skimpy vinyl crap, he would have appreciated the hell out of it, but not Delaney. Seeing her shrink-wrapped tighter than a deli snack had made him itch to peel back the plastic and take a bite. He'd gone from zero to hard in about three seconds.

He kicked the stand up with the heel of his boot and pressed the ignition button. The v-twin engine roared to life, shattered the still night air, and vibrated his thighs. Getting hard for a woman he wasn't planning on taking to bed didn't bother him. Getting hard over *that* particular woman did.

He gunned the bike and shot down the alley, barely slowing as he turned onto First. He felt restless and was home only long enough to take a shower. The silence set him on edge, and he didn't know why. He needed a diversion, a distraction, and he ended up at Hennesey's with a beer in his hand and Lonna Howell in his lap.

His table looked out onto the dance floor, pitched in darkness and filled with slow shifting bodies, moving to the sensual rhythm and languid blues flowing from five-foot speakers. Slivers of light shone on the band and several rows of track lighting illuminated the front of the bar. But mostly the tavern was as dark as sin so a person could get away with sinful things.

Nick didn't have any particular sin planned, but the night was still young and Lonna was more than willing.

Delaney locked her fingers behind her old boyfriend's neck and moved with him to the slow pulse of blues guitar. Being so close to Tommy again felt a little like déjà vu, only different because the arms holding her now belonged to a man, not a boy. As a boy he'd had no rhythm, he still didn't. Back then, he'd always smelled like Irish Spring soap. Now he wore cologne, not the fresh scent she'd always associated with him. He'd been her first love. He'd made her heart pound and her pulse race. She felt neither of those things now.

'Remind me again,' he spoke next to Delaney's ear, 'why can't we be friends?'

'Because your wife hates me.'

'Oh, yeah.' He pulled her a little closer, but kept his hands on the small of her back. 'But I like you.'

His shameless flirting had started an hour ago, right after Lisa had left. He'd propositioned her twice, but was so charming about it, she couldn't get angry with him. He made her laugh and made her forget that he'd broken her heart by choosing Helen.

'Why wouldn't you sleep with me in high school?' he asked.

She'd wanted to – really wanted to. She'd been madly in love and filled with the juices of raging teen hormones. But overpowering her desire for Tommy had been the terror that her mother and Henry would find out she'd been with a boy. 'You dumped me.'

'No. *You* dumped me.'

'Only after I caught you boffing Helen.'

'Oh, yeah.'

She pulled back far enough to look into his face, barely visible on the darkened dance floor. His laughter joined hers when she said, 'That was horrible.'

'It sucked. I always felt really bad about what happened, but I never knew what I should say to you after that,' he confessed.

'I knew what I wanted to say, but I didn't think you'd like it.'

'What?'

His teeth flashed white in the murky light. 'That I was sorry you caught me "boffing" Helen, but could we still go out anyway?'

There had been a time when she'd written his name all over her notebooks, when she'd envisioned living the picket-fence dream with Tommy Markham.

'Would you have gone for it?'

'No,' she answered, truly grateful he wasn't her husband.

He leaned forward and placed a soft kiss on her forehead. 'That's what I remember the most about you. The word "no",' he said against her skin. The music stopped and he pulled back and smiled into her face. 'I'm glad you're back.' He escorted her to the table and grabbed his jacket. 'See ya around.'

Delaney watched him leave and reached for the beer she'd left on the table. As she raised the bottle to her lips, she lifted her hair from her neck with her free hand. Tommy hadn't changed much since high school. He was still good-looking. Still charming and still a hound. She almost felt sorry for Helen – almost.

'Planning a date with your old boyfriend?'

She knew the voice even before she turned around. She lowered the bottle and looked up at the only man who'd caused her more misery than all her old boyfriends combined. 'Jealous?' But unlike Tommy, she would never forget what had happened one hot August night with Nick Allegrezza.

'Pea green.'

'Did you come over here to fight with me? Because I don't want to fight. Like you said the other day, we're both going to be in your brother's wedding. Maybe we should try to get along. Be more friendly.'

A slow sensuous smile curved his lips. 'How friendly?'

'Friends. Just friends,' she said although she doubted it would ever happen. But maybe they could quit taking swipes at each other. Especially since she always seemed to lose.

'Buddies?'

That might be pushing it. 'Okay.'

'Pals?'

'Sure.'

He shook his head. 'It'll never happen.'

'Why?'

He didn't answer. Instead he plucked the bottle from her hand and set it on the table. The singer of the small blues band dug into a slow sweet rendering of 'I've Been Loving You Too Long' as Nick dragged her onto the crowded dance floor. He pulled her against him, then swayed his hips to the sensuous soul music. She was jostled from behind as she tried to put a little distance between her breasts and his chest, but his big hands on her back kept her just where he wanted her. She had no choice but to lightly place her palms on his broad shoulders. The ends of his hair brushed her knuckles like the whisper of cool silk, and the heat from his hot, hard body seeped through layers of denim and flannel and sweater to warm her skin. Unlike Tommy, rhythm poured through Nick, easy and natural, like a languid stream in no great hurry to get anywhere. 'You could've *asked* me to dance,' she said, speaking past the heavy thud of her heart.

'You're right. I could have.'

'This is the nineties. Most men have abandoned the cave.' The scent of him filled her head with the smell of clean cotton and warm man.

'Most men like your old boyfriend?'

'Yes.'

'Tommy thinks with his dick.'

'So do you.'

'There you go again,' he paused and his voice lowered a fraction, 'thinking you know so much about me.'

Her stomach knotted in a tangle of conflicting emotion. Anger and desire, breathless anticipation, and gut-level fear. Tommy Markham, her first love, hadn't created such chaos within her. Why Nick? He'd been nasty to her more times than he'd been nice. They had a past she'd thought she'd buried. 'Everyone in town knows you spend time with quite a few women.'

He pulled back far enough to look down at her. Light from the stage sliced across the left half of his handsome face. 'Even if that were true, there's a difference. I'm not married.'

'Married or not, indiscriminate sex is still disgusting.'

'Is that what you told your boyfriend?'

'My relationship with Tommy is none of your business.'

'Relationship? Are you going to meet him later for some of that indiscriminate sex you find so disgusting?' His hands moved up her back to the base of her skull. 'Did he get you hot?' He plowed his fingers through her hair from beneath, holding her head in his palms. His eyes were as hard as granite.

She pushed at his shoulders, but he tightened his grasp, pressing his strong fingers into her scalp. He wasn't hurting her, but he wasn't letting her go either. 'You're sick.'

He lowered his face and asked against her lips, 'Does he turn you on?'

She sucked in her breath.

'Make you ache?'

Delaney's heart pounded in her chest and she couldn't answer. He lightly brushed his mouth over hers and slid the tip of his tongue across the seam of her lips. A current of pleasure swept across her breasts. Her body's immediate reaction surprised and alarmed her. Nick was the last man for whom she wanted to feel such aching desire. Their past was too ugly. She meant to push him away, but he turned up the heat, and the kiss turned carnal. His tongue entered her mouth for a long hot assault, devouring her, consuming her resistance, and creating a delicious suction with his lips.

She wanted to hate him. She wanted to hate him even as she kissed him back. Even as her tongue encouraged him. Even as she wound her arms around his neck and clung to him as the only steady thing in a dizzy chaotic world. His lips were warm. Firm. Demanding she kiss him back with the same fiery passion.

He slid his big hands down her sides, then slipped them beneath the loose edge of her sweater. She felt his fingers lightly caress the small of her back, the stroke of each across her skin. Then his warm callused palms slipped to her waist, and his thumbs skimmed her abdomen, fanning lightly over her heated flesh. The knot in her stomach tightened even more and the sensation of pinpricks tingled her chest, drawing her nipples taut as if he'd touched her there. He made her forget she stood on a crowded dance floor. He made her forget everything. Her hands drifted to the sides of his neck, and she tangled her fingers in his hair. Then the kiss changed, became almost gentle, and he softly pressed his thumbs into her navel. He slid his thumbs beneath the waistband of her jeans and pulled her tight against the long hard bulge just to the right of his button fly.

Her own choked moan brought an instant of sanity, and she

tore her mouth from his. She gasped for breath, ashamed and appalled at her body's uncontrolled reaction. He'd done this to her before, only that time she hadn't stopped him.

She pushed at him and his hands fell to his sides. When she finally looked into his face, his gaze was hooded and watchful. Then his jaw hardened and his eyes narrowed.

'You shouldn't have come back. You should have stayed gone,' he said, then he turned and forced his way through the throng of people.

Stunned by her behavior and his and the desire still surging through her veins, Delaney was unable to move for several long moments. Blues continued to pump from the big speaker, and the couples around her swayed to the beat as if nothing disturbing had just happened. Only Delaney knew that it had. It wasn't until the music stopped that she stumbled back to her table. Maybe he was right. Maybe she should have stayed gone, but she'd sold her soul for money. A lot of money, and she couldn't leave now.

Delaney shoved her arms into her jacket and made her way to the front entrance. There was only one way she was going to survive the next seven months. Revert back to plan A and avoid Nick as much as possible. With her head down, she stepped out into the brisk air. Her breath hung in front of her face as she zipped her coat.

The unmistakable rumble of Nick's Harley shook the night, and Delaney glanced over her shoulder. He stood with the big bike between his widespread legs, his back to her, and a worn black leather jacket stretched across his shoulders. He held his hand out and one of the Howell twins jumped on behind, bonding her perfect self to his butt like super glue.

Delaney's head snapped back around and she shoved her hands in her pockets for the short walk home. Nick had the morals of a tomcat. He always had, but why he'd kissed her when he had one of the Howell girls with him was beyond

Delaney's understanding. In fact, why he'd kiss her at all was past comprehension. He didn't like her. That much was clear.

Of course, he hadn't liked her ten years ago, either. He'd used her to get back at Henry, but Henry was dead now, and getting involved with her could mean he'd lose the bequest Henry had given him. Nick was many things, all of them complicated, but he wasn't stupid.

She took a left at the alleyway and walked toward the stairs leading to her apartment. It didn't make sense, but many things Nick did had never made any sense to her.

In any other city, Delaney might have been afraid to walk the streets after dark, but not in Truly. Occasionally one of the summer homes at the north side of the lake got broken into. But nothing really *bad* ever happened here. People didn't lock their cars, and more often than not, didn't bother to lock their homes, either.

Delaney had lived in too many big cities to leave without locking her apartment. Once she'd climbed the stairs and was inside, she secured the door behind her and tossed the keys on the glass and black coffee table. While she unlaced her boots, she thought about Nick and her crazy reaction to him. For a few unguarded moments, she'd wanted him. And he'd wanted her, too. She'd felt it in the way he touched her and in the hard bulge of his erection.

The boot in Delaney's hand hit the floor, and she frowned into the darkness. On a crowded dance floor, she'd kissed him like he was a fresh batch of sin and she was dying for a taste. He'd made her burn, and she'd wanted him like she hadn't wanted any other man in a long time. Like she'd wanted him once before. Like no one existed beyond him and nothing else mattered. Nick was the only man she'd ever known who could make her forget everything. There was something about him that went straight to her head. He'd gotten to her tonight, just as he had the night before she'd left Truly ten years ago.

She didn't like to think about what had happened, but she was exhausted and her mind did an unstoppable turnback to the memories she'd always tried to forget, but never could.

The summer after high school graduation had started out bad, then proceeded to go to hell. She'd just turned eighteen and figured it was finally time for her to have a say in her life. She didn't want to attend college right away. She wanted to take a year off to decide what she really wanted to do, but Henry had already preregistered her at the University of Idaho, where he'd been a member of the Alumni Hall of Fame. He'd chosen her classes and signed her up for a full load of freshman courses.

At the end of June she got up the nerve to talk to Henry about a compromise. She would go part-time to Boise State University where Lisa was going, and she wanted to take classes she thought sounded fun.

He said no. End of subject.

With the August registration date breathing down her neck, she approached Henry again in July.

'Don't be silly. I know what's best for you,' he said. 'Your mother and I have discussed this, Delaney. Your plans for your future are aimless. You're obviously much too young to know what you want.'

But she'd known. She'd known for a long time, and somehow she'd always thought that on her eighteenth birthday she would get it. For some mixed-up reason, she'd thought that with her freedom to vote would come real freedom. But when her February birthday had passed without the slightest change in her life, she figured graduation from high school had to mean liberation from Henry's control. She would get the freedom to break out and be Delaney. The freedom to be wild and crazy if she wanted to. To take silly college classes. To wear holey jeans or too much makeup. To wear the clothes she wanted. To look like a preppie, a bum, or a whore.

She didn't get those freedoms. In August Henry and her mother drove her four hours north to the University of Idaho in the town of Moscow, Idaho, and she registered for the fall semester. On the way back home, Henry kept saying, 'Trust me to know what's best for you.' And 'Someday you'll thank me. When you get your business degree, you'll help run my companies.' Her mother accused her of being 'spoiled and immature.'

The next night, Delaney snuck out of her bedroom window for the first and last time of her life. She could have asked Henry to use his car, and he probably would have let her, but she didn't want to ask him for anything. She didn't want to tell her parents where she was going, who she was going to be with, or what time she'd be home. She didn't have a plan, just a vague idea of doing something she'd never done before. Something other eighteen-year-olds did. Something reckless and exciting.

She curled her straight blond hair on big fat rollers and put on a pink sundress that buttoned up the front. The dress reached just above the knee and was the most daring thing she owned. The straps were thin and she didn't wear a bra. She thought she appeared older than her age, not that it mattered. She was the mayor's daughter and everyone knew how old she was anyway. She walked all the way into town in a pair of huarache sandals and carrying a white cardigan. It was a warm Saturday night, and there had to be something going on. Something she'd always been afraid to do for fear of getting caught and disappointing Henry.

She found that something outside the Hollywood Market on Fifth Street where she stopped to call Lisa from a pay phone. She stood beneath a weak light screwed into the front of the brick building. 'Come on,' she pleaded into the receiver she held to her ear. 'Meet me.'

'I told you, I feel like my head is going to explode,' Lisa said, sounding pathetic with a bad summer cold.

Delaney stared at the metal numbers on the face of the phone and frowned. How could she rebel by herself? 'Baby.'

'I'm not a baby,' Lisa defended herself. 'I'm sick.'

She sighed and glanced up, her attention drawn to the two boys moving across the parking lot toward her. 'Oh, my God.' She hung her sweater over one arm and cupped her hand around the receiver. 'The Finley boys are walking toward me.' There were only two other brothers who had worse reputations than Scooter and Wes Finley. The Finleys were eighteen and twenty and had just graduated high school.

'Don't make eye contact,' Lisa had warned, then lapsed into a coughing fit.

'Hey there, Delaney Shaw,' Scooter drawled and leaned one shoulder against the building beside her. 'What are you doing out by yourself?'

She glanced into his pale blue eyes. 'Looking for fun.'

'Huh huh,' he laughed. 'Guess you found it.'

Delaney had graduated from Lincoln High with the Finleys and found them slightly amusing and somewhat dense. They'd kept the school year interesting with false fire alarms or pulling down their pants to show their very white butts. The Finleys were big on mooning. 'What did you have in mind, Scooter?'

'Delaney – Delaney –' Lisa called into the receiver. 'Run. Run as fast as you can away from the Finleys.'

'Drink a little brew,' Wes answered for his brother. 'Find a party.'

Drinking 'brew' with the Finleys was certainly something she'd never done before. 'I gotta go,' she said to Lisa.

'Delaney—'

'If they find my body floating in the lake, tell the police I was last seen with the Finleys.' As she hung up the receiver, an old convertible Mustang with rust spots and rustier pipes pulled into the parking lot, the twin beams spotlighting

Delaney and her new friends. The lights and engine died, the door swung open, and out stepped six feet, two inches of bad attitude. Nick Allegrezza had tucked an 'Eat the Worm' T-shirt into a pair of old jeans. He looked Scooter and Wes over, then turned his gaze on Delaney. In the past three years, Delaney had seen little of Nick. He spent most of his time in Boise where he worked and attended the university. But he hadn't changed that much. His hair was still shiny black, cut short at his ears and the back of his neck. He was still breathtaking.

'We could have our own party,' Scooter suggested.

'Just the three of us?' she asked loud enough for Nick to hear. He used to call her a baby, usually right after he'd thrown a grasshopper at her. She wasn't a baby now.

A frown pulled at the corners of his mouth, then he turned and disappeared into the market.

'We could go back to our house,' Wes continued. 'Our parents are out of town.'

Delaney returned her attention to the brothers. 'Ah . . . are you going to invite anyone else?'

'Why?'

'For a party,' she answered.

'Do you have any girlfriends you can call?'

She thought about her only friend home sick with a cold and shook her head. 'Don't you know some other people you can invite?'

Scooter smiled and took a step closer. 'Why would I want to do that?'

For the first time, apprehension fluttered in Delaney's stomach. 'Because you want to party, remember?'

'We'll party. Don't you worry.'

'You're scaring her, Scoot.' Wes pushed his brother and knocked him aside. 'Come back to our house and we'll call people from there.'

Delaney didn't believe him and lowered her gaze to her

sandals. She'd wanted to be like other eighteen-year-old girls. She'd wanted to do something reckless, but she wasn't up for a threesome. And there was no doubt that's what they had in mind. If and when Delaney decided to lose her virginity, it wouldn't be with one or both of the Finleys. She'd seen their pale butts – and thank you, no.

Getting rid of them was going to be difficult, and she wondered how long she would have to stand in front of the Hollywood Market before they finally gave up and went away.

When she looked up, Nick stood by the side of his car shoving a six-pack of beer in the backseat. He straightened, rested his weight on one foot and pinned his gaze on Delaney. He stared at her for several long moments, then said, 'Come here, princess.'

There'd been a time when she'd been both frightened and fascinated by him at the same time. He'd always been so cocky, so sure of himself, and so forbidden. She was no longer afraid, and the way she saw it, she had two choices: trust him or trust the Finleys. Neither option was great, but despite his nasty reputation, she knew Nick wouldn't force her to do something she didn't want to do. She wasn't so sure she could say the same for Scooter and Wes. 'See you guys around,' she said, then slowly walked to the baddest of the bad boys. The leap in her pulse had nothing to do with fear and everything to do with the smooth rich tone of his voice.

'Where's your car?'

'I walked into town.'

He opened the driver's side door. 'Climb in.'

She looked up into his smoky eyes. He wasn't a boy anymore, no doubt about it. 'Where are we going?'

He nodded toward the Finleys. 'Does it matter?'

It probably should have. 'You aren't going to take me on a snipe hunt and dump me in the forest, are you?'

'Not tonight. You're safe.'

She tossed her sweater into the back and climbed across the console and into the passenger seat with as much dignity as possible. Nick fired up the Mustang, and the dash lights flashed to life. He backed out of the parking lot and pulled onto Fifth. 'Are you going to tell me where we're going now?' she asked, excitement tingling her nerve endings. She couldn't believe she was actually sitting in Nick's car. She couldn't wait to tell Lisa. It was just too incredible.

'I'm taking you back home.'

'No!' She turned toward him. 'You can't. I don't want to go back there. I can't go back yet.'

He glanced at her then returned his gaze to the dark road before him. 'Why not?'

'Stop and let me out,' she said instead of answering his question. How could she explain to anyone, let alone Nick, that she couldn't breathe there anymore? It felt like Henry had his foot on her throat, and she couldn't get air deep inside her lungs. How could she explain to Nick that she'd waited most of her life to break free of Henry, but now she knew that day would never happen? How could she explain that this was her way of finally fighting back? He'd probably laugh at her and think she was immature, like Henry and her mother did. She knew she was naive, and she hated it. Her eyes began to water, and she turned away. The thought of crying like a baby in front of Nick horrified her. 'Just let me out here.'

Instead of stopping, he turned the Mustang onto the road leading to Delaney's house. The street ahead of the car's headlights was like an inky tube, shadowed by towering pine and lit only by the reflection of the center divider.

'If you take me home, I'll just leave again.'

'Are you crying over there?'

'No,' she lied, forcing her eyes real wide, hoping the wind would hurry and dry them out.

'What were you doing with the Finleys?'

She glanced over at him, his face cast in the gold lights of the dashboard. 'Looking for something to do.'

'Those two guys are bad news.'

'I can handle Scooter and Wes,' she bragged, although she wasn't so sure.

'Bullshit,' he said and stopped the Mustang at the end of the long drive leading to her house. 'Now, go on home where you belong.'

'Don't tell me where I belong,' she said as she reached for the handle and shoved the door with her shoulder. She was sick to death of everyone telling her where to go and what to do. She jumped from the car and slammed the door behind her. With her head high, she headed back toward town. She was too angry for tears.

'Where do you think you're going?' he called after her.

Delaney flipped him the bird and it felt good. Freeing. She kept walking and heard him swear right before the sound of his voice was drowned out by the squeal of tires.

'Get in,' he shouted as the car pulled alongside her.

'Go to hell.'

'I said get in!'

'And I said go to hell!'

The car stopped but she kept on walking. She didn't know where she was going this time, but she *wasn't* going back home until she was good and ready. She didn't want to go to the University of Idaho. She didn't want a degree in business. And she didn't want to spend any more of her life in a little town where she couldn't breathe.

Nick grabbed her arm and spun her around. The headlights lit him from behind, and he looked huge and imposing. 'For Christ sake, what is your problem?'

She pushed at him and he grabbed her other arm. 'Why should I tell you? You don't care. You just want to dump me.'

Tears pooled on her lower lashes, and she was mortified. 'Don't you dare call me a baby. I'm eighteen.'

His gaze drifted from her forehead to her mouth. 'I know how old you are.'

She blinked and stared at him through blurred vision, at the finely etched bow of his top lip, his straight nose, and his clear eyes. Months of angry frustration poured out of her like water through a sieve. 'I'm old enough to know what I want to do with my life. And I don't want to go to college. I don't want to go into business, and I don't want anyone to tell me what's best for me.' She took a deep breath, then continued. 'I want to live my own life. I want to think about myself first. I'm tired of trying to be perfect, and I want to screw up like everybody else.' She thought a moment, then said, 'I want everyone to back off. I want to experience life – *my life*. I want to suck the marrow. Take a walk on the wild side. I want to take a bite out of my life.'

Nick pulled her up to the tips of her toes and looked into her eyes. 'I want to take a bite out of you,' he said, then he lowered his mouth to hers and softly bit the fleshy part of her bottom lip.

For several long heartbeats Delaney stood perfectly still, too stunned to move. Her head clogged with a myriad of astonished sensations. Nick Allegrezza was softly biting her lips and her breath caught in the top of her lungs. His mouth was warm and firm, and he kissed her like a man who'd had a lifetime of experience. His hands moved to cup her face, and he slipped his thumbs along her jaw to her chin. Then he pressed downward until her mouth opened. His warm tongue swept inside and touched hers, and he tasted like beer. Hot shivers ran up her spine and she kissed him like she'd never kissed anyone else. No one had ever made her feel like her skin was too tight at the base of her skull and across her breasts. No one had ever made her want to act first and deal with the consequences later. She placed her hands on the solid wall of his chest and sucked his tongue into her mouth.

And always in the back of her mind was the absolute incredibility of it all. This was Nick, the boy who'd spent equal time terrorizing and fascinating her. Nick, the man, made her feel hot and breathless.

He ended the kiss before Delaney was ready, and she slid her palms to the sides of his neck.

'Let's get out of here,' he said and grabbed her hand.

This time she didn't ask him where they were going.

She didn't care.

7

They drove three miles out of town and parked on the sandy shore of Angel Beach. The property was secluded and they had to open a wire gate to get to it. It was an area Delaney knew fairly well. Dense forest gave way to white sand, and it all belonged to Henry.

Nick leaned his behind against the hood of the Mustang, then planted one foot on the bumper. He pulled two Coors out of the six-pack, then set the rest next to him. 'Have you ever drank a beer?' he asked, popping the two tops and handing one to Delaney.

She'd been allowed to taste Henry's. 'Yeah, sure. All the time.'

He slanted her a glance from beneath his lashes. 'All the time, huh?' He raised the can to his lips and took a long pull.

Delaney watched him and took a sip of her own beer. She hid her grimace by turning her back and looking out at Lake Mary twenty feet in front of her. A shimmering path led across the dark ripples to the full moon hanging low above the water. The trail looked magical, like you could step from the shore onto it and never get wet. Like you could walk across the water and end up someplace exotic. She tried her beer again, and this time she succeeded in keeping the frown from her face. A cool breeze whispered across her skin, but she wasn't cold.

'I take it you don't want to go to the U of I.'

She turned back toward Nick. Streaks of moonlight glistened in his dark hair. 'No, I don't want to go to college right now.'

'Then don't.'

She laughed and took a few more sips of her beer. 'Yeah, right. When has what I wanted ever counted for anything? Henry didn't even ask me which classes I'd like to take this fall. He just signed me up and paid for it all.'

Nick was quiet for a moment and Delaney didn't have to ask him what he was thinking. The irony spoke louder than words. Nick worked his way through college to pay for the privilege his father was forcing on Delaney. 'Tell the old man to shove it. I would.'

'I know *you* would, but I can't.'

He raised the can and asked, 'Why not?'

Because she'd always felt like she owed Henry for rescuing her mother and her from that tiny Air-stream trailer on the outskirts of Las Vegas. 'I just can't.' Her gaze took in the black outline of the mountains before resting once again on Nick. 'This is so weird,' she said. 'I never would have thought you and I would be drinking buddies.'

'Why's that?'

She looked at him like he was slightly retarded. 'Because you're who you are. And I'm me,' she said and took a few more sips.

His gaze narrowed. 'You mean because you're the mayor's daughter and I'm his bastard son?'

His bluntness surprised her. Most of the people she knew didn't come right out and say things like that. They kissed the air above your cheek and said you looked good when you didn't. She wondered what it was like to have that kind of freedom. 'Well, I wouldn't put it that way.'

'How would you put it then?'

'That your family hates me, and my family doesn't care for you.'

He tilted his head back and drained half his beer. He studied her over the top of the can until he lowered it again. 'It's a little more complex than that.'

'True. You've spent most of your life torturing me.'

One corner of his full mouth lifted. 'I never tortured you. I may have teased you occasionally.'

'Ha! When I was in third grade you told me that Reggie Overton stole little blond-haired girls and fed them to his Dobermans. I was terrified of Reggie for years.'

'And you've spent most of your life walking around with your nose in the air as if I smell bad.'

'No, I haven't.' Delaney didn't think she'd ever looked at anyone like that.

'Yes, you have,' he assured her.

'Than why did you kiss me tonight?'

His gaze slid to her mouth. 'Curious.'

'Curious to see if I'd let you?'

He chuckled quietly and let his eyes move down the row of buttons closing her dress. 'No,' he said as if a rejection had never occurred to him. He looked back up into her eyes. 'Curious to see if you taste as sweet as you look.'

She stood as tall as she could and took a few chugs of beer for courage before she asked, 'What did you decide?'

He crooked his finger at her and said in a low and sensual voice, 'Come here, wild thing.'

Something in his voice, what he said and the way he said it, drew her to him like they were connected by string and he was just reeling her in. A funny little tickle pulled at her stomach.

'I've decided you taste like my Uncle Josu's huckleberry wine. Definitely sweet, but with a warm kick.'

She hid her smile behind the Coors can. She wanted to be like wine. 'Is that bad?'

He took the beer from her hand and set it behind him on the hood of the car. 'Depends on what you want to do about it.' He set his beer next to hers and stood in one smooth motion. He placed two fingers beneath her chin and stared into her eyes. 'Has anyone ever kissed you until you were so hot you were burning up?'

She didn't answer, not wanting to admit that she'd never been so consumed or burned up with passion that she'd lost her head or her fear of Henry.

Nick moved his hands to the sides of her neck, and he looked into her eyes. 'Until you didn't care about anything else?' He lowered his face to her ear. 'Has anyone ever touched your breasts?' he whispered. 'Under the shirt, beneath your bra? Where your skin is warm and soft?'

Her tongue stuck to the roof of her mouth.

'Slipped his hand inside your panties?' His hot open mouth moved across her cheek. 'Felt between your legs where you're slick and ready?'

Besides health class, no one had ever really talked to Delaney about sex before. What she knew, she'd learned from movies and from eaves-dropping on other girls at school. Even Lisa assumed she was a prude, but apparently not Nick. Nick saw what no one else did, and instead of being offended at his language, she turned her face and kissed him. For years she'd heard rumors about his sexual conquests. She didn't want him to think her naive and boring in comparison, and she purposely turned up the passion and devoured him with her lips and tongue. She let herself fall head first into the dizzy heat burning her flesh. Her young body filled with the hot juices of desire, and for the first time in her life, she let go of everything else.

The kiss shattered their differences, sweeping them away

on a glut of passion. His hands moved to her back and slid to her behind. He palmed each cheek, then dragged her on to the balls of her feet and crushed her breasts against his chest. He pulled her against his pelvis and let her feel his long hard erection. She wasn't afraid. Instead she felt free. Free to explore for herself what other girls her age knew. Free to be a desirable eighteen-year-old on the verge of becoming a grown woman. She was flushed with new sensations and wonder, and she wanted him to touch her like he would any other girl. To lose herself in him.

He pulled back and let her slide down his body. 'We better stop right there, wild thing.'

Delaney didn't want to stop. Not yet. She slid right back up his chest, fitting her body to his. She licked her lips and tasted him there. 'No.' A shudder ran through him and he stared at her as if he wanted to shove her away but couldn't quite bring himself to do it. She looked into his eyes then let her gaze skim his handsome face. She kissed his cheek and just below his ear. 'I'm staying right here.' She opened her mouth and licked his warm flesh. He smelled of soap and skin and cool mountain breezes.

His hands moved to her waist, then slipped up her sides, bunching the material of her dress. The hem rode up to the top of her thighs, and he pressed his erection into her abdomen. 'Are you sure this is what you want?'

She nodded.

'Tell me. Tell me so there's no mistake.'

'Touch me like you said.'

He filled his palm with her right breast. 'Here?'

Her nipple tightened into a hard point. 'Yes.'

'You never answered my question. Has anyone ever touched you like this?'

She looked into his eyes, and it was like she was seeing a whole other side of Nick. For the first time she saw past the breathtaking face to the man inside. She didn't know this Nick. His gaze was intense, yet he caressed her as if she were made of something delicate. 'No.'

'Why?' He lightly brushed his thumb over the tip of her breast, and she bit her lip to keep from moaning out loud. 'You're beautiful, Delaney, and you could have anyone you want. Why me?'

She knew she wasn't beautiful, not like her mother. But the way he looked at her and touched her, and the tone of his voice when he said it made her almost believe him. He made her believe anything was possible. 'Because you make me not want to say no.'

He groaned deep in his throat and lowered his mouth to hers once again. The kiss started as a light brush of lips but quickly turned hard, wet, rough. The carnal thrust of his tongue touched something equally carnal within her and she squirmed against him. She wanted to crawl inside Nick, feel surrounded by him. When he finally set her away from him, her breathing was heavy. He reached for the buttons that closed her dress, and he gazed into her eyes as he worked downward until the pink cotton lay open past her waist. A twinge of apprehension penetrated the warm haze clouding her head. No man had ever seen her naked, and while she wanted him to touch her, she didn't necessarily want him to *look* at her. Not a man like Nick who'd seen more than his fair share of naked women, but then he pushed the dress apart and it was too late. The cool air beaded her already taut nipples, and he lowered his gaze to her bare breasts. He stared at her so long her apprehension grew and she raised her hands to shield herself from him.

'Don't hide from me.' He grabbed hold of her wrists and held them behind her back. Her spine arched, and the straps of her dress fell down her arms. He again leaned his behind against the hood of the car, bringing his face level with her naked breasts. He whispered her name, then kissed between her cleavage. His cool cheek brushed the inside slope of her breast, and she forgot all about her apprehension. 'You're beautiful.' His words warmed her skin and tugged at her heart, and this time she believed he meant what he said. He rested his forehead against her, his dark hair in stark contrast to her white flesh. 'I knew you would be. I've always known. Always.' Then his hot mouth drifted across her breast and he slid the seam of his lips across the very tip. 'I knew you'd be pink right here.'

For one fleeting second Delaney wondered how he knew, but then his tongue circled her nipple and her brain shut to cohesive thought. Her breathing became shallow as she watched his tongue curl, licking her.

'Do you like this?'

Behind her, Delaney's hands tightened into fists. 'Yes.'

'How much?'

'A . . . a lot.'

'Do you want more?'

Delaney closed her eyes and her head fell to one side. 'Yes,' she answered, and he drew her nipple into his mouth. His lips tugged and she felt the pull between her legs. It felt good. So good she didn't want him to stop. Ever. His mouth moved to her other breast and he sucked that nipple also. His tongue licked and stabbed and drove her fidgety for more. 'Nick,' she whispered and pulled her wrists free of his grasp. Her dress fell to the ground and pooled about her feet. She dug her fingers into his hair, holding him to her breast.

'More?'

'Yes.' She didn't really know exactly what she wanted, but she definitely wanted more of the hot ache pooling in her abdomen. She wanted more of him.

One of his big warm hands slid between her legs and he gently cupped her crotch. The thin cotton of her underwear was the only barrier separating his palm from her sensitive flesh. 'You're wet.'

The hot ache intensified and she could hardly speak. 'I'm sorry,' she managed.

'Don't be. I've always wanted to make your panties wet.' He stood once again and gave her a quick kiss. Then he grasped her waist and set her on the hood of the Mustang he'd just vacated. He moved her feet to the chrome bumper and said, 'Lie down, Delaney.'

'Why?' She put a hand on his chest then moved it to the front of his jeans. She pressed against the hard bulge beneath his zipper.

He sucked in his breath and pushed her shoulders until she lay with her back against the cool metal. 'Because I'm going to make you feel real good.'

'I already feel good.' She held out her arms for him as he stepped between her thighs.

'Then I'm going to make you feel even better.' He planted both of his palms by the sides of her head and kissed her like he wanted to consume her. When he raised his mouth again he said, 'I'm going to set you on fire.'

Delaney looked up into his beautiful face and she wanted him to make love to her. She wanted to know what other young women her age knew. She wanted Nick to teach her. 'Yes,' she said to anything he wanted.

He smiled as his skillful hands eased her panties from her legs. She felt the cotton slide down her calves and then her underwear was gone. His palms drifted up the insides of her thighs, and one of his thumbs touched her where she was slick. The pleasure was indescribable. His fingers brushed her moist flesh until she wanted to scream.

'More?'

'Yes,' she murmured and her eyes slid shut. 'More.' His touch felt so good it was almost painful, the building pressure in her groin intense. She wanted it to end, yet at the same time continue forever. She wanted him naked and on top of her, filling her arms with his warm body. She opened her eyes and gazed up at him, standing there between her knees, looking down at her through heavy lids. 'Make love to me, Nick.'

'I'll give you something better than love.' He knelt on one knee and softly kissed the inside of her thigh. 'I'm going to make you come.' Delaney froze, extremely grateful she was surrounded by darkness. When she'd said yes, she hadn't meant *that*. She would have clamped her legs together but Nick was in the way. She wasn't sure what he would do, but she was pretty sure he wouldn't do *that*.

But he did. He slid his hands beneath her behind, then raised her to his hot open mouth. Shock held her still. She couldn't believe what he'd done. What he was doing. She wanted to tell him to stop, but she couldn't get the words past the warm pleasure swirling through her body. She couldn't control the shiver tingling up her spine and instead of pulling away, she arched her back. His tongue and mouth gently caressed between her legs in much the same way he'd kissed her breasts.

'Nick,' she moaned and touched her hands to the sides of his head. The pleasure grew and tightened and each touch of his tongue pushed her toward the peak of climax. He moved one of her heels to his shoulder and tilted her hips. He took her more fully into his mouth and drew on her sensitive flesh. The incredible sensations built and coiled in her body, then shoved her over the top.

The stars above her head blurred as she felt herself pulled under wave after hot wave of ecstasy. She called his name over and over as heat flushed her thighs and breasts. Involuntary contractions shook her, and when it was over she felt changed. She was shocked by what she'd done and who'd done it to her, but she wasn't sorry. She'd never felt so close to anyone else in her life, and she wanted him to hold her.

'Nick?'

He gently kissed the inside of her thigh. 'Mmm.'

At the touch of his lips, she suddenly became very aware of her embarrassing position. She felt her cheeks burn as she slid her foot from his shoulder and sat up.

He stood and cupped her face in his hands. 'More?'

She was naive, not stupid, and she knew what he was asking. She wanted to give him the same awesome pleasure he'd just given her. 'More.' She pulled his T-shirt from the waistband of his jeans and released the buttons of his fly. His hands wrapped around her wrists and stopped her.

'Be still a minute,' he said right before a beam of light struck him full in the face. 'Shit!'

Delaney glanced over her shoulder and was blinded by two headlights gunning toward them. Pure adrenaline shot through her veins, and she pushed Nick and jumped off the hood at the same time. Her dress lay at his feet and she reached for it just as Henry's silver Lincoln slid to a stop beside the Mustang. She pulled the summer dress over her head but her hands shook so bad she couldn't button it. 'Help me,' she cried to no one in particular.

Nick turned, and he reached for the buttons at the waist of her dress. He whispered something to her, but she couldn't hear him over the pounding in her ears.

'Get away from her!' Henry bellowed the second he opened the car door.

She managed the top two buttons but was helpless to control the panic welling within her. She glanced at the ground and saw Nick's big foot in the crotch of her panties. Distressed little sobs filled the top of her lungs.

'Get your filthy damn hands off her!'

Delaney looked up just as Henry reached them. He shoved

Nick and pushed her behind him. Both men were of the same height, same build, same flashing gray eyes. The Lincoln's headlights lit every excruciating detail. The stripe on Henry's dress shirt, the silver in his hair.

'I never thought you'd sink this low,' Henry said as he pointed at Nick. 'I've always known you hated me, but I never thought you'd sink this low just to get back at me.'

'Maybe this has nothing to do with you,' Nick said, his brows lowered on his forehead.

'My aching ass this has nothing to do with me. You've hated me all your life, and you've been jealous of Delaney since the day I married her mother.'

'You're right. I have hated you all of my life. You're a son of a bitch, and the biggest favor you ever did my mother was deny you ever slept with her.'

'And you finally got your revenge. The only reason you screwed Delaney was to get back at me.'

Nick folded his arms over his chest and rested his weight on one foot. 'Maybe I screwed her because she makes me hard.'

'I should beat the hell out of you.'

'Give it your best shot, old man.'

'Oh, God,' Delaney groaned as she finished the buttons on her dress. 'Henry, we didn't—'

'Get in the car,' Henry interrupted her.

She looked at Nick, and gone was the gentle lover who'd made her feel beautiful. 'Tell him!' A few moments ago she'd felt so close to him, now she didn't know him at all. He appeared relaxed, but it was an illusion. Or maybe she did know this Nick. This surly man before her was the Nick she'd grown up with; the man who'd picked her up earlier had been the illusion. 'Please, tell him nothing happened,' she pleaded with him to help her out of the worst of it. 'Tell him we didn't do anything!'

One knowing brow rose up his forehead. 'What exactly do you want me to lie about, wild thing?' he asked. 'He saw you sitting on my car like a hood ornament. If he'd been a few minutes earlier, he would have seen a hell of a lot more.'

'You got your revenge, didn't you?' Henry grabbed Delaney's arm and pushed her toward Nick. 'You took an innocent girl and you made her dirty just to get even with me.'

Delaney looked into Nick's hard gaze and she didn't know what to believe. She wanted him to care just a little bit, but the eyes that stared back at her were so cold. Several minutes ago she would have said Henry was mistaken, but she didn't know what to think now. 'Is that true?' she asked as one tear ran down her hot cheeks. 'Did you use me to get back at Henry?'

'Is that what you think?'

What he'd done to her was so private, so intimate, she didn't think she could bear knowing he'd used her. She wanted him to tell Henry he was wrong, that he'd kissed her and touched her because he wanted her, not because he hated Henry. 'I don't know!'

'Don't you?'

'No.'

He didn't speak for what seemed like an eternity, then he said, 'Believe Henry then.'

A sob caught in her throat and she stumbled toward the Lincoln. Her chest felt as if it were caving in on itself, and she managed to get into the car before the second tear slid down her cheek. The cold leather beneath her bare behind reminded her she was completely naked under her dress. She stared out the window at both men, and above the pounding of her heart, she heard Henry threaten Nick.

'You stay away from my daughter,' he yelled. 'You stay away or I'll make your life hell.'

'You can try,' Nick said, his words barely audible through the thick glass. 'But there is nothing you can do to me.'

'We'll see about that.' Henry moved to the driver's side of the Lincoln. 'Stay away from Delaney,' he warned one last time and slid into the front seat. He slipped the car into reverse, and the headlights shone on Nick for a few short seconds. And in those few seconds, his T-shirt glowed a bright white, the soft cotton untucked at his waist, and the top button on his jeans was undone. He leaned down to pick up something, but Henry cranked the wheel and the car turned toward the road before she could see what he'd retrieved from the ground. But she didn't have to see, she already knew. Carefully, she tucked her dress beneath her bare behind.

'This is going to kill your mother,' Henry seethed.

Probably, Delaney thought. She looked down at her hands and a tear fell on her thumb.

'She went to your room to tell you good night, but you weren't there.' The Lincoln turned onto the main road, and Henry gunned the big engine. 'She's worried sick. She's afraid you've been kidnapped.'

Delaney bit her lip to keep the customary apology inside. She didn't care that she'd worried her mother.

'Just wait until she learns the truth is worse than anything she could have imagined.'

'How did you find me?'

'Not that it matters, but several people down at the market saw you crawl into Allegrezza's car. If you hadn't left the gate open at Angel Beach, it would have taken me a lot longer, but I would have found you.'

Delaney didn't doubt him. She turned her gaze to the passenger window and stared out into the dark night. 'I can't believe you hunted me down. I'm eighteen and I can't believe you drove around town looking for me as if I were ten years old.'

'And I can't believe I found you naked as a two-bit hooker,' he said and kept up his verbal battering until he pulled the Lincoln into the garage.

As calm as possible under the circumstances, Delaney got out of the car and walked into the house. Her mother met her in the kitchen.

'Where have you been?' Gwen asked, her gaze sliding from Delaney's face to her feet then back up again.

Delaney walked past without answering. Henry would tell her mother. He always did. Then together they would decide her fate. They would probably ground her as if she were a child. She moved up the stairs to her bedroom and shut the door behind her. She wasn't trying to hide. She knew better, and even if she hadn't, tonight's lesson showed her the futility of independence.

She looked at her reflection in the cheval mirror. Mascara trailed down her cheeks, her eyes were red, and her face pale. Otherwise she looked as she always did. She didn't look as if her world had shifted beneath her feet and now she stood in a new place. Her room looked the same as it had hours ago when she'd sneaked out the window. The pictures stuck to the mirror, and the roses on her bedspread were the same as they'd always been, but everything was different. She was different.

She'd let Nick do things to her that she'd never imagined in her wildest dreams. Oh, she'd heard about oral sex. A few girls in her math class had bragged about knowing how to give blow jobs, but until tonight, Delaney had never believed people actually did that sort of thing. Now she knew better. Now she knew a man didn't even have to like the girl he was with. Now she knew that a man could do incredibly intimate things to a woman for reasons other than passion or mutual attraction. Now she knew what it was like to be used.

When she thought of Nick's warm mouth pressed to the inside of her thigh, her pale cheeks turned red and she turned her gaze away from her reflection. What she saw embarrassed her. She'd wanted to feel free. Free from Henry's control. Free from her life.

She was a fool.

Delaney changed into a pair of jeans and T-shirt, then washed her face. When she was finished, she went to Henry's office, where she knew her parents would be waiting for her. They stood behind the mahogany desk, and by the look on Gwen's face, Henry had filled her in on every excruciating detail.

Gwen's blue eyes were wide as she looked at her daughter. 'Well, I don't know what to say to you.'

Delaney sat in one of the leather chairs opposite the desk. Not knowing what to say had never stopped her mother before. It didn't stop her now.

'Tell me Henry is mistaken. Tell me he didn't see you in a sexually compromising situation with that Allegrezza boy.'

Delaney didn't say anything. She knew she wouldn't win. She never did.

'How could you?' Gwen shook her head and placed a hand at her throat. 'How could you do such a thing to this family? While you were crawling out your bedroom window did you give a thought to your father's position in this community? While you were letting that Allegrezza boy put his hands on you, did you stop – for even one second – to think how your father would suffer for your actions?'

'No,' Delaney answered. When Nick's head had been between her thighs, she hadn't given a thought to her parents. She'd been busy humiliating herself.

'You know how this town loves to gossip. By ten o'clock tomorrow, everyone in town will know about your shameful behavior. How could you do this?'

'You've hurt your mother deeply,' Henry added. They were like tag team wrestlers, one ready to jump in when the other ran out of steam. 'If your disgraceful behavior gets out, I don't know how she'll hold her head up in this town.' He pointed a finger at her. 'We never expected this of you. You were always such a good girl. We never expected that you would do something so vulgar. I never thought you'd bring shame on this family. I guess you aren't the person we thought you were. I guess we don't even know you.'

Delaney's hands clenched into fists. She knew better than to say anything. She knew defending herself only made things worse. She knew if she said anything, Henry would consider it arguing, and Henry hated for anyone to argue with him. But Delaney couldn't help it. 'That's because you've never wanted to know me. You're only interested in how I make you look. You don't care how I feel.'

'Laney,' Gwen gasped.

'You don't care that I don't want to go to college right away. I told you I didn't want to go, and you're making me go anyway.'

'So that's what tonight was all about,' Henry said as if he were an omnipotent God. 'You wanted to get back at me for knowing what's best for you.'

'Tonight was about me,' she said as she stood. 'I wanted to go out and be a regular eighteen-year-old. I wanted to have a life. I wanted to feel free.'

'You mean feel free to screw up your life.'

'Yes! Free to screw up my life if I want to, just like everyone else. I never have the freedom to do anything. You choose everything for me. I never have a choice.'

'And it's a good thing,' Gwen took over. 'You're immature and selfish, and tonight you chose the one boy who could hurt this family the most. You gave yourself to a person whose only interest in you was to get back at Henry.'

What Nick had done was a hot lump of humiliation burning a hole in her stomach, but the despair choking the life out of her was worse. As she looked at both of her parents she knew it was no use. They would never understand. Never change. And she would never escape.

'You've degraded yourself, and I can hardly stand to look at you,' her mother continued.

'Then don't. You were going to take me to the University of Idaho in a week. Take me tomorrow instead.' Delaney walked from the room, the weight of resignation settling about her shoulders. She moved up the stairs, her feet felt leaden, her heart empty, too drained to cry. She didn't bother to pull off her jeans before she crawled into bed. She stared up at the pink canopy above her head and knew she wouldn't be able to sleep, and she was right. Her mind raced with every dreadful detail of the past few hours. What her parents had said. What she'd said, and how nothing ever changed. And no matter how hard she tried to avoid thoughts of Nick, her mind turned again and again to him. She remembered his hot touch, the cool silky texture of his hair through her fingers, and the taste of his skin. She closed her eyes and could practically feel his warm wet mouth on her breasts and lower. She didn't know why she'd let him do those things to her. She'd had enough previous experience with him to know he could pass for pleasant one minute and turn mean as a snake the next. So why Nick Allegrezza of all people?

Delaney punched her pillow and turned on her side. Maybe because he'd always been so free, and he'd always fascinated her with his heavenly face and wild hellion ways. Maybe because he was so beautiful he took her breath away, and tonight he'd made her feel like maybe she was beautiful too. He'd looked at her like a man who wanted to make love to a woman. He'd touched her as if he wanted *her*. But it had all been a lie. An illusion, and she'd been a naive fool.

I'll give you something better than love, he'd said. *I'm going to make you come*. Why he'd chosen that particular method she didn't know. But he couldn't have chosen anything more humiliating if he'd had years to plan it. He'd stripped her naked while he'd remained clothed. He'd touched her all over, and she'd never even gotten a glimpse of his bare chest.

Her only consolation was that no one knew, not even Henry, exactly what had happened on the hood of Nick's Mustang. And unless Nick spoke of it, no one would ever know. Maybe her mother was wrong. Maybe no one would talk about it.

But Gwen had only been wrong about the amount of time it would take for the gossip to reach her. It was noon, not ten, the next day when Lisa called and told Delaney that someone had seen her and Nick at the Charm-Inn in the nearby city of Garden. Another had them running buck naked through Larkspur Park and having sex on the kiddie slide. And yet in a third, she and Nick had been sighted in the alley behind the liquor store, drinking tequila shooters and going at it in the backseat of his car.

Suddenly being sent away to college didn't seem so bad. The University of Idaho wasn't Delaney's first choice, but it was four hours from Truly. Four hours from her parents and their tight control. Four hours from the gossip blowing through town like a hurricane. Four hours from ever having to lay eyes on Nick or any member of his family.

No, maybe the U of I wouldn't be so horrible after all.

'If you get good grades and behave yourself,' Henry told her on the drive to Moscow, 'maybe we'll lighten your class load next year.'

'That would really be great,' she'd said without enthusiasm. Next year was twelve months away, and she was sure she'd do something in the interim to displease Henry. But she would try. Just like she always did.

She tried for one month, but her first taste of real freedom went straight to her head, and she pulled straight Ds her first semester. She lost her virginity to a wide receiver named Rex and got a job waitressing at Ducky's Bar and Grill, which was more bar than actual grill.

The money from her job gave her even more freedom, and when she turned nineteen that February, she quit school all together. Her parents had been livid, but she didn't care anymore. She moved in with her first boyfriend, a weightlifter named Rocky Baroli. She sought higher education reading Rocky's incredible pecs and adding up how many straight shots she could consume at the all-night parties she attended off campus. She learned the difference between a Tom Collins and a vodka Collins, between imported and home-grown.

She'd taken her new independence and she'd run with it. She'd grabbed hold with both hands and taken a great big bite, and she was never going back. She'd lived as if she had to experience everything at once, before her freedom was snatched away from her. Whenever she thought back on those years, she knew she was lucky to be alive.

The last time she'd seen Henry, he'd tracked her down with the sole purpose of dragging her back home. By then she'd dumped Rocky and had moved into a basement apartment in Spokane with two other girls. Henry had taken one look at the garage sale furniture, overflowing ash trays, and collection of empty booze bottles, and ordered her to pack her clothes. She'd refused and the confrontation had turned ugly. He'd told her if she didn't get in his car, he would disown her, forget she was his daughter. She'd called him a controlling pompous son of a bitch.

'I don't want to be your daughter anymore. It's too exhausting. You were always more dictator than father. Don't ever hunt me down again,' were the last words she'd spoken to Henry.

After that, whenever Gwen called her on the telephone, she made sure Henry was never home. Her mother visited

Delaney occasionally in whichever city she happened to be living, but of course Henry never came with her. He'd been true to his word. He'd disowned Delaney completely, and she'd never felt so free – free of his control, free to screw up her life with abandon. And sometimes she really screwed up, but in the process, she also grew up.

She'd been free to drift from state to state and job to job until she figured out what to do with her life. She'd finally figured it out six years ago when she enrolled in beauty school. After the first week, she'd known she'd found her niche. She loved the tactile sensations and the whole process of creating something wonderful right before her eyes. She had the freedom to dress outrageously if she wanted to, because there was always someone a little bolder than herself.

It may have taken Delaney longer than most to settle on a career, but at last she'd found something she was good at and loved to do.

Being a stylist gave her the freedom to be creative. It also gave her the freedom to move when she began to feel trapped in one place, although she hadn't felt claustrophobic in a while.

Not until a few months ago when Henry had flexed his muscle one last time and left that appalling will, controlling her life once again.

Delaney picked up her boots and headed into the bedroom. She flipped on the light and tossed her boots toward the closet. What was wrong with her? What would make her kiss Nick out on a crowded dance floor in spite of their sordid past? There were other available men around. True, some were married or divorced with five kids, and none of them were as fine as Nick, but she didn't have a painful past with other men.

Nick the snake. That's who he was, like that big python with the mesmerizing eyes in *The Jungle Book*, and she was just one more helpless victim.

Delaney looked at herself in the mirror above her dresser

and frowned. Maybe if she weren't so lonely and aimless she wouldn't be so susceptible to Nick's hypnotic charms. There had been a time in her life when aimlessness had been her goal. Not anymore. She was living in a town she didn't want to live in, working in a salon with no real intentions of success. Her only goals were to survive and aggravate Helen. Something had to change, and she had to change it.

Monday morning Delaney thought about advertising for a manicurist in the small daily newspaper, but she resisted the idea because the salon would be open for only seven months. She'd stayed awake last night thinking of ways to make a success out of the business, even though she would have it for only a short time. She wanted to feel proud of herself. She was going to end her secret hair war with Helen and stay as far away from Nick as humanly possible.

After Delaney opened the salon, she grabbed a poster of Claudia Schiffer, her perfect body squeezed into a lace Valentino, her golden hair curled and blowing artfully about her beautiful face. There was nothing like a glamorous poster to draw attention.

Delaney kicked off her shoes with the huge buckles and climbed up on the window bay. She'd just stuck the poster on the plate glass when the bell over the door rang. She glanced to her left and set the tape on the ledge. One of the Howell twins stood just inside the entrance gazing about the salon, her light brown hair held back from her pretty face by a wide red headband.

'Can I help you?' Delaney asked as she carefully climbed out of the window, wondering if this was the twin who had jumped on the back of Nick's Harley last Saturday night.

If she was, the woman had bigger problems than split ends.

Her blue eyes raked Delaney from head to toe, scrutinizing her green and black striped tights, green lederhosen, and black turtleneck. 'Do you take walk-ins?' she asked.

Delaney was desperate for clients, desperate for anyone who didn't qualify for a senior citizen discount, but she really didn't care for the woman's close examination, as if she were looking for faults. Delaney didn't care if she lost this potential customer, and so she said, 'Yes, but I charge twenty-five dollars.'

'Are you good?'

'I'm the best you'll find around here.' Delaney shoved her feet into her shoes, a little surprised that the woman wasn't already out the door, running down the street toward a ten-dollar haircut.

'That isn't saying much. Helen sucks.'

Perhaps she'd rushed to judgment. 'Well, I don't suck,' she said simply. 'In fact, I'm very good.'

The woman reached for the headband and pulled it from her hair. 'I want the bottom trimmed and layered up to here,' she said, indicating her jawline. 'No bangs.'

Delaney cocked her head to the side. The woman standing before her had a great jawline and nice high cheekbones. Her forehead was in proportion to the rest of her face. The cut she wanted would look good on her, but with her big blue eyes, Delaney knew something short and boyish would look stunning. 'Come on back.'

'We met briefly at a party on the Fourth of July,' the twin said as she followed Delaney. 'I'm Lanna Howell.'

Delaney stopped in front of a shampoo chair. 'Yes, I recognized you.' Lanna sat and Delaney draped the woman's shoulders in a silver shampoo cape and white fluffy towel. 'You have a twin sister, right?' she asked, when what she really wanted to know was if this was the sister who'd glued herself to Nick the other night.

'Yeah, Lonna.'

'That's right,' she said as she analyzed her client's hair between her fingers and thumb. Then she adjusted the cape over the rear of the chair and carefully eased Lanna back until her neck rested comfortably in the dip of the shampoo sink. 'What did you use to lighten your hair?' She grabbed the spray nozzle, then tested the water temperature with her hand.

'Sun-In and lemon juice.'

Delaney mentally rolled her eyes at the logic of some women who spent big bucks at the cosmetics counter, then went home and dumped a five-dollar bottle of peroxide on their heads.

With one hand she protected Lanna's face, neck, and ears from the spray while the other saturated the hair with warm water. She used a mild shampoo and natural conditioner, and as she worked, the two women chatted idly about the weather and the beautiful colors of autumn. When she was finished, she wrapped Lanna's head in a towel and led her to the salon chair.

'My sister said she saw you the other night in Hennesey's,' Lanna stated as Delaney blotted the water from her hair.

Delaney glanced in the big wall mirror, studying Lanna's reflection. So, she thought as grabbed her comb, it was the other twin who had been with Nick. 'Yeah, I was there. They had a pretty good R&B band up from Boise.'

'That's what I heard. I work in the restaurant at the microbrewery, so I couldn't make it.'

As Delaney combed out the tangles and secured the hair into five sections with duckbill clamps, she purposely moved the subject away from Hennesey's. She asked Lanna about her job, and the conversation turned to the big ice sculpture festival the town held every December. According to Lanna, the festival had turned into quite an event.

As a child, Delaney and been shy and introverted, but after years of attempting to put her clients at ease, she could shoot the bull with anyone about anything. She could moon over Brad Pitt as easily as she could commiserate over cramps. Stylists were a lot like bartenders and priests. Some people just seemed compelled to spill their guts and confess shocking details of their lives. Styling chair confessions were just one of the many things she missed about her life before she'd accepted the terms of Henry's will. She also missed the competition and camaraderie between stylists and the juicy gossip that made Delaney's life look tame in comparison.

'How well do you know Nick Allegrezza?'

Delaney's hand stilled, and then she blunt cut a section of hair at the center of Lanna's nape. 'We grew up here in Truly at the same time.'

'But did you know him very well?'

She glanced into the mirror again, then back down at her hands, snipping a guideline from left to right. 'I don't think anyone really knows Nick. Why?'

'My friend Gail thinks she's in love with him.'

'Then she has my sympathy.'

Lanna laughed. 'You don't care?'

'Of course not.' Even if she thought Nick was capable of loving any woman, he wasn't her concern. 'Why should I care?' she asked and removed the clip at the back of Lanna's head and clamped it on the bib of her lederhosen.

'Gail told me all about Nick and you and what happened when you lived here.'

Delaney wasn't all that surprised as she combed out tangles and cut the new section. 'Which story did you hear?'

'The one where you had to leave town years ago to have Nick's baby.'

Delaney felt as if she'd been hit in the stomach and her hands stilled again. She shouldn't have asked. There had been several rumors churning the gossip mill of Truly when she'd left, but she'd never heard that one. Her mother had never mentioned it, but then she wouldn't. Gwen didn't like to talk about the real reason Delaney had left Truly. Her mother always referred to that time as 'when you went away to school.' Delaney didn't know why such old news should bother her now, but it did. 'Really? That's news to me,' she said, ducking her head and sliding strands of Lanna's hair between her fingers. She laid the open scissor across her knuckle and cut a straight line. She couldn't believe the town had thought she was pregnant. Well, actually, she guessed she could. She wondered if Lisa knew of the rumor – or Nick.

'I'm sorry.' Lanna broke into her thoughts. 'I thought you knew about it. I guess I've stuck my foot in my mouth.'

Delaney glanced up. Lanna looked sincere, but Delaney didn't know the woman so she wasn't real sure. 'It's just a little shocking to hear I've had a baby when I've never been pregnant.' She let down another section and combed it free of tangles. 'Especially with Nick. We don't even like each other.'

'That will relieve Gail's mind. Lonna's too. The two of them are kind of competing for the same man.'

'I thought they were friends.'

'They are. If you go out with Nick, he lets you know right up front it's not marriage he's interested in. Lonna doesn't really mind, but Gail's trying to get in the house.'

'Get in the house? What do you mean?'

'Lonna says Nick never takes women to his house for sex. They go to motels or wherever. Gail thinks if she can get him to make love to her in his house, than she'll get him to do other things too. Like buy her a big diamond and walk down the aisle.'

'Nick must have a huge motel bill.'

'Probably.' Lanna laughed.

'Doesn't that bother you?'

'Me? Maybe if I were the one going out with him, but I'm not. Me and my sister never date the same men.'

Delaney felt relieved, and she really didn't know why she should care if Nick had kinky group sex with a pair of beautiful twins. 'Well, doesn't it bother your sister?'

'Not really. She's not looking for a husband. Not like Gail. Gail thinks she'll change his mind, but she won't. When Lonna saw you and Nick dancing the other night, she wondered if you were another of his women.'

Delaney turned the chair and let down the last section. 'Did you really come here to get your hair cut, or are you here to get information for your sister?'

'Both,' Lanna laughed. 'But I liked your hair the first time I saw it.'

'Thank you. Have you ever thought of getting yours cut short?' she asked, again purposely changing the subject from Nick. 'Really short, like Halle Berry in *The Flintstones*?'

'I don't think I'd look good in short hair.'

'Believe me, you'd look awesome. You've got big eyes and the perfect shaped head. Mine's kind of narrow so I need lots of volume.'

'I'd have to think about it for a *really* long time.'

Delaney put down her scissors and reached for a can of mousse. She wrapped the ends of Lanna's hair around a large round brush and blew it dry. When she was finished, she handed her an oval mirror. 'What do you think?' she asked, knowing full well that it looked damn good.

'I think,' Lanna answered slowly as she studied the back of her hair, 'that I don't need to drive the hundred and fifty miles to Boise just to get my hair cut anymore.'

After Lanna left, Delaney swept up the hair and rinsed the shampoo sink. She thought about the old rumor that had her leaving town ten years ago because she carried Nick's child. She wondered what other gossip had circulated when she'd left town and been stuck in a dormitory at the University of Idaho. Maybe she would ask her mother tonight when she drove out there for dinner.

But she didn't get the chance to ask. Max Harrison answered the door with a highball in his hand and a welcoming smile on his face.

'Gwen is in the kitchen doing something to the lamb,' he said as he shut the door behind her. 'I hope you don't mind that your mother invited me tonight.'

'Of course not.' The wonderful smells of her mother's cooking filled Delaney's head and made her mouth water. No one cooked a leg of lamb like Gwen, and the scents from the kitchen wrapped Delaney in warm memories of special occasions at the Shaw house, like Easters or her birthday when she'd been allowed to choose her favorite meal.

'How's that salon of yours working out?' Max asked as he helped her out of her long wool coat, then hung it on the hall tree.

'Okay.' Lately, it seemed that Gwen was spending quite a bit of time with Max, and Delaney wondered what was going on between her mother and Henry's estate lawyer. She just couldn't picture her mother as any man's lover. She was too uptight, and Delaney figured it couldn't be anything but friendship. 'You should come in and let me cut your hair.'

His quiet laughter made Delaney smile. 'I just might do that,' he said as they walked toward the back of the house.

When they entered the kitchen, Gwen looked up from the bag of baby carrots she held in her hand. An almost imperceptible frown narrowed Gwen's eyes a fraction, and Delaney knew something was wrong.

Shit! Someone was in trouble, and she doubted it was Max. 'What's the special occasion?'

'No special occasion. I wanted to make you your favorite.' Gwen looked at Max and told him, 'Every birthday, Laney always requested my lamb. Other children would have wanted pizza or burgers, but not her.'

Maybe she wasn't in trouble, but she pushed up a cheerful smile just in case. 'How can I help you?'

'You can get the salad out of the refrigerator and dress it, please.'

Delaney did as she was asked, then carried the bowls into the dining room. The table was set with beautiful roses, beeswax candles, Royal Doulton, and fine damask. It looked like a special occasion to her. Which could mean two completely different things. That she should worry, or that she was worrying about nothing. Either her mother simply wanted to enjoy a nice meal, or she was covering for a crack in the facade.

Delaney knew within moments of sitting down that the latter was the case. There was something wrong with the perfect picture. The conversation during dinner was pleasant on the surface, but a current of tension hid just beneath. Max didn't seem to notice, but Delaney felt it at the base of her skull. She felt it during the first course and while she ate her mother's lamb with mint. She smiled and laughed and entertained Max with stories of all the places she'd lived. She knew how to keep up a good front, but by the time she helped carry the dinner plates to the kitchen, her headache had moved to her eyebrows. Maybe with Max there, she could make a quick escape before her head exploded. 'Well,' she said as she set the plates next to the sink, 'I hate to eat and run, but—'

'Max,' Gwen interrupted, 'could you leave us girls alone for a few moments?'

Damn.

'Sure, I'll go examine those contracts you wanted me to take a look at.'

'Thank you. I won't be long.'

Gwen waited until she heard the doors of Henry's office close before she said, 'I need to talk to you about your scandalous behavior.'

'What scandalous behavior?'

'Trudie Duran called me this afternoon to inform me that you and Tommy Markham were getting drunk together while his wife was out of town. According to Trudie, everyone at the Shop-n-Kart was talking about it.'

'Who's Trudie Duran?' Delaney asked, her skull tightening.

'That doesn't matter! Is it true?'

She folded her arms across her breasts and frowned. 'No. I ran into Tommy at Hennesey's the other night, and we talked for a little bit. Lisa was there most of the time.'

'Well, I'm relieved.' Gwen grabbed a roll of tinfoil and ripped off a long piece. 'And then, if that weren't bad enough, she told me her daughter Gina saw you kissing Nick Allegrezza out on the dance floor.' She calmly set the roll of foil on the counter. 'I told her she must be mistaken, because I'm sure you would never do anything so stupid. Tell me she was mistaken.'

'Okay, she was mistaken.'

'Is that the truth?'

Delaney thought about her answer but knew sooner or later the lie would catch up with her. Besides, she wasn't a little girl who had to fear punishment, and she wasn't going to allow her mother to treat her like a kid. 'No.'

'What were you thinking? My God, that boy and his whole entire family have meant nothing but trouble for us since the moment we arrived in this town. They are rude and jealous. Especially toward you, although Benita has certainly shown me her ugly side on more than one occasion. Have you forgotten what happened ten years ago? Have you forgotten what Nick did? What pain and humiliation he caused all of us?'

'It wasn't all of us. It was me, and no, I haven't forgotten. But you're making a big deal out of absolutely nothing,' she assured her mother, but it hadn't felt like nothing. '*Nothing* happened. It was *so* nothing, I don't want to talk about it. I don't even want to think about it either.'

'Well, you better think about it. You *know* how the people of this town love to gossip, especially about us.'

Delaney silently agreed that most everyone in Truly loved to gossip – including Gwen – but she didn't think the Shaws were singled out any more than others. Juicy gossip got attention, but as always, her mother overestimated her importance in the food chain. 'Okay, I'll think about it.' She closed her eyes and pressed her fingers to her brows.

'I hope you do, and for goodness sake, stay away from Nick Allegrezza.'

Three million dollars, she told herself. *I can do this for three million*.

'What's wrong with you? Are you sick?'

'It's just a headache.' She took a deep breath and dropped her hands. 'I have to go.'

'Are you sure? Can't you just stay for tort? I bought it at the Bakery Basket over on Sixth.'

Delaney declined and started down the hall to Henry's office. She bid Max good night, then grabbed her coat and shoved her arms into the sleeves.

Her mother pushed Delaney's hands out of the way and buttoned it for her as if she were five again. 'I love you, and I worry about you in that little apartment downtown.' Delaney opened her mouth to argue, but Gwen put a restraining finger to her lips. 'I know you don't want to move back here now, but I just want you to know that if you change your mind, I'd love to have you.'

Just when Delaney was convinced her mother was Mommy Dearest, the woman changed. It had always been that way. 'I'll keep that in mind,' Delaney said, hurrying out the door before things changed back again.

Gwen stared at the closed door and sighed. She didn't understand Delaney. Not at all.

She didn't understand why her daughter insisted on living in that horrid little apartment when she didn't have to. She didn't understand why someone who'd been given so much opportunity had rejected it all for the life of a wandering *beautician*. And she couldn't help but be a little disappointed in her, too.

Henry had wanted to give Delaney everything, and she'd thrown it away. All she'd had to do was let him guide her, but Delaney had wanted her freedom. As far as Gwen was concerned, freedom was overrated. It didn't feed you or your child, and it didn't take away the fear that gripped your stomach in the middle of the night. Some women could take care of themselves just fine, but Gwen wasn't one of those women. She needed and wanted a man to take care of her.

The first night she'd met Henry Shaw, she'd known he was just the man for her. Forceful and rich. She'd been shampooing wigs and styling hair on the heads of Las Vegas showgirls, and she'd hated it. After one of the shows, Henry had come to the dressing room of his latest girlfriend and he'd left with Gwen. He'd looked so handsome and so classy. A week later, she married him.

She'd loved Henry Shaw, but more than she'd ever loved him, she'd been grateful. With his help, she lived the life she'd always dreamed. With Henry, the hardest decision she ever had to make was what to serve for dinner and which club to join. Gwen turned and headed down the hall toward Henry's office. Of course there'd been a tradeoff for all the privileges. Henry had wanted a legitimate child, and when she didn't conceive, he blamed her. After years of trying, she'd finally convinced him to see a fertility specialist, and just as Gwen had suspected, Henry was virtually infertile. He had a very low sperm count, and of the few he did have, most of those were deformed and sluggish. The diagnosis had insulted and enraged Henry, and he'd wanted to make love all the time just to prove the doctors all wrong. He'd been so bullheaded and so sure he could conceive a child. Of course the doctors hadn't been wrong. They'd had sex all the time, even when she hadn't felt like it. But it had never been real bad, and the payback had been worth it. People looked up to her in the community, and she had a life filled with beautiful things.

And then a few years ago, he gave up on the idea of having a child with her. Nick had moved back to town and Henry turned his attention to the child he already had. Gwen didn't like Nick. She didn't like that whole family, but she had been grateful when Henry had finally turned his obsession toward his son.

When Gwen entered the room, she found Max standing behind Henry's desk looking at a few documents sitting on the desk. He looked up and a smile creased the corners of his blue eyes. Silver was just beginning to turn the hair at his temples, and not for the first time lately, she wondered what it would be like to be touched by a man who was closer to her own age. A man as handsome as Max.

'Is Delaney gone?' he asked as he walked around the desk toward her.

'She just left. I worry about her. She's so aimless, so irresponsible. I don't think she'll ever grow up.'

'Don't worry. She's a bright girl.'

'Yes, but she's almost thirty. She'll –'

Max brushed his index finger across her lips and cheek and silenced her words. 'I don't want to talk about Delaney. She's a grown woman. You've done your job, now you need to step back and think about something else.'

Gwen's gaze narrowed. Max didn't know what he was

talking about. Delaney needed her mother's guidance. She'd lived like a gypsy much too long. 'How can you say that? She's my daughter. How can I possibly not think about her?'

'Think about me instead,' he said as he dipped his head and softly kissed her mouth.

At first, the lips pressed to hers felt foreign. She couldn't even remember a time when a man other than Henry had kissed her. Max opened his mouth over hers, and she felt the first tentative stroke of his tongue. Pleasure swept across her flesh, and her heart seemed to triple its beat. She'd wanted to know what it felt like to be touched by Max, and now she knew. It felt better than she'd imagined.

On the way home from her mother's, Delaney stopped at the Value Rite Drug for a bottle of Tylenol, a four-pack of toilet paper, and a packet of Reese's Peanut Butter Cups. She threw in two boxes of tampons because they were on sale, then she stopped at the magazine rack. She picked up a slick publication that reeked of perfume and promised to reveal 'The Secrets of Men.' She flipped through the pages and tossed it in the cart, planning to read it in the bathtub when she got home. In aisle four she threw in a scented candle, and when she headed down aisle five toward the checkout, she practically ran over Helen Markham.

Helen looked tired, and by the hate glaring from her eyes, she'd obviously heard the latest.

Delaney almost felt sorry for her. Helen's life couldn't be easy, and Delaney figured she had two choices: make her old enemy squirm, or let her off the hook. 'I hope you don't believe the gossip about me and Tommy,' she said. 'It's not true.'

'Stay away from my husband. He doesn't want you coming on to him anymore.'

So much for trying to be nice. 'I never came on to Tommy.'

'You've always been jealous of me. Always, and now you

think you can take my husband, but it won't work.'

'I don't want your husband,' she said, excruciatingly aware of the two boxes of tampons in her cart, like one wouldn't be enough.

'You've wanted him since we were in high school. You never could stand that he chose me.'

Delaney's gaze swept the contents of Helen's cart. A bottle of Robitusson, tweezers, a jumbo pack of Stay-free, and a box of Correctol. Delaney smiled, feeling a slight advantage. Feminine hygiene *and* laxative. 'He only chose you because I wouldn't sleep with him, and you know it. Everyone knew it then, and everyone knows it now. If you hadn't acted like a Sealy Posturepedic, he wouldn't have gone to bed with you.'

'You're pathetic, Delaney Shaw. You always have been. Now you think you can come back, take away my husband *and* my business.'

'I told you I don't want Tommy.' She pointed her finger at Helen and leaned forward. 'But watch out because I am going to take your business.' Her smile conveyed a smugness she didn't feel as she pushed her cart past Helen toward the front of the store. So much for ending the hair war. She was going to kick Helen's butt.

Delaney's hands shook as she set her purchases on the checkout counter. They were still shaking as she drove home and when she placed her key in the lock to her apartment door. She turned on the ten o'clock news for noise and dumped out her shopping bag on the counter in her kitchen. The day had started out okay, but had gone to hell in a hurry. First her mother, then Helen. Gossip about her was burning up the phone lines of Truly, and there was nothing she could do about it.

Her head pounded like it was going to explode, and she downed four Tylenols. This was Tommy's fault – and Nick's. She'd been minding her own business when both men had approached her. If they'd left her alone, tonight wouldn't have happened. She wouldn't have had to defend herself to her mother, and she'd wouldn't have had it out with Helen in the Value Rite.

Delaney grabbed her magazine, then headed for the bathroom and filled the tub. As soon as she'd peeled to her skin, she sank into the warm water. A shudder worked its way up her spine, and she sighed. She tried to read, but her mind raced with ways to steal Helen's business. She wondered if Tommy, the dog, had really told his wife that Delaney had 'come on' to *him*, but she guessed it really didn't matter.

The thoughts spinning in her head turned to Nick and the rumors. It was starting again. Ten years ago, the two of them had been a hot topic, apparently even after she'd left town. She didn't want to be linked with Nick. She didn't want to be viewed as one of his women. And she probably wouldn't be if he hadn't dragged her out on the dance floor and kissed her until she felt it clear to the soles of her feet. With very little effort, he'd made her heart race and her body tingle. She didn't know why Nick of all men could turn her inside out with just a kiss, but she obviously wasn't alone. There were Gail and Lonna Howell, and those were just two that she knew about.

She turned to an article in her magazine on pheromones and the powerful effect they had on the opposite sex. If what she read was true, Nick had more than his share. He was the pied piper of pheromones, and Delaney was just another susceptible rat.

She stayed in the tub until the water turned cold before she got out and dressed for bed in a flannel nightshirt and thick socks that reached her knees. She set her alarm for eight-thirty, then slid beneath her new thick duvet. She tried to clear her head of Nick and Tommy, Gwen and Helen, but after three hours of watching the digital clock tick off the minutes, she went to her medicine cabinet and looked for anything to help her sleep. All she had was a bottle of Nyquil she'd moved with her from Phoenix. She took a couple of slugs and finally drifted to sleep.

But she found no rest in her sleep. She dreamed of being stuck in Truly for life. Time stood still. The days refused to progress. The calendar was forever stuck on May thirty-first. There was no way out.

When Delaney woke, it was to a pounding in her head and the buzzing of her alarm clock. She felt relieved to be wakened from her nightmare. She hit the off button on her clock and closed her eyes. The pounding continued and she realized that it wasn't *in* her head, but on her front door. Groggy from lack of sleep and the big slugs of Nyquil, she stumbled into the living room. With her socks around her ankles, she yanked open the door. Immediately she threw her arm up like a vampire, protecting her eyes from the morning sun burning her corneas. Through her squint and the haze clogging her vision, she watched a slow grin tilt Nick Allegrezza's mouth. Cold air hit her face and nearly took her breath away. 'What do *you* want?' she wheezed.

'Good morning, sunshine.'

He did that laughing *at* her thing again and she slammed the door. Nick was the very last person she wanted to see right now.

His laughter continued as he hollered out, 'I need the key to the back door of your salon.'

'Why?'

'I thought you wanted the locks changed.'

Delaney stared at the closed door for several heartbeats. No way was she going to open it again. She'd vowed to stay away from Nick. He was nothing but trouble, and she was pretty sure she had a bad case of bed head. But she did want new locks. 'I'll leave the keys in your office later,' she yelled.

'I'm busy later. It's now or next week, wild thing.'

She yanked the door open again and glared at the disgustingly handsome man standing there with his hair pulled back and hands in the pockets of his biker's jacket. 'I told you not to call me that!'

'That's right, you did,' he said, walking past her into the apartment as if he owned the place, bringing the smell of autumn and leather.

Cold air swirled about Delaney's shins and up her nightshirt, reminding her that she wasn't dressed for company, but she wasn't exactly showing anything, either. She shivered and shut the door. 'Hey, I didn't invite you in.'

'But you wanted to,' he said as he unzipped the big silver teeth of his jacket.

Her brows drew together and she shook her head. 'No, I didn't.' Suddenly her apartment seemed so small. He filled it with his size, the scent of his skin, and his massive machismo.

'And now you want to make coffee, too.' He wore a gray and

blue plaid flannel. Flannel shirts were obviously a big staple in his wardrobe. And Levi's. Soft Levi's, worn at interesting places.

'Are you always this cranky in the morning?' he asked, his gaze scanning the apartment, taking in everything. Her boots lying on the worn beige carpet. The old appliances in the kitchen. The two boxes of tampons on the counter.

'No,' she snapped. 'I'm usually very pleasant.'

His gaze returned to her, and he cocked his head to one side. 'Bad hair day?'

Delaney put a hand to the side of her head and stifled a groan. 'I'll get the key,' she said as she walked into the kitchen and grabbed her purse. She pulled out her 'Names to Take, Butts to Kick' key ring. When she turned around, Nick was so close she jumped back and her behind hit the cabinets. She stared at his hand, thrust toward her. His long blunt fingers, the lines and calluses in his palm. A silver zipper closed his black leather sleeve from elbow to wrist. The aluminum tab lay across the heel of his hand.

'Where are the closest outlets to your doors?'

'What?'

'The electrical outlets in your salon.'

She dropped the keys into his palm then squeezed past him. 'By the cash register in front, and behind the microwave in the storeroom.' And because he looked like a breathing fantasy, and she was sure she looked horrible, she snapped, 'Don't touch anything.'

'What do you think I'm going to do?' he called out to her as she practically ran down the hall. 'Give myself a perm?'

'I never know *what* you're going to do,' she said and shut the bedroom door behind her. She looked in the mirror above her dresser and raised a hand to her mouth. 'Oh my God,' she cried. She had bed head all right. The back was flat; the front fuzzy. She had a pillowcase crease on her right cheek, and a black smudge beneath her eye. She'd answered the door looking like one of those blurry eyed people who'd survived a natural disaster. Worse, she'd answered the door looking like crap with *Nick* standing on the other side.

As soon as Delaney heard her front door close, she ran into the bathroom and took a quick shower. The hot water helped clear her head, and by the time she got out, she was fully awake. She could hear the whine of Nick's drill coming from the front of her salon, and she went into the kitchen and started a pot of coffee. Whatever his reason, he was actually doing her a favor. He was being nice. She didn't know why, or how long it would last, but she was grateful and meant to take full advantage.

She dressed in a black ribbed sweater that zipped up the front and had a zebra print collar and cuffs and a matching skirt. She wore calf boots and black tights, fingered mousse in her hair, and dried it with a diffuser. She quickly put on her makeup, then wrapped herself up in her big wool coat, scarf, and gloves. Forty-five minutes after she'd been awakened by Nick's pounding, she walked down the stairs from her apartment with a thermos under one arm and two steaming mugs of coffee.

The back door to the salon was wide open, and Nick stood with his back to her, his feet wide apart, a tool belt slung low across his hips. He'd pulled on a pair of leather work gloves, and the drill lay silent just inside the salon. A circular hole had been cut in the door, and he was in the process of removing the old handle. He looked up as she approached, his gray eyes touching her everywhere.

'I brought you coffee,' she said and held a mug toward him.

He bit the middle finger of the glove and pulled his hand out. He shoved the glove in the pocket of his jacket and reached for the coffee. 'Thanks.' He blew into the mug and looked at her over the steam. 'It's only October, what are you going to do in December when the snow's up around your little butt?' he asked, then took a drink.

'Freeze to death.' She set the thermos by the door. 'But I suppose that's good news for you.'

'How's that?'

'Then you inherit my share of Henry's estate.' She straightened and wrapped her hands around her mug. 'Unless of course I'm buried here in Truly without ever leaving town. Then things might get a little dicey. But if you want, you can throw my body outside the city limits.' She thought for a moment, then added a stipulation, 'Just don't let any animals chew on my face. I'd really hate that.'

One corner of his mouth lifted. 'I don't want your share.'

'Yeah, right,' she scoffed. How could any sane person not want part of an estate worth serious cash? 'You were pretty ticked off the day Henry's will was read.'

'So were you.'

'Only because he was manipulating me.'

'You haven't a clue.'

She sipped her coffee. 'What do you mean?'

'Never mind.' He set his mug next to the thermos and shoved his hand back inside his glove. 'Let's just say I got exactly what I wanted out of Henry. I got property any builder would cough up a gonad to own, and I got it free and clear.' He fished around in the pouch of his tool belt for a screwdriver.

Not quite free and clear, she thought. Not yet anyway. He had to wait a year just like she did. 'So you weren't angry that you only got two pieces of property, and I got his businesses and money?'

'No.' He removed a screw and tossed it in the box to his right. 'You and your mother are welcome to the headache.'

She didn't know if she believed him. 'What does your mother think of Henry's will?'

His gaze cut to hers then returned to the door handle. 'My

mother? Why do you care what my mother thinks?' he asked as he removed both knobs and threw them in the box.

'I don't really, but she looks at me like I mutilated her cat. Sort of furious and disdainful at the same time.'

'She doesn't have a cat.'

'You know what I mean.'

He used the screwdriver to pry out the latch bolt. 'I guess I know what you mean.' He reached for the new part and removed it from its packaging. 'What do you expect her to think? I'm her son, and you're the *neska izugarri*.'

'What does *neska iz – izu*, whatever mean?'

He laughed silently. 'Don't take it personal, but it means you're a horrible girl.'

'Oh.' She took a drink of coffee and looked at her feet. She guessed being called a 'horrible girl' wasn't too bad. 'I've been called worse, of course usually in English.' She glanced back at Nick and watched him screw the shiny new knobs in place. 'I always wanted to be bilingual so I could swear and my mother wouldn't know it. You're lucky.'

'I'm not bilingual.'

A chilly breeze picked up the ends of Delaney's hair and she burrowed deeper inside her coat. 'You speak Basque.'

'No I don't. I understand a few words. That's about it.'

'Well, Louie does.'

'He knows as much as I do.' Nick bent down and picked up a dead bolt. 'We understand a little because my mother speaks Basque with her relatives. She tried to teach us Euskara and Spanish, but we really weren't interested. Mostly Louie and I know swear words and body parts because we looked them up in her dictionary.' He glanced at Delaney, then shoved the dead bolt through the hole he'd drilled in the door. 'The really important stuff,' he added.

'Louie calls Lisa his sweetheart in Basque.'

Nick shrugged. 'Then maybe he knows more than I thought he did.'

'He calls her something like *alu gozo.*'

Nick chuckled deep in his chest and shook his head. 'Then he's not calling her "swee*theart*." '

Delaney leaned forward and asked, 'So, what is he *really* calling her then?'

'No way am I telling you.' He dug in the pouch of his tool belt for screws then clamped two between his lips.

She fought an urge to punch him. 'Come on. You can't leave me hanging.'

'You'd tell Lisa,' he muttered around the screws, 'and get me in trouble with Louie.'

'I won't tell – pleeaase,' she wheedled.

A chirping from the vicinity of Nick's chest stopped her pleas. He spit out the screws and bit the middle finger of his glove again. Then he reached inside his jacket and pulled out a slim cell phone. 'Yeah, it's Nick,' he answered and shoved his glove into his pocket. He listened for a minute, then rolled his eyes skyward. 'So when can he get out there?' He wedged the phone between his shoulder and ear and continued securing the dead bolt. 'That's too damn late. If he doesn't want to sub with us, he needs to say so, otherwise he better get his ass, and his PVC, on the job no later than Thursday. We've been lucky so far with the weather, and I don't want to push it.' He talked of square feet and board feet and Delaney didn't understand any of it. He fastened the strike plate to the door frame then shoved the screwdriver into his tool belt one last time. 'Call Ann Marie, and she'll give you the numbers on that. It was either eighty or eighty-five thousand, I'm not sure.' He pressed the off button on the cell phone, then slipped it back beneath his jacket. He dug around in the front pocket of his jeans, then handed her a set of keys. 'Try it,' he ordered as he stepped into the salon and slid the latch bolts into place.

When she did as he requested, both locks opened easily. She retrieved Nick's coffee mug and the thermos from the ground and entered the back of the shop. With her hands full, she kicked the door shut and walked into the storage room. Nick's tool belt and jacket sat on the counter next to the microwave. His drill lay on the floor still plugged into the socket, but he was nowhere to be seen.

From behind the closed bathroom door, she heard the toilet flush as she shucked out of her coat and gloves. She hung them on the coat rack by the door, then grabbed a fresh cup of coffee for herself and hurried to the front of the salon. For some weird reason, standing across the hall while Nick used her bathroom made her feel like a voyeur, like the time she'd hidden behind a display of sun-glasses at the Value Rite and watched him buy a box of a dozen – large, ribbed for her pleasure – condoms. He'd been about seventeen.

Delaney opened her appointment book and stared at the blank page. She'd had her share of boyfriends, and they'd certainly used her bathroom. But for a reason she couldn't explain to herself, it was different with Nick. More personal . . . almost intimate. As if he were her lover instead of the guy who'd provoked her most of her life, then used her to get back at Henry.

She heard the door to the bathroom open, and she took a long sip of coffee.

'Did you try the front door?' he asked, the heels of his boots thudding on her linoleum as he walked toward her.

'Not yet.' She glanced over her shoulder at him and watched his approach. 'Thanks for the new locks. How much do I owe you?'

'It works. I already checked it for you,' he said instead of answering her question. He stopped beside her, then leaned his hip into the counter next to her right elbow. 'That was on the floor when I changed the front lock,' he said and pointed to an envelope lying on the top of the cash register. 'Someone must have slipped it beneath your door.'

Her name was the only thing typed on the white paper, and she figured it was probably some kind of notice for a downtown business association meeting or something equally exciting.

'Your cheeks are red.'

'It's a little cold in here,' she said, but wasn't sure temperature had anything to do with it.

'You're not going to last the winter.' He wrapped his hands around her coffee mug for a few seconds, then cupped her cheeks in his palms. 'Any other parts you need warmed up?'

Uh-oh. 'No.'

'Sure?' The tips of his fingers brushed her hair behind her ears. 'I'll warm you up real good.' His thumb slipped over her chin, then fanned her lower lip. 'Wild thing.'

She made a fist and punched him in the stomach.

Instead of becoming angry, he laughed and dropped his hands to his sides. 'You used to be more fun.'

'When was that?'

'When you used to get all wide-eyed and mad and look like you wanted to hit me but were such a little goody-goody you never would. Your jaw would get all clenched and your lips puckered. In grade school, all I had to do was look at you, and you'd run away.'

'That's because you practically knocked me unconscious with a snowball.'

A frown creased his brow and he straightened. 'That snowball thing was an accident.'

'Really, which part? When you accidentally packed snow into a hard ball, or when you accidentally threw it at me?'

'I didn't mean to hit you that hard.'

'Why did you hit me at all?'

He thought a moment then said, 'You were there.'

She rolled her eyes. 'That's brilliant, Nick.'

'It's the truth.'

'I'll have to remember that next time I see you in a crosswalk and my foot gets a little itch to mow you down.'

His smile showed his straight white teeth. 'You've become a regular smart ass since you've been away.'

'I've become my own person.'

'I think I like it.'

'Gee, I guess I can die happy.'

'Kind of makes me wonder what else is different.' He reached out and flipped up the tab of her zipper. The cool metal hit her collarbone and rested against her skin.

Delaney took a shallow breath but refused to look away. He raised his gaze from her throat, and she looked up into his eyes. Within the space of a second, he'd gone from being a somewhat regular guy to the ornery boy she'd grown up with. She'd seen that silvery glint too many times not to know he was about to stomp his foot and yell boo and make her run like crazy. Make her think he was going to throw a worm on her, or something equally hideous. She refused to let him intimidate her. She'd always let him win, and she stood her ground now for all those times she'd lost. 'I'm not the same girl you used to antagonize all the time. I'm not afraid of you.'

He lifted one black brow up his tan forehead. 'No?'

'No.'

His gaze locked with hers as he reached for the metal tab of her zipper again. He slowly eased it half an inch down its silent track. 'Are you afraid now?'

Her hands clenched at her sides. He was testing her. He was trying to make her flinch first. She shook her head.

The tab moved down another few teeth then stopped. 'Now?'

'No. You'll never scare me. I know what you are.'

'Uh-huh.' The zipper slid another inch, and the heavy zebra collar fell open. 'Tell me what you think you know.'

'You're full of bull. You're not going to hurt me. Right now you want me to think you're going to strip me naked while people walk by my big window. I'm supposed to get all uptight, and then you can go away and have a really big laugh. But guess what?'

He pulled the tab to the gold satin rose that closed the front of her bra. 'What?'

She took a big breath and called his bluff. 'You won't do it.'

Zzziiiiip.

Delaney's mouth fell open, and she looked down at the front of her sweater. The black ribbed cotton lay undone, the edges gaping an inch apart, revealing her leopard print bra and the inside swells of her breasts. Then before Delaney knew how it happened, she found herself picked up and plopped back down on top her appointment book. The soft fabric of his jeans brushed her knees, and the green Formica top felt cool beneath her thighs. 'What do you think you're doing?' she gasped as she clutched the front of her sweater.

'Shh . . .' He touched his finger to her lips. His gaze was pinned to the big window ten feet behind Delaney. 'The owner of the bookstore is walking by. You don't want him to hear you and press his nose against the glass, do you?'

Delaney glanced over her shoulder, but the side-walk was empty. 'Let me down,' she demanded.

'Are you afraid now?'

'No.'

'I don't believe you. You look like you're about ready to jump out of your skin.'

'I'm not afraid. I'm just too smart to play your games.'

'We haven't started to play yet.'

But they had, and he was one man she didn't want to play with. He was far too dangerous and she found him far too alluring. 'Do you get some sort of warped thrill out of this?'

A slow sensual smile curved his lips. 'Absolutely. That leopard bra you've got on is pretty wild.'

Delaney let go of the front of the sweater long enough to zip it up again. Once it was closed she relaxed a little. 'Well, don't get excited. I know I'm not.'

His deep quiet laughter surrounded her. 'Are you sure?'

'Absolutely.'

His gaze drifted to her mouth. 'I guess I'll have to see what I can do about that.'

'It wasn't a challenge.'

'It was a challenge, Delaney.' He brushed his knuckles across her cheek, and her breathing became a little shallow. 'A man knows when he's being challenged by a woman.'

'I take it back.' She wrapped her hand around his wrist.

He shook his head. 'You can't. You already put it out there.'

'Oh, no.' Delaney lowered her gaze to his strong, stubborn chin. Someplace safe, away from his hypnotic eyes. 'No. I never put out anything.'

'Maybe that's why you're so uptight. You need to get laid.'

Her gaze snapped to his and she forced his hand from her cheek. 'I don't need to get laid. I get laid all the time,' she lied.

He slanted her a doubtful look.

'I do!'

He lowered his face to hers. 'Then maybe you need someone who knows what he's doing.'

'Are you offering your services?'

His mouth lightly brushed hers as he shook his head. 'No.'

Delaney's breath got stuck in her throat. 'Then why are you doing this to me?'

'It feels good,' he said barely above a whisper and placed soft kisses at the corner of her lips. 'Tastes good, too. You always tasted good, Delaney.' He brushed his lips against hers. 'All over,' he said and opened his mouth wide over hers. His head tilted to one side and in an instant everything changed. The kiss turned hot and wet like he was sucking the juice from a peach. He ate at her mouth and demanded she feed him in turn. He sucked her tongue into his mouth. The inside of his mouth was warm and slick, and she felt her bones melt. She was helpless to stop him now. She let herself go and kissed him, matching his hunger. He was so good. So good at making her feel like this. Making her more than happy to do things she had no intention of doing. Making her breathless. Making her skin itchy and tight.

His hands moved to her knees and he pushed them apart. She felt the brush of his Levi's as he stepped between her thighs, felt his grasp on her wrists as he lifted her hands to his shoulders. One of his hands cupped her breast and she moaned deep in her throat. Her stomach clinched and her nipple tightened. Through her sweater and satin bra, she felt the heat of his palm. She arched toward him, wanting more. Her hands slid across his wide shoulders to the sides of his head. Her thumbs brushed his jaw, and she slipped her palms down the sides of his neck. She felt the heavy thumping of his pulse and uneven pull of air into his lungs, and pure female satisfaction poured through her. Her fingers moved to the front of his shirt and went to work on the buttons. Ten years ago he'd seen almost every inch of her naked body, and she hadn't gotten even a glimpse of his chest. She opened the flannel to satisfy an old curiosity. Then she pulled back from the kiss for a good look at him and wasn't disappointed. He had the kind of chest that inspired women to shove money down his pants. Dark brown nipples and corrugated muscles, taut skin and black hair that trailed down his flat stomach, circled his navel, then disappeared into the waistband of his jeans. Her eyes lowered to the front of his pants and the thick bulge beneath his button fly. She raised her gaze to his face. He looked back at her from beneath lowered lids, his mouth still wet from their kiss. Her hands slipped across his chest, and her fingers made furrows in his soft hair. Beneath her touch, his muscles bunched.

'Be still a minute,' he said, his voice all husky, like he'd just gotten out of bed. 'Unless you want the blue-haired lady at the door to know what we're doing.'

She froze. 'You're kidding, right?'

'No. It looks like my first grade teacher, Mrs Vaughn.'

'Laverne!' she whispered loudly and looked over her shoulder. 'What's she want?'

'Maybe a haircut,' he said and brushed his thumbs across her nipples.

'Stop that.' She turned back and slapped his hands aside. 'I can't believe I let this happen to me again. Is she still there?'

'Yep.'

'Can she see us, do you think?' she asked.

'I don't know.'

'What's she doing?'

'Staring at me.'

'I can't believe this. Just last night my mother bitched me out for my scandalous behavior with you at Hennesey's.' She shook her head. 'Now this. Laverne will tell everyone.'

'Probably.'

She looked up at him, still standing between her thighs. 'Don't you care?'

'Exactly what am I supposed to care about? That we were just getting to the fun stuff? That my hand was on your breasts, and your hands were all over my chest, and both of us were having a good time? Damn right I care about that. I wasn't finished. But don't expect me to care that a little old lady looked in the window and watched. Why should I care what people are going to say about that? People have talked about me since the day I was born. I stopped caring a long time ago.'

Delaney pushed at his shoulders until he took a step

backward. With desire still pulsating along her nerves, she jumped down from the counter and turned around in time to see Mrs Vaughn totter away in a pink housecoat and support hose. 'People in this town already think we're sleeping together. And you should care since you stand to lose the property Henry left you.'

'How's that? The last time I checked, at some point during sex, someone gets off. Otherwise it's nothing more than a grope.'

Delaney groaned and put her head in her hands. 'I don't belong here. I hate this town. I hate everything about it. I can't wait to leave. I want my life back.'

'Look on the bright side,' he said, and she heard the thud of his boot as he made his way toward the back. 'When you leave, you'll leave a wealthy woman. You sold out for Henry's money, but I'm sure you'll think it's worth it in the end.'

She looked up at him. 'You're a hypocrite. You agreed to your part of the will, too.'

He walked into her storage room and popped back out a few seconds later. 'True, but there's a difference.' With his shirt still unbuttoned, he shrugged into his leather jacket. 'That particular stipulation is no hardship for me.'

'Then why were you trying to take off my sweater?'

He bent down and picked up his drill. 'Because you let me. Don't take it personally, but you could have been anyone.'

His words hit her like a punch in the stomach. She bit the inside of her cheek to keep from crying or screaming or both. 'I hate you,' she said barely above a whisper, but he heard her.

'Sure you do, wild thing,' he said as he wrapped the cord around the drill.

'You should grow up and became an adult, Nick. Grown-up men don't have to grope women just to see if they can. Real men don't look at women as sexual playthings anymore.'

He stared at her across the distance that separated them. 'If you believe that, then you're the same silly naive girl you always were.' He yanked the back door open. 'Maybe you should take your own advice,' he said, then closed the door behind him.

'Grow up, Nick!' she yelled after him. 'And . . . and . . . get a haircut.' She didn't know why she added the last part. Perhaps because she wanted to hurt him, which was ridiculous. The man had no feelings. She turned around and stared at her blank appointment book. Her life was going from crap to downright shitty. Two hours, she thought. She'd give the gossip two hours to reach her mother, and then only because it would take Laverne an hour to get to her car.

Angry tears blurred Delaney's vision and her gaze fell to the envelope on top of the cash register. She tore it open. A page fell out with three bold words typed in the center. **I'M WATCHING YOU**, it said. Delaney crumpled the paper and threw it across the salon. Great! That was all she needed. Helen the psycho woman watching her and slipping notes under her door.

Nick gripped the steering wheel until his knuckles turned white. The insistent throb in his groin urged him to turn his Jeep around and relieve his aching need between Delaney's soft thighs. Impossible, of course. For so many reasons.

If he wanted, he could ring Gail on his cell phone and have her meet him. There were a few others he could call, too, but he didn't want that. He didn't want to have sex with one woman while thinking of another. While wanting another. He wasn't that big a bastard. He wasn't that sick, either.

Instead of calling anyone, he pulled his Jeep to a stop next to the burned remains of Henry's barn. He left the engine running and shifted into neutral. He didn't know why he'd come here. Maybe he'd come looking for answers in the blackened rubble. Answers he knew he'd never find.

I don't belong here. I hate this town. I hate everything about it. I can't wait to leave. I want my life back. Her words still echoed in his head. Still made him want to grab her and shake her.

But she was right. She didn't belong in Truly. From the moment he'd looked across Henry's casket and seen her standing there in that green suit and dark sunglasses, she'd complicated his life. When she'd moved back, she'd brought the past with her. All the old complicated bullshit he'd never understood.

Nick looked down at the front of his shirt and raised his hands to the buttons. The Jeep's engine and the steady hum of the heater were the only sounds disturbing the late morning air.

I hate you, she'd whispered, and he believed her. Earlier, when he'd arrived on her doorstep with her new locks, he hadn't purposely set out to make her hate him, but he'd done a pretty good job of it. Her hatred was best, and he actually felt a little relieved. No more kissing her and touching her. No more filling his hand with her firm breast, her nipple hard beneath his thumb.

He leaned his head back against the seat and stared at the beige canvas rag top. All she had to do was look at him and he had an urge to mess up her hair. Squeeze her between his hands, and eat the lip gloss off her mouth. Maybe Henry had been right. Maybe he'd known what Nick refused to admit, even to himself. He was still drawn most to the things he couldn't have. In the past, once he'd gotten those unattainable things, he'd easily moved on to the next. But with Delaney, he couldn't. He couldn't have her and he couldn't move on. If it weren't for Henry's will, he would have had sex with her already, and he would have forgotten about her by now. She really wasn't the kind of female he liked to spend time with anyway. Her clothes were weird, and she had a mean mouth on her. She wasn't the most beautiful female he'd known. In fact, she looked horrible in the morning. He'd seen his share of women who weren't looking their best when they first rolled out of the sack, but damn, she'd looked downright scary.

Nick raised his head and stared out the windshield. But it didn't seem to matter what she'd looked like. He'd wanted her. He'd wanted to kiss her sleepy mouth and soft skin. He'd wanted to take her back to her bed where her sheets were still warm. He'd wanted to strip her naked and bury himself deep within her hot thighs.

He'd wanted to touch her like he had in any one of the thousand fantasies he'd had growing up. As he had the night she'd jumped in his car. The night he'd driven them to Angel Beach. She'd acted like she'd wanted him that night, too, but she'd left with Henry. She'd left him alone and aching for her. Just one more unfulfilled fantasy.

He swore to himself and shifted the Jeep into gear. The wide tires chewed up the dirt road as the four-by-four sped toward town. He had some building contracts waiting for him to sign at his offices, and his mother and Louie were expecting him for lunch. Instead, he drove to a job site fifty miles north in Garden. The subcontractors were surprised to see him. The framers were even more surprised when he pulled on his work gloves and picked up a nail gun. He shot the hell out of the subfloor and wall studs. It had been several years since he and Louie had taken part in the physical part of construction. Most of his time was spent driving or talking with contractors and suppliers. If he wasn't driving or talking or doing both at the same time, he was creating new business. But after the day he'd had, it felt good to shoot something again.

By the time he got home, it was past dark outside. He tossed his leather jacket and car keys on the marble countertop in the kitchen, then reached for a Bud. He could hear the television in another part of the house but wasn't concerned. His entire family had a key to his front door, and Sophie often came over to watch a movie on his big screen. His boots echoed on the hardwood floors as he made his way to the great room.

The television blinked off and Louie rose from the beige leather sofa. He tossed the remote on the pine coffee table. 'You should call Mother and tell her you're not dead in a ditch.'

Nick took a pull off his beer and eyed his older brother. 'I will.'

'Both of us have been trying to reach you since noon. Did you forget about lunch?'

'No. I decided to drive to Garden.'

'Why didn't you call?'

He hadn't wanted to hear the disappointment in his mother's voice or listen to the guilt she'd heap on his head. 'I got busy.'

'Why didn't you answer your cell phone?'

'I didn't feel like it.'

'Why, Nick?'

'I told you why. What in the hell is this all about? You haven't been waiting for me because I didn't answer my cell phone.'

Louie's brows lowered over his brown eyes. 'Where were you?'

'I told you.'

'Tell me again.'

Nick's scowl matched his brother's. 'Go to hell.'

'It's true then. What everyone is saying about you is true. You were screwing Delaney Shaw on the counter in her salon. Right there on Main Street for anybody walking by to see.'

A slow smile started at the corners of Nick's mouth, then he burst into laughter.

Louie didn't see the humor. 'God damn you,' he swore. 'When Mom told me she'd heard you were kissing Delaney at Hennesey's, I told her not to believe it. I told her you weren't that stupid. Jesus, Joseph, and Mary, you are!'

'No I'm not. I didn't screw Delaney in her shop or anyplace else.'

Louie sniffed and scratched the side of his neck.

'Maybe not yet, but you will. You're going to go right ahead and lose it all.'

Nick raised the beer and took a drink. 'Now we get to the real reason you're here. Money. You don't care who I screw, as long as you get to develop Silver Creek.'

'Sure. Why not? I'll admit it. I want it so bad the thought of it keeps me up at night just thinking of all those million-dollar houses and ways to spend all that money I stand to make. But even if that piece of property wasn't worth a pile of shit, I'd still be here because I'm your brother. Because I slithered through bushes with you. Spied with you, flattened the tires on her bike with you, and I thought we did it because she got a nice new Schwinn. She got what you should have had. And because I thought you hated her. But you didn't. You flattened those tires because you wanted to walk her home. You said you walked with her so Henry would see you and get all pissed off, but that was a lie. You were infatuated with her. You've had a hard on for Delaney Shaw since you could get it up, and everyone knows you think with your dick.'

Slowly Nick set his bottle on the stone mantel of the fireplace. 'I think you better leave before I kick your ass all the way out of my house.'

Louie crossed his arms over his barrel chest, not looking like he planned to leave any time soon. 'That's another thing. This house. Look at it.'

'Yeah?'

'Look around. You live in a thirty-eight-hundred-square-foot house. You've got four bedrooms and five bathrooms. You're one guy Nick. One.'

Nick glanced about at the fireplace made of smooth river rock, the high ceiling with exposed beams, and the bank of cathedral windows that looked out at the lake. 'What's your point?'

'Who'd you build it for? You say you're never going to get married. So why do you need such a big house?'

'You tell me. You seem to know all the answers.'

Louie rocked back on his heel. 'You wanted to show Henry.'

It was close enough to the truth that Nick didn't deny it. 'That's old news.'

'You wanted to show her, too.'

'You're full of shit,' he scoffed. 'She didn't even live here.'

'She does now, and you're going to screw up your life for a piece of high-price ass.'

Nick pointed toward the front door. 'Get out before you really piss me off.'

Louie walked forward, stopping within an arm's distance. 'You going to throw me out, little brother?'

'You going to make me?' Nick was taller, but Louie was built like a bull. Not only did Nick not want to fight his own brother, he knew Louie hit like a bulldozer. He was relieved when Louie shook his head and walked past.

'If you're going to have sex with her, do it now.' Louie sighed as he picked up his jacket from the back of a leather arm chair. 'Do it before you get other contractors involved in Silver Creek. Do it before you contact more lenders, and do it before I waste any more of my time.'

'You're worrying about nothing,' Nick assured his brother as they walked to the front door. 'I'm not going anywhere near Delaney, and I have a feeling she'll be avoiding me for a long time.'

'Then what happened in her salon today?'

Nick opened the heavy wood door. 'Nothing. I changed her locks for her. That's it.'

'I doubt it.' Louie shrugged into his jacket and headed down the steps. 'Call Mom,' he said. 'The sooner you get it over with, the better.'

Nick shook his head and walked back into the great room. He wasn't in the mood to call his mother. He didn't want to hear her rant about Delaney. He snagged his beer off the mantle, then headed through a pair of French doors to the deck. Steam rose from the octagonal hot tub, and he flipped the switch to start the jets. His right shoulder ached from the work he'd done in Garden. He stripped naked and goose bumps broke over his arms and chest before he stepped into the bubbling hot water. The windows from the house threw oblong patches of light but didn't reach his corner of the deck.

Louie had been right about some things and dead wrong about others. Nick had originally built his house as an 'up yours' gesture toward Henry. But before construction had been halfway completed, he'd lost interest in proving anything to anybody. As far as Delaney was concerned, he hadn't really expected to see her again. His brother was way off the mark with that theory. He'd been close to the truth with the bicycle conspiracy theory of his though. Originally Nick hadn't planned to push the bike all the way to Henry's, but then he'd looked at her face when she'd seen her tires. She'd looked as if she were about to burst into tears and he'd felt so guilty, he'd helped her. He'd even given her a Tootsie Roll, and she'd given him a stick of gum. Peppermint.

Louie had been right about the other – although he'd call it a strong interest rather than infatuation. But contrary to his brother's opinion, he wasn't going to have sex with her. He might not be able to control his body's reaction, but he sure as hell could control what he did, or didn't do, about it.

People said a lot of things about him. Some were true. Some weren't. For the most part he didn't care. But Delaney would. She would be hurt by the gossip.

Nick took a drink of his beer and looked at the reflection of stars in the black water of the lake. He didn't want her hurt. He didn't want to hurt her. It was time he stayed away from Delaney Shaw.

The telephone inside the house rang, and he wondered how long it would take his mother to give up on the phone calls. He knew she'd want to talk about the gossip like she had some sort of maternal squatter's rights on his life. Louie didn't seem to mind the constant prying as much as Nick. Louie called it love. Maybe it was, but when Nick had been a boy, she'd sometimes held him so tight he couldn't breathe.

Nick set his beer on the side of the hot tub and sank further into the hot water. His mother didn't like to drive after dark so he figured he was safe for the night. He'd call her in the morning and get it over with.

Gwen placed the telephone to her ear for about the fifth time in the last hour. 'Delaney has obviously taken her phone off the hook.'

Max walked across a thick Aubusson rug and stopped behind her. He took the receiver from her hand and hung it up. 'Then she obviously has her reasons.' He rubbed Gwen's shoulders and pressed his thumbs into the base of her skull. 'You're too tense.'

Gwen sighed and lazed her head to one side. Her soft blond hair brushed across his knuckles, and the smell of roses filled his nose. 'It's the latest rumor about her and Nick,' she said. 'He's out to ruin my daughter.'

'She'll handle Nick.'

'You don't understand. He's always hated her.'

Max remembered the day Nick had barged into his office. The man had been angry, but Max hadn't received the impression that Nick held any animosity toward Delaney. 'Your daughter is a grown woman. She can take care of herself.' He slid his hands to her waist and pulled her back against his chest. It seemed their time together was always the same. Gwen fussing about Delaney, and him wanting to touch her like a lover. He'd seen quite a bit of her since Henry's death, and he'd found pleasure in her bed on several occasions. She was beautiful and had a lot to offer a man. Yet he was growing tired of her immersion in her daughter's business.

'How? By creating a scandal?'

'If that's her choice. You've done your job. You've raised her. Let it go or you might lose her again.'

Gwen turned and Max saw fear in her eyes. 'I am afraid she's going to leave me. I always thought she stayed away because of Henry, but now I'm not sure. A few years ago I went to visit her when she lived in Denver, and she said that I always took Henry's side when she was growing up. She thinks I never stood up for her. I would have, but Henry was right. She needed to get good grades and go to college and not run around town like a hoyden.' Gwen paused and took a deep breath. 'Delaney is stubborn and holds a grudge for a long time. I just know that she'll leave in June and never come back.'

'Maybe.'

'She can't go. Henry could have made her stay longer.'

Max dropped his hands to his sides. 'He wanted to, but I advised him that a judge might strike down the will if Henry stipulated a lengthier period.'

Gwen turned and walked to the fireplace. She gripped the brick mantel and gazed back at Max through the mirror in front of her. 'He should have done something.'

Henry had done everything he could to control the people in his life from the grave. He'd stayed just to the right of what a court would consider fair and reasonable restraints. The whole thing had been extremely distasteful to Max, and it bothered him that Gwen supported her late husband's manipulations.

'Delaney needs to stay here. She needs to grow up.'

Max looked at Gwen's reflection; her beautiful blue eyes and pouty pink mouth, perfectly flawless white skin and hair like ribbons of caramel and butterscotch. Desire settled in the pit of his groin. Maybe she just needed something else in her life to think about. He walked toward her, determined to give her that something else.

*

Nick didn't get the chance to call his mother the next morning. She rang his doorbell at seven A.M.

Benita Allegrezza set her purse on the white marble counter and looked at her son. Nick obviously thought he could avoid her, but she was his mother. She'd given birth to him, which gave her the right to drag him out of bed. No matter that he was thirty-three and no longer lived with her.

He'd pulled on a pair of ragged Levi's and an old black sweatshirt, and his feet were bare. Benita frowned. He could afford to dress better. Nick never took very good care of himself. He didn't eat when he should, and he spent time with loose women. He didn't think she knew about the women, but she did. 'Why can't you just avoid that *neska izugarri?*'

'I don't know what you've heard, but nothing happened with Delaney,' he said, his voice rough from sleep. He took her coat and hung it in the hall closet.

Obviously, he thought she could be fooled, too. Benita followed him into the kitchen and watched him pull two mugs from the cupboard. 'Then why were you there, Nick?'

He waited until he'd filled the two mugs with coffee before he answered her. 'I installed some locks at her shop.'

She took the mug he offered her and looked at him standing by the kitchen sink as if nothing had happened in that beauty salon. She knew better. She knew the less he said, the more he left unsaid. Sometimes she needed a Mack truck to pull anything out of him. He'd been that way for a long time now. 'That's what your brother told me. Why couldn't she hire a locksmith like everyone else? Why does she need *you?*'

'I told her I'd do it.' He leaned one hip against the counter and shrugged the opposite shoulder. 'It was no big deal.'

'How can you say that? The whole town is talking about it.

You haven't returned my phone calls and you've been hiding from me.'

His brows drew together, and he frowned at her. 'I haven't been hiding from you.'

Yes, he had, and it was Delaney Shaw's fault. From the day she'd moved to Truly, she'd made Nick's life harder than it had been before she'd arrived.

Before Henry married Gwen, Benita could tell herself and everyone else that Henry ignored Nick because he didn't want to have children. Afterward, everyone knew that wasn't true. Henry just didn't want Nick. He could lavish love and attention on a stepdaughter, yet reject his own son.

Before Delaney's arrival in Henry's life, Benita would sit with Nick on her lap and hold him close. She'd kiss his sweet forehead and dry his tears. Afterward, there were no more tears or hugs. No more softness in her son. He'd grow stiff in her arms and tell her he was too big for kisses. Benita blamed Henry for the pain he caused his own son, but in her eyes, Delaney became the living, breathing symbol of deep betrayal and rejection. Delaney had been given everything that should have been given to Nick, but everything hadn't been enough for her. She'd been a troublemaker to boot.

She'd always had a way of making Nick look bad. Like the time he'd hit her with a snowball. Although he shouldn't have thrown a snowball at her, Benita was sure *that girl* must have done *something*, but the grade school hadn't even questioned her. They'd just blamed the whole incident on Nick.

And then there was that horrible episode when those awful rumors had spread through town about Nick taking advantage of Delaney. Ten years later, Benita still didn't know what had taken place that night. She knew Nick was no saint when it came to women, but she was sure he hadn't taken anything Delaney hadn't been more than willing to give him. Then like a coward, she'd fled and escaped the stinging gossip, while

Nick had stayed behind and braved the worst of it. And the rumor about Nick taking advantage of that girl hadn't been the worst of it.

She looked at him now – her tall, handsome boy. Both her sons had succeeded on their own. No one had handed them anything, and she was extremely proud of them. But Nick . . . Nick would always need her to watch out for him, even though he didn't think he needed her at all.

Now all she really wanted for Nick was for him to settle down with a nice Catholic girl, marry in the church, and be happy. She didn't think it was too much for a mother to ask. If he married, the loose women would quit chasing him – especially Delaney Shaw. 'You probably wouldn't tell your mother if something did happen with that girl anyway,' she said. 'What am I to believe?'

Nick raised his mug and took a drink. 'I'll tell you what. If something did happen, it won't happen again.'

'Promise me.'

He gave her an easy smile meant to appease her. 'Of course, *Ama*.'

Benita wasn't appeased. Now that girl was back and the rumors were starting again.

Delaney took her telephone off the hook. She kept it off the hook until she left her apartment for work the next morning. She hoped that somehow the impossible had happened and Mrs Vaughn hadn't been able to see into the shop. Maybe she'd been lucky.

But when she unlocked the front door of her salon, Wannetta Van Damme was waiting and within seconds it became apparent Delaney's luck had run out months ago. 'Is this where it happened?' Wannetta asked as she hobbled in. The sound of her silver walker, chink-thump, chink-thump, filled the inside of the salon.

Delaney was a little afraid to ask the obvious, but she was too curious not to know. 'What happened?' she asked and took the older woman's coat. She hung it on a tree in the small reception area.

Wannetta pointed to the counter. 'Is that where Laverne saw you and that Allegrezza boy . . . you know?'

A lump formed in Delaney's throat. 'What?'

'Hanky-panky,' whispered the older woman.

The lump fell to her stomach as she felt her brows rise to her hairline. 'Hanky-panky?'

'Whoopie.'

'Whoopie?' Delaney pointed to the counter. 'Right here?'

'That's what Laverne told everyone last night at the bingo game over there at that church on Seventh, Jesus the Divine Savior.'

Delaney walked to a salon chair and sank into it. Her face grew hot and her ears began to ring. She'd known there would be gossip, but she'd had no idea how bad. 'Bingo? Jesus the Divine Savior?' Her voice raised and got squeaky. 'Oh, my God!' She should have known. Anything involving Nick had always been bad and she wished she could blame him completely. But she couldn't. He hadn't unbuttoned his own shirt. She'd done that.

Wannetta moved toward her, chink-thump, chink-thump. 'Is it true?'

'No!'

'Oh.' Wannetta looked as disappointed as she sounded. 'That youngest Basque boy is a looker. Even though he has a nasty reputation, I might find him hard to resist myself.'

Delaney put a palm to her forehead and took a deep breath. 'He's evil. Evil. Evil. Evil. You stay away from him, Wannetta, or you just might wake up and find yourself the subject of horrible rumors.' Her mother was going to kill her.

'Most mornings I'm just glad to wake up. And at my age, I don't think I'd find those rumors too horrible,' she said as she moved toward the back of the salon. 'Can you squeeze me in today?'

'What? You want your hair done?'

'Of course. I didn't go to all the trouble of getting myself down here just to talk.'

Delaney rose and followed Mrs Van Damme to the shampoo sink. She helped her into the chair then set her walker aside. 'How many people were at the bingo game?' she asked fearing the answer.

'Oh, maybe sixty or so.'

Sixty. Then those sixty would tell sixty more and it

would spread like a brushfire. 'Maybe I should just kill myself,' she muttered. Death might be preferable to her mother's reaction.

'Are you going to use that shampoo that smells so nice?'

'Yes.' Delaney draped Wannetta, then lowered her back toward the sink. She turned on the water and tested it on her wrist. She'd spent the previous day and night hiding in her apartment like a mole. She'd felt emotionally battered and bruised by what had happened with Nick. And so extremely embarrassed by her own abandon.

She wet Wannetta's hair and cleaned it with Paul Mitchell. When she was finished with the conditioning, she helped her walk to the styling chair. 'Same thing?' she asked.

'Yep. I stick to what works.'

'I remember.' As Delaney combed out the tangles, Nick's parting words still echoed in her head. They'd been echoing in her head since he'd said them. *To see if I could*. He'd kissed her and touched her breasts, just to see if he could. He'd made her breasts tingle and her thighs burn just to see if he could. And she'd let him. Just like she'd let him ten years ago.

What was it about her? What personality defect did she possess that allowed Nick to slide past her defenses? During the long hours she'd spent contemplating that question, she'd come up with only one explanation other than loneliness. Her biological clock was ticking. It had to be. She couldn't hear it ticking, but she was twenty-nine, not married, with no prospects in the immediate future. Maybe her body was a hormonal time bomb and she didn't even know it.

'Leroy liked when I wore silky drawers,' Wannetta said, interrupting Delaney's silent contemplations about ticking hormones. 'He hated the cotton kind.'

Delaney snapped on a pair of latex gloves. She didn't want to envision Wannetta in silky underwear.

'You should buy yourself some silky drawers.'

'You mean the kind that come up past your navel?' *The kind that look like car seatcovers?*

'Yep.'

'Why?'

''Cause men like 'em. Men like women to wear pretty things. If you get yourself some silky drawers, you can get yourself a husband.'

'No, thank you,' she said as she reached for the waving solution and snipped the top off. Even if she were interested in finding a husband in Truly, which was of course ludicrous, she was only going to be in town until June. 'I don't want a husband.' She thought of Nick and all the problems he'd caused since she'd been back. 'And to tell you the truth,' she added, 'I don't think men are worth all the problems they cause. They are highly overrated.'

Wannetta grew silent as Delaney poured the solution on one side of her head, and just when Delaney began to worry that her client had fallen asleep with her eyes open, or worse, passed on, Wannetta opened her mouth and asked in a hushed voice, 'Are you one of those lipstick lesbians? You can tell me. I won't tell a soul.'

And the moon is made of green cheese, Delaney thought. If only she *were* a lesbian, she wouldn't have found herself kissing Nick and her hands tearing at his shirt. She wouldn't have found herself fascinated by his hairy chest. She met Wannetta's gaze in the mirror and thought about telling her yes. A rumor like that might neutralize the rumor about herself and Nick. But her mother would freak even more. 'No,' she finally sighed. 'But it would probably make my life easier.'

Mrs Van Damme's finger waves took Delaney just under an hour. When she was finished, she watched the older woman write out a check, then she helped her with her coat.

'Thanks for coming in,' she said as she walked her to the door.

'Silky drawers,' Wannetta reminded her and slowly moved down the street.

Ten minutes after Mrs Van Damme left, a woman came in with her three-year-old son. Delaney hadn't given a child a cut since beauty school, but she hadn't forgotten how. After the first snip, she wished she had. The little boy pulled at the small plastic cape she'd found in the storage room as if she were choking him. He writhed and fussed and continually yelled NO! at her. Cutting his hair turned into a wrestling match. She was sure if she could just tie him up and sit on him, she could get the job done in a hurry.

'Brandon's such a good boy,' his mother cooed from the neighboring chair. 'Mommy's so proud.'

Incredulous, Delaney stared at the woman who'd decked herself out in Eddie Bauer and REI. The woman looked to be in her early to mid-forties, and reminded Delaney of a magazine article she'd read in the dentist's office questioning the wisdom of older women producing children from old eggs.

'Does Brandon want a good-boy fruit snack?'

'No!' screeched the product of her old egg.

'Done,' Delaney said when she finished and threw her hands upward like a champion calf roper. She charged the lady fifteen dollars with the hope Brandon would plague Helen next time. She swept up the child's white-blond curls, then flipped the OUT TO LUNCH sign and walked to the corner deli for her usual, turkey on whole wheat. For several months she'd eaten her lunch at the deli and had gotten to know the owner, Bernard Dalton, on a first-name basis. Bernard was in his late thirties and a bachelor. He was short, balding, and looked like a man who enjoyed his own cooking. His face was always slightly pink, as if he were a little out of breath, and the shape of his dark mustache made him appear as if he always wore a smile.

The lunch rush was slowing as Delaney stepped into the

restaurant. The shop smelled of ham, pasta, and chocolate chip cookies. Bernard looked up from the dessert case, but his gaze quickly slid away. His face turned several shades pinker than usual.

He'd heard. He'd heard the rumor and he obviously believed it.

She cast a glance about the deli, at the other customers staring at her, and she wondered how many had listened to the gossip. She suddenly felt naked and forced herself to walk to the front counter. 'Hello, Bernard,' she said, keeping her voice even. 'I'll have a turkey on whole wheat like I usually have.'

'Diet Pepsi?' he asked, moving toward the meat case.

'Yes, please.' She kept her gaze pinned to the little 'Extra Pennies' cup by the cash register. She wondered if the whole town believed she'd had sex with Nick in her front window. She heard hushed voices behind her and was afraid to turn around. She wondered if they were talking about her, or if she was just being paranoid.

Usually she took her sandwich to a small table by the window, but today she paid for her lunch and hurried back to her salon. Her stomach was in knots and she had to force herself to eat a portion of her meal.

Nick. This mess was his fault. Whenever she let her guard down around him, she always paid for it. Whenever he decided to charm her, she always lost her dignity, if not her clothes.

At a little after two, she had a client who needed her straight black hair trimmed, and at three-thirty Steve, the backhoe driver she'd met at Louie and Lisa's Fourth of July party, walked into the salon bringing in a wisp of cool autumn with him. He wore a jean jacket with sheared sheep lining. His cheeks were pink and his eyes bright, and his smile told her he was glad to see her. Delaney was glad to see a friendly face. 'I need a haircut,' he confessed.

With one quick glance, she took in the shaggy condition of his hair. 'You sure do,' she said and motioned toward her booth. 'Hang up your coat and come on back.'

'I want it short.' He followed her and pointed to a spot above his right ear. 'This short. I wear a lot of ski hats in the winter.'

Delaney had something in mind that would look awesome on him, and she'd get to use her clippers, too. Something she'd been dying to do again for months now. His hair would have to be dry so she sat him in the salon chair. 'I haven't seen you around much,' she said as she combed out his golden tangles.

'We've been working a lot to get done before the first snow, but now things have slowed down.'

'What do you do in the winter for a job?' she asked, and fired up the clippers.

'Collect unemployment and ski,' he spoke over the steady buzz.

Unemployment and skiing would have appealed to her when she'd been twenty-two, also. 'Sounds like fun,' she said, cutting up and away in an arching motion and leaving the hair longer at his crown.

'It is. We should ski together.'

She would have loved to, but the closest resort was outside Truly city limits. 'I don't ski,' she lied.

'Then what if I come and pick you up tonight? We could grab a bite to eat then drive down to Cascade for a movie.'

She couldn't go to Cascade, either. 'I can't.'

'Tomorrow night?'

Delaney held the clipper aloft and looked in the mirror at him. His chin was on his chest and he looked up at her through eyes so big and blue she could drive a boat through them. Maybe he wasn't too young. Maybe she should give him another chance. Then maybe she wouldn't be so lonely and vulnerable to the pied piper of pheromones. 'Dinner,' she said and resumed her cutting. 'No movie. And we can only be friends.'

His smile was a combination of innocence and guile. 'You might change your mind.'

'I won't.'

'What if I tried to change it for you?'

She laughed. 'Only if you don't get too obnoxious about it.'

'Deal. We'll go slow.'

Before Steve left, she gave him her home telephone number. By four-thirty, she'd had four clients total and an appointment to do a foil weave for the next afternoon. The day hadn't been all bad.

She was tired and looked forward to a long soak in the bathtub. With half an hour remaining before she could close, she kicked back in a salon chair with some of her hair braiding books for brides. Lisa's wedding was less than a month away, and Delaney was looking forward to styling her friend's hair.

The bell above the front door rang, and she looked up as Louie walked in. Deep red mottled his cheeks like he'd been outside all day, and his hands were stuck in the pockets of his blue canvas coat. A deep wrinkle furrowed his brow, and he didn't look like he'd come to get his hair cut.

'What can I do for you, Louie?' She stood and walked behind the counter.

He quickly looked about the salon, then settled his dark gaze on her. 'I wanted to talk to you before you closed for the day.'

'Okay.' She set down her braiding book and opened the cash register. She shoved money into a black Naugahyde bag, and when he didn't speak right away, she looked up at him. 'Shoot.'

'I want you to stay away from my brother.'

Delaney blinked twice and slowly zipped the money bag closed. 'Oh,' was all she managed.

'In less than a year you'll be gone, but Nick will still live here. He'll have to run his business here, and he'll have to live with all the gossip you two create.'

'I didn't mean to create anything.'

'But you did.'

Delaney felt her cheeks grow hot. 'Nick assured me he doesn't care what people say about him.'

'Yeah, that's Nick. He says a lot of things. Some of them he actually means, too.' Louie paused and scratched his nose. 'Look, like I said, you're leaving in under a year, but Nick will have to listen to the gossip about you after you're gone. He'll have to live it down – again.'

'Again?'

'The last time you left, there was some crazy stuff said about you and Nick. Stuff that hurt my mother, and I think Nick a little, too. Although he said he didn't care except for the grief it caused my mother.'

'Do you mean the gossip about me having Nick's baby?'

'Yes, but the part about the abortion was worse.'

Delaney blinked. 'Abortion?'

'Don't tell me you didn't know.'

'No.' She looked down at her hands clutching the money bag. The old gossip hurt and she didn't know why. It wasn't as if she cared what people thought of her.

'Well, someone must have seen you somewhere and noticed you weren't pregnant. People said you had an abortion because the baby was Nick's. Others thought maybe Henry had you get rid of it.'

Her gaze shot to his and an odd little ache settled next to her heart. She hadn't been pregnant so she didn't know why she cared at all. 'I hadn't heard that part.'

'Didn't your mother ever tell you? I always assumed that was probably why you never came back.'

'No one ever mentioned it.' But she wasn't surprised.

Delaney was silent for a moment before she asked, 'Did anyone actually believe it?'

'Some.'

To imply she'd terminated a pregnancy because of Nick, or that Henry had forced an abortion was beyond insulting. Delaney believed in a woman's right to choose, but she didn't believe she could ever have an abortion herself. Certainly not because she no longer liked the father, and especially not because of anything Henry would have had to say about it. 'What did Nick think?'

Louie's dark eyes stared into hers before he answered, 'He acted like he always does. Like he didn't care, but he beat the hell out of Scooter Finley when Scooter was stupid enough to mention it in front of him.'

Nick would have known she wasn't pregnant with his baby, and she was stunned that the rumor had bothered him at all, let alone bothered him enough to deck Scooter.

'And now you're back and a whole new batch of rumors has begun. I don't want my wedding to turn into another excuse for you and my brother to create more gossip.'

'I would never do that.'

'Good because I want Lisa to be the center of attention.'

'I think Nick and I are probably going to avoid each other for the rest of our lives.'

Louie dug in his coat pocket and pulled out a set of keys. 'I hope so. Otherwise, you'll just hurt each other again.'

Delaney didn't ask him what he meant by that comment. She'd never hurt Nick. Impossible. In order for Nick to be hurt by anything, he'd have to have human feelings like everyone else, and he didn't. He had a heart of stone.

After Louie left, Delaney locked up, then stood at the counter and studied several more books on braids for the upcoming wedding. She had some great ideas, but she couldn't concentrate long enough to visualize the important details.

People said you had an abortion because the baby was Nick's. Others thought maybe Henry had you get rid of it. Delaney put the books aside and turned out the lights. The old gossip was so mean-spirited with its insinuation that Nick's own father had forced her to get an abortion because the baby was *Nick's*. She wondered what kind of person would spread something so cruel, and she wondered if they ever felt remorse or ever bothered to apologize to Nick.

Delaney grabbed her coat and locked the salon behind her. Nick's Jeep was parked next to her car in the small dark parking lot. *He acted like he always does. Like he didn't care.*

She tried not to wonder if he'd really been hurt as much as Louie had implied. She tried not to care. After the way he'd treated her the day before, she hated him.

She got as far as the stairs before she turned and walked to the back of his office. She knocked three times before the door swung open, and Nick stood there looking more intimidating than ever in a black thermal crew. He shifted his weight to one foot and tilted his head to the side. Surprise lifted one of his brows, but he didn't say anything.

Now that he stood before her, with the light from his office spilling into the parking lot, Delaney wasn't sure why she'd knocked. After what had happened yesterday, she really wasn't sure what to say, either. 'I heard something, and I wondered if—' She stopped and took a deep breath. Her nerves felt jumpy and her stomach queasy, like she'd consumed a triple shot German chocolate latte with an espresso chaser. She clasped her hands and looked at her thumbs. She didn't know where to begin. 'Someone told me about something horrible, and . . . I wondered if you'd . . .'

'Yes,' he interrupted. 'I've heard all about it several times today. In fact, Frank Stuart chased me down at a job site this morning to ask me if I'd broken the terms of Henry's will. He might ask you about it, too.'

She looked up. 'What?'

'You were right. Mrs Vaughn told everyone, and apparently she added a few juicy details of her own.'

'Oh.' She felt her cheeks burn and stepped a little to the left, out of the light. 'I don't want to talk about that. I don't ever want to talk about what happened yesterday.'

He leaned one shoulder against the door jam and looked at her through the night shadows. 'Then why are you here?'

'I don't really know, but I heard about an old rumor today, and I wanted to ask you about it.'

'What's that?'

'Supposedly, I was pregnant when I left ten years ago.'

'But we both know that was impossible, don't we? Unless of course you weren't really a virgin.'

She took another step backward, deeper into the dark lot. 'I heard a rumor that I had an abortion because you were the father of the baby.' She watched him straighten, and suddenly she knew why she'd knocked on his door. 'I'm sorry, Nick.'

'It happened a long time ago.'

'I know, but I heard it for the first time today.' She walked to the bottom of the stairs and put a hand on the rail. 'You want everyone to think nothing can touch you, but I think that rumor hurt more than you'll ever admit. Otherwise, you wouldn't have hit Scooter Finley.'

Nick rocked back on his heels and stuck his hands in his front pockets. 'Scooter's an asshole, and he pissed me off.'

She sighed and looked across her shoulder at him. 'I just want you to know I wouldn't have had an abortion, that's all.'

'Why do you think I care what people say about me?'

'Maybe you don't, but no matter how I feel about you, or how you feel about me, that was a really cruel thing for someone to say. I guess I just wanted you to know that I know it was mean and someone should say they're sorry.' She dug in her coat pocket for her keys and started up the stairs. 'Forget it.' Louie had been wrong. Nick acted like he didn't care because he really didn't.

'Delaney.'

'What?' She stuck her key in the lock, then paused with her hand on the doorknob.

'I lied to you yesterday.' She looked over her shoulder, but she couldn't see him.

'When?'

'When I said you could have been anyone. I would know you with my eyes closed.' His deep voice carried across the darkness more intimate than a whisper when he added, 'I would know you, Delaney.' Then there was the squeak of hinges followed by the click of a dead bolt and Delaney knew he was gone.

She leaned over the railing, but the door was closed like Nick had never been there. His words were swallowed in the night like he'd never spoken them.

Once inside her apartment, Delaney kicked off her shoes and popped a Lean Cuisine into the microwave. She turned on the television and tried to watch the local news, but she had a difficult time concentrating on the weather report. Her mind kept returning to her conversation with Nick. She kept remembering what he'd said about knowing her with his eyes closed, and she reminded herself that Nick was far more dangerous when he was nice.

She took her dinner out of the microwave and wondered if Frank Stuart would really want to talk to her about the latest rumor. Just like ten years ago, the town was whispering about her again. Whispering about her and Nick and 'hanky-panky' on the counter in her salon. But unlike ten years ago, she couldn't run from it. She couldn't escape.

Before she'd agreed to the terms of Henry's will, she'd moved all over the place. She'd always had the freedom to pick up and move when the mood struck. She'd always been in control of her life. She'd always had a goal. Now everything was hazy and confused and out of control. And Nick Allegrezza was smack in the middle of it all. He was one of the biggest reasons her life was so messed up.

Delaney stood and walked into her bedroom. She wished she could blame everything on Nick. She wished she could hate him completely, but for some reason she couldn't hate Nick. He'd made her more angry than anyone in her life, but she'd never been able to really hate him. Her life would be so much easier if she could.

When she fell asleep that night, she had another dream that quickly turned into a nightmare. She dreamed it was June and she'd fulfilled the terms of Henry's will. She was finally able to leave Truly.

She was free and buzzing with pleasure. The sun poured all over her, bathing her in a light so bright she could hardly see. She was finally warm and wore a killer pair of purple platforms. Life just didn't get much better.

Max was in her dream, and he handed her one of those big checks like she'd won The Publisher's Clearing House Sweepstakes. She shoved it in the passenger seat of her Miata and jumped in the car. With the three million dollars beside her, she headed out of town feeling as if a mammoth weight had been lifted from her spirit, and the closer she drove to the Truly city limits, the lighter she felt.

She drove toward the city limits for what seemed like hours, and just when freedom was less than a mile away, her Miata turned into a Matchbox car, leaving her on the side of the road with her big check tucked under one arm. Delaney looked at the tiny car by the toe of her right purple platform and shrugged as if that sort of thing happened all the time. She stuck the car into her pocket so it wouldn't get stolen and continued toward the city limits. But no matter how long or how fast she walked, the LEAVING TRULY sign remained barely visible in the distance. She began to run, leaning to one side to counterbalance the weight of her three-million-dollar check. The check grew increasingly burdensome, but she refused to leave it behind. She ran until her sides ached and she could move no further. The city limits remained in the distance, and Delaney knew without a doubt, she was stuck in Truly forever.

She sat straight up in bed. A silent scream on her lips. She was sweaty and her breathing choppy.

She'd just had the worst nightmare of her life.

12

'The Monster Mash' blared from five-foot speakers in the back of Mayor Tanasee's Dodge pickup. Fake spider-webs wrapped the truck in a gossamer tangle and two grave-stones stood in the bed. The Dodge crawled up Main Street with witches and vampires, clowns and princesses, trailing behind. The excited chatter of ghosts and goblins mixed with the music and kicked off the annual Halloween parade.

Delaney stood in the sparse crowd in front of her salon. She shivered and snuggled deep into her green wool coat with the big glittery buttons. She was freezing, unlike Lisa who stood next to her in a B.U.M. sweatshirt and a pair of cotton gloves. The newspaper predicted unseasonable warmth for the last day in October. The temperature was supposed to shoot up to a whopping forty degrees.

As a child, Delaney had loved the Halloween parade. She'd loved dressing up and marching through town to the high school gymnasium where the costume contest would begin. She'd never won, but loved it any way. It had given her a chance to play dress-up and cake on the cosmetics. She wondered if they still served cider and glazed doughnuts and if the new mayor handed out little bags of candy like Henry had done.

'Remember when we were in the sixth grade and shaved

our eyebrows and dressed as psychotic killers and had blood squirting out of our necks?' Lisa asked from beside Delaney. 'And your mother lost it big time?'

She remembered all right. Her mother had made her a stupid bride costume that year. Delaney had pretended to love the dress, only to turn up at the parade as a blood-soaked killer with no eyebrows. Thinking back, she didn't know how she'd gathered the nerve to do something she'd known would anger her mother.

The next year Delaney had been forced to dress as a Smurf.

'Look at that kid and his dog,' Delaney said, pointing to a boy dressed as a box of McDonald's French fries and his little dachshund decked out as a package of ketchup. It had been a long time since Delaney had driven through McDonald's. 'I'm craving a Quarter Pounder with cheese right now.' She sighed, visions of a greasy beef patty making her mouth water.

'Maybe one will walk down the street next.'

Delaney looked at her friend out of the corner of her eye. 'I'll fight you for it.'

'You're no match for me, city girl. Look at you shivering to death in your big ol' coat.'

'I just need to acclimatize,' Delaney grumbled, watching a woman and her baby dinosaur step from the sidewalk and join the parade. A door opened and closed somewhere behind her, and she turned, but no one had entered her salon.

'Where's Louie?'

'He's in the parade with Sophie.'

'As what?'

'You'll see. It's a surprise.'

Delaney smiled. She had a surprise of her own coming up. She'd had to get up real early this morning, but if everything went according to her plan, her business would take off.

A second truck slowly moved past with a big smoking cauldron and cackling witch on its flatbed. Despite the crazy black hair and green face, the crone looked slightly familiar.

'Who's that witch?' Delaney asked.

'Hmm. Oh it's Neva. You remember Neva Miller, don't you?'

'Of course.' Neva had been wild and outrageous. She'd regaled Delaney with stories of stealing booze, smoking pot, and having sex with the football team. And Delaney had hung on every word. She leaned toward Lisa and whispered, 'Remember when she told us about blowing Roger Bonner while he pulled his little brother water skiing? And you didn't know what a blow job was so she told us in graphic detail?'

'Yeah, and you started to gag.' Lisa pointed to the man driving the truck. 'That's her husband, Pastor Jim.'

'Pastor? Holy hell!'

'Yep, she got saved or born again or whatever. Pastor Jim preaches over at that little church on Seventh Street.'

'It's Pastor Tim,' corrected a painfully familiar voice directly behind Delaney.

Delaney did a mental groan. It was so typical of Nick to sneak up on her when she least expected him.

'How do you know it's Tim?' Lisa wanted to know.

'We built his house a few years ago.' Nick's voice was low, like he hadn't used it much that morning.

'Oh, I thought maybe he prays for your soul.'

'No. My mother prays for my soul.'

Delaney cast a quick glance over her shoulder. 'Maybe she should make a pilgrimage to Lourdes, or to that tortilla shrine in New Mexico.'

An easy smile curved Nick's mouth. He'd pulled a thick hooded sweatshirt over his head; the white strings hung down his chest. His hair was pulled back from his face. 'Maybe,' was all he said.

Delaney turned to the parade again. She raised her shoulders and buried her cold nose in the collar of her coat. There was only one thing worse than being baited by Nick, and that was wondering why he wasn't baiting her at all. She'd seen very little of him since the day she'd knocked on the back door of his business. By tacit agreement, they were avoiding each other.

'Where did you come from?' Lisa asked him.

'I was making a few calls from the office. Has Sophie come by yet?'

'Not yet.'

Four boys dressed as bloody hockey players wheeled past on Roller Blades and were followed closely by Tommy Markham pulling his wife in a rickshaw. Helen was dressed as Lady Godiva, and on the back of the rickshaw hung a sign that read HELEN'S HAIR HUT. QUALITY CUTS FOR TEN DOLLARS. Helen waved and threw kisses to the crowd, and on her head sat a rhinestone crown Delaney recognized all too well.

Delaney dropped her shoulders and uncovered the lower half of her face. 'That's pathetic! She's still wearing her homecoming crown.'

'She wears it every year like she's the Queen of England or something.'

'Remember how she campaigned for homecoming queen, and I didn't because campaigning was against the rules? Then after she won the school wouldn't disqualify her? That crown should have been mine.'

'Are you still mad about that?'

Delaney folded her arms over her chest. 'No.' But she was. She was annoyed with herself for giving Helen the power to irritate her after so many years. Delaney was cold, possibly neurotic, and very aware of the man standing behind her. Too aware. She didn't have to see him to know how close he stood. She could feel him like a big human wall.

Except for the time Nick had ridden his bike in the parade like some crazed stunt rider and ended up with stitches in the top of his head, he'd always been a pirate – always. And every year she'd taken one look at his eye patch and fake sword, and her hands would get all clammy. A weird reaction considering that he usually told her she looked stupid.

She turned her head and glanced up at him again with his dark hair pulled back in a ponytail and small gold hoop in his ear. He still looked like a pirate, and she was getting a warm little tingle in her stomach.

'I didn't see your car in back,' he said, his eyes staring into hers.

'Um, no. Steve has it.'

A frown creased his brow. 'Steve?'

'Steve Ames. He works for you.'

'Real young guy with dyed blond hair?'

'He's not that young.'

'Uh-huh.' Nick shifted his weight to one foot and tilted his head slightly to the side. 'Sure he's not.'

'Well, he's nice.'

'He's a nancy boy.'

Delaney turned and scowled at her friend. 'Do you think Steve's a nancy boy?'

Lisa looked from Nick to Delaney. 'You know I love you, but geez, the guy plays air guitar.'

Delaney shoved her hands into her pockets and turned to watch Sleeping Beauty, Cinderella, and a Hershey's Kiss walk by. It was true. She'd gone out with him twice and the guy played air guitar to everything. Nirvana. Metal Head. Mormon Tabernacle Choir. Steve played it all, and it was *so* embarrassing. But he was the closest thing she had to a boyfriend, although she wouldn't even call him that. He was the only available man who'd paid attention to her since she'd arrived in Truly.

Except Nick. But he wasn't available. Not to her anyway. Delaney leaned forward to look down the street and saw her

Miata turn the corner. Steve steered the sports car with one hand, his hair dyed and cut short in a spiky crewcut. Two teenage girls sat like beauty queens directly behind him while one more girl waved from the passenger seat. Their hair was cut and styled to make them look as if they'd just stepped out of a teen magazine. Smooth and free-flowing and trendy. Delaney had scoured the high school, purposely searching for girls who weren't cheerleaders or pep club officers. She'd wanted average girls she could make over to look fantastic.

She'd found them last week. After receiving their mothers' approval, she'd gone to work on each of them earlier that morning. All three looked wonderful and were living, breathing advertisements for her salon. And if the girls weren't enough, Delaney had taped a sign on the sides of her car that read: THE CUTTING EDGE FIXES TEN-DOLLAR HAIRCUTS.

'That's going to drive Helen nuts,' Lisa muttered.

'I hope so.'

A collection of grim reapers, werewolves, and corpses passed, then a fifty-seven Chevy turned the corner with Louie at the wheel. Delaney took one look at his dark hair greased into a jelly roll and burst out laughing. He wore a tight white T-shirt with a pack of cigarettes rolled up in the sleeve. In the seat next to him sat Sophie with her hair in a high ponytail, bright red lipstick, and cat's-eye sun-glasses. She smacked bubble gum and snuggled inside Nick's big leather jacket.

'Uncle Nick,' she called out and threw him a kiss.

Delaney heard his deep chuckle just before Louie revved the big engine for the crowd. The antique car shook and rumbled, then for a grand finale, backfired.

Startled, Delaney jumped back and collided with the immovable wall of Nick's chest. His big hands grabbed her upper arms, and when she looked up at him, her hair brushed his throat. 'Sorry,' she muttered.

His grasp on her tightened, and through her coat she felt

his long fingers curl into the wool sleeve. His gaze swept across her cheeks, then lowered to her mouth. 'Don't be,' he said, and she felt the brush of his thumbs on the backs of her arms.

His gaze lifted to hers once again, and there was something hot and intense in the way he looked at her. Like he wanted to give her one of those kisses that devoured her resistance. Like they were lovers and the most natural thing in the world would be for her to put one hand on the back of his head and lower his face to hers. But they weren't lovers. They weren't even friends. And in the end he stepped back and dropped his hands to his sides.

She turned around and sucked air deep into her lungs. She could feel his gaze on the back of her head, feel the air between them charged with tension. The pull was so strong she was sure everyone around them could feel it, too. But when she glanced at Lisa, her friend was waving like a mad woman to Louie. Lisa hadn't noticed.

Nick said something to Lisa and Delaney felt rather than heard him leave. She let out the breath she hadn't realized she'd been holding. She glanced over her shoulder one last time and watched him disappear into the building behind them.

'Isn't he cute?'

Delaney looked at her friend and shook her head. By no stretch of the imagination was Nick Allegrezza *cute*. He was hot. One hundred percent, testosterone-pumping, drool-inspiring hot.

'I helped him do his hair this morning.'

'Nick?'

'Louie.'

The light dawned. 'Oh.'

'Why would I do Nick's hair?'

'Forget it. Are you going to party at the Grange tonight?'

'Probably.'

Delaney checked her watch. She only had a few minutes before her one o'clock appointment. She bid Lisa good-bye and spent the rest of the afternoon on a three-color weave and two walk-ins.

When she was finished for the day, she quickly swept up hair from the last girl, then grabbed her coat and climbed up the back stairs to her apartment. She had plans to meet Steve at the costume party being held out in the old Grange hall. Steve had found a police uniform somewhere, and since he planned to impersonate a law enforcement officer, it seemed a given that she should impersonate a hooker. She already had the skirt and fishnet stockings, and she'd found a fluffy pink boa with matching handcuffs in the gag gift aisle at Howdy's Trading Post.

Delaney stuck her key into the lock and noticed a white envelope on the step next to the toe of her black boot. She had a bad feeling she knew what it was even before she bent to pick it up. She opened it and pulled out a white piece of paper with four typewritten words: **GET OUT OF TOWN**, it said this time. She crushed the paper in her fist and glanced over her shoulder. The parking lot was empty of course. Whoever had left the envelope had done it while Delaney had been busy cutting hair. It would have been so easy.

Delaney retraced her steps to the parking lot and knocked on the back door of Allegrezza Construction. Nick's Jeep wasn't in the back lot.

The door swung open and Nick's secretary, Ann Marie, appeared.

'Hi,' Delaney began. 'I was wondering if you might have seen anyone back here today.'

'The garbage men emptied the Dumpster this afternoon.'

Delaney doubted she'd pissed off the garbage men. 'How about Helen Markham?'

Ann Marie shook her head. 'I didn't see her today.'

Which didn't mean Helen hadn't left the note. After Delaney's entry into the parade, Helen was probably livid. 'Okay, thanks. If you see anyone hanging around that shouldn't be here, will you let me know?'

'Sure. Did something happen?'

Delaney shoved the note into her coat pocket. 'No, not really.'

The old Grange hall had been decorated with bales of hay, orange and black crepe paper, and cauldrons filled with dried ice. A bartender from Mort's poured beer or cola at one end, and a Country and Western band played at the other. The ages of those gathered at the Halloween party ranged from teens who were too old to trick-or-treat to Wannetta Van Damme, who was tieing one on with the two remaining World War vets.

By the time Delaney arrived, the band was well into its first set. She'd dressed in a black satin skirt, matching bustier, and black lace garters. The matching satin blazer she left at home. Her black stilettos had five-inch heels, and she'd spent twenty minutes making sure the lines on her stockings ran straight up the backs of her legs. Her boa was draped around her neck and the handcuffs were tucked in the waistband of her skirt. Except for her teased hair and thick mascara, most of her efforts were concealed by her wool coat.

She wanted nothing more than to go back home and fall head first into a coma. She'd thought of not coming at all. She was sure the note had come from Helen and was bugged by it more than she liked to admit. Sure, she'd stalked Helen a little bit. She'd hidden in her Dumpster and scoured her garbage, but that was different. She hadn't left psychotic notes. If Delaney hadn't told Steve she'd meet him, she'd be curled up right now in her favorite flannel nightgown, after a warm bath filled with fragrant bubbles.

Delaney reached for the buttons on her coat as her gaze scanned the crowd dressed in a wide variety of interesting costumes. She spied Steve dancing with a hippie chick who looked to be about twenty. They looked good together. She knew Steve saw women besides her and wasn't bothered by it. He was a nice diversion sometimes when she needed to get out of her apartment. He was a nice guy, too.

She decided to keep her coat on as she made her way into the crowd. She squeezed by two coneheads and a mermaid and almost ran smack into a *Star Trek* character covered in makeup with a slight yellow tinge.

'Hey, Delaney,' he said above the sound of county music. 'I heard you moved back.'

The voice sounded vaguely familiar and he obviously knew her. She hadn't a clue. His hair was slicked back with black spray-in color, and he wore a red and black uniform with a symbol that looked like an A on his chest. She'd never watched *Star Trek* and frankly didn't understand the attraction. 'Uh, yeah. I moved back in June.'

'Wes said that was you when you walked in.'

Delaney stared into eyes so light they hardly were blue at all. 'Oh, my God,' she gasped. 'Scooter!' There was only one thing scarier than a Finley. A Finley dressed up as a Trekkie.

'Yeah, it's me. Long time no see.' Scooter's makeup was cracking on his forehead, and his choice in face color picked up the yellow in his teeth. 'You're lookin' good,' he continued, his head nodding like one of those wooden Chinese dolls with the spring necks.

Delaney glanced around the area for someone to rescue her. 'Yeah, you too Scooter,' she lied. She didn't see anyone she recognized and her gaze rested on him once again. 'What have you been up to?' she asked, making simple conversation until she could make her escape.

'Me and Wes own a fish farm over in Garden. We bought it

from Wes's old girlfriend after she ran off with a long-haul trucker. We're going to make a fortune selling catfish.'

Delaney could only stare. 'You have a fish farm?'

'Heck yeah. Where do you think all that fresh catfish comes from?'

What fresh catfish? Delaney didn't recall seeing a lot of catfish at any meat counter in town. 'Is there a big demand for that around here?'

'Not yet, but Wes and me figure that with *E. coli* and that chicken flu, people will start eating butt-loads of fish.' He raised a red Solo cup and took a long pull. 'Are you married?'

Usually she hated that question, but she couldn't get over the obvious fact that Scooter was an even bigger moron than she remembered. 'Ah, no. Are you?'

'Divorced twice.'

'Go figure,' she said as she shook her head and shrugged. 'See ya around, Scooter.' She moved past him but he followed.

'Wanna beer?'

'No, I'm meeting someone here.'

'Bring her along.'

'It's not a her.'

'Oh.' He hung back and called after her. 'See ya around, Delaney. Maybe I'll call you sometime.'

His threat might have scared her if she'd been listed in the telephone book. She wove her way through a group dressed as punkers, to the edge of the dance floor. Abraham Lincoln asked her to dance, but she declined. Her head was beginning to pound and she wanted to go home, but she figured she owed it to Steve to tell him she was leaving. She spied him with Cleopatra this time, playing air guitar to Wynonna Judd's 'No One Else on Earth.'

Her eyes scrunched and she glanced away from Steve. He could be so extremely embarrassing sometimes. Her gaze stopped on a familiar couple dressed as a fifties tough and his girlfriend in a poodle skirt. From the perimeter of dancing couples, Delaney watched Louie swing Lisa behind his back then around front again. He pulled her against his chest and dipped her so low her ponytail brushed the ground. Delaney smiled and her gaze moved to the couple closest to Lisa and Louie. There was no mistaking the tall man spinning his niece like a top. As far as Delaney could tell, Nick's only concession to the holiday was his *txapel*, his Basque beret. He wore jeans and a tan chambray shirt. Even without a costume, he managed to look like a two-stepping pirate, with that black beret pulled partway down his forehead.

For the first time since she'd moved away, Delaney seriously longed to be a part of a family again. Not a superficial controlling family like hers, but a real family. A family that laughed and danced and loved one another without conditions.

Delaney turned away and ran into Elvis. 'Excuse me,' she said and looked up into Tommy Markham's face complete with fake sideburns.

Tommy glanced from her to the woman at his side. Helen was still dressed as Lady Godiva, still had the crown on her head.

'Hello, Delaney,' she greeted her, a smug smile on her face as if she were superior. It was the same 'kiss my ass' smile she'd been giving Delaney since the first grade.

Delaney was too tired to pretend a civility she didn't feel. Her head pounded, fueled by Helen's stupid smile. 'How did you like my parade entry?'

Helen's smile fell. 'Pathetic, but predictable.'

'Not as pathetic as your mangy wig and cheap crown.' The music stopped as she stepped forward and shoved her face in Helen's. 'And if you ever leave me another threatening note, I'll shove it up your nose.'

Helen's brows lowered and she blinked. 'You're mental. I never left you any note.'

'Notes.' Delaney didn't believe her for one second. 'There were two.'

'I don't think Helen would –'

'Shut up, Tommy,' Delaney interrupted without taking her gaze from her old enemy. 'Your stupid notes don't scare me, Helen. I'm more annoyed than anything else.' She gave one last warning before she walked away, 'Stay away from me and anything that belongs to me.' Then she turned and pressed her way through the crowd, dodging and weaving, her head pounding. What if it wasn't Helen? Impossible. Helen hated her.

She made it as far as the door before Steve caught up with her.

'Where are you going?' he asked, matching his stride to hers.

'Home. I have a headache.'

'Can't you stay for just a little while?'

'No.'

They walked into the parking lot and stopped by Delaney's car. 'We haven't danced yet.'

At the moment the mere thought of dancing with a man who played the front of his pants was just too disturbing for her to handle. 'I don't want to dance. I've had a long day and I'm tired. I'm going to bed.'

'Want some company?'

Delaney looked into his cute surfer-boy face and chuckled silently. 'Nice try.' He leaned forward to kiss her, but her hand on his chest stopped him.

'Okay.' He laughed. 'Maybe next time.'

'Good night, Steve,' she said and got into her car. On the way home, Delaney stopped at the Value Rite and bought a king-sized Reese's, a bottle of Coke, and some vanilla-scented bubble bath. Even after a hot soak, she could be in bed by ten.

I never left you any note. Helen had to be lying. Of course she wouldn't admit to writing the notes. Not in front of Tommy.

What if she wasn't lying? For the first time, real fear settled like a bubble in her chest, but she tried to ignore it. Delaney didn't want to think that the author of the note could be anyone other than her old enemy. Someone she didn't know.

When she pulled into the parking lot behind her salon, Nick's Jeep was parked behind his business. His dark silhouette leaned against the back fender, his familiar posture relaxed. The headlights of her Miata cut across his leather jacket as he pushed himself away from the four-wheel drive.

Delaney cut the car's engine and reached for the plastic grocery bag. 'Are you following me?' she asked as she got out of the car and shut the door.

'Of course.'

'Why?' The heels of her stilettoes stirred the gravel as she started toward the stairs.

'Tell me about the notes.' He reached out and grabbed the grocery bag from her hand as she passed.

'Hey, I can carry that,' she protested even as she realized it had been a long time since a man had offered to carry anything for her. Not that Nick had offered, of course.

'Tell me about the notes.'

'How did you know about those?' He followed so close behind her up the steps, she felt his heavier tread beneath the soles of her shoes. 'Did Ann Marie tell you?'

'No. I heard your conversation with Helen tonight.'

Delaney wondered how many others had heard it as well. Her breath hung in front of her face as she quickly unlocked her door. Since it would have been a total waste of breath, she didn't bother to tell Nick he couldn't come in. 'Helen has written me a couple of little notes.' She walked into the kitchen and flipped on the light.

Nick followed, unzipping his jacket and filling the small space with his size and presence. He set her groceries on the counter. 'What do they say?'

'Read for yourself.' She dug into her coat pocket and handed him the envelope she'd shoved in there earlier. 'The other one said something like, "I'm watching you."' She brushed past him and moved into the short hall leading to the bedroom.

'Have you called the sheriff?'

'No.' She hung her coat in the closet, then retraced her steps. 'I can't prove Helen is the one leaving them, although I'm certain it's her. And besides, the notes aren't really threatening, just annoying.' From the doorway, she watched him study the note in his hand. His *txapel* made him look like an exotic Basque freedom fighter.

'Where did you find this?'

'By my front door.'

'Do you still have the oth—' He looked up and stopped in mid-sentence. His eyes widened a fraction, then his gaze swept her from hair to stilettoes. For the first time in her life, she'd rendered Nick speechless. It had taken a hooker outfit to do it.

'What's the matter?'

'Not a thing.'

'Don't you have at least one smart or smarmy comment?' She tried to stand perfectly still, as if she couldn't feel his gaze touching her everywhere. But in the end she blew it and moved the boa to cover her cleavage pressed against the satin bustier.

'At least one.'

'I'm not surprised.'

He pointed to her waist. 'What do you do with the cuffs?'

'You'd know better than me.'

'Wild thing,' he said, a salacious smile tilting the corners of his mouth, 'I don't need extra hardware to get the job done.'

She rolled her eyes toward the ceiling. 'Spare me the details of your sex life.'

'Are you sure? You might learn something good.'

She folded her arms beneath her breasts. 'I doubt you know anything I'd want to learn.' Then she quickly added, 'That wasn't a challenge.'

His soft laughter filled the short distance between them. 'It was a challenge, Delaney.'

'I'll take your word for it.' He took a step toward her, and she held up her hand like a traffic cop. 'I don't want to go there with you, Nick. I thought you came up here to look at the note Helen left me.'

'I did.' He stopped when her palm hit his chest. Cool leather pressed into her hand. 'But you make it real hard to think about anything but your zippers.'

'You're a big boy. Try to concentrate.' Delaney dropped her hand and moved past him to the refrigerator. 'Wanna beer?'

'Sure.'

She twisted off the tops, then handed him a pumpkin beer she'd bought at the microbrewery. He looked at the designer brew as if he didn't quite know what to do with it. 'It's really good,' she assured him and took a big swallow.

Nick raised the beer to his lips, and his gray eyes watched her over the top of the bottle as he took a drink. He immediately lowered the beer and wiped the back of his hand across his mouth. 'Jesus, Joseph, and Mary that's foul.'

'I like it.' She smiled and took an extra long swig.

'Do you have any real beer?' He set both the bottle and the note on the counter.

'I have a raspberry ale.'

He looked at her as if she were suggesting he chop off his testicles. 'Got a Bud?'

'Nope. But I have a Coke in that bag.' She waved her bottle

toward the plastic sack then moved past Nick to the living room.

'Where did you find the first note?' he called after her.

'In the salon.' She switched on a light above the stereo, then moved to a table lamp next to the couch. 'Actually, you pointed it out to me.'

'When?'

'The day you changed my locks.' She looked over her shoulder as she pulled the lamp's chain. Nick stood in the middle of the room chugging the Coke she'd bought at the Value Rite. 'Remember?'

He lowered the bottle and sucked a brown drop from his bottom lip. 'Perfectly.'

Unbidden, the memory of his lips pressed to hers and the texture of his warm skin beneath her hands flooded her senses. 'I was talking about the note.'

'So was I.'

No he wasn't. 'Why do you think Helen is responsible?'

Delaney sat on the couch, carefully making sure her satin skirt didn't slide to her crotch and make her a porno star. 'Who else could it be?'

He set the Coke on the coffee table and shrugged out of his jacket. 'Who else would want you gone?'

Delaney couldn't think of anyone besides Nick and his entire family. 'You.'

He tossed his jacket on the arm of the sofa and looked at her from beneath lowered brows. 'Do you really believe that?'

'Not really. I don't know.'

'If you think I sneak around threatening women, why did you let me in your apartment?'

'Could I have stopped you?'

'Maybe, but I didn't leave those notes and you know it.' He sat next to Delaney and leaned forward to rest his elbows on his knees. He'd rolled the sleeves of his chambray shirt up his forearms, and he wore a wristwatch with a worn black band. 'Someone's real upset with you. Have you given a bad haircut lately?'

Her eyes narrowed, and she set her pumpkin beer on the coffee table with a heavy thump. 'First of all, Nick, I never give bad haircuts. And second, what do you think, that some infuriated psycho is running around leaving me notes because I trimmed her bangs too short or overprocessed a perm?'

Nick looked across his shoulder at her and laughed. It started low in his chest and grew louder, feeding Delaney's temper. 'Why are you so pissed off?'

'You insulted me.'

He placed an innocent hand on the front of his shirt, pushing the soft fabric to the side and exposing a slice of tan chest. 'I did not.'

Delaney lifted her gaze to his amused eyes. 'You absolutely did.'

'Sorry.' Then he ruined the apology by adding insult to injury, 'Wild thing.'

She punched his arm. 'Jerk.'

Nick grabbed her wrist and pulled her toward him. 'Has anyone told you that you're a great-looking hooker?'

The scent of sandalwood soap and warm skin filled her senses. His strong fingers sent tingling pinpricks up the inside of her arm, and she tried to pull away. He let her go only to grab her boa in both his hands and tug her closer. Her nose bumped his, and she felt herself sucked into his smoky gaze. She opened her mouth meaning to say something stinging and sarcastic, but her brain and voice betrayed her and what came out instead was a breathy, 'Gee, thanks, Nick. I bet you say that to all your women of the night.'

'Are you my woman for the night?' he asked just above her mouth, holding her with nothing more than a string of fluffy pink feathers and his smooth voice.

She didn't think she'd said that, or meant that, or some-thing . . . 'No. You know we can never be together.'

'You should never say never.' The feathers brushed across her cheek and neck as he slid one hand to the top edge of her bustier. 'Your heart is pounding.'

'I have pretty high blood pressure.' Her eyelids were heavy and she felt the tip of his tongue touch her bottom lip.

'You were always a really bad liar.' Then before Delaney knew quite how it happened, she was in Nick's lap and his mouth was all over hers, in a kiss that started sweet but quickly shattered Delaney's pitiful resistance. He had a hand on the back of her head, the other on the outside of her thigh, caressing her through black hose. His slick tongue stroked hers, urging a hotter, more passionate response, and she gave him a kiss that sent a shudder of raw lust through them. She slid her hands up the sides of his neck and worked the rubber band from his ponytail. The beret fell from his head as she combed her fingers through his cool, fine hair. She felt his fingers drift up her garter to the edge of her skirt, drawing a line of fire that heated the insides of her thighs and flamed the hunger deep in her abdomen. Then his fingers dipped beneath the black lace and elastic and he grasped her bare flesh. She shoved one hand inside the open collar of his shirt and touched his shoulder where he was warm, his muscles hard, but it wasn't enough and she tugged at the buttons until his shirt lay open. He was hard and smooth, his skin hot and slightly damp. Beneath her bottom, his thick erection pressed into her and she squirmed deeper into his lap. His fingers bit into her thigh, and she felt his deep groan beneath her palm.

He moved one hand to her waist, and his strong fingers squeezed her through the thin satin. A moan stuck in the top of her chest as his palm slipped upward, over her breast, to her throat. His knuckles brushed her collarbone and across the edge of her bustier. Then he slid his sensual mouth to her throat and his hand inside the tight satin top. He cupped her bare breast, and Delaney arched, pressing her hard nipple into his hot, hot palm. Her hands moved to his shoulder, and she grasped the soft fabric of his shirt in tight fists.

She ached all over and, with her last shred of sanity whispered, 'Nick, we have to stop this.'

'We will,' he murmured as he pushed the bustier practically to her waist and lowered his head. He brushed his lips across the pink tip of her breast, then sucked it into his mouth, his tongue hot and wet and relentless. His big warm hand slipped between her thighs and he pressed his palm into her sensitive flesh. Through her damp cotton panties, his fingers felt her, and she squeezed her legs together, locking his hand in her crotch. Delaney's eyes closed and his name escaped her lips, part moan, part sigh. It was the sound of need and desire. She wanted him to make love to her. She wanted to feel his naked body pressed to her. She had nothing to lose but self-respect. What was a little self-respect compared to a quality orgasm?

Then his mouth was gone and cool air swept across her breast. She forced her eyes open and followed his fiery gaze to her glistening nipple. He slid his hand from her thighs and picked up one end of her boa, slowly brushing it across her sensitive flesh. 'Tell me you want me.'

'Isn't it obvious?'

'Say it anyway.' He looked up, his eyes heavy with lust and determination. 'Say it.' The feathers made another downy pass across her breasts.

Delaney sucked in her breath. 'I want you.'

His gaze skimmed her face, then settled on her mouth. He placed a soft kiss on her lips and pulled her bustier back in place, covering her breasts once again.

He wasn't going to make love to her. Of course he wasn't. He had a lot more to lose than she did. 'Why do we keep doing this?' she asked when he lifted his mouth. 'I never mean for this to happen with us, but it always does.'

'Don't you know?'

'I wish I did.'

'Unfinished business.'

She took a deep breath and leaned against him. 'What are you talking about? Unfinished business.'

'That night at Angel Beach. We never got to finish what we started before you ran off.'

'Ran off?' She felt her brows lower then rise up her forehead. 'I didn't have a choice.'

'You had a choice and you made it. You left with Henry.'

With as much dignity as possible under the circumstances, Delaney removed herself from his lap. Her left shoe was missing and her boa was stuck inside her bustier. 'I left because you were using me.'

'Exactly when was that?' He stood and towered over her. 'When you begged me to touch you all over?'

Delaney tugged her skirt down. 'Shut up.'

'Or when my head was between your legs?'

'Shut up, Nick.' She yanked the boa free. 'You were only out to humiliate me.'

'Bullshit.'

'You used me to get back at Henry.'

He rocked back on his heels and his gaze narrowed. 'I never used you. I told you not to worry and that I'd take care of you, but you looked at me like I was some kind of rapist and left with Henry.'

She didn't believe him. 'I never looked at you like you were a rapist, and I would have remembered if you'd said one nice word. But you didn't.'

'Yes I did, only you chose to leave with the old man. And the way I see it, you owe me.'

She picked up his jacket from the back of the couch and

threw it at him. 'I don't owe you anything.'

'You better not be around here on June fourth, otherwise I'm going to take what you've owed me for ten years.' He shoved his arms into his jacket and walked to the door. 'And paybacks are a real bitch, wild thing.'

Delaney stared at the closed door long after she heard his Jeep tear out of the alley. Her body still burned from his touch, and the thought of some sort of sexual payback didn't sound all that unappealing. She turned back toward the room and picked up Nick's *txapel* from the floor. She raised the beret to her nose. It smelled of leather and wool and Nick.

'Uncle Nick, did you see that movie on TV the other night about a girl who was kidnapped as a baby and she never knew it until she was like about twenty or something?'

Nick stared at his computer screen, going over the budget he'd projected on a home on the north shore of the lake. The foundation had been poured before the ground froze, and the roof put on before the snow. The home was close to completion, but the owner had decided on different fixtures throughout, and the finish carpentry was way over budget. Since business was slowing down, Ann Marie and Hilda only worked mornings. He and Sophie were alone in the building.

'Uncle Nick.'

'Hmm, what?' He deleted several figures, then typed in the new cost.

Sophie took a deep drawn-out breath and sighed, 'You're not listening to me.'

He glanced from the screen to his niece, then returned his gaze to his work. 'Sure I am, Sophie.'

'What did I say?'

He added a restocking fee and reached for a calculator on the edge of his desk, but when he glanced at his niece again, his hand stilled. Her big brown eyes looked back at him as if he'd stomped her feelings beneath his work boots. 'I wasn't listening.' He pulled his hand back. 'Sorry.'

'Can I ask you something?'

He figured she hadn't dropped by his office on her way home from school to watch him work. 'Sure.'

'Okay, what would you do if you liked a girl and she didn't know you liked her.' She paused and looked somewhere over the top of his head. 'And she liked someone else with really great clothes and blond hair and everybody liked her and she was a cheerleader and everything?' She returned her gaze to his. 'Would you give up?'

Nick was confused. 'Do you like a boy who dresses like a cheerleader?'

'No! Geez, I like a boy who *dates* a cheerleader. She's pretty and popular and has the best body in eighth grade, and Kyle doesn't know I'm alive. I want him to notice me, so what should I do?'

Nick looked across his desk at his niece, who was all shiny braces and had her mother's Italian eyes that were way too big for her face. She had an enormous red pimple on her forehead that, despite her best efforts, would not remain concealed with the makeup she'd slapped on it. Someday Sophia Allegrezza would turn heads, but not today, thank God. She was too young to worry about boys, anyway. 'Don't do anything. You're gorgeous, Sophie.'

She rolled her eyes and reached for her backpack sitting on the floor by her chair. 'You're no better help than Dad.'

'What did Louie say?'

'That I'm too young to worry about boys.'

'Oh.' He leaned forward and grabbed her hand. 'Well, I would never say that,' he lied.

'I know. That's why I came to talk to you. And it's not just Kyle. *No* boys ever notice me.' She dragged her backpack into her lap and slumped in the chair, a lump of misery. 'I hate it.'

And he hated to see her so unhappy. He'd helped Louie raise Sophie, and she was the only female he'd ever felt completely free to show affection and love to. The two of them could sit and watch a movie together or play Monopoly, and she never pried into his life or hung on to his neck too tight. 'What do you want me to do?'

'Tell me what boys like in girls.'

'Eighth grade boys?' He scratched the side of his jaw and paused to think a moment. He didn't want to lie, yet he didn't want to spoil her innocent illusions, either.

'I thought since you have a lot of girlfriends, you would know.'

'A lot of girlfriends?' He watched her pull a bottle of green fingernail polish from her backpack. 'I don't have a *lot* of girlfriends. Who told you something like that?'

'No one had to *tell* me.' She shrugged. 'Gail is a girlfriend.'

He hadn't seen Gail since a few weeks before Halloween, and that had been a week ago. 'She was just a friend,' he said. 'And we broke it off last month.' Actually, he'd broken things off with her and she hadn't been pleased.

'Well, what did you like about her?' she asked as she added a coat of green polish over an existing layer of navy blue.

The few things he'd liked about Gail, he could hardly tell his thirteen-year-old niece. 'She had nice hair.'

'That's it? You would date a girl just because you liked her hair?'

Probably not. 'Yep.'

'What's your favorite hair color?'

Red. Different shades of red all streaked together and tangled up in his fingers. 'Brown.'

'What else do you like?'

Pink lips and pink boas. 'A good smile.'

Sophie looked up at him and grinned, her mouth filled with metal and mauve rubber bands. 'Like this?'

'Yep.'

'What else?'

This time he answered with the truth. 'Big brown eyes, and I like a girl who can stand up to me.' And, he realized, he'd developed an appreciation of sarcasm.

She dipped the brush into the polish and went to work on her other hand. 'Do you think girls should call boys?'

'Sure. Why not?'

'Grandma says girls who call boys are wild. She says you and Dad never got into trouble with wild girls because she never let you talk on the phone when they called.'

His mother was the only person he knew who had the ability to see only what she chose and nothing else. Growing up, both Nick and Louie had found their fair share of trouble without the telephone. Louie had gone on to get a girl pregnant in his last year of college. And when a Basque boy got a good Catholic girl pregnant, the result was an inevitable wedding at St John's Cathedral. 'Your grandmother remembers only what she wants to remember,' he told Sophie. 'If you want to talk to a boy on the phone, I don't see why you shouldn't, but you better ask your dad first.' He watched her blow on her wet nails. 'Maybe you should talk to Lisa about all this girl stuff. She's going to be your stepmom in about a week.'

Sophie shook her head. 'I'd rather talk to you.'

'I thought you liked Lisa.'

'She's okay, but I like talking to you better. Besides, she stuck me at the end of the bridesmaid line.'

'Probably because you're shortest.'

'Maybe.' She studied her polish a moment, then looked up. 'Do you want me to paint your nails?'

'No way. The last time you did that, I forgot to take it off and the clerk at the Gas-n-Go gave me a funny look.'

'Pleeaase.'

'Forget it, Sophie.'

She frowned and carefully screwed the cap back on her polish. 'Not only am I last in the line now, I have to stand next to you-know-who.'

'Who?'

'Her.' Sophie pointed to the wall. 'Over there.'

'Delaney?' When she nodded Nick asked her, 'Why should that matter?'

'You *know*.'

'No. Why don't you tell me.'

'Grandma said that girl over there lived with your dad, and he was nice to her and mean to you. And he gave her nice clothes and stuff and you had to wear old jeans.'

'I like old jeans.' He reached for his pencil and studied Sophie's face. Her mouth was pinched at the corners like his mother's whenever she spoke of Delaney. Henry had certainly given Benita reasons for bitterness, but Nick didn't like to see Sophie affected by it. 'Whatever happened, or didn't happen, between me and my father, had nothing to do with Delaney.'

'You don't hate her?'

Hating Delaney had never been his problem. 'No, I don't hate her.'

'Oh.' She stuffed the fingernail polish into her backpack and reached for her coat on the back of her chair. 'Will you take me to my orthodontist appointment at the end of the month?'

Nick stood and helped her with her coat. Sophie's appointment was almost a two-hour drive one way. 'Can't your dad take you?'

'He'll be on his honeymoon.'

'Oh, yeah. I'll take you then.'

As he walked her to the door she wrapped one arm around his waist. 'Are you sure you're never getting married, Uncle Nick?'

'Yes.'

'Grandma says you just need to find a nice Catholic girl. Then you'll be happy.'

'I'm already happy.'

'Grandma says you need to fall in love with a Basque woman.'

'Sounds like you've been spending way too much time talking about me with Grandma.'

'Well, I'm glad you're never getting married.'

He reached up and pulled a hunk of her smooth black hair. 'Why?'

' 'Cause I like having you all to myself.'

Nick stood on the sidewalk in front of his office and watch his niece walk down the street. Sophie was spending too much time with his mother. He figured it was only a matter of time before Benita lured her to the dark side, and Sophie began to nag him about marrying a nice 'Basque' woman, too.

He shoved his hands up to his knuckles in the front pockets of his jeans. Louie was the marrying kind. Not Nick. Louie's first marriage hadn't lasted more than six years, but his brother had liked being married. He'd liked the comfort of living with a woman. Louie had always known he would remarry. He'd always known he would fall in love, but it had taken him close to eight years after his divorce to find the right woman. Nick didn't doubt that his brother would be happy with Lisa.

The door to Delaney's salon swung open and an old lady with one of those silver-dome hairdos ambled out. As she passed, she stared at him as if she knew he was up to no good. He laughed beneath his breath and lifted his gaze to the window. Through the glass he watched Delaney sweep the floor, then head toward the back with a dustpan. He watched her straight shoulders and back, and the sway of her hips beneath a sweater skirt that clung to her round behind. A heavy ache settled in his groin, and he thought about perfect white breasts and pink feathers. He thought of her big brown eyes, her long lashes, and the lust pulling at her heavy lids, her mouth wet and swollen from his kiss.

I want you, she'd said, or rather he'd coerced her into saying it like he was some lovesick loser begging her to want him. Never in his life had he demanded a woman tell him she wanted him. He didn't have to. It had never mattered if those words were whispered from a woman's soft pink lips. Apparently it did now.

No maybes about it anymore. Henry knew what he was doing when he drew up that will. He'd reminded Nick of just what it felt like to want something he could never have, to ache for something held just beyond his grasp. Something he might touch but never really possess.

A few light snowflakes drifted in front of Nick's face, and he walked back into his office and grabbed his jacket off the back of the chair. Some men made the mistake of confusing lust for love. Not Nick. He didn't love Delaney. What he felt for her was worse than love. It was gut-twisting lust, and it was turning him inside out. He was walking around and behaving like a complete asshole with a monster-sized hard-on for a woman who hated him most of the time.

Delaney pushed the tomatoes to one side of her plate, then speared a piece of endive and chicken.

'How's business?' Gwen asked, immediately arousing Delaney's suspicion. Gwen never asked about the salon.

'Pretty good.' She looked across the table and stuck the lettuce into her mouth. Her mother was up to something. She never should have agreed to meet for lunch in a restaurant where she couldn't yell without causing a scene. 'Why?' she asked.

'Helen always does the hair for the Christmas fashion show, but this year I spoke with the other members of the board, and I've convinced them to let you do the hair.' Gwen poked around at her fettucini, then set her fork aside. 'I thought you could use the publicity.'

More than likely it was a way for her mother to rope her into serving on some sort of dumb committee. 'Just the hair? That's it?'

Gwen reached for her hot tea with lemon. 'Well, I thought you could be in the show, too.'

There it was. The real reason. Styling hair for the show was a bone. What Gwen really wanted was to parade around in matching mother-daughter lamé like they were twins. There were two rules of the fashion show, the dress or costumes had to be made by hand and had to reflect the season. 'You and me together?'

'Of course I'd be there.'

'Dressed alike?'

'Similar.'

Not a chance. Delaney clearly remembered the year she'd been forced to dress as Rudolph. She might not have minded if she hadn't been sixteen. 'I couldn't possibly be in the show and do the hair.'

'Helen does.'

'I'm not Helen.' She reached for a breadstick. 'I'll do the hair, but I want the name of my salon printed in the program and announced at both the start and finish of the show.'

Gwen looked a little less than pleased. 'I'll have someone on the board get hold of you.'

'Great. When is the show?'

'During the Winter Festival. It's always the third Saturday, a few days before the ice sculpture contest.' She set her cup back on the saucer and sighed. 'Remember when Henry was mayor and we used to walk beside him and help with the judging?'

Of course she remembered. Each December businesses in Truly made huge snow sculptures in Larkspur Park, drawing tourists for hundreds of miles. Delaney remembered her frozen cheeks and nose, and her big fluffy coat and furry hat as she walked beside Henry and her mother. She remembered the crisp smell of ice and winter and the feel of hot chocolate warming her hands.

'Remember the year he let you choose the winner?'

She'd probably been twelve, and she'd chosen Quality Meats and Poultry's fifteen-foot Lamb Chop. Delaney took another stab at her salad. She'd forgotten about Lamb Chop.

'I need to talk to you about Christmas,' Gwen said.

Delaney assumed she would spend it at her mother's, complete with a *real* tree, shiny presents, eggnog, chestnuts roasting on an open fire. The whole bit.

'Max and I are leaving on a Caribbean cruise on the twentieth, the day after the Winter Festival starts.'

'What?' She carefully set her fork back on her plate. 'I didn't know the two of you were that serious.'

'Max and I are getting close, and he suggested a warm vacation to find out just how strongly we feel for each other.'

Gwen had been a widow for all of six months and already had a serious boyfriend. Delaney couldn't remember the last time she'd had a serious *date*. Suddenly she felt real pathetic, like an old spinster cat lady.

'I thought you and I could celebrate Christmas when I get back.'

'Okay.' She hadn't realized how much she might have enjoyed a Christmas at home until she no longer had the option. Well, spending the holidays alone was nothing she hadn't done before.

'And now that it has begun to snow, you should park your little car in my garage and drive Henry's Cadillac.'

Delaney waited to hear the conditions, like she'd have to spend the night on weekends, attend a council meeting of some sort, or wear practical pumps. When Gwen didn't elaborate, and reached for her fork instead, Delaney asked, 'What's the catch?'

'Why are you so suspicious all the time? I just want you to be safe this winter.'

'Oh.' It had been years since she'd driven in the snow, and she found it wasn't like riding a bike. She'd forgotten how. She'd much rather slide through stop signs in Henry's big silver car rather than her Miata. 'Thanks, I'll pick it up tomorrow.'

After lunch, she took the rest of the day off and drove to Lisa's to drop off some books on braids and pick up her brides-maid dress. The red stretch velvet dress was the color of wine in one light but changed to a deep burgundy in another. It was beautiful, and if it hadn't been for Delaney's hair, it would have looked great on her, but so many different shades of red all on one person made her look like a Picasso. She ran a hand over her stomach, smoothing the cool material beneath her palm.

'I didn't think about your hair,' Lisa admitted as she stood back and viewed Delaney in her bedroom mirror. 'Maybe you could wear one of those big straw hats.'

'Not a chance.' She tilted her head to the side and studied her reflection. 'I could always go back to my natural color.'

'What is your natural color?'

'I'm not really sure anymore. When I retouch my roots, it's sort of a warm blond.'

'Can you change it back without having your hair fall out?'

Delaney put her hands on her hips and turned to face her friend. 'What is wrong with you people in this town? Of course I can remove the tint without my hair falling out. I know what I'm doing. I've been doing this for years.' As she spoke, the volume of her voice rose. 'I'm not Helen. I don't give bad cuts!'

'Geez, I just asked.'

'Yeah, you and everyone else.' She unzipped the back of the dress and stepped out of it.

'Who else?'

The image of Nick sitting on her couch popped into her head. His hot mouth on hers. His fingers pressed into her thigh. She wished she could hate him for making her want him, for making her tell him that she wanted him, then leaving her alone to dream about him all night. But she couldn't hate him, and she was so confused about what happened that she didn't want to talk about it with anyone until she figured it out. Not even with Lisa. She laid the dress on the plaid quilt covering Lisa's bed then stepped into a pair of jeans. 'Never mind. It's not important.'

'What? Is your mother still bugging you about being a stylist?'

'No, in fact she asked me to style hair for the Christmas fashion show.' Delaney looked up from the button on her pants. 'She thought she could trick me and get me to do that mother-daughter thing I had to do when I was growing up.'

Lisa laughed. 'Remember that gold lamé dress with the big sash and that bow on the back?'

'How could I forget.' She pulled an angora sweater over her head then sat on the edge of the bed and shoved her feet into her Doc Marten's. 'And then my mother is going on a Caribbean cruise over Christmas with Max Harrison.'

'Your mother and Max?' Lisa sat next to Delaney. 'That's weird. I can't picture your mother with anyone but Henry.'

'I think Max is good for her.' She tied one boot, then worked on the other. 'Anyway, this is the first time I've been home for ten Christmases, and she leaves. That's pretty typical, when I think about it.'

'You can come to my house. I'll be living with Louie and Sophie, and we'll have Christmas there.'

Delaney stood and reached for her dress. 'I can just see myself breaking bread with the Allegrezzas.'

'You'll be "breaking bread" with us at my wedding dinner.'

Apprehension settled in Delaney's stomach as she slowly put the dress on the hanger. 'It's a buffet, right?'

'No. It's a sit-down dinner at the Lake Shore Hotel.'

'I thought the dinner was after the rehearsal.'

'No, that's the buffet.'

'How many people will be at this dinner?'

'Seventy-five.'

Delaney relaxed. With so many guests, it would be quite easy to avoid certain members of Louie's family. 'Well, don't seat me by Benita. She'll probably stab me with her butter knife.' And Nick? He was so unpredictable, she couldn't guess what he might do.

'She's not that bad.'

'Not to you.' Delaney gathered her coat and headed outside.

'Think about Christmas,' Lisa called after her.

'Okay,' she promised just before she drove away, but there wasn't even a remote chance she would sit across the table from Nick. What a nightmare. She'd have to spend the entire time trying not to get drawn in by him, looking anywhere but his eyes and mouth and hands. *You better not be around here on June fourth, otherwise I'm going to take what you've owed me for ten years.*

She didn't owe him anything. He'd used her to get back at Henry, and they both knew it. *Exactly when was that? When you begged me to touch you all over?* She hadn't begged him. More like asked. And she'd been young and naive.

Delaney pulled her little car next to Nick's Jeep and bolted up the stairs. She wasn't prepared to see him. Each time she thought of his mouth on her breast and his hand between her thighs, her cheeks got hot. She would have had sex with him right there on her couch, no doubt about it. All he had to do was look at her and he sucked her in like a Hoover. All he had to do was touch her and she wanted to suck him like a Hoover.

He had the ability to make her forget who he was. Who she was, and their past together. *I told you not to worry and that I'd take care of you, but you looked at me like I was some kind of rapist and left with Henry.* She didn't really believe him now any more than she had the other night. He had to be lying. But why would he lie? It wasn't like he'd been trying to sweet-talk her out of her clothes. She'd pretty much abandoned all modesty by that point.

She laid her dress on the couch and reached for Nick's *txapel* sitting on the coffee table where she'd left it. Her fingertips traced the leather band and smooth wool. It didn't matter now. Nothing had changed. That night at Angel Beach was old history and best left in the past. Even if it weren't for Henry's will, there was no future for the two of them. He was a womanizer and she was leaving just as soon as possible.

With the beret in one hand Delaney walked back outside to the parking lot. Nick's Jeep was still there, and she opened the driver's side door. The beige leather interior was still warm as if he'd arrived just before she'd returned to her apartment. The Jeep key was in the ignition, and his Basque cross hung from the rearview mirror. A big box of tools, an extension cord, and three jars of wood putty were tossed in the back. He'd obviously been living in Truly too long, but she supposed if she were a thief, she'd think twice about stealing from an Allegrezza. She set his beret on the leather seat, then turned and hurried back up to her apartment. She didn't want him to have any reason to walk up her stairs. Obviously, she had no willpower where he was concerned, and it was just best to avoid him as much as possible.

Delaney sat on her couch and tried to tell herself she wasn't listening for sounds from below. She wasn't listening for the rattle of keys or the crunch of gravel beneath heavy boots. She wasn't listening, but she heard his office door open and close, his keys and the scuff of boots. She heard nothing but silence when he discovered his *txapel* and she imagined him pausing to look up the stairs at her apartment. The silence grew as she listened for his footsteps. Finally, the Jeep's engine rumbled to life and he rolled out of the parking lot below.

Delaney slowly let out a breath and closed her eyes. Now all she had to do was get through Lisa's wedding. With seventy-five guests, she could easily ignore Nick. How hard could it be?

14

It was a nightmare. Only this time, Delaney was definitely awake. The evening had started out wonderfully enough. The wedding ceremony had gone smoothly. Lisa looked beautiful, and the pictures afterward hadn't lasted too long. She'd left Henry's Cadillac at the church and ridden to the Lake Shore with Lisa's cousin Ali, who owned a salon in Boise. For the first time in a long while, Delaney had been able to chat hair trends with another professional, but most important, she'd been able to avoid Nick.

Until now. She'd known about the wedding dinner of course, but she hadn't known the tables would be organized in a large open rectangle with all the guests seated on the outside so everyone could see everyone else. And she hadn't known about the arranged seating or she would have switched her engraved placecard to avoid the nightmare she was living.

Beneath the table, something brushed the side of Delaney's foot, and she would bet it wasn't an amorous mouse. She pulled both feet beneath her chair and stared down at the remains of her filet mignon, wild rice, and asparagus spears. Somehow, she'd been seated on the groom's side, sandwiched between Narcisa Hormaechea, who clearly didn't care for her, and the man who refused to cooperate and let her ignore him any longer. The harder she tried to pretend Nick didn't exist, the more pleasure he took in provoking her. Like *accidentally* bumping her arm and making her rice shoot off her fork.

'Did you bring your handcuffs?' he asked next to her left ear as he reached across her for a bottle of Basque Red. His tuxedo lapel brushed her bare arm.

Like an erotic movie wrapped for continuous play, visions of his hot mouth on her naked breast played in her head. She couldn't even look at him without blushing like an embarrassed virgin, but she didn't need to actually see him to know when he raised his wine to his lips, or when his thumb stroked the clear stem, or when he shoved his black bow tie into a pocket and removed the black stud at his throat. She didn't have to look at him to know he wore his pleated cotton shirt and tuxedo jacket with the same casual ease he wore flannel and denim.

'Excuse me.' Narcisa touched Delaney's shoulder, and she turned her attention to the older woman, who had two white streaks on the sides in her perfect dome of black hair. Her brows were lowered and her brown eyes were magnified behind a pair of thick octagon-shaped glasses, making her appear a little like a myopic Bride of Frankenstein. 'Could you pass the butter, please?' she asked and pointed to a small bowl sitting by Nick's knife.

Delaney reached for the butter, careful to keep any part of her from touching Nick. She held her breath, waiting for him to say something rude, crude, or socially unacceptable. He didn't utter a word, and she immediately grew suspicious, wondering what he planned next.

'It was a beautiful wedding, don't you think?' Narcisa asked someone further down the table. She took the bowl from Delaney, then ignored her completely.

Delaney didn't really expect warm fuzzies from Benita's sister and turned her gaze to the bride and groom, who were surrounded by parents and grandparents on both sides.

Earlier, she'd braided Lisa's brown hair in an inside-out coronet. She'd stuck in a few sprigs of baby's breath, and wove in a piece of tulle. Lisa looked great in a white off-the-shoulder gown, and Louie was quite dapper in his black tails. Everyone seated near the bride and groom appeared happy, and even Benita Allegrezza smiled. Delaney didn't think she'd ever seen the woman smile, and she was surprised at how much younger Benita looked when she wasn't glaring. Sophie sat next to her father with her hair pulled up in a simple ponytail. Delaney would have loved to have gotten her hands and scissors on all that thick dark hair, but Sophie had insisted her grandmother fix it for her.

'When is it your turn to get married, Nick?' The booming question came from down the table.

Nick's quiet laughter mixed with the other noise in the room. 'I'm too young, Josu.'

'Too wild, you mean.'

Delaney glanced a few feet down the table. She hadn't seen Nick's uncle in a long time. Josu was stocky like a bull and had florid cheeks, due in part to the amount of vino he'd poured back.

'You just haven't found the right woman, but I'm sure you'll find a nice Basque girl,' Narcisa predicted.

'No Basque girls, Tia. You're all too stubborn.'

'You need someone stubborn. You're too handsome for your own good, and you need a girl who will tell you no. Someone who won't say yes to you all the time about everything. You need a good girl.'

Out of the corner of her eye, Delaney watched Nick's long blunt fingers brush the linen tablecloth. When he responded, his voice was smooth and sensual, 'Even good girls say yes eventually.'

'You're bad, Nick Allegrezza. My sister was too easy on you, and you've grown into a libertine. Your cousin Skip is always chasing skirts, too, so maybe it's genetic.' She paused and let out a long-suffering sigh. 'Well, how about you?'

It was probably too much to hope that Narcisa was talking to someone else. Delaney lifted her gaze to Nick's aunt and stared into her magnified eyes. 'Me?'

'Are you married?'

Delaney shook her head.

'Why not?' she asked, then looked Delaney over as if the answer was written somewhere. 'You're attractive enough.'

Not only was Delaney sick of that particular question, she was getting really tired of being treated as if there had to be something wrong with her because she was single. She leaned toward Narcisa and said just above a whisper, 'One man could never satisfy me. I need lots.'

'You're kidding?'

Delaney choked back her laughter. 'Don't tell anyone because I do have my standards.'

Narcisa blinked twice. 'What?'

She put her mouth even closer to Narcisa's ear. 'Well, he has to have teeth, for one.'

The older woman leaned back to get a good look at Delaney, and her mouth fell open. 'My lord.'

Delaney smiled and raised her glass to her lips. She hoped she'd scared Narcisa off the subject of marriage for a while.

Nick nudged her arm with his elbow and her wine sloshed. 'Have you found any more notes since Halloween?'

She lowered her glass and wiped a bead of wine from the corner of her mouth. She shook her head, doing her best to ignore him as much as possible.

'Did you part your hair with a lightening bolt?' Nick asked loud enough for those around them to hear.

Before the wedding, she'd done a zig-zag part, pulled the flat bangs behind her ears, and teased the crown into a nice little bouffant. With her hair back to blond, she thought she looked like a 60s go-go dancer. Delaney lifted her gaze up the pleats of his cotton shirt, to the exposed hollow of his tan throat. No way was she going to get sucked in by his eyes. 'I like it.'

'You dyed it again.'

'I dyed it back.' Unable to resist, she raised her gaze past his chin to his lips. 'I'm a natural blond.'

The corners of his sensuous mouth curved upward. 'I remember that about you, wild thing,' he said, then picked up his spoon and tapped it on the edge of his glass. When the room fell silent, he rose to his feet, looking like a model out of one of those bride magazines. 'As my brother's best man, it is my duty and honor to toast him and his new bride,' he began. 'When my big brother sees something he wants, he always goes after it with unyielding determination. The first time he met Lisa Collins, he knew he wanted her in his life. She didn't know it then, but she didn't stand a chance against his tenacity. I watched him proceed with an absolute certainty that left me bewildered and, I admit, envious.

'As always, I am in awe of my brother. He has found real joy with a wonderful woman, and I am happy for him.' He reached for his glass. 'To Louie and Lisa Allegrezza. *Ongi-etorri*, Lisa. Welcome.'

'To Louie and Lisa,' Delaney toasted with the other guests. She cast a glance upward and watched Nick tip back his head and drain his wine. Then he sat once again, relaxed and easy with his hands in the pockets of his wool pants. He pressed his leg against the length of hers, as if it were as unintentional as breathing. She knew better.

'*Ongi-etorri*,' Josu echoed, then unleashed a Basque yell that started out like mocking laughter but quickly changed into a cross between the ooh of a wolf's howl and the expiring ahh of a braying donkey. Other male relatives joined Josu and the dining room reverberated with the sounds. While each family member tried to outdo the other, Nick leaned in front of Delaney and grabbed her glass. He filled it and then his own, in typical Nick style: he didn't ask first. For one brief moment, he enveloped her in the smell of his skin and cologne. Her heart beat a little faster and her head got a little lighter as she breathed him in. Then he was gone and she could almost relax again.

Lisa's father hit his spoon against his glass and the room fell silent. 'Today my little girl . . .' he began, and Delaney shoved her plate away and folded her arms on the table. If she concentrated on Mr Collins, she could almost ignore Nick. If she concentrated on Mr Collins's hair, which was a lot whiter than she remembered, and his—

Nick lightly brushed his fingers over the top of her thigh, and she froze. Through the sheer barrier of nylon, his fingertips swept her from knee to the hem of her dress. Unfortunately, it was a short dress.

Delaney grabbed his wrist beneath the table and stopped his hand from sliding up the inside of her thigh. She looked into his face, but he wasn't looking back at her. His attention was focused on Lisa's father.

'. . . to my daughter and my new son, Louie,' Mr Collins finished.

With his free hand, Nick raised his wine glass and toasted the couple. As he took two big swallows, his thumb stroked the top of Delaney's leg. Back and forth his fingers caressed over the smooth nylon. Sensations she couldn't ignore settled low in her abdomen and she squeezed her legs together. 'Aren't you going to toast the happy couple?' he asked.

As carefully as possible, she shoved his hand, but his grasp tightened. She pushed a little harder and accidentally bumped Nick's aunt.

'What's that matter?' Narcisa asked. 'Why are you wiggling around?'

Because your libertine nephew is inching his hand up my thigh. 'No reason.'

Nick leaned toward her and whispered, 'Be still or people will think I'm copping a feel under the table.'

'You are!'

'I know.' He smiled and turned his attention to his uncle. 'Josu, how many sheep are you running this year?'

'Twenty thousand. Are you interested in working for me like when you were a boy?'

'Hell no.' He slanted her a look from the corner of his eye and chuckled deep in his chest. 'I have my hands full right here.' His hot palm warmed her flesh through her pantyhose, and Delaney sat perfectly still, trying to appear as if the heat from Nick's hand wasn't pouring through her body like a warm flood. It swept up her chest and down her thighs, tingling her breasts and pooling desire between her legs. Her grasp on his wrist tightened, but she was no longer sure if she was holding his hand to keep it from moving further up her leg, or to keep it from moving away.

'Nick.'

He tilted his head toward hers. 'Yes?'

'Let go.' She pasted a smile on her face like she and Nick were chatting up a good time, and let her gaze skim the crowd. 'Someone could see you.'

'Tablecloth is too long. I checked.'

'How did I end up sitting next to you anyway?'

He reached for his wine and said behind the glass, 'I switched your little name card with my Aunt Angeles's. She's the mean-looking lady sitting over there clutching her purse like someone's going to mug her. She's a Rottweiler.' He took a drink. 'You're more fun.'

Angeles stuck out like a storm cloud on an otherwise sunny day. Her hair was scraped up into a black bun, and her scowl lowered her dark brows. She obviously didn't like being stuck among Lisa's family. Delaney moved her gaze down the table, past the bride and groom to Nick's mother. Benita's dark eyes stared back at her, and Delaney recognized the look that used to unnerve her as a child. 'I know you're up to no good,' it said.

Delaney turned to Nick and whispered, 'You have to stop. Your mother is watching us. I think she knows.'

He looked into her face, then gazed past her to his mother. 'What does she know?'

'She's giving me the evil eye. She knows where you've got your hand.' Delaney glanced over her shoulder at Narcisa, but the older woman had turned and was talking to someone else. No one but Benita seemed to be paying any attention to them.

'Relax.' His palm slid up another half an inch, and the tips of his fingers drifted along the elastic leg of her underwear.

Relax. Delaney wanted to shut her eyes and moan.

'She doesn't know anything.' He paused a moment, then said, 'Except maybe that your nipples are hard and it isn't cold in here.'

Delaney looked down at her breasts and the two very distinct points in the red velvet. 'Jerk.' She shoved his hand at the same time she shoved her chair backward. Grabbing her velvet handbag, she walked from the dining room and hurried down two different narrow hallways before she found the women's restroom. Once inside, she took a deep breath and looked at herself in the mirror. Beneath the fluorescent lighting, her cheeks looked flushed, her eyes overly bright.

There was definitely something wrong with her. Something that made her brain-dead where Nick was concerned. Something that allowed him to caress her in a room filled with people.

She tossed her red velvet handbag on the counter and ran a paper towel under cold water. She pressed it against her warm face and sucked in a breath. Maybe she'd been on the wagon so long, she was suffering from sexual deprivation. Starving for attention and affection like an abandoned cat.

A toilet flushed behind her and a hotel employee appeared from a stall. As the woman washed her hands, Delaney opened her bag and pulled out a tube of Rebel Red lipstick.

'If you're with the wedding party, they're cutting the cake now.'

Delaney looked at the woman through the mirror and smeared red across her bottom lip. 'Thanks. I guess I better get back then.' She watched the hotel employee leave and dropped her lipstick back into her little purse. Using her wet fingers, she smoothed the front of her hair and fluffed the back. If Lisa and Louie were cutting their wedding cake, then dinner was officially over and she wouldn't have to sit by Nick any longer.

She grabbed her bag and swung open the door. Nick leaned back against the opposite wall in the narrow hallway. The sides of his tuxedo jacket were brushed aside, and his hands were buried in his front pockets. When he saw her, he pushed away from the wall.

'Stay away from me, Nick.' She held out a hand to hold him off.

He grabbed her arm and pulled her against his chest. 'I can't,' he said softly. He crushed her to him, and his mouth slashed across hers in a fiery kiss that left her numb. He tasted like unchecked passion and warm wine. His tongue caressed and plundered, and when he pulled back, his breathing was uneven, like he'd just run the mile.

Delaney placed a hand over her racing heart and licked the taste of him from her lips. 'We can't do this here.'

'You're right.' He grabbed her arm and propelled her down the hall until he found an unlocked linen closet. Once inside, he pressed her backward against the closed door, and Delaney had an impression of white towels and mop buckets before he was on her. Kissing her. Touching her anywhere his hands landed. Her palms slid up the pleats of his shirt to the warm sides of his neck, and she combed her fingers through the side of his hair. The kiss became an avaricious feeding frenzy of mouths and lips and tongues. They tore at each other. Her handbag fell to the floor, and she pushed at the shoulders of his jacket. She kicked the little velvet pumps from her feet and raised onto the balls of her feet. Like a complete wanton, she hooked a leg over his hip and strained against the swollen ridge of his erection.

He groaned his pleasure deep, deep within his chest, and pulled back to look at her through eyes heavy with lust. 'Delaney,' he said, his voice rough, then he repeated her name as if he couldn't quite believe she was with him. He kissed her face. Her throat. Her ear. 'Tell me you want me.'

'I do,' she whispered, pushing his jacket from his shoulders.

'Say it.' He shrugged out of the jacket and tossed it to the side. Then his hands were on her breasts, and he brushed her hard nipples through the velvet dress and lace bra. 'Say my name.'

'Nick.' She trailed kisses down his neck to the hollow of his throat. 'I want you, Nick.'

'Here?' His hands moved to her hips, her behind, holding her against him, grinding against her soft inner thigh.

'Yes.'

'Now? Where anyone could walk in and find us?'

'Yes.' She was beyond caring. She ached with desire and emptiness and the need for him to fill her with pleasure. 'Tell me you want me, too.'

'I've always wanted you,' he breathed into her hair. 'Always.'

The tension inside her built and pulled and made her mindless to anything but him. She wanted to climb on top of him. Inside him, and stay there forever. He rubbed his straining erection back and forth against her aroused flesh.

Nick removed her leg from him and bunched the hem of her dress and slip in one fist, holding them up as he shoved her hose and silky panties down her thighs to her knees. He planted his foot in the crotch of her underwear and nylons, pushing the garments to her feet. Delaney kicked them free, and his hand moved between their bodies, and he touched her between her legs. His fingers slid into her slick flesh and she shuddered, feeling herself slowly propelled toward climax with each caress. A moan slipped past her lips, a husky sound of need.

'I want deep inside you.' His gaze locked on hers and he shrugged off his suspenders, leaving them to hang at his sides. His hands tore at the waistband, fumbling with the button and zipper closing his wool pants. Delaney reached for him and pushed his cotton briefs. His penis jutted free in her palm, huge and hard and smooth as polished teakwood. His skin stretched tight and he slowly pushed himself into her tight grasp. 'I have to have you – *now*.'

Nick lifted her and she wrapped her legs around his waist and her arms around his neck. The voluptuous head of his hot erection nudged her slick opening. Their flesh touched, and he reached between their bodies and wrapped his hand around the shaft of his penis. He forced her down as he thrust upward inside, stretching her until a stitch of pain invaded Delaney's erotic haze, but he withdrew, then buried himself deep, and there was nothing but intense pleasure. The penetration was so powerful and complete, his knees buckled and for one tense moment she feared he might drop her, but he didn't. His grip on her hips tightened; he withdrew then plunged into her again, deeper. 'Sweet Jesus,' he gasped as his powerful body crushed her against the door. His chest heaved as he fought to pull air into his lungs, and his uneven breath whispered across her temple, the sound of his passion and pleasure all the same.

Her legs tightened around his waist and she moved with

him, slowly at first, then faster and faster as the pressure built. Her heart beat in her ears as he hammered into her, over and over, pushing her closer to orgasm with each thrust of his pumping hips. Like their frantic mating, there was nothing slow or easy about the intense pleasure that grabbed her, pulled her down, and turned her inside out. Tremor upon tremor shook her, rippled across her flesh, and robbed her of breath. She felt weightless, and a sound like a hurricane thundered in her head. Her back arched and she clutched at his shirt. She opened her mouth to scream, but the sound died in her dry throat. His strong arms crushed her against his chest, his big shoulders shook, and he held her tight as wave after luscious wave continued to roll through her. Her muscles contracted, gripping him tight within her. Her spasms had barely slowed when his began. A deep groan rumbled in his chest as he plunged into her. His muscles turned as hard as stone, and he whispered her name one last time.

When it was over, she felt battered and bruised, as if she'd just lived through a battle. Nick rested his forehead on the door behind her until his breathing slowed and he pulled back far enough to look into her face. He was still embedded deep within her body and their clothes were in disarray. Carefully he eased himself out of her, and she lowered her feet to the ground. Her dress slid down her hips and thighs. His gray eyes looked into hers, but he didn't utter a word. He studied her for a moment longer, his gaze more guarded with each passing second, then he reached for his pants and pulled them to his waist.

'Aren't you going to say anything?'

He glanced at her, then returned his gaze to his pants. 'Don't tell me you're one of those women who like to talk afterward?'

Something wonderful and awful had just happened, she wasn't quite sure which. Something more than sex. She'd had her share of orgasms in the past, some really good ones, too, but what she'd just experienced was more than getting off. More than waves crashing and the earth quaking. Nick Allegrezza had taken her someplace she'd never been before, and she felt like sitting down and crying about it. A sob escaped her throat, and she pressed her fingers to her lips. She didn't want to cry. She didn't want him to see her cry.

His gaze shot to her as he shoved his shirttails into his pants. 'Are you crying?'

She shook her head, but her eyes began to water.

'Yes, you are.' He threaded his arms through his suspenders and snapped them in place.

'I'm not.' He'd just given her the most intense pleasure of her life, and now he calmly got dressed as if this sort of thing happened to him all the time. Maybe it did. She wanted to scream. To curl up her fist and hit him. She'd thought they'd shared something special, but obviously they hadn't. She felt raw and exposed, her body still aching from his touch. If he said something nasty, she was afraid she'd shatter. 'Don't do this to me, Nick.'

'The damage is done,' he said as he retrieved his jacket from the floor. 'Tell me you're taking some form of birth control.'

She could feel the blood drain from her face and she shook her head. She thought back to her last period and felt a glimmer of relief. 'It's the wrong time of the month for me to get pregnant.'

'Honey, I'm Catholic. A lot of us are conceived at the wrong time of the month.' He pushed his arms through the sleeves of his jacket and straightened the collar. 'I haven't forgotten a condom in about ten years. How about you?'

'Ah . . .' She was a woman of the nineties. In charge of her life and her body, but for some reason she couldn't talk about this with Nick without getting embarrassed. 'Yeah.'

'What exactly does "ah . . . yeah" mean?'

'You're the first in a really long time, and before this, I was careful.'

He studied her for a moment. 'Okay,' he said and tossed her underwear and pantyhose to her. 'Where's your coat?'

She clutched the garments to her chest, suddenly feeling shy and embarrassed. An odd delayed reaction, considering what she'd held in her hand a few moments before. 'On a rack by the front doors. Why?'

'I'm taking you home.'

Home had never sounded so good.

'Get dressed before a maid decides she needs some towels or something.' His unreadable gaze stared into hers as he pulled on his cuffs. 'I'll be right back,' he said, then slowly opened the door. 'Don't go anywhere.'

Once she was alone, Delaney looked around the room. She spotted her handbag by her left foot, a velvet pump beneath a step chair, and the other beside an empty bucket. Without Nick to distract her, thoughts and self-recriminations came rushing at her. She couldn't believe what she'd done. She'd had unprotected sex with Nick Allegrezza in a linen closet in the Lake Shore Hotel. He'd made her lose complete control with nothing more than a kiss, and if it weren't for the lingering physical proof, she probably wouldn't believe it even now.

She carefully sat on the step chair and put on her underwear and pantyhose. Just last month she'd assured Louie that she and Nick wouldn't do anything to cause gossip at his wedding, yet she'd had wild sex with his brother behind an unlocked door where anyone could have caught them. If anyone found out, she'd never live it down. She'd probably have to kill herself.

Just as she pulled her hose to her waist and shoved her feet into the shoes, the door swung open and Nick entered the small room. She had trouble looking at him as he held her coat open for her. 'I need to tell Lisa I'm leaving.'

'I told her you got sick and I'm taking you home.'

'Did she believe you?' She glanced up quickly, then shoved her arms into her wool coat.

'Narcisa saw you run out of the dining room and told everyone you looked like death.'

'Gee, maybe I should thank her.'

They left out a side door, and white downy snow drifted from the black sky and settled on their hair and shoulders. A new layer slid inside Delaney's pumps as she made her way across the parking lot toward Nick's Jeep. Her feet slipped from beneath her, and she would have fallen on her behind if he hadn't reached out and grabbed her upper arm. His grasp tightened as they walked across the slick ground, but neither of them spoke, the only sound the crunch of snow beneath the soles of their shoes.

He helped her into the Jeep, but didn't wait for the engine to warm before he shoved the four-wheel drive into gear and headed away from the Lake Shore. The inside of the Jeep was pitched in darkness and smelled of leather seats and Nick. He stopped at the corner of Chipmunk and Main and reached for her, practically pulling her into his lap. The tips of his fingers touched her cheek as he looked down into her face. Then slowly his head lowered and he pressed his mouth to hers. He kissed her once, twice, and stayed the third time to leave a soft lingering kiss on her lips.

He pulled back and whispered, 'Buckle your seatbelt.' The wide tires spun until the knobby tread found traction, and cool air blasted Delaney's warm cheeks from the heater vent. She buried her chin in the collar of her coat and cast a sideways glance at him. The dash light cast his face and hands in a green glow. Melted snow glistened like tiny emeralds in his black hair and on the shoulders of his tuxedo jacket. A street lamp illuminated the inside of the Jeep for several seconds as he blew past her salon.

'You missed the turn to my apartment.'

'No I didn't.'

'Aren't you taking me home?'

'Yep. My home. Did you think we were finished?' He shifted into a lower gear and took a left along the east end of the lake. 'We haven't even begun.'

She turned in her seat and looked at him. 'Begun doing what exactly?'

'What we did in that closet wasn't near enough.'

The thought of his fully nude body pressed to hers wasn't exactly abhorrent, in fact it turned her insides warm. As Nick had said earlier, the damage was done. Why not spend the night with a man who was very good at making her body come alive in ways she'd never known possible? She'd been on the wagon a long time and wasn't likely to get a better offer in the foreseeable future. One night. One night she would probably regret, but she'd worry about that tomorrow. 'Are you trying to tell me – in your own typically macho way – that you want to make love again?'

He glanced at her. 'I'm not *trying* to tell you anything. I want you. You want me. Someone is going to end up wearing nothing but a satisfied smile on her lips.'

'I don't know, Nick, I might talk afterward. Do you think you can handle it?'

'I can handle anything you can think up, and a few things you've probably never even thought of.'

'Do I have a choice?'

'Sure, wild thing. I have four bedrooms. You can choose which one we use first.'

Nick didn't scare her. She knew he wouldn't force her to do anything against her will. Of course, around him, she seemed to pretty much abandon anything resembling a will of her own.

The Jeep slowed and turned into a wide driveway lined on both sides with Ponderosa and lodge pole pine. Out of the dense forest rose a huge house made of split log and lake rock. Its cathedral windows spilled panels of light on the freshly fallen snow. Nick reached for his visor and the middle of three garage doors opened. The four-wheel drive rolled between his Bayliner and Harley.

The inside of the house was just as impressive as the outside. Lots of exposed beams, muted colors, and natural fibers. Delaney stood in front of a wall of windows and looked outside onto the deck. It was still snowing, and the white flakes accumulated on the rail and landed in the Jacuzzi. Nick had taken her coat, and with the ceiling so high and the rooms so open, she was surprised she wasn't cold.

'What do you think?'

She turned and watched him approach her from the kitchen. He'd taken off his jacket and his shoes. One more black stud had been removed from his pleated white shirt, and he'd rolled the sleeves up his forearms. The black suspenders lay flat against his wide chest. He handed her a Budweiser, then took a drink from his own. His eyes watched her over the bottle, and she got the feeling he cared about her answer more than he wanted her to know.

'It's beautiful, but huge. Do you live here alone?'

He lowered the beer. 'Of course. Who else?'

'Oh, I don't know. Maybe a family of five.' She glanced up at the balcony which she presumed lead to those four bedrooms he'd mentioned. 'Are you planning for a large family with lots of children someday?'

'I don't plan to get married.'

His answer pleased her, but she didn't understand why. It wasn't like she cared if he wanted to spend his life with another woman, or kiss her, or make love to her, or overwhelm her with his touch.

'No kids, either . . . unless you're pregnant.' He glanced at her stomach as if he could tell by looking. 'When will you know for sure?'

'I already know I'm not.'

'I hope you're right.' He moved to the window and looked out into the night. 'I know single women are getting pregnant on purpose these days. Being illegitimate doesn't have the stigma it used to have, but that doesn't make it easy. I know what it's like to grow up like that. I don't want to do that to some poor kid.'

The Y of his suspenders lay against his back and up over his big shoulders. She remembered the times she'd seen his mother and Josu sitting in the gymnasium watching school plays and holiday programs. Henry and Gwen would have been there, too, somewhere. She'd never thought about what that must have been like for Nick. She set her bottle on a cherrywood coffee table and moved to him.

'You're not like Henry. You wouldn't deny your own child.' She wanted to slide her hands around his waist to his flat stomach and press her cheek against his spine, but she held back. 'Henry's probably spinning in his grave.'

'He's probably congratulating himself.'

'Why? He didn't want us to—' Her eyes widened. 'Oh, no, Nick. I forgot about the will. I guess you forgot, too.'

He turned to face her. 'For a few crucial moments, it did slip my mind.'

She looked into his eyes. He didn't appear all that upset. 'I won't tell anyone. I don't want that property. I promise.'

'That's up to you.' He brushed a stray piece of hair from her face and softly traced her ear with his fingertips. Then he took her hand and led her upstairs to his bedroom.

As they moved up the steps, she thought about Henry's will and the repercussions of tonight. Nick didn't strike her as the type of man who let anything slip his mind, especially not his multimillion dollar inheritance. He had to care for her as much as she feared she was beginning to care for him. He risked a lot to be with her, while she risked nothing but a little self-respect. And actually, when she thought of it, she didn't feel dirty or used or regret anything. Not now – maybe she would in the morning.

Delaney stepped into a room with a thick beige carpet and a set of closed French doors leading to an upper deck. There was a huge hardwood mission bed with pillows and comforters of striped sage-green and beige. Keys were thrown on one dresser, and a newspaper lay unopened on the other. There wasn't a flower printed on anything, no spots of lace or strings of fringe in sight. Not even on the bolsters. It was a man's room. Elk antlers hung above the rock mantel. The bed was unmade, and a pair of Levi's was thrown over a chair.

As he set their beer bottles on a nightstand, Delaney raised her hands to the black studs and worked them free until the shirt lay open to his waist. 'It's time I got to see you naked,' she said, then slid her palms up his warm skin. Her fingers combed through the fine hair growing in a dark line up his belly and across his chest. She pushed the white cotton and suspenders from his shoulders and down his arms.

He balled the shirt in one hand and tossed it to the floor. She ran her gaze over his taut skin, powerful chest, and flat brown nipples surrounded by dark hair. She swallowed and thought maybe she should check for drool. Only one word came to mind. 'Wow,' she said and pressed her hand against his flat stomach. She ran her palm up his ribs and looked into his gray eyes. He watched her from beneath lowered lids as she stripped him to his BVDs. He was beautiful. His legs were long and thick with muscles. Her fingers traced the tattoo circling his biceps. She touched his chest and shoulders, and slid her hands over his back and rounded behind. When her examination moved south, he grabbed her wrist and took over.

He slowly undressed her, then laid her on soft flannel sheets. His warm skin pressed the length of hers, and he took his time making love to her.

His touch was different from before. His hands lingered over her body, and he seduced her with stirring, languid kisses. He teased her breasts with his hot mouth and slick tongue, and when he entered her, his thrusts were slow and controlled. He held her face between his palms and his gaze locked with hers, holding himself back as he drove her wild.

She felt herself propelled toward orgasm, and her eyes drifted shut.

'Open your eyes,' he said, his voice husky. 'Look at me. I want you to see my face when I make you come.'

Her lids opened and she looked into his intense gaze. Something bothered her about his request, but she didn't have time to think about it before he thrust harder, deeper, and she wrapped one leg around his behind and forgot about everything but the hot tingles building with steady pressure in her body.

It wasn't until just before dawn the next morning as he kissed her good-bye at her door, that she thought about it again. As she watched him drive away, she remembered the look in his eyes as he'd held her face between his palms. It was as if he were watching her from a distance, yet at the same time wanting her to know it was Nick Allegrezza who held her and kissed her and drove her wild.

He made love to her in his bed and later in the Jacuzzi, but neither time had been like that hurried, hungry mating in the linen closet when he'd touched her with an urgency and need he hadn't been able to control. She'd never felt so wanted as she had smashed against his chest in the Lake Shore Hotel. '*I have to have you – now*,' he'd said, as desperate for her as she'd been for him. His touch had been needy and greedy, and she craved it more than the slow lingering caresses.

Delaney shut her apartment door behind her and unbuttoned her coat. They hadn't talked of seeing each other again. He hadn't said he'd call her, and even though she knew it was probably for the best, disappointment tugged at her heart. Nick was the kind of guy a girl couldn't depend on for anything but great sex, and it was best not to even think about things like next time. Best but impossible.

The sun rose over dense jagged pine, topped with snow. Silvery rays spread across the partially frozen lake to the bottom of Nick's retaining wall. He stood behind the French doors in his bedroom and watched brilliant light stretch across his deck, chasing away dusky shadows. The snow sparkled like it was embedded with tiny diamonds, so bright he was forced to turn away. His gaze fell on his bed, the sheets and comforter shoved to the very end.

Now he knew. Now he knew what it was like to hold her and touch her as he'd always wanted. Now he knew what it was like to live out his oldest fantasy, to have Delaney in his bed, looking into his eyes with him buried deep inside her. Her wanting him. Him pleasing her.

Nick had been with his share of women. Maybe more than some men, but less than he'd been given credit for. He'd been with women who liked their sex slow or fast, raunchy or strictly missionary. Women who thought he should do most of the work, and those who'd gone overboard to please him. Some of the women he'd shared friendships with, others he'd never seen again. Most had known what to do with their mouths and hands, a few were just drunken episodes he'd mostly forgotten, but none of them had made him lose control. Not until Delaney.

Once he'd pulled her into that closet, there'd been no turning back. Once she'd kissed him like she wanted to eat him alive, hooking her leg over his hip and grinding against his hard-on, nothing had mattered but losing himself in her hot slick body – not Henry's will, and certainly not the chance of discovery by a hotel employee. Nothing had mattered but possessing her. Then he did and the feeling nearly sent him to his knees. It shook him to the core, changing everything he thought he knew about sex. Sex was sometimes slow and easy, other times fast and sweaty, but never like with Delaney. Never had it slammed into him like a hot fist.

Now he knew, and he wished he didn't. It ate a hole in his gut and made him hate her as much as he wanted to hold her close and never let her leave him. But she would leave. She would leave Truly, blowing out of town in her little yellow car.

Now he knew, and it was hell.

15

Delaney combed her fingers through the back of Lanna's damp hair and eyed her critically in the salon mirror. 'What about if we cut it to here?' she asked, moving her hands to about ear level. 'You have a short enough jaw line that you'd look really good in a short bob. I could bevel the back and you could flip it up.'

Lanna tilted her head to one side and studied her reflection. 'What about bangs?'

'Your forehead is wide so you really don't need bangs.'

Lanna took a deep breath and let it out slowly. 'Go for it.'

Delaney reached for her comb. 'You don't have to act like I'm going to be drilling on your teeth.'

'I haven't had short hair since fourth grade.' Lanna slid her hand from beneath the silver cape and scratched her chin. 'I don't think Lonna's ever had hers short.'

Delaney sectioned Lanna's hair, then clipped it. 'Really?' She picked up her scissors. 'Is your sister still seeing Nick Allegrezza?' she asked as if she had no more than a passing interest.

'Yeah. She sees him off and on.'

'Oh.' Delaney hadn't seen him in over two weeks, not since the night of Lisa's wedding. Well, she'd *seen* him. She'd seen him across a crowded room at a Downtown Business

Association meeting, and she'd seen him as she'd slid through a stop sign at the intersection of Main and First, nearly broadsiding his Jeep with Henry's big Cadillac. She'd managed to hook a right, he a left. That same evening he left a message on her answering machine: 'Get some damn snowtires,' he said, then hung up. She hadn't seen him again until yesterday when he and Sophie had walked out the back door of his office as she'd been throwing trash in the Dumpster. He'd stopped by the driver's side of his Jeep and looked at her, his eyes hot, touching her everywhere. And she'd stood there, the waste basket in her arms forgotten, stunned by the emotion twisting her stomach. 'Uncle Nick,' Sophie had called to him, but he hadn't answered. He hadn't said anything. 'Let's go, Uncle Nick.' He glanced over his shoulder at his niece, then back to Delaney.

'I see you still don't have snowtires.'

'Ah . . . no.' She stared into his eyes and felt her head get light and her stomach fuzzy.

'Come on, Uncle Nick.'

'Okay Sophie,' he'd said, his gaze moving over her one last time before he'd turned away.

'I don't think Lonna has seen Nick for a few weeks,' Lanna said, breaking into Delaney's thoughts. 'At least I don't think he's called and wanted her to meet him somewhere. She would have told me if he had.'

Delaney cut a line along the nape of Lanna's neck. 'Do you two have that twin connection going on and tell each other everything?'

'We don't tell each other *everything*. We do talk about the men we sleep with though. But she's more promiscuous and has more interesting stories. She and Gail used to sit around and swap stories about Nick. Of course that was back when Gail still thought she had a chance of becoming Mrs Allegrezza.'

Delaney reached for a duck clip and slowly combed out a section of hair. 'She doesn't think that anymore?'

'Not so much now, and she was so sure he'd move her in, but he never even invited her to spend the night.'

He hadn't invited Delaney, either. At the time, she'd had no intention of actually spending the night with Nick. She knew how bad she looked every morning, and she'd had no intention of waking up with someone she suspected got out of bed looking like a cover model. But she didn't want to be just another of *his women*, either. She'd let herself think that maybe she was special since he risked losing his Angel Beach and Silver Creek property to be with her. She remembered something else Lanna had told her once, too. Nick didn't take women home with him, but he'd taken her. She'd hoped maybe she'd been different from the others, but he hadn't even given her a call, so she guessed she wasn't.

'Are you going to be in the Christmas fashion show?' Delaney asked her client. She just didn't want to talk about Nick anymore.

'No, but I'm going to help the microbrewery build their ice sculpture for the Winter Festival.'

The subject of Nick was dropped, and they talked about where each of them had spent Thanksgiving. Delaney had gone to her mother's, of course. Max had been there, and it was the first completely relaxed holiday she could remember. Well, almost completely relaxed. Her mother did try to drill her about the Christmas fashion show. She'd wanted to know what Delaney planned, starting with hair clips and ending with the style of shoes. Gwen recommended pumps. Delaney horrified her mother by mentioning hip boots even though she didn't own a pair. Gwen suggested a 'nice Anne Klein suit.' Delaney thought she might wear a 'nice plastic cat suit,' which she did own but had outgrown since she'd been stuck in Truly. Max had stepped in and proposed he carve the turkey.

When Delaney was finished, Lanna liked her new cut so much she tipped her ten bucks. In Truly, that was a rare compliment. Once the salon was empty again, she swept up hair and checked her appointment book. She had a little less than an hour before her three-thirty cut and blow-dry. The appointment was with her second male client since she'd opened the salon, and she was a little apprehensive. Some men tended to think since she'd spent half an hour running her fingers through their hair, she'd naturally want to go for a drink at Motel 6 afterward. She never knew which client would interpret her job as a sexual advance. Marital status was never a factor. It was weird, but wasn't uncommon.

While she waited, she counted products in the storeroom, telling herself she wasn't listening for the sound of a certain black Jeep, but she was.

She counted shampoo towels and wrote out an order for several dozen more. She needed more finger-waving solution, thanks to Wannetta, and just as she finished checking her inventory, the muted crunch of gravel reached her from the back lot. She stilled and listened until she heard it again. Before she could think about it, she grabbed a small trash can and slowly opened the back door.

Sophie stood by the front of the silver Cadillac, raising the windshield wiper with one hand. In the other she held a white envelope. She slid the envelope under the wiper blade, and Delaney didn't have to see the typewritten note to know what it said.

'It's you.'

Sophie spun around, her eyes huge, and lifted a hand to the chest of her blue parka. Her mouth fell open, then snapped shut. She looked as stunned as Delaney felt. Delaney didn't know whether to thank her for not being a psycho stalker or scream at her for being a brat.

'I was just ... just ...' she stammered as she grabbed the envelope and shoved it in her pocket.

'I know what you were just doing. You were leaving me another warning.'

Sophie crossed her arms over her chest. She tried to look tough, but her face was only a few shades darker than the snow at her feet.

'Maybe I should go call your father.'

'He's on his honeymoon,' she said instead of denying anything.

'Not forever. I'll wait until he gets back.'

'Go ahead. He won't believe you. He's only nice to you because of Lisa.'

'Your Uncle Nick will believe me. He knows about the other two notes.'

Her arms fell to her sides. 'You told him?' she cried as if Delaney was the person who'd done something wrong.

'Yep, and he'll believe me.' She conveyed a certainty she didn't at all feel. 'He's not going to like it when I tell him you're the one leaving the threatening notes.'

Sophie shook her head. 'You can't tell him.'

'Tell me why you've been sneaking around trying to scare me, and I might not call Nick.'

Sophie stared at her for a few long moments then took several steps backward. 'Go ahead and call him then. I'll just deny it.'

Delaney watched the girl disappear from the parking lot, then she turned and entered her salon. She couldn't let Sophie get away with what she'd done, but the problem was, she didn't know what to do about it. She had no experience with children, and she didn't want to drop something like this on Lisa when she arrived back from her honeymoon. Also, she suspected Lisa might have her own problems with Sophie, and she didn't want to add to them. That left Nick. She wondered if *he'd* believe her.

She was still wondering the next afternoon when Sophie walked into the salon at three-thirty. Delaney looked up from Mrs Stokesberry's wig and spotted the girl hovering near the front door. She'd clipped the sides of her thick hair into flower barrettes, and her dark eyes were huge in her small face. She looked like a scared little girl in a big puffy coat. 'I'll be with you in a minute,' she called to her, then turned her attention to her client. She fit the white wig on the older woman, then handed her a black helmet of hair stuck on a Styrofoam head. She gave Mrs Stokesberry her senior citizen discount, then helped her out the door.

Delaney turned her attention to Sophie and waited for the girl to speak. After a moment of hesitation Sophie said, 'You didn't call Uncle Nick last night.'

'Maybe I did and you just don't know yet.'

'You didn't because I'm staying with him until Dad and Lisa get back.'

'You're right. I didn't call him.'

'Have you talked to him today?'

'No.'

'When are you going to?'

'I don't know yet.'

A deep furrow settled between her brows. 'Are you trying to torture me?'

Delaney hadn't thought about the agony the thirteen-year-old must be going through waiting for the bomb to drop. 'Yes.' She smiled. 'You're never going to know when or where I'm going to say something.'

'Okay, you win. I wanted to scare you so you'd leave town.' Sophie folded her arms over her chest and looked at a point somewhere behind Delaney's head. 'Sorry.'

She didn't sound sorry. 'Why'd you do it?'

'Because then my uncle would get everything that you always took from him. His father gave you everything and he had to wear holey jeans and T-shirts.'

Delaney didn't remember Nick wearing anything holey. 'I was Henry's stepdaughter, do you think I should have gone naked because my mother married Nick's father? Do you really think what Nick wore was my fault?'

'Well, if your mother hadn't married Henry then—'

'Then he would have become a great dad?' Delaney interrupted. 'He would have loved Nick and bought him anything he wanted? Married your grandmother?' She could see by the look on Sophie's face that was exactly what she thought. 'It wouldn't have happened. Nick was ten when I moved to Truly, and in those ten years his father never acknowledged him. Never said one nice word.'

'He might have.'

'Yes, and monkeys might have flown out his butt, but the chances weren't good.' She shook her head. 'Take off your coat and come on back,' she ordered. She didn't think she could look at Sophie's split ends for another minute.

'Why?'

'I'm going to wash your hair.'

'I washed it this morning before school.'

'I'm also going to trim those dead ends for you.' Delaney stopped by the sink and stared toward the front of the salon. Sophie hadn't budged. 'I'm still not sure I shouldn't call Nick and tell him about the notes you've been leaving.'

With her scowl back in place, the girl shrugged out of her coat and walked to the back. 'I don't want my hair cut. I like it long.'

'It'll still be long. It just won't look like a frayed rope.' Delaney used a mild shampoo and conditioner, then moved the girl to the salon chair. She combed and clipped, and if all that glorious dark hair had been attached to another head besides the girl frowning at her through the mirror, she might have been in stylist heaven. 'You might not believe this, but your Uncle Nick doesn't want what Henry left me in his will. And I certainly don't want what he got.'

'Then why are you always hanging around him, dancing and kissing and making him take you home when you get sick? I know all about the will, and I saw you staring at him. Grandma has seen it, too. You want him to be your boyfriend.'

Had she really looked at him in that way? 'Nick and I are friends,' she said, as she snipped two inches of dried split hair. But were they? She didn't know how she really felt about him and was afraid of what he might feel for her. Afraid he might feel nothing one way or the other. 'Don't you have boys who are just friends?'

'A few, but that's different.'

They both fell silent and Delaney thought about Nick and what she felt about him. Jealousy for sure. The thought of him with another woman made her stomach knot. Anxious, wondering when she might see him again, and disappointment at knowing it was probably best if she didn't.

She let down the remainder of Sophie's hair and slightly beveled the ends so it would curl under easily at her shoulders. She grabbed a big round brush and blew it dry. Mostly Delaney felt confused.

'Why are you being nice?'

'How do you know I am? You haven't seen the back of your hair yet.' She gave Sophie a hand mirror and spun her around.

Relief flooded the girl's eyes when she saw her hair hadn't been butchered. 'I don't have money to pay you.'

'I don't want your money.' Delaney removed the cape and neck strip and lowered the chair. 'When someone asks you where you got your hair cut, you tell them at the Cutting Edge, but if you go home and start washing your beautiful hair with something harsh and it starts looking like hell again, you tell everyone you got it cut at Helen's Hair Hut.' She thought she detected a slight smile but wasn't quite sure. 'No more notes, and I'll accept your apology when you really mean it.'

Stone-faced, Sophie studied her reflection. Her eyes met Delaney's, then she walked to the front of the salon and grabbed her coat. After she walked out the door, Delaney watched her move down the sidewalk. Sophie waited half a block before she ran her fingers through her hair and tossed her head. Delaney smiled. She recognized the signs of a pleased customer.

She turned from the window and wondered what Sophie's family would think.

The next morning she found out as she decorated her salon for the Christmas season. Nick walked into the front door of her salon wearing his leather jacket and platinum Oakley's. Delaney had just started coffee brewing and was preparing for her nine-thirty appointment. She had half an hour before Wannetta Van Damme teetered in for her monthly finger wave.

'Sophie told me you cut her hair.'

Delaney set a roll of clear tape and a string of green garland on her styling station counter. Her heart hitched a beat and she placed a hand on her stomach. 'Yes, I did.'

He reached for his sunglasses and slid his gaze down her black turtleneck and short kilt skirt to her black riding boots. 'How much do I owe you?' he asked as he shoved his Oakley's in his jacket pocket and pulled out a checkbook.

'Nothing.' He raised his gaze to hers once again, and she lowered hers to the middle of his chest. She couldn't look in his eyes and think at the same time. 'I cut hair sometimes just for promotion.' She turned to her station and straightened a jar of sanitized combs. She heard his footsteps behind her but kept her attention on her work.

'She also told me she's the one who left those threatening notes.'

Delaney looked up into his reflection in the mirror as he moved toward her. He unzipped his jacket, and beneath it, he wore a blue flannel shirt tucked into his Levi's and a leather woven belt. 'I'm surprised she told you.'

'After you cut her hair, she started feeling so guilty she broke down and confessed last night.' He stopped directly behind her. 'I don't think she should be rewarded with a free hair cut.'

'I didn't see it as . . . a . . .' She looked at him through the glass and forgot what she'd been about to say. He was so bad for her mental health. He was so close, if she leaned back just a little, she could press herself into his big chest.

'You didn't see it as what?'

The smell of crisp morning air clung to him. She took a deep breath, pulling the scent of him deep into her lungs.

'Delaney?'

'Hmm?' Then she did lean back, her shoulders into his chest, her behind pressed into his groin. He was solid and fully aroused. He brought one hand around to her stomach and he drew her tight against him. Delaney followed his gaze to his long fingers splayed wide across her abdomen. His thumb brushed the underside of her right breast.

'When is your first appointment this morning?' he asked close to her ear. He pushed the edge of her turtleneck and kissed the side of her throat.

Her eyes drifted closed, and she tilted her head to one side to give him better access. He cared about her. He had to. 'In about twenty minutes.'

'I could give us what we both need in fifteen.' His fingers brushed her sensitive flesh through the cotton of her shirt.

She was falling in love with him. She could feel it happen like a fierce undertow, pulling at her, sweeping her feet from beneath her, and there was nothing she could do about it except maybe save herself a little pain. She looked into his stunning face and said, 'I don't want to be just another of your women, Nick. I want more.'

He raised his gaze to hers. 'What do you want?'

'While I'm here, I want to be the only woman you're with. Just me.' She paused and took a deep breath. 'I want you to make love only to me. I want you to get rid of your other women.'

His hand stilled and he studied her for several long moments. 'You want me to "get rid" of all the women I'm supposed to be screwing to make some sort of commitment to you for what . . . six months?'

'Yes.'

'What do I get in return?'

She'd been afraid he'd ask that question. There was only one answer she could give him, and she was aware he might not think it enough. 'Me.'

'For six months.'

'Yes.'

'Why should I?'

'Because I want to make love with you, but I don't want to share you with anyone.'

'You say the word "love" a lot.' He straightened and dropped his hand from her abdomen. 'Do you love me?'

She was scared as hell she did and afraid of what it meant. 'No.'

'Good, because I don't love you.' He took a step back and zipped his jacket. 'You know what they say about me, wild thing. I can't be faithful to one woman, and you haven't said anything that would make me want to try.' He took a few more steps backward. 'If you want hot, sweaty sex, you know where to find me. If you want someone to beg for crumbs at your table for a few months, find someone else.'

She didn't want him to beg for anything and didn't really know what he meant, only that she wasn't enough for him.

After he left Delaney wanted nothing more than to curl up in a tight ball and cry. Maybe she should have taken those fifteen minutes he offered, but she was more selfish than that. She didn't share. Not men, and especially not Nick. She wanted him all to herself. Unfortunately, he didn't feel the same. Because of the risk he'd taken to be with her, she'd been so sure he cared. She guessed not.

Now she didn't have to think about what loving Nick meant. She didn't have to consider the repercussions or what to do about them. All she had to do was get through the next six months.

16

The holiday parade kicked off the Truly Winter Festival and started a scandal that would last for decades when the man chosen to play Santa, Marty Wheeler, got so wasted he took a header out of the sleigh and knocked himself unconscious. Marty was short, as stocky as a pug dog, and as hairy as a primate. He overhauled engines at the Chevron on Sixth and was an instructor at the kung fu dojo – a real man's man. The fact that Marty got tanked before and during the parade shocked no one. His choice of underwear, however, left the crowd speechless. When the paramedics opened his Santa suit and revealed his bright pink merry widow, everyone was stunned. Everyone but Wannetta Van Damme, who'd always figured the forty-three-year-old bachelor was 'a mite queer.'

Delaney was almost sorry she'd missed seeing Marty in his underwear, but she'd been busy at the Grange hall decorating for the fashion show. She helped decorate the stage with silver stars and tinsel and the runway with pine boughs and Christmas lights. Backstage, she set up lighted mirrors and chairs. She brought gel and mousse, big cans of hair spray and little sprigs of holly. She figured the people of Truly weren't ready for anything as extreme as style show hair. No rose bushes or bird's nests for these ladies. She brought pictures of braids and twists and ponytails she could arrange in ten to fifteen minutes per head.

The show was set to start at seven, and by six-thirty, Delaney was deep into her work. She braided hair into ropes and knots, turned them inside out and upside down. She twisted and tucked and rolled and listened to the latest dish, secretly relieved Marty had taken her place on the menu.

'One of the nurses at the hospital told Patsy Thomason who told me that Marty had on one of those lace thongs, too,' the mayor's wife, Lillie Tanasee, informed Delaney as she braided a coronet in the woman's auburn hair. Lillie had decked herself and her young daughter out in matching red and green taffeta. 'Patsy said the merry widow and panties were from Victoria's Secret. Can you imagine anything so tawdry?'

Delaney had worked with many gay hairdressers over the years, but she'd never met a cross dresser – not that she knew, anyway. 'At least he isn't cheap. I don't mind tawdry as much as I mind cheap.'

'My husband bought me one of those nylon crotchless numbers,' confessed a woman waiting her turn in the chair. She covered the ears of the little girl dressed as an elf standing next to her. 'It was three sizes too small and so cheap I felt like a low-rent prostitute.'

Delaney shook her head as she wove a few holly berries into Lillie's hair. 'Nothing like cheap lingerie to make a woman feel like a hooker.' She grabbed a tall can and sprayed down Lillie's head. The mayor's daughter Misty jumped into the chair next, and Delaney styled her hair to replicate her mother's. Several women who'd done their own hair stood away from the others; Benita Allegrezza was one of them. Out of the corner of her eye, Delaney watched Nick's mother speak with a group of her friends. She figured Benita was in her mid-fifties, but looked a good ten years older. She wondered if it was genes or bitterness that had etched the lines in her forehead and around her mouth. She glanced around for her mother and wasn't surprised when she spied her in the middle of the action, her hair already perfect. Helen was nowhere to be seen, but Delaney wasn't surprised by her absence.

Those who chose to sit in Delaney's chair ranged in age and style of dress. Some wore elegant velvets, others elaborate costumes. Delaney's favorite was a young mother dressed as Mrs Winter and her toddler in a snowflake costume. She got her biggest surprise when Lisa arrived impersonating a sugarplum and wanting her hair braided in a French rope. Delaney had talked to her friend several times since she'd returned from her honeymoon a few weeks past. They'd had lunch a couple of times, but Lisa hadn't mentioned she planned to participate. 'When did you decide to be in the show?'

'Last weekend. I thought it might be nice for me and Sophie to do something together.'

Delaney looked around. 'Where is Sophie?' For a brief moment she wondered if Lisa knew about the notes Sophie had been leaving, but she supposed Lisa would have mentioned it by now.

'Changing. She was helping Louie and Nick work on their ice sculpture. When I picked her up from Larkspur Park, she wasn't wearing a hat and her coat was unzipped. It'll be a miracle if she isn't sick tomorrow.'

'What is she changing into?'

'A nightgown we made. We were inspired by "The Night Before Christmas." '

'How do you get along with Sophie now that you live with her?' Delaney asked as she gathered a handful of Lisa's hair and divided it into three sections at the crown of her head.

'It's a pretty big adjustment for both of us. I like her to eat at the kitchen table, and she's been allowed to graze like a free-range chicken all of her life. Just little stuff like that. If she weren't thirteen it might be easier.' Lisa looked in the mirror and adjusted the felt leaves around her neck. 'Louie and I want a baby, but we think we should wait until Sophie gets used to having me around before we bring another child into the family.'

A baby. She used all her fingers as she braided and twisted Lisa's hair down the back. Lisa and Louie were planning a family. Delaney didn't even have a boyfriend, and when she thought of a man in her life, there was only one who entered her head – Nick. She thought about him a lot lately. Even while she slept. She'd had another bad dream the other night, only this time the days progressed and her car hadn't disappeared. She'd been free to leave Truly, but the thought of never seeing Nick again tore at her heart. She didn't know which was worse, living in the same town and ignoring him, or not living in the same town and not forcing herself to ignore him. She was confused and pathetic and thought maybe she should just give into the inevitable and buy a cat. 'I suppose you heard about Marty Wheeler,' she said in an effort to divert her thoughts.

'Of course. I wonder what makes a man want to slip on a merry widow under his Santa suit. You know, those things are really uncomfortable.'

'Did you hear about the lace thong?' Delaney grabbed an elastic band and secured the end of the French rope. Then she tucked it under with a bobby pin.

Lisa stood and straightened her costume. 'Go figure. Can you imagine the wedgie?'

'It hurts just to think about it.' She caught sight of Sophie standing a few feet away, trying not to look embarrassed and guilty in her long nightgown and the kerchief on her head. 'Do you want me to braid your hair?' she asked the thirteen-year-old.

Sophie shook her head and looked away. 'It's almost our turn, Lisa.'

After Lisa left to take her stroll down the catwalk, Delaney rolled Neva Miller's hair in an inverted ponytail, then gave her four daughters upside-down braids. Neva talked nonstop about her church, her husband Pastor Tim, and the Lord. Her mouth took on that born again, Jesus-loves-me-more-than-you smile, tempting Delaney to ask Neva if she remembered blowing the football team during halftime.

'You should come to our church tomorrow,' Neva said as she herded her girls toward the stage. 'We meet from nine till noon.'

Delaney would rather burn in hell for eternity. She packed up her remaining supplies and went in search of her mother. She wouldn't see Gwen until after the new year, and she wanted to say goodbye and wish her a nice trip. For years she'd spent the holidays with friends who took pity on her and invited her over for Christmas dinner. This year she'd be completely alone, and she realized as she hugged her mother and promised to look after Duke and Dolores that she really did want to spend Christmas at home like she used to. Especially now that Max was in the picture. The lawyer seemed to be able to distract her mother from criticizing everything in Delaney's life.

Snow fell on her head as she loaded everything into Henry's Cadillac. She didn't have her gloves and her hands froze as she scraped windows. She was exhausted and her shoulders ached, and she hooked the corner behind her salon a little too fast. The Caddie slid sideways into the parking lot and finally stopped with the rear fender blocking the door to Allegrezza Construction. Delaney figured the brothers wouldn't be working the next day, and she was too tired to care anyway. She changed into a nightshirt and crawled into bed. It seemed to her as if she hadn't slept long before someone pounded on her door. She squinted at the clock on her bedside table as the pounding continued. It was nine-thirty Sunday morning, and she didn't have to actually see Nick to know who stood on her porch beating down the door. She grabbed her red silk robe but didn't bother to wash her face or brush her hair. She figured he deserved to be scared for waking her up so early on her day off.

'What in the hell is wrong with you?' were the first words out of his mouth as he stormed into her apartment looking like the wrath of God.

'Me? I'm not the one pounding down your door like a lunatic.'

He folded his arms across his chest and tilted his head to the side. 'Do you plan to slide your way through town all winter, or just until you kill yourself?'

'Don't tell me you're worried.' She tied the silk belt securely around her waist, then walked past him toward the kitchen. 'That might mean you actually care about me.'

He wrapped his hand around her upper arm and stopped her. 'There are certain parts of your body I care about.'

She looked into his face, at his lips compressed into a straight line, the slash of his brow, and the desire raging in his eyes. He was angrier than she'd ever seen him, but he couldn't hide wanting her. 'If you want me, you know my terms. No other women.'

'Yeah, and we both know it would take me about two minutes to get you to change your mind.'

She'd learned months ago that if she argued he'd take it as a challenge just to prove her wrong. She wanted to believe she could resist temptation, but deep down she feared he'd have a minute and thirty seconds to spare. She twisted from his grasp and walked into the kitchen.

'Give me the keys to Henry's car,' he called after her.

'Why?' She pulled the reservoir from her coffee maker and filled it with water. 'What are you going to do, steal it?'

The slam of the front door answered her. She set the reservoir on the counter and walked into the living room. Her purse was dumped out on the coffee table and she had a feeling her keys were missing. She ran out onto her porch, and her feet sunk in snow at the edge of the first step. 'Hey,' she called down to the top of his head, 'what do you think you're doing? Give me my keys back, you jerk!'

His laughter drifted up to her. 'Come on down here and take 'em.'

There were several good reasons she could think of to walk barefoot in the snow. A burning building, rat infestation, a slice of chocolate cheese cake, but Henry's Cadillac wasn't one of them.

Nick jumped into the silver car and fired it up. He scraped a portion of the windshield, and then he was gone. By the time he got back an hour later, Delaney was fully dressed and waiting for him at her front door.

'You're lucky I didn't call the sheriff,' she told him as he walked up the stairs toward her.

He took her hand and dropped the keys in her palm. His eyes were on the same level as hers, and his mouth inches from her lips. 'Slow down.'

Slow down? Her heart raced and her breath caught in her throat as she waited for him to kiss her. He was so close, if she leaned forward just a little . . .

'Slow down before you kill yourself,' he said, then turned and headed back down the stairs.

Disappointment slowed her racing heart to a distressing thud. Over the side of the rail, she watched him walk into his office, then she moved to the Cadillac parked below. She peered through the windows at the cans of hair spray and gel she'd thrown in the back the night before. No dents. No dings.

The car looked the same as it always had – except it now had four studded snow tires, so new they shone.

Monday morning started slowly enough that Delaney could hang Christmas lights on the little tree she'd bought for the reception area. It was only three feet tall, but it filled the salon with the scent of pine. By noon business had picked up and remained steady until she closed at five-thirty. The judging for the ice sculptures would begin in Larkspur Park at six, and she hurried and changed into jeans, her beige cotton sweater with the American flag on the front, and her Doc Marten's. She wasn't so much interested in the ice sculptures as she was in finding a certain Basque man who'd changed the tires on Henry's car yesterday.

By the time she arrived at Larkspur, the parking lot was nearly filled and the judging was under way. The sun had set and the park lights shone on the wonderland of towering crystal shapes. Delaney walked past a ten-foot Beauty and the Beast, a burly mountain man with his pack mule, and Puff the Magic Dragon. Exquisite detail had been given to each sculpture, bringing them to life in the black night and bright lights. She moved through the crowd past Dorothy and Toto, a huge duck, and a cow the size of a mini-van. The crisp air chilled her ears, and she shoved her bare hands into the pockets of her wool coat. She found the Allegrezza Construction entry at the far west end, surrounded by people and judges. Nick and Louie had sculpted a gingerbread house complete with ice gumdrops and candy canes. The house was big enough to walk through, but was roped off until after the judges made their decision. Delaney looked around for Nick and saw him standing to one side with his brother. He wore a black North Face parka with a white lining, jeans, and work boots. Gail Oliver stood next to him, her arm threaded through his. A hot lump of jealousy churned in Delaney's stomach, and she might have lost her nerve and walked past if he hadn't glanced up, locking his gaze on her.

She forced herself to move toward him but spoke to Louie because it was easier. 'Is Lisa around here somewhere?'

'She and Sophie went to the bathroom,' Louie answered, his brown eyes moving from Delaney to Nick, then back again. 'Stick around though, she'll be right back.'

'Actually I wanted to talk to Nick.' She turned and looked up at the man responsible for the chaotic feelings colliding in her heart. She stared into his face, and she knew she'd somehow fallen madly in love with the boy who used to fascinate and torment her at the same time. They were both adults now, but nothing had changed. He'd just found new and better ways of torturing her. 'If you have a minute, I need to talk to you.'

Without a word he disengaged himself from Gail and moved toward her. 'What's up, wild thing?'

She glanced at the people around them, then looked into his face. His cheeks were red and she could see his breath against the darkness. 'I wanted to thank you for the snow tires. I watched for you today, but you didn't go to your office. So I thought I might find you here.' She rocked back on her heel and looked down at the toes of her boots. 'Why did you do it?'

'What?'

'Put snow tires on Henry's car. No man has ever given me tires.' Nervous laughter escaped her lips. 'It was a really nice thing to do.'

'I'm a really nice guy.'

One corner of her mouth lifted. 'No, you're not.' She shook her head and lifted her gaze to his. 'You're rude and overbearing most of the time.'

His smile showed his white teeth and creased the corners of his eyes. 'What am I when I'm not rude and overbearing?'

She made a fist and blew her breath into her cold hand. 'Conceited.'

'And?' He reached out and sandwiched her fingers between his warm palms.

Out of the corner of her eye she caught a glimpse of Gail moving toward them. 'And I can see that I've come at a bad time.' She pulled her hand free and shoved it into her pocket. 'I'll talk to you some other time when you're not busy.'

'I'm not busy right now,' he said just as Gail came to stand next to him.

'Hi, Delaney.'

'Gail.'

'I couldn't make it to the fashion show Saturday night.' Gail glanced up at Nick and smiled. 'I had something else going on, but I heard you did a real good job with the hair this year.'

'I think everyone had a nice time.' Delaney took a step backward. Jealousy twisted like a hot knife in her gut, and she needed to get away from Nick and Gail and the sight of them together. 'See ya around.'

'Where are you going?' he asked.

'I have to check in on Duke and Dolores,' she answered, sounding pitiful to her own ears. 'Then I'm meeting some friends,' she added the lie to salvage her pride and lifted her hand in an abbreviated wave, then turned to leave.

In three long strides Nick caught up to her. 'I'll walk you to your car.'

'You don't have to.' She looked up at him, then over her shoulder at Gail, who stared after them as they moved toward the parking lot. 'You'll make your date mad.'

'Gail isn't my date, and you don't need to worry about her.' He took Delaney's hand in his and slid it into his coat pocket. 'Why do you have to check on Henry's dogs?'

They walked by an ice genie sitting on his lamp. She didn't know if she believed him about Gail, but decided to let the subject drop for now. 'My mother left town with Max Harrison.' He wove his fingers through hers and hot tingles spread to her wrist. 'They're going to celebrate their Christmas on one of those love boats.'

Nick slowed as they moved around a crowd gathered in front of the genie. 'What about your Christmas?'

The tingles swept to her elbow and further up her arm. 'We'll celebrate when she gets back. No big deal. I'm used to being alone during the holidays. I haven't had a real Christmas since I left town anyway.'

He didn't say anything for a few moments as they walked from beneath a park light and through a patch of night. 'Sounds lonely.'

'Not really. I usually found someone who took pity on me. And besides, it was always my choice to stay away. I could have come back and apologized for being such a disappointment and pretended to be the daughter my parents wanted, but a few presents and a yule log weren't worth my pride or my freedom.' She shrugged and purposely changed the subject. 'You never did answer my question.'

'What was that?'

'The tires. Why did you do it?'

'No one was safe with you driving that big boat of Henry's. It was only a matter of time before you took out a couple of kids.'

She looked up at him, at his dark profile. 'Liar.'

'Believe what you want,' he said, refusing to admit he might care for her.

'How much do I owe you?'

'Consider them a Christmas present.'

They stepped off the curb into the parking lot and walked between a Bronco and a van. 'I don't have anything to give you.'

'Yes, you do.' He stopped and raised her hand to his mouth. He brushed his lips across her knuckles. 'When I'm not rude and overbearing and conceited . . . what am I?'

She couldn't see his features clearly through the darkness,

but she didn't need to see his eyes to know he stared at her over the back of her hand. She could feel his gaze just as surely as she could feel his touch. 'You're . . .' She could feel herself melt, right there in the parking lot with her toes frozen and the temperature below zero. She wanted to be with him. 'You're the man I think about all the time.' She pulled her hand free and raised onto the balls of her feet. 'I think about your handsome face, wide shoulders, and your lips.' She wrapped her arms around his neck and pressed into him. He ran his hand up and down her back, holding her close. Her heart pounded in her ears and she buried her cold nose just below his ear. 'Then I think about licking you.'

His hands stilled.

'All over.' She touched the tip of her tongue to the side of his throat.

'Jesus, Joseph, and Mary,' he groaned. 'When do you have to meet your friends?'

'What friends?'

'You said you were meeting friends tonight.'

'Oh, yeah.' She'd forgotten about her lie. 'It's not important. They won't miss me if I don't show up.'

He pulled back to look at her. 'What about the dogs?'

'I really do have to let them out for a while. What about Gail?'

'I told you not to worry about her.'

'Are you seeing her?'

'I *see* her.'

'Are you having sex with her?'

She could see the dark corners of his mouth pull into a frown. 'No.'

Delaney's heart swelled, and she planted her mouth on his, devouring him with a hot kiss that left them both breathless. 'Come with me.'

'To Henry's?'

'Yes.'

He didn't speak for a moment, and she couldn't tell what he might be thinking. 'I'll meet you there,' he finally said: 'I need to talk to Louie, then swing by the drugstore.'

She didn't have to ask why. He pressed his lips to hers, then he was gone. She watched him walk away, his long, confident strides carrying him back into the park.

On the drive to her mother's, she tried to tell herself that Nick was hers for tonight, and nothing else mattered. She felt the slight vibration of the metal studs digging into snow and striking pavement and told herself that tonight was enough, and she tried to believe it.

When she opened the front door of her mother's house, Duke and Dolores greeted her with wagging tails and wet tongues. She let them out and stood on the sidewalk as they jumped into snow up to their bellies, two brown dogs in a thick blanket of white. She'd remembered her gloves this time and packed a few snowballs for Duke to catch in his mouth.

Maybe she could convince Nick she was enough for him. She wanted to believe he wasn't involved with anyone else. She wanted to believe him when he'd said he wasn't having sex with Gail, but she couldn't trust him completely. She tossed a snowball to Dolores. It hit the dog's side and the Weimaraner looked around without a clue. Delaney knew there was more between them than sex, and Nick had to know it, too. She could see it in his eyes when he looked at her. It was hot and intense, and after tonight, maybe he would want only her.

I can't be faithful to one woman, and you haven't said anything to make me want to try.

He wanted her. She wanted him. He didn't love her. She loved him so much she ached. Her feelings hadn't happened like a slow blissful glide through the tunnel of love. As with everything else involving Nick, loving him had blindsided her, smacked her for a loop and left her stunned. And so confused she felt like laughing and crying and maybe lying down and not getting back up until she had it all worked out in her head.

As she made another snowball, she heard the Jeep's engine before she saw the headlights pulling into the drive. The four-wheel drive stopped beneath a pool of light in front of the garage, and Duke and Dolores bounded across the yard to the driver's side, barking like mad. The door swung open and Nick stepped out. 'Hey, dogs.' He bent to scratch them behind their ears before he looked up. 'Hey, wild thing.'

'Are you ever going to stop calling me that?'

He glanced back down at Duke and Dolores. 'No.'

Delaney threw the snowball and nailed the top of his head. The light snow disintegrated on impact and powdered his dark hair and the shoulders of his black parka. Slowly he straightened, then shook his head, showering the night with white flakes. 'I would think you'd know better than to get into a snowball fight with me.'

'What are you going to do, give me a black eye?'

'Nope.' He moved toward her up the sidewalk, the heels of his boots sounding ominous in the still air.

She reached for more snow and packed it lightly in her gloved hands. 'If you try anything funny, you'll be really sorry.'

'You got me scared, wild thing.'

She threw the snowball and it exploded across his chest. 'I owed you that.' She took a step backward into the yard and sank in white powder up to her knees.

'You owe me a lot.' He grabbed her upper arms and lifted her until the toes of her Doc Marten's hardly touched the ground. 'By the time I'm finished collecting from you, you're not going to able to walk for a week.'

'You got me scared,' she drawled. He looked at her through lowered lids, and she thought he would pull her against the length of his body and kiss her. He didn't. He tossed her backward. A startled squeal escaped her lips as she flew a few feet and fell spread-eagle in the snow. It was like landing on a down pillow, and she lay there stunned, staring up at the black sky crammed full of gleaming stars. Duke and Dolores barked, jumped on top of her, and licked her face. Over the heavy panting of excited dogs, she heard the sound of deep rich laughter. She pushed the dogs away and sat up. 'Jerk.' She dug snow out of the back of her collar and the top of her gloves. 'Help me up.' She held up a hand and waited until he'd pulled her to her feet before she used all her weight and dragged him with her to the ground. He landed on top of her with an *oomph*. Bemusement creased his brow as if he couldn't quite believe what had happened.

She tried to draw a deep breath and couldn't. 'You're kind of heavy.'

He rolled to his back, taking her with him, which was exactly where she wanted to be. Her legs rested beside his, and she grabbed his collar in both her fists. 'Say uncle and I won't have to hurt you.'

He looked up at her as if she were crazy. 'To a girl? Not in this life.'

The dogs jumped over them as if they were hurdles, and she picked up a handful of snow and dropped it on his face. 'Come and look at this, Duke. It's Frosty the Basque Snowman.'

With his bare hand, he brushed the white flakes from his tan skin and licked them from his lips. 'I'm going to have a real good time making you pay for this.'

She lowered her face and slipped the tip of her tongue across his bottom lip. 'Let me do that for you.' She felt his response in the catch in his breath and the tight grasp on her arms. She kissed his hot mouth and sucked his tongue. When she was finished, she sat up across his hips, her wool coat fanned out around them. Through her jeans she felt his full arousal pushing into her, long and hard and blatant. 'Is that an icicle in your pocket, or are you happy to see me?'

'Icicle?' He slid his hands beneath her coat and up her thighs. 'Icicles are cold. You're sitting on twelve hot inches.'

She lifted her eyes to the night sky. 'Twelve inches.' He was big, but he wasn't that big.

'It's a known fact.'

Delaney laughed and rolled off him. He might be right about that hot part, though. He certainly knew how to set her on fire.

'My ass is frozen.' He sat up and Duke and Dolores jumped on him. 'Hey, now,' he said as he pushed them away and helped Delaney to her feet. She brushed the snow off his parka; he brushed it out of her hair. On the porch they stomped their feet, then went inside. Delaney took his coat and hung it on the rack by the front door. As he looked around, she took the opportunity to study him. He wore a flannel shirt, of course. Solid red flannel tucked inside his faded Levi's.

'Have you ever been in here before?'

'Once.' He returned his gaze to hers. 'The day Henry's will was read.'

'Oh, yeah.' She glanced about, trying to see the foyer through new eyes, as if she'd never stood there before. It was a typical Victorian. White paint and wallpaper, dark wood and wainscoting, thick handwoven rugs from Persia, antique grandfather clock. Everything was rich and somewhat oppressive, and they were both aware that if Henry had been interested in being a father, Nick would have grown up in the huge house. She wondered if he considered himself lucky.

They took off their wet, frozen boots by the door, and she suggested he build a fire in the parlor while she moved to the kitchen and made Irish coffee. When she returned ten minutes later, she found him standing before the traditional hearth, staring at the portrait of Henry's mother hanging above the mantel. There was only a slight resemblance between Alva Morgan Shaw and her only grandson. Nick looked out of place among his ancestral trappings. His own home suited him much better, exposed beams and river rock and soft flannel sheets.

'What do you think?' she asked as she set a glass tray on the sideboard.

'About what?'

She pointed to the picture of Henry's mother, who'd relocated to the capital city long before Delaney's arrival in Truly. Henry had taken Gwen and Delaney to visit the old woman several times a year until she'd died in 1980, and as far as Delaney could remember, the portrait was quite flattering. Alva had been a tall skinny woman with bony features like a stork, and Delaney recalled her smelling of stale tobacco and Aqua-Net. 'Your grandmother.'

Nick cocked his head to one side. 'I think I'm glad I favor my mother's side, and you're lucky you were adopted.'

'Don't hold back.' Delaney laughed. 'Tell me what you really think.'

Nick turned to look at her and wondered what she would do if he told her. He ran his gaze over her blond hair and big brown eyes, the arch of her brow and her pink lips. He'd been thinking about a lot of things lately, things that would never happen, things it was best not to think about. Things like waking up with Delaney every morning for the rest of his life and watching her hair turn gray. 'I'm thinking the old man is pretty happy with himself just about now.'

She handed him a mug, then raised her own and blew into it. 'How do you figure that?'

He took a mouthful of the coffee and felt the whiskey burn clear to his stomach. He liked the feeling. It reminded him of her.

'Henry didn't want us to be together.'

He wondered if he should tell her the truth, and decided why the hell not. 'You're wrong. He *wanted* us to end up together. That's why you're stuck here in Truly. Not to keep your mother company.' The creases in her forehead told him she didn't believe him for a minute. 'Trust me on this.'

'Okay, why?'

'You really want to know?'

'Yes.'

'All right. A few months before he died, he offered me everything. He said he'd have to leave a little something to Gwen, but he'd leave everything else to me if I gave him a grandchild. He would have cut you out completely.' He paused before he added, 'I told him to go to hell.'

'Why would he do that?'

'I guess he figured a bastard son was better than no son, and if I don't have children, then all that superior Shaw blood dies with me.'

She frowned and shook her head. 'Okay, but that doesn't have anything to do with me.'

'Sure it does.' He reached for her free hand and pulled her closer. 'It's crazy, but he thought, because of what happened out at Angel Beach, I was in love with you.' He rubbed the back of her knuckles with his thumb.

Her gaze searched his face then she looked away. 'You're right. It's crazy.'

He dropped her hand. 'If you don't believe me, ask Max. He knows all about it. He drafted the will.'

'It still doesn't make a lot of sense. It's so risky, and Henry was too controlling to leave this to chance. I mean, what if I'd married before he died? He could have lived for years, and in the meantime, I could have become a nun or something.'

'Henry killed himself.'

'No way.' She shook her head again. 'He loved himself too

much to do something like that. He loved being a big fish in a small pond.'

'He was dying of prostate cancer and only had a few months to live anyway.'

Her mouth fell open a little, and she blinked several times. 'No one told me.' Her brows scrunched together, and she rubbed the side of her neck. 'Does my mother know any of this?'

'She knows about his cancer and the suicide.'

'Why didn't she tell me?'

'I don't know. You'll have to ask her.'

'This sounds so bizarre and controlling that the more I think about it, the more it sounds just like something Henry would do.'

'The ends always justified the means with him, and everything had a price.' He turned back to the fire and took a drink. 'The will was his way of controlling everyone even after he was gone.'

'You mean he used me to control you.'

'Yes.'

'And you hate him for it.'

'Yes. He was a son of a bitch.'

'Then I don't understand.' She came to stand beside him and he could hear the confusion in her voice. 'Why are you here tonight? Why haven't you avoided me?'

'I tried.' He set his mug on the mantel and stared into the flames. 'But it's not that easy. Henry was right about one thing, he knew I wanted you. He knew I would want you despite the risk.'

Several long moments of silence stretched between them, then she asked, 'Why are you here now – tonight? We've been together.'

'It's not over. Not yet.'

'Why risk it again?'

Why was she pushing him? If she wanted the answer, he'd give it to her, but he doubted she'd like it much. 'Because I've thought about you naked and willing since you were about thirteen or fourteen.' He took a deep breath and let it out slowly. 'Since the time Louie and I were out at the public beach with a few friends, and you were there, too, with some other girls. I don't remember them, just you. You had on a shiny swimming suit the color of green apples. It was one piece and by no stretch of the imagination skimpy, but it had a zipper up the front that drove me crazy. I remember watching you talking with your friends and listening to music, and I couldn't take my eyes off that zipper. That was the first time I noticed your breasts. They were small and pointed and all I could think about was pulling down that zipper so I could see them, so I could look at the changes in your body. I got so hard, I hurt, and I had to lie on my stomach so no one would see I had a Ponderosa-sized woody.

'That night when I went home, I fantasized about crawling in your bedroom window. I fantasized that I watched you sleep with your blond hair all fanned out across your pillow. Then I imagined you waking up and telling me you'd been waiting for me, holding out your arms and welcoming me into your bed. I pictured myself slipping between the sheets, pushing up your shirt, and pulling down your panties. You let me touch your little breasts all I wanted. You let me touch you between your legs, too. I fantasized about that for hours.

'I was sixteen and knew more than I should have about sex. You were young and naive and didn't know anything. You were the princess of Truly, and I was the mayor's illegitimate son. I wasn't good enough to kiss your feet, but that didn't stop me from wanting you so much my guts ached. I could have called one of a number of girls I knew, but I didn't. I wanted to fantasize about you.' He took another deep breath. 'You probably think I'm a pervert.'

'Yes,' she softly laughed. 'A Ponderosa-sized pervert.'

He looked across his shoulder at the amusement in her big brown eyes. 'You aren't mad?'

She shook her head.

'You don't think I'm sick as hell?' He'd often wondered about that himself.

'Actually, I'm flattered. I guess every woman likes to imagine that at some time in her life there's been at least one man out there fantasizing about her.'

She didn't know the half of it. 'Yeah, well, I thought about you from time to time.'

She turned to him and reached for the button on the front of his shirt. 'I've thought about you, too.'

Beneath his lids, he watched her white hands against red flannel, her thin fingers moving toward his waist. 'When?'

'Since I've been back.' She pulled the ends of his shirt from his jeans. 'Last week I thought about this.' She leaned forward and brushed her tongue across his flat nipple. It hardened like leather, and he plowed his fingers through the sides of her hair.

'What else?'

'This.' She unbuttoned his fly and shoved one hand beneath his briefs. When she wrapped her soft palm around his hard shaft and squeezed, he felt it in his gut. She stroked him from base to head, up and down, and he stood there and took it all in. The texture of her soft hair through his fingers, the feel of her wet mouth on his chest and throat. He could smell some sort of light powdery perfume on her skin, and when she kissed him, she tasted of whiskey and coffee and lust. He loved having her tongue in his mouth and her hand down his pants. He loved looking into her face as she touched him.

He took off her sweater and unhooked her beige bra and thought of the hundreds of fantasies he'd had about this one woman. Combined, none of them could hold a candle to the real thing. He cupped her round white breasts in his hands, and caressed her perfect pink nipples.

'I told you I wanted to lick you all over,' she whispered as she shoved his pants and briefs down his thighs. 'I've been thinking about that, too.' She knelt before him in her jeans and socks and took him into her hot wet mouth. His breath left his lungs and he spread his feet shoulder width apart for balance. She kissed the head of his penis and gently caressed his testicles. He shuddered and held Delaney's fine hair away from her face as he looked down at her long eyelashes and soft cheeks.

Nick usually preferred oral sex to anything else. He didn't always wear a condom during, leaving the choice up to the woman. But he didn't want to get off in Delaney's mouth. He wanted to look in her eyes as he buried himself deep inside her. He wanted to know she felt him there. He wanted to feel her grip him deep within her body and feel her wild pulsations. He wanted to forget about using protection and leave something of himself deep inside her long after he was gone. He'd never felt that way with any other woman. He wanted more. He wanted those things he never dared think were possible. He wanted to make her his for more than just a night. For the first time in his life, he wanted more from a woman than she wanted from him.

In the end, he pulled her to her feet and retrieved a condom from the pocket of his jeans. He placed it in her palm. 'Suit me up, wild thing,' he said.

17

Delaney awoke to the soft brush of fingertips caressing her spine. She opened her eyes and stared at Nick's broad hairy chest less than an inch from her nose. She lay on her stomach, and a patch of bright morning sun streamed across his tan skin.

'Good morning.'

She wasn't sure, but she thought she felt him kiss the top of her head. 'What time is it?'

'About eight-thirty.'

'Crap.' She rolled to her side and would have fallen to the floor if he hadn't grabbed the top of her arm and thrown a bare leg over her hips. A thin floral sheet was the only thing separating them. She raised her gaze to the same pink canopy she'd awakened to most mornings as a girl. The twin-sized bed was small for one person, let alone one person and a guy Nick's size. 'I have a nine o'clock appointment.' She gathered her courage and looked at him, her worst fear confirmed. He was gorgeous in the morning. His shoulder-length hair fell to one side and a shadow of a beard darkened his jaw. From beneath his thick lashes, his eyes were too intense and alert for eight-thirty in the morning.

'Can you cancel it?'

She shook her head and glanced around for her clothes. 'If

I leave within the next ten minutes, I might make it on time.'
She returned her gaze to his face and caught him staring at her,
looking as if he were either memorizing her features or
inspecting for flaws. She could feel her cheeks grow warm, and
she sat up, holding the sheet to her chest. 'I know I look like
shit,' she said, but he didn't look at her as if she were half dead.
Maybe for once in her life she'd lucked out and didn't have
dark circles. 'Don't I?'

'Do you want the truth?'

'Yes.'

'Okay.' He reached for her hand and kissed her palm. 'You
look better than you did when you were a Smurf.'

A wrinkle appeared in the corners of his eyes, and Delaney
felt a rush of warm tingles tickle her fingertips and spread
across her breasts. This was the Nick she loved. The Nick who
teased as he kissed. The man who could make her laugh even
as he made her want to cry. 'I should have asked you to lie,' she
said and pulled her hand away before she forgot her nine
o'clock appointment. She spotted her clothes thrown on the
floor beside her. With her back to him, she reached for them
and got dressed as quickly as possible.

Behind her the bedsprings dipped as Nick rose to his feet.
He moved about the room, retrieving his clothes from the
floor, completely unconcerned by his nudity. With a sock in
one hand, she watched him shove his legs into his Levi's and
button the fly. Beneath the harsh morning light, Nick
Allegrezza was one hundred percent prime American
beefcake. Life wasn't fair.

'Give me your keys, and I'll warm your car for you.'

Delaney shoved her foot in her sock. No man had ever
offered to warm up her car for her, and she was touched by the
simple gesture. 'In my coat pocket.' After he left the bedroom,
Delaney washed her face and brushed her teeth and hair. By
the time she locked the house behind her, the windows of

Henry's Cadillac were clear. No man had ever scraped her windows, either. Her new snow tires shined a polished black against the backdrop of silver and white. She felt like crying. No one had ever cared about her safety and well-being, except maybe her old boyfriend Eddy Castillo. He'd been an exercise freak, concerned about her diet. He'd given her a Salad Shooter for her birthday, but a kitchen appliance didn't compare to snow tires.

She didn't ask when she'd see Nick again. He didn't offer. They'd spent the night as lovers, yet neither of them mentioned love or even dinner plans.

Delaney arrived at her salon moments before her first client, Gina Fisher, who'd graduated a year behind Delaney in school and had three children under the age of five. Gina had worn her thick hair to her waist since the seventh grade. Delaney cut it to her shoulders and gave her long layers. She brushed in red highlights and made the young mother look youthful again. After Gina, she cut the hair of a girl who wanted to look like Claire Danes. She had a walk-in at eleven, then closed the salon at noon so she could finally take a shower. She told herself she wasn't waiting for Nick's call or the sound of his Jeep, but of course she was.

When she hadn't heard from him by six that evening, she jumped in the Cadillac to do a little Christmas shopping. She hadn't bought a gift yet for her mother and ended up at one of those high-priced tourist traps that catered to the Eddie Bauer crowd. She didn't find anything for her mother, but she did blow seventy bucks on a size fifteen and a half flannel, the same exact gray of Nick's eyes. She had it gift-wrapped in red foil paper, and took it home and sat it on her dining room table. There were no messages on her machine. She pressed call return just to make sure, but he hadn't called.

She didn't hear from him the next day, and by Christmas morning, she was feeling more alone than she ever had in her life. She got up the nerve and dialed Nick to wish him Merry Christmas, but he didn't answer. She thought about driving by his house to see if he was home and avoiding her. In the end, she drove to her mother's to visit Duke and Dolores. At least the two Weimaraners were happy to see her.

By noon, she'd fallen into a zombie state watching *A Christmas Story*, relating to Ralphie as never before. She knew what it was like to want something she wasn't likely to get. And she knew what it was like to have a mother who made a kid wear a horrid bunny costume, too. Just as Ralphie was about to shoot his eyes out with his Red Ryder B-B gun, the doorbell rang. The Weimaraners lifted their heads, then laid them back down, proving they weren't much good as watchdogs.

Nick stood on the porch in his leather jacket and Oakley's. His breath hung in front of his face as a slow sensuous smile curved his lips upward. He looked good enough to roll in sugar and eat whole. Delaney didn't know whether to let him in or slam the door in his face for leaving her hanging the past two days. The shiny gold box in his hand decided his fate. She let him in.

He shoved his sunglasses in his pocket and pulled out a piece of mistletoe and held it over her head. 'Merry Christmas,' he said. His warm mouth covered hers, and she felt the kiss to the soles of her feet. When he pulled back to look at her, she placed her palms on his cheeks and brought him down for more. She didn't even bother to hide her feelings. She wasn't so sure she could have, anyway. She ran her hands over his shoulders and across his chest, and when she was through, she confessed, 'I've missed you.'

'I was in Boise until late last night.' He shifted his weight to one foot and shoved the box at her. 'This is for you. It took me a while to find it.'

She stared at the gold box and ran a hand over the smooth

paper. 'Maybe I should wait. I have a gift for you at my apartment.'

'No,' he insisted like a death row inmate who just wanted to hurry and get his sentence over with as quickly as possible. 'Go ahead and open it now.'

Beneath her hands, the smooth paper ripped apart with one excited pull. Nestled in a bed of tissue paper inside sat a rhinestone crown like those given out in beauty pageants.

'I thought since Helen stole that homecoming crown from you in high school, I'd get you a better one.'

It was big and gaudy and absolutely the most beautiful thing she'd ever seen. She bit her lower lip to keep it from trembling as she pulled the crown from its bed of tissue and shoved the box at Nick. 'I love it.' The rhinestones caught the light and shot sparks through the foyer. She placed it on her head and looked at herself in the mirror next to the coat rack. The shiny stones were fashioned into a row of hearts and ribbons with one central heart bigger than the rest. She blinked back her tears as she raised her gaze to his in the mirror. 'This is the best Christmas present anyone has ever given me.'

'I'm glad you like it.' He placed his big palms on her stomach, then slid them beneath her sweater to her breasts. Through her lacy bra, he cupped her, his fingers pressing into her flesh as he pulled her back against his chest. 'On the long drive from Boise last night, I thought about you wearing that thing and nothing else.'

'Have you ever made love to a queen?'

He shook his head and grinned. 'You're my first.'

She grabbed his wrist and led him to the sun-room where she'd been watching television. He undressed her with slow languid hands and made her feel beautiful and desired and loved right there on her mother's lemon yellow sofa. She ran her fingertips down his warm back and bare behind and kissed his smooth shoulder. She wanted to feel as she did at that moment forever. Her skin tingled and her body flushed. Her heart swelled when he kissed her sensitive breasts, and when he buried his hot erection deep inside her body, she was more than ready. He placed his hands on the sides of her face and stared in her eyes as he slowly drove into her again and again.

She stared up into his face, into his gray eyes, alive with the passion he felt for her, his lips moist from their kiss, his breathing labored. 'I love you, Nick,' she whispered. He stilled for a moment, then plunged deeper, harder, again and again, and she whispered her love with each stroke until she fell head first into the sweetest ecstasy of her life. She heard his deep primal groan and the mixture of prayer words and curses. Then his full weight collapsed on her.

A twinge of unease settled in her chest as she listened to his breathing slow. She'd told him she loved him. And while he'd made her feel loved, he hadn't uttered the words. She needed to know how he felt about her now, yet at the same time, she feared the answer. 'Nick?'

'Hmm?'

'We need to talk.'

He lifted his head and looked into her eyes. 'Give me a minute.' He withdrew from her and walked naked from the room to rid himself of the condom he hadn't forgotten since that first frenzied time in the closet at the Lakeshore. Delaney searched for her panties and found them under a rattan cocktail table. She stepped into them, and with each passing moment her unease grew. What if he didn't love her? How could she stand it, and what was she going to do if he didn't? He returned just as she'd discovered her bra behind a couch cushion. He took the bra from her hand and tossed it aside. He wrapped her in his embrace and held her against his chest, holding her tighter than ever before. Within his warm arms, with the scent of his skin filling her head, she told herself that he loved her. Even though she wasn't good at being patient, she could wait for him to say the words she needed to hear. Instead she heard the squeak of wood and hinges, like the front door swinging open, and she stilled. 'Did you hear something?' she whispered.

He put a finger to his lips and listened. The door slammed shut, galvanizing her into action.

'Holy hell!' She jumped from Nick's arms and reached for the closest article of clothing, his flannel shirt. Footsteps tapped up the hall as she shoved her arms in the holes. Nick's jeans lay somewhere behind the couch, and he stepped behind Delaney just as Gwen walked into the room. An eerie feeling of déjà vu climbed up Delaney's spine. Her mother stood within a shaft of light, the sun shining in her hair like she was a Christmas angel.

Gwen looked from Delaney to Nick then back again, shock rounding her blue eyes. 'What is going on here?'

Delaney closed the front of the shirt with her hand. 'Mom . . . I . . .' Her fingers worked the buttons as an unreal feeling fogged her head. 'What are you doing home?'

'I live here!'

Nick placed a hand on her abdomen and pulled her back against him, hiding his goods from Delaney's mother. 'I know, but you're supposed to be on the love boat.'

Gwen pointed a finger at Nick. 'What is he doing in my house?'

Carefully she finished with the buttons. 'Well, he was kind enough to spend Christmas with me.'

'He's naked!'

'Well, yes.' She spread the hem of his shirt wider in an effort to cover him better. 'He . . . ah . . .' She closed her mouth and shrugged. There was no help for it, she'd been caught. Only this time she wasn't a naive eighteen-year-old girl. She was a few months shy of thirty and she loved Nick Allegrezza.

She was a mature independent woman, but she would have preferred that her mother had not found them naked in her sunroom, 'Nick and I are dating.'

'I'd say you're more than dating. How could you do this, Delaney? How could you take up with a man like him? He's a womanizer and he hates this family.' She turned her attention to Nick. 'You put your hands on my daughter again, but this time you've fixed yourself good. You violated the terms of Henry's will. I'll see to it you lose everything.'

'I never gave a damn about the will.' His fingers brushed over the flannel covering Delaney's stomach.

Delaney knew her mother well enough to know she'd make good on her threat. She also knew how to stop her. 'If you tell anyone about this, then I'll never speak to you again. Once I leave in June, you'll never see me. If you thought you never saw me after I left ten years ago, you just wait. When I leave this time, I won't even tell you where I am. When I leave, I'll have three million dollars and I'll never come back to visit you.'

Gwen's lips pursed and she folded her arms over her breasts. 'We'll talk about this later.'

Nick's hand fell away. 'If you don't want to see my bare ass, then you better leave the room while I get dressed.'

The tone of his voice was razor-sharp. She'd heard it once before. The last time the three of them had been in Henry's office. The day the will had been read. Delaney couldn't blame him for being edgy. The situation was unbearably awkward, and her mother brought out the worst in some people under the best of circumstances.

As soon as Gwen turned on her heel, Delaney spun around. 'I'm sorry, Nick. I'm sorry she said those things to you, and I promise I won't let her do anything to jeopardize what Henry left you.'

'Forget about it.' He found his pants and shoved his legs inside. They dressed in silence, and when she walked him to the front door, he left quickly and neglected to kiss her good-bye. She told herself it didn't matter and went in search of her mother. Gwen wasn't going to like what she had to say, but Delaney had quit living her life for her mother a long time ago. She found her in the kitchen, waiting.

'Why are you home, Mom?'

'I've discovered that Max is not the man for me. He's too critical,' she said through clenched jaws. 'Never mind about that now. What was that *man* doing in my house?'

'I told you, he was spending Christmas with me.'

'I thought that was his Jeep parked in front of the garage, but I was sure I had to be mistaken. Not in a million years did I expect to find him . . . you . . . in my home. Nick Allegrezza of all men. He's—'

'I'm in love with him,' Delaney interrupted.

Gwen grabbed the back of a kitchen chair. 'That is not funny. You're just saying it to get back at me. You're angry with me because I left you alone for Christmas.'

Sometimes her mother's logic boggled the mind, but it was always predictable. 'My feelings for Nick have nothing to do with you. I want to be with him, and I'm going to be with him.'

'I see.' Her mother's face hardened. 'Are you saying you don't care how I feel about it?'

'Of course I care. I don't want you to hate the man I love. I know you can't be really happy for me right now, but maybe you could just accept that I am involved with Nick, and I'm happy with him.'

'That's impossible. You can't be happy with a man like Nick. Don't do this to yourself or your family.'

Delaney shook her head and her crown slid to one side. She pulled it from her head and brushed her fingers across the cool rhinestones. It was no use. Her mother would never change. 'Henry's dead. I am your only family now.' She looked up at Gwen. 'I want Nick. Don't make me choose.'

*

Nick stood by the stone fireplace and stared at the blinking lights Sophie had helped him hang on his tree. He raised a bottle of beer to his lips and the lights blurred as he tipped his head back.

He'd known better. For the past few days he'd lived his fantasy. He'd held her while she'd slept in that tiny pink bed and let himself imagine a house, and a dog, and a couple of kids. He'd let himself imagine her in his life, for the rest of his life, and he'd wanted it more than breathing.

Once I leave in June, you'll never see me. If you thought you never saw me after I left ten years ago, you just wait. When I leave this time, I won't tell you where I am. When I leave, I'll have three million dollars and I'll never come back to visit you.

He was a fool. He'd known she would leave, but he'd let himself start to think that he was enough to make her stay. She'd said she loved him. So had a lot of women at that particular moment, when he'd been buried inside giving them both pleasure. It didn't always mean anything, and he wasn't the kind of guy to wait around and watch for signs from the buckbrush to see if it did.

The doorbell rang and he expected to see Delaney. He found Gail instead.

'Merry Christmas,' she said and held a brightly colored box toward him. He let her in because he needed a distraction.

'I didn't get you anything.' He hung her coat by the door, then led her into the kitchen.

'That's okay. It's just cookies, nothing big. Josh and I had some extra.' Nick set the box on the counter and looked her over. She wore a tight red dress and red stiletto heels. He'd bet she had on her red garter and nothing else. She'd come over to deliver more than gingersnaps, but he wasn't even mildly interested.

'Where is your son?'

'His daddy has him tonight. All night. I thought you and I could spend some quality time together in your hot tub.'

The doorbell rang for a second time in five minutes, and this time it was Delaney. She stood on his porch, a foil red present in her hands and a smile on her lips. Her smile died when Gail walked up behind him and hung her wrist over his shoulder. He could have removed it. He didn't.

'Come on in,' he said. 'Gail and I were just about to jump in the hot tub.'

'I –' Her stunned gaze moved between them. 'I didn't bring my swimsuit.'

'Neither did Gail.' He knew what she thought and he let her think it. 'You won't need one, either.'

'What's going on, Nick?'

He wrapped an arm around Gail's waist and pulled her up against his side. He took a drink from the bottle and looked at the woman he loved so much it was like a writhing ache in his chest. 'You're a big girl. Figure it out.'

'Why are you behaving this way? Are you angry about what happened earlier? I told you I'll make sure my mother doesn't say anything.'

'I don't give a rat's ass about any of that.' Even if he'd wanted to stop himself from hurting her, he couldn't. He felt like a powerless kid again, watching her and wanting her so much it drove him crazy. 'Why don't you join us in the hot tub?'

She shook her head. 'Three's a crowd, Nick.'

'No, three's one hell of a good time.' He knew he'd never forget the pain in her eyes, and he turned his gaze to Gail. 'What do you say? Are you up for a threesome?'

'A –'

He looked back at Delaney and raised a brow. 'Well?'

She lifted her free hand and grabbed her wool coat above her heart. She took a step backward and her mouth moved but no words came out. He watched her turn, the shiny red package forgotten in her hand, and run down the sidewalk to her car. Better to let her go before he begged her to stay. Better to end it now. Nick Allegrezza didn't beg anyone to love him. He never had and he never would.

He made himself stand there, and he made himself watch her drive out of his life. He made himself feel his insides rip apart, then he handed Gail her coat. 'I'm not good company,' he said, and for once she had the sense not to try and change his mind.

Alone, he walked into the kitchen and popped the cap off another beer. By midnight he'd graduated to Jim Beam. Nick wasn't necessarily a mean drunk, but he was in a mean mood. He drank to forget, but the more he drank the more he remembered. He remembered the scent of her skin, the soft texture of her hair and the taste of her mouth. He fell asleep on the sofa with the sound of her laughter in his ears and his name on her lips. When he woke at eight, his head pounded, and knew he needed a little something for breakfast. He grabbed a bottle of Bufferin and added a little orange juice to his vodka. He was on his third drink and seventh aspirin when his brother walked into his house.

Nick lay sprawled on the leather couch, channel surfing with the remote to the big screen television in one hand. He didn't bother to look up.

'You look like shit.'

Nick switched the channel and drained his glass. 'Feel like shit, too, so why don't you leave.'

Louie crossed to the television and shut it off. 'We expected to see you last night for Christmas dinner.'

Nick set his empty glass and the remote on an end table. He finally looked at Louie standing there across the room, surrounded by a hazy glow, kind of like the picture of Jesus his mother had hanging on the wall in her dining room. 'Didn't make it.'

'Obviously. What's going on?'

'None of your business.' His head pounded and he wanted to be left alone. Maybe if he stayed drunk for a couple of months, the alcohol would kill that persistent voice in his head that had started nagging him sometime around midnight, calling him an idiot and telling him he'd made the biggest mistake of his life.

'Lisa talked to Delaney this morning. I guess she's pretty upset about something. Would you happen to know anything about that?'

'Yep.'

'Well – what did you do?'

Nick stood and the room spun twice before stopping. 'Mind your own business.' He moved to walk past Louie, but his brother reached out and grabbed a fistful of his shirt. He looked down at Louie's fingers tangled in his flannel, and he couldn't believe it. The two of them hadn't physically fought since they'd knocked their mother's back door off the hinges fifteen years ago.

'What in the hell is wrong with you?' Louie began. 'For most of your life you've wanted one thing. One. Delaney Shaw. As soon as it looks like you're finally going to get what you want, you do something to screw it up. You hurt her on purpose so she'll hate you. Just like always. And guess what? She does.'

'What do you care?' Nick raised his gaze to his brother's deep brown eyes. 'You don't even like her.'

'I like her okay, but how I feel doesn't really matter. You're in love with her.'

'Doesn't matter. She's leaving in June.'

'Did she say that?'

'Yep.'

'Did you ask her to stay? Did you try to work anything out with her?'

'It wouldn't have made any difference.'

'You don't know that, and instead of finding out, you're going to let the one woman you've loved your whole life walk out. What's that matter with you? Are you chicken shit?'

'Fuck you, Louie.' He barely saw Louie's fist before he buried it in his face. Light exploded behind Nick's eyes and he went down hard, cracking the back of his head on the wood floor. His vision darkened and he thought he might pass out. Unfortunately the exposed ceiling beams came into focus, and with his cleared vision, his skull felt like it had been split in two. His cheekbone began to throb, and his brain pounded. He groaned and gingerly touched his eye. 'You're a little prick, Louie, and when I get up, I'm gonna kick your ass.'

His brother moved to stand over him. 'You couldn't kick old man Baxter's ass, and he's been pushing around one of those oxygen cylinders for ten years.'

'You cracked my head open.'

'No, your head's too hard. Probably cracked your floor though.' Louie pulled a set of keys from his pants pocket. 'I don't know why you made Delaney hate you, but you're going to sober up and realize you made a big mistake. I hope it's not too late.' He frowned and pointed a finger at his brother. 'Take a shower, Nick. You stink like a distillery.'

After Louie left, Nick picked himself off the floor and stumbled upstairs to bed. He slept until the next morning and woke up feeling like he'd been run over by a monster truck. He took a shower, but didn't feel much better. The back of his head hurt and he had a black eye. That wasn't the worst of it. Knowing that Louie was right was worse. He'd pushed Delaney out of his life. He'd thought he could push her out of his head, too. He'd thought he'd feel better. He'd never felt so low.

Are you chicken shit? Instead of fighting for Delaney, he'd fallen back on old habits. Instead of taking a chance, he'd hurt her before she could hurt him. Instead of taking a risk, he'd taken a swing. Instead of grabbing her with both hands, he'd pushed her away.

She'd said she loved him, and he wondered if he'd ruined everything. He might not deserve her love, but he wanted it. And if she no longer loved him? that nagging little voice asked. He'd made her love him once. He could do it again.

He dressed and headed out the door to take the biggest risk of his life. He drove to Delaney's apartment, but she wasn't home. It was Saturday, and her salon was closed, too. Not a good sign.

He drove to her mother's, but Gwen wouldn't talk to him. He looked in the garage to see if Delaney was hiding out and refusing to see him. Henry's Cadillac sat inside. The little yellow Miata was gone.

He searched for her all over town, and the longer he looked, the more desperate he became to find her. He wanted to make her happy. He wanted to build her a house on the Angel Beach property or anywhere she wanted. If she wanted to live in Phoenix or Seattle or Chattanooga, Tennessee, he didn't care, as long as he lived there with her. He wanted the dream. He wanted everything. Now all he had to do was find her.

He talked to Lisa, but she hadn't heard from Delaney. When she didn't show up to open her salon that Monday morning, Nick paid a visit to Max Harrison.

'Have you heard from Delaney?' he asked, walking into the lawyer's office.

Max looked him over and took his time before answering. 'She called me yesterday.'

'Where is she?'

Again he took his time. 'I guess you'll find out soon enough. She's left town.'

The words hit him in the chest like a two-by-four. 'Shit.'

Nick sank into a chair and rubbed a hand over his jaw. 'Where'd she go?'

'She didn't say.'

'What do you mean, she didn't say?' He dropped his hand to his thigh. 'You said she called.'

'She did. She called to tell me she'd left town, and she was breaking the will. She didn't say why or where she was going. I asked, but she wouldn't tell me. I think she thought I'd tell her mother before she was ready for Gwen to know.' Max tilted his head to one side. 'This means you get Delaney's provision. Congratulations, come June, you'll get everything.'

Nick shook his head and laughed without humor. Without Delaney there was nothing. He had nothing. He looked at Henry's estate lawyer and said, 'Delaney and I had a sexual relationship before she left town. Tell Frank Stuart and the two of you do whatever you have to do to make sure she gets that property at Silver Creek and Angel Beach.'

Max looked disgusted and tired of the whole mess. Nick knew the feeling.

Two weeks after his visit to Max, he still hadn't heard a word. He'd haunted Gwen and Max Harrison, and he'd called the old salon Delaney had worked for in Scottsdale. They hadn't heard from her since she'd quit the previous June. Nick was going crazy. He didn't know where to look next. He never suspected that he should have looked within his own family.

'I hear Delaney Shaw is working down in Boise,' Louie mentioned as he casually took a swallow of his soup.

Everything within Nick stilled and he looked up at his brother. He and Louie and Sophie sat at his mother's dining room table eating lunch. 'Where did you hear that?'

'Lisa. She told me Delaney's working in her cousin Ali's salon.'

Slowly Nick lowered his spoon. 'How long have you known?'

'A few days.'

'And you didn't tell me?'

Louie shrugged. 'Didn't think you'd want to know.'

Nick stood. He couldn't decide if he should hug his brother or punch him in the head. 'You knew I'd want to know.'

'Maybe I thought you needed to get yourself together before you see her again.'

'Why would Nick want to see that girl?' Benita asked. 'The best thing she ever did was to leave town. The right thing is finally being done.'

'The right thing would have been for Henry to accept his responsibility a long time ago. But he had no interest in me until it was too late.'

'If it weren't for that girl and her mother, he would have tried to provide for you years ago.'

'And monkeys might have flown out his butt,' Sophie said as she reached for the salt and pepper, 'but I doubt it.'

Louie raised a stunned brow while Nick laughed.

'Sophia,' Benita gasped. 'Where did you hear such foul language?'

There were any number of places, starting with her father and uncle and ending with the television. Her answer surprised Nick. 'Delaney.'

'See!' Benita rose and moved toward Nick. 'That girl is no good. Stay away from her.'

'That's going to be a little difficult since I'm going to drive to Boise and find her. I love her, and I'm going to beg her to marry me.'

Benita stopped and raised a hand to her throat as if Nick were choking her.

'You've always said you wanted me to be happy. Delaney makes me happy, and I'm not going to live without her anymore. I'm going to do whatever it takes to get her back in my life.' He paused and looked into this mother's stunned face. 'If you can't be happy for me, then stay away until you can at least fake it.'

Delaney hated to admit it, and certainly would never cop to it out loud, but she missed finger waves. Actually, she missed Wannetta. But it went deeper than missing one nosy old woman. She missed living in Truly. She missed living in a place where people knew her, and where she knew most everyone.

She removed the clips from the bib of her lederhosen and set them on her work station. On both sides of her, stylists cut and combed in the upscale salon in downtown Boise. Ali's Salon was located in a renovated warehouse, and everything about it was trendy and new. The kind of salon she'd always loved working in before, but it was different now. It wasn't hers.

She reached for a broom and swept up the hair of her last client. For the past ten years she'd lived in places where she had no past, no history, no girlfriends who'd lived through the agony of junior high with her. She'd lived in four different states, always looking for that elusive something, for the perfect place to grow some roots. Her life had come full circle, and it was ironic as hell that she'd found the perfect place exactly where she'd left it. She felt like Dorothy in *The Wizard of Oz*, only she could never go home. Not now.

Boise was a nice city and had a lot to offer. But it didn't have a cross-dressing Santa or parades every holiday. It didn't have the same pulse and heartbeat as a small town.

It didn't have Nick.

She finished sweeping the hair into a pile, then reached for a dustpan. Not having Nick in the same town should have made her feel better. It didn't. She loved him, and she knew she always would. She wished she could move on and forget about Nick Allegrezza, but she couldn't even force herself to leave the state. She loved him, but she couldn't live near him.

Not even for three million dollars. The decision to leave hadn't been all that difficult. There was no way she could live through the next five months seeing Nick with other women. Not for all the money in the world.

The bell above the door rang as Delaney emptied the hair into a trash basket. She heard a collective intake of female breath from the other work stations and the thud of boots.

'Can I help you?'

'Thanks,' said an achingly familiar voice. 'I found what I'm looking for.'

She turned and looked at Nick an arm's length away. 'What do you want?'

'I want to talk to you.'

He'd cut his hair short. One dark lock curled and touched his brow. He took her breath away. 'I'm busy.'

'Give me five minutes.'

'Do I have a choice?' she asked, fully expecting him to say no, so she could then tell him to go to hell.

He shifted his weight to one foot and shoved his hands in the front pockets of his jeans. 'Yes.'

His answer threw her and she turned to Ali, who worked at the next station. 'I'll be back in five minutes,' she said and walked toward the door. With Nick right behind her, she walked into the hall and stopped beside a pay telephone. 'You've got five minutes.' She leaned back against the wall and folded her arms over her breasts.

'Why did you leave town in such a hurry?'

She looked down at her new suede platforms. She'd bought them to make herself feel better, but they hadn't helped. 'I needed to get away.'

'Why? You wanted all that money pretty bad.'

'Evidently I needed to get away more than I wanted the money.'

'I told Max about you and me. Angel Beach and Silver Creek belong to you now.'

She hugged herself tighter, fighting to hold it all together. She couldn't believe they were talking about some stupid property she didn't care about. 'Why did you tell him?'

'It didn't seem right that I inherit everything.'

'Is that what you came to tell me?'

'No. I came to tell you that I know I hurt you and I'm sorry.'

She closed her eyes. 'I don't care,' she said because she didn't *want* to care. 'I told you I loved you, then you called Gail to come over to your house to have sex.'

'I didn't call her. She just showed up, and we didn't have sex.'

'I saw what was going on.'

'Nothing happened. Nothing was ever going to happen. You saw what I wanted you to see, to think what I wanted you to think.'

She lifted her gaze to his. 'Why?'

He took a deep breath. 'Because I love you.'

'That isn't funny.'

'I know. I've never loved any woman but you.'

She didn't believe him. She *couldn't* believe him and risk her heart again. It hurt too much when he broke it. 'No, you love to confuse me and drive me crazy. You don't really love me. You don't know what love is.'

'Yeah, I think I do.' His brows lowered, and he took a step toward her. 'I have loved you my whole life, Delaney. I can't remember a day when I didn't love you. I loved you the day I practically knocked you out with a snowball. I loved you when I flattened the tires on your bike so I could walk you home. I loved you when I saw you hiding behind the sunglasses at the Value Rite, and I loved you when you loved that loser son of a bitch Tommy Markham. I never forgot the smell of your hair or the texture of your skin the night I laid you on the hood of my car at Angel Beach. So don't tell me I don't love you. Don't tell me –' His voice shook and he pointed a finger at her. 'Just don't tell me that.'

Her vision blurred and her fingers dug into her arms. She didn't want to believe him, but at the same time, she wanted to believe him more than she wanted to live. She wanted to throw herself into his arms as much as she wanted to punch him. 'This is just so typical of you. Just when I'm convinced you're a big jerk, you trick me into thinking you're not.' A tear spilled over her bottom lash and she brushed it away. 'But you really are a jerk, Nick. You broke my heart, and now you think you can come here and tell me you love me and I'm supposed t-to forget ev-erything?' she finished just before she lost control and burst into tears.

Nick wrapped his arms around her and held her against his chest. She didn't know it, but he didn't plan to let her go. Not now. Not ever. 'I know. I know I've been a jerk, and I don't have a good excuse. But touching you and loving you, and knowing you were planning to leave me, made me crazy. After we made love the second time, I began to think maybe you'd decide to stay with me. I started to think about you and me waking up every day together for the rest of our lives. I even thought about kids and taking some of those breathing classes when you got pregnant. Maybe buying one of those mini-vans. But then Gwen came home, and you said you were leaving, and I figured I'd been fantasizing again. I was afraid you really would leave, so I made you leave me sooner. I just didn't think you'd leave *town*.' From within the folds of his leather jacket she sniffed but didn't speak. She hadn't told him she loved him and he was dying inside. 'Please say something.'

'A mini-van? Do I strike you as the mini-van type?'

It wasn't exactly what he'd hoped for, but it wasn't a bad sign, either. She hadn't told him to go to hell yet. 'I'll buy you whatever you want if you tell me you love me.'

She looked up at him. Her eyes were wet and her makeup was running. 'You don't have to bribe me. I love you so much I can't think of anything else.'

Relief flooded him and he closed his eyes. 'Thank God, I was afraid you'd hate me forever.'

'No, that's always been my problem. I never could hate you as long as I probably should have,' she said on a sigh and ran her fingers through the side of his short hair. 'Why did you cut your hair?'

'You told me once I should cut it.' He brushed her tears away with his thumbs. 'I thought it might help win you over.'

'It's nice.'

'You're nice.' He kissed her gently, tasting her lips. His tongue entered her mouth and touched hers with a soft caress meant to drug her while he reached for her left hand and slid a three-carat diamond solitaire on her ring finger.

She pulled back and looked down at her hand. 'You could have asked.'

'And take the chance you'd say no? Not hardly.'

Delaney shook her head and returned her gaze to him. 'I won't say no.'

He took a deep breath. 'Marry me?'

'Yes.' She wrapped her arms around his neck and kissed the side of his throat. 'Now take me home.'

'I don't know where you live.'

'No. I mean Truly. Take me home.'

'Are you sure?' he asked, knowing he didn't deserve her or the happiness gripping his chest but taking it anyway. 'We could live anywhere you want. I could move the business back to Boise if you'd like.'

'I want to go home. With you.'

He pulled back far enough to look into her eyes. 'What could I possibly ever give you compared to what you've given me?'

'Just love me.'

'That's too easy.'

She shook her head. 'No it's not. You've seen what I look like in the morning.' She flattened her left hand on his chest and studied her finger. 'What can I give you? I get a handsome guy who *does* look good in the morning, *and* I get a great ring. What do you get?'

'The only thing I've ever wanted.' He held her tight and smiled. 'I get you, wild thing.'